PEACE MAKER

ALSO BY AMBER BIRD
Peace Fire

PEACE MAKER

PEACEFORGERS: BOOK TWO

AMBER BIRD

BARYCENTRE
PRESS

Worldwide Rights
Printed in the United States of America

First Edition

Cover Design by George C. Cotronis | www.cotronis.com

ISBN: 978-1-945636-15-8

www.AmberBird.com

For my parents,
who sacrificed so I could
grow up with sci-fi and
computers.

For Simon, as everything
worthwhile is these days.

PEACE MAKER

CHAPTER 1

If there had ever been a time I should have been at my most watchful and perceptive, right after having blown up the Secure World Systems headquarters seemed like a strong candidate. I mean, we'd just committed a major crime—even if it was for the greater good—and were on the run. (Though not running as far as we'd planned.) Most of us were injured, one of us was dead (newly dead, taking the total up to three of us in the last week), and there was...well, it kind of sounded like the person in the seat next to me was an alien. Like the shady corporation we'd been trying to take down had *actually* been part of a dangerous alien plot.

It was prime "notice everything and be paranoid" time...But, somehow, I was too slow. Not actually peak observant. I'd noticed too late to do more than brace for the shot. To cringe as if pulling myself in would somehow save me from the expected effects. From the noise and the spattering of blood. Though, go figure, my brain swore immediately afterwards that it was time that was slow in the moment, giving me no excuse.

That time had slowed enough to take in the whole story. Bryan and Riley both turned around (in what was supposed to be our damned *escape* vehicle). Bry in the driver seat and Riles in the passenger seat, their guns trained on the back seat. On the blindfolded stranger with pale, poreless flesh who sat beside me. Who sat so still that they must have sensed they'd said something unwise. Rye's gun pressed into their forehead was probably a solid clue.

Bryan looked...well, he was Bryan. He looked steady and calm. Scary calm. But he was only keeping one eye on the stranger. The other eye was on Riles. Slowly, he lowered his gun, put it down on the console between their seats. I *was* observant enough to notice that and feel a moment of confusion.

Our Riley was the most deeply feeling of us, and zir loss was freshest. That newly dead one of us had been zir partner, Kitty.

Bryan had had days, almost a week now, to start to recover a little from his 'Randa's murder. I had my Jonny, beat up but alive, on my other side. (Lover to my left, danger to my right.) But Rye's Kitty was freshly buried in the rubble of the SWS HQ. Before the cameras went down, zie'd watched Kitty's last moments as she'd struggled with a beefy SWS CorpSec guy.

Struggled to escape an explosion that *we'd* planned and triggered. That zie had known was coming and hadn't warned Kitty about. That zie had been so sure she'd be clear of when things blew.

So, yeah, Rye was feeling at least as wrecked as zie looked. Wrecked and angry, jaw clenched and nostrils flared as zie snarled at the stranger, "Say that again."

We were *all* frozen in that moment, not just the stranger.

Riles raged, "Say that again!" and spittle flew from zir mouth. Rabid with fury and deep, still bleeding loss. I could see the hungry, unpredictable flames of hysterical grief in zir eyes. Zie moved enough with zir heated demand that zir gun pulled slightly away from the stranger's forehead.

They must have realized the decrease in gun-related pressure wasn't necessarily a good sign, because their voice was strained as the stranger uncertainly complied with Riley's command. "Your world will burn with the peace fire?"

Riles was suddenly too calm, a scarier calm than Bryan's. "No, *you'll* burn." And something in zir eyes clicked.

Snapped.

Switched, like a safety coming off.

And zir fingers curled on the trigger.

I noticed. I cringed.

And, fortunately for us all, Bryan acted. As if by some kind of instinct (where the hell do you get an instinct like that?), he snapped his hand out and squeezed Rye's wrist. The one that wasn't quite recovered from the sprain, making it just weak enough. Weak enough to make it harder to pull the trigger, harder enough that it slowed zir down. So it was just tender enough that Riles sucked in a quick hiss of breath and reflexively let go of the gun before zie could actually fire the shot.

Good thing Bry's instinct included catching the gun in his other hand. The thing we needed less than a mess of alien brains on the upholstery was an un-aimed bullet doing random damage or, with our recent luck, killing another one of us.

The noise didn't come. The blood didn't spatter.

It took me a second to register that the gun wasn't going to fire. And another second to un-cringe, to straighten up. But my dumbass hater of a brain took almost no time to tell me things had just gone slo-mo, that I totally could have beat Bryan to stopping Riles (I couldn't have), and that I'd been irresponsibly distracted. Distracted by how wrong things had already gone (fair point, brain).

We were supposed to be speeding away from Seattle, leaving the smoking remains of a villainous corporation and the need for violence behind us. Bragging about the code we'd hacked, the digital counter-attacks we'd blocked, the plots we'd stopped. We were supposed to be all alive, healthy, and jubilant or smug or some mix of the two.

We were supposed to be at the end of adventures and at the start of a very dull tale of lying low and lazily evading anyone looking for us.

Instead, we were in a deserted side street in an industrial area of Seattle (again), guns drawn. Instead, we were mourning Kitty's death and 'Randa's murder and wondering if Jonny would heal enough to be conscious for good. (*Please, please, let him heal,* I quietly pleaded with whatever sort of deity might exist.) We were nursing our own injuries. We were being given reason to believe that, in fact, we'd just fucked up and made an ugly story worse. And we were feeling...well, not jubilant or smug.

Freaked out? Angry? Worried? Maybe a little like this was too much and it wasn't fair and would the adrenaline ever get a chance to subside? I knew I was feeling those things, so it seemed safe to assume that my friends, the ones who were conscious, were feeling about the same.

I shook my head, trying to get myself to unclench mentally and physically. But my brain was still running as if Riles had gotten off the shot it expected. I darted quick looks around, outside the vehicle, looking for flashing lights. I strained to hear the sirens that usually heralded such lights. I didn't detect any emergency vehicles, but there did seem to be loads of helicopters in the air...and it looked like smoke, like there must be multiple fires burning out in the Seattle evening.

I grunted, "Helicopters!" and pointed towards them.

Bryan growled, "Dammit!" and pivoted back to the wheel. He started the vehicle and got us moving.

I checked my mobile to see if there were any headline reports to explain the smoke. It looked like someone else had decided to follow our lead. Not just some*one*...Multiple small domestic terror groups had blown up and/or burned down other SWS buildings, fortunately empty for the night, and all were proudly taking credit. They hadn't wasted any time acting on the information we'd released and, just this once, I felt an urge to cheer them on. It seemed less like terror and more like people fighting for their freedom from a clear threat. Even if it wasn't, it turned out, all that clear what the threat really was.

In mere seconds, Bryan had us in a dark alley with enough overhang from the roofs above to shield the vehicle from the helicopters. Sure, they were probably too busy with the numerous fires to notice one average black mini-SUV outside empty buildings on the outskirts, but this was no time to dial back the paranoia.

For a moment, the only sound in the vehicle was breathing. Bryan and I were quiet, but Jonny was breathing the breath of the recently battered and mainly unconscious, Riles was breathing the jagged breath of someone whose girlfriend had just been killed trying to fight (bizarre as it sounded) an alien invasion, and the stranger was...What the hell was the stranger doing?

The stranger was sort of quietly humming. It was just one extended tone and it sounded like it was probably meant to be a calming sound. Like doing a long "om" during meditation. Their cheeks were puffing out with the extended hum, sucked in during silence, and then out again for more humming. My ears must be inching towards normal if I could hear all that, right? (I'd kind of worried about how long they'd be fucked up after being so close to a massive explosion.)

After a moment of this low volume waiting, the stranger ventured, "I didn't mean to upset you. I swear, I'm on your side.

If, as it seems, you're the ones who took action against SWS tonight. But...but on your side as humans, even if not."

Bryan nodded, as if he'd already been puzzling some things out in his head, and said, "Okay. It's time for us to make a choice. Do we head out now or delay?"

Riles mimed shooting the stranger with zir fingers, then asked, "Delay based on *their* bizarre claims that we've just angered secret alien overlords?" Zie snorted and sneered, "Mate, it's just interstellar illuminati bullshit."

I didn't want to upset zir, but I asked, "Don't you think we should at least get the story?" I thought (hoped) I sounded kind. I could only imagine that zie wanted to put as many miles as possible between zirself and the scene of all the bad shit.

Bryan clarified, "I'm not talking about weeks or even days of delay. We've done enough of that leading up to today, I know. Just...one night. Just a little time to let them," he waved a hand in the stranger's direction, "give us all the info they seem to think they have for us. And, unless we all decide it's a good idea to stay longer, we head out tomorrow. Okay?"

Rye squinted in the growing dark, "Unanimous decision? Promise?" When Bryan and I both nodded, zie said, "Okay. But I plan to vote we go unless the reasons to stay are really damned good. I've given enough." Zie sounded thoroughly defeated, and I didn't disagree.

I wanted to hear the story because I knew I'd regret taking action without all the information, but I was with Riles; we'd done enough, lost enough, tried enough. Certainly we'd saved enough lives—if not from death than from mental captivity—that our ledgers should be clean. All past misdeeds paid off, with interest. Dammit.

Bryan held up Riley's gun. "If I give this back to you, am I going to regret it?"

"You're not my damned father," zie sulked, but then, with a huff, said, "I've got a hold on myself. It won't happen again."

Bryan just nodded and handed back the gun. "Let's see if we can duck into this place," he nodded towards one of the walls that formed the alley, "and have a 'chat' with this one." He gestured towards the stranger again, as if we might not know who he meant.

Bryan holstered his gun and ducked out to quickly check and open a door in the wall he'd indicated. He walked casually, like someone who knew what he was doing. Like someone who belonged there. If it was me, I have no doubt I'd have looked like a complete amateur, tiptoeing from shadow to shadow and getting whiplash from swinging my head side to side trying to keep an eye on everything.

He was back soon, opening the door to my left, shouldering his bag and gently picking up Jonny. "We can't just leave him here." He motioned with his head. "Grab the pasty one and follow me."

I waited until Riles opened the door to my right, then pushed the stranger out. We probably could have been *slightly* less obvious with our guns as we prodded them, still blindfolded, after Bryan. We also probably could have been gentler with our guiding hands on their arms. Probably.

We found ourselves in a dim little back office. It looked like maybe the company was in construction equipment rentals. That or sexy (by somebody's standards) women who would lie on construction equipment, if the calendar on the wall was any indication.

Bryan had set Jonny on a dingy couch of itchy orange fabric that looked as old as Gran and about a million times as used up. Ew.

For the stranger, he was pulling out the desk chair. "Put them here," he directed.

I zip-tied the stranger to the chair, then Bryan pointed his mobile's camera at them once I moved away. Rye dug in zir bag and handed us each a germ/air pollution mask to wear. I put mine on and gently laid one on Jonny's face (but I couldn't see actually putting it on right and making it any harder for him to breathe).

When that was all set, there was a pause, and Bryan caught my eye, then Riley's, a clear question. Were we cool? Did we have our shit together enough to not do anything stupid? After we nodded, he motioned that I should take off the stranger's blindfold. I pulled up my hood and kept my back to the camera as I did, just in case Bry had already started recording. Riles ducked in to aim a desk lamp at them, making sure we'd get a clear view of their face.

Then we stood together, behind the camera, and glared at the stranger.

The stranger looked at the camera in confusion, and Bryan said, "I have a feeling you've got a story that we'll want to be able to mull over."

I got a good look at their eyes. Grey eyes with no perceptible differentiation of parts (no white, iris, or pupil that I could see), just some shimmery tracework. Like when you realize too late that you're about to walk face-first into a dewy spiderweb in the fog. Pretty but maybe reason to panic. If those were contacts, they were quality.

The stranger was sounding slightly less patient. "How long are you going to hold me hostage? This...this really isn't necessary. I swear that I'm on your side."

"They raise a good question," I said. "We should probably step aside and make a choice."

There wasn't a lot of room to actually step aside, but I liked the illusion of having a quiet conference. Bry paused his camera.

With all heads leaned in, I quietly said "I don't want to do this again."

Bryan sounded half confused and half defensive, "Do what?"

"I can't play fucking hostage-holders again. We need a plan that *doesn't* involve that." I set my jaw, hoping he could see that around the g/ap mask.

"I vote we get their story and then kill them, make sure they can't bring the rest their bastard friends back for us. Eye for eye, life for life." Riley was still in vicious mode.

"Um..." I ventured carefully, "I can't vote for more death. Not right now. I mean, hopefully we don't have to vote for it again ever. I feel for you, poppet. And, hey, I'm okay if you want to get in some good hits. I just...I think, if I've learned anything from watching too much TV, you'll probably feel worse in the long-run."

Bryan put a strong arm around Rye's shoulder, and zie let him pull zir in. Zie sagged against him a little, but I saw in zir eyes that zie chose to cling to anger. I couldn't really argue with that; sadness was just another flavor of paralyzed. Anger seemed more likely to let zir do hard things. (Please, let us not have more hard things to do today.)

Bryan said, "Well, once we get their story...I can blindfold them again and drop them off somewhere not near here. I'm not sure that they could report back much of anything that isn't already suspected about us."

(I wanted to argue that they could describe our faces, but he was right. The aliens already suspected we were the true faces of some of the hackers whose 'nyms they had on the top of their Enemies of the Peace list or whatever.)

"I hate to break the illusion of privacy," the stranger interjected, "but I can hear you. And I'm not going to report back anything. Not...not like you think. I don't mean you any harm."

We turned back towards them. From what I saw of my mates' faces as we turned, I knew we all had looks that would best be classified as "we could *not* be more dubious and also we want to hit you a lot."

I put my hands on my hips and asked, "So, we're supposed to just take you at your word?" My tone might have strongly implied that I thought that was ridiculous.

They shrugged and said, "You might want to turn on your camera." When Bryan hesitated, they said, "No, I'm serious. You'll want to capture this."

Bryan held up his mobile, and we all stayed just behind him as he moved around, though he still looked doubtful, and started recording again. "It's on."

The stranger smiled. "Cool. So, listen, if I'd wanted to do you harm, I'd have done it already. I wouldn't have helped you get away from the ruins of HQ after you blew it up. I wouldn't have let you tie me up. And I wouldn't still be sitting here. I'd have been gone in that first alley we pulled into."

Riles argued, "But you're tied up. What the hell are you talking about?" Zie snorted. "And if you're going to claim laser eyes or psychic powers for your so-called alien race, you better be prepared to prove it."

"I'm saying that I could have gotten away at any time." They told Bryan, "Zoom out." Then said, "Watch." With that, they turned their head to the side and their tongue shot out three feet. We heard a ping as it hit a soda can on a windowsill before snapping back into their mouth.

Holy shit.

Riles smacked me on the shoulder. "Did you just see that too?" Zie sounded shocked, maybe a little impressed.

"Yeah, poppet. I don't know what I saw, but I saw it." I checked to make sure my mouth wasn't hanging open.

The stranger and Bryan seemed to be sizing each other up, wordlessly.

After a moment, the stranger said, "So, one of the things you can't see that's different about me—about, uh, my people—is that my tongue is...a bit longer than yours. And it has a sort of cartilaginous tip that's hard and strong enough that I can make it pierce soft things. Like human skin. And you *definitely* can't see that I have a gland from which I can extrude a paralytic venom onto my skin-piercing tongue."

Bryan sounded quietly impressed. "No shit?"

The stranger (alien, maybe? probably...) nodded.

"Is there venom on that can you just hit?" Bryan pointed at the can in question.

The stranger shook their head. "No. Learning to control the release of our venom is seen as a righteous and civilized necessity."

"Yeah," Rye noted, "I'm now totally believing they aren't human." Zie put a hand on zir cheek, a touch of wonder in zir voice. "I'm meeting an alien."

Somewhere back in time, since time probably isn't actually linear, our younger selves were feeling a thrill. Aliens! Pretty much confirmed aliens! I seriously wished circumstances would let us enjoy that now.

"So, not to press the point," the alien (alien!) said, "but maybe you could cut me loose now? At least you won't have to hold a hostage." They looked at me. "Right?"

Bryan took out his knife, but paused. "I'm about persuaded, but I have one question." He scratched his cheek with his knife hand, considering. "I guess I want to know how it is you just happened to be there to drag some of our people out of the mess."

"That's fair. I guess that's pretty suspicious, isn't it?"

We all gave the sort of half-nod with an eyebrow lift that means, "No shit," but didn't interrupt. Because, yeah, how had they just happened to be there?

"I know you probably won't believe it, but I live right by there. It's a...convenient location for me. And..." To my eyes, they now looked ashamed. "When you guys did whatever you did, I was watching a transmission covering what they were doing at SWS and—"

Bryan cut them off. "A transmission? What kind of transmission?"

"Today was supposed to be a big step, so all of us who live here got looped in to watch a special live transmission of the SWS execs pushing buttons." Their brow kind of furrowed. "And then they started to panic because someone had set off the building destruct sequence. When they said that, I threw on my hoodie and ran out." They shook their head. "You're just lucky that everyone else who lives near was probably too busy being upset about our dead and the damage to the mission to think to come out as quickly as I did."

"Huh." Next to me, Riley sounded almost convinced. "So, you could tell us your address and we could verify where you came from?"

"Yeah. Of course." They rattled off an address, including their unit number, like we were going to mail them a care package or some shit. "Though I don't have a way for you to verify *why* I came. Not to shoot myself in the foot here..." They sort of nervously laughed. "But, again, I could have held you back or at least left you. Or just kept an eye on you and followed you. Or, you know, just have used the tongue at any point."

Even though zie was busy on zir mobile, looking into the alien's claim about where they lived, Riles leaned forward, voice dripping with curiosity and a little cheekiness. "Is your tongue prehensile?"

Because the only thing that can distract Rye from sadness and anger is sex, and anyone who knew zir knew that was the real application zie had in mind when asking just how...handy the tongue was.

I gently put my elbow in zir ribs. "Really?!"

"Hey, I'm just asking important questions." All innocence and wrongfully questioned reputation, zie explained, "Like, what if they could use their tongue to grab a knife and cut a zip tie to free their hands? Totally important and not at all what I'm sure you're implying." Zie overplayed the offense just enough to make it clear that, in fact, not even in a serious situation like this could zie keep zir mind entirely out of the gutter.

The alien (alien!) agreed, "It actually *is* an important question. Strategically necessary information. Know your enemy, right?"

"See?" Riley was pleased to be backed up, even if it was by someone zie'd recently wanted to kill. Someone who was probably (definitely) giving zir more credit than zie deserved.

"If my tongue were a monkey tail, you'd say it's partially prehensile. I can aim it. I can wrap it around and grasp things, but I can't really manipulate things well." They shrugged. "You should probably just be paranoid about our tongues though."

"Fuck it," sighed Rye. "I say cut them free." Zie sounded more sad than angry now. "I won't get real or satisfactory revenge from anything I do to *this* one." Obviously, zie thought there might be some of the aliens (seriously, aliens!) zie *would* enjoy fucking up.

Bryan had tucked his knife away and grabbed Riley's mobile when the tongue questions distracted zir. He'd been quietly working, a mobile in either hand like some kind of dual-fisted mobile menace. I saw that he'd been pulling up footage of the area around the SWS headquarters at the time of the explosion. He tapped his thumb on the screen as he handed Rye's mobile back. "Got it."

We leaned in to watch as our alien rushed out the front door of a building that was all flats, no retail or office spaces, and ran towards the building we were (at the time of the footage) blowing up. They kept to shadows and overhangs, but we never lost them. We saw them pause a beat in the shadow of the building that, in moments, they would pull us up against, once they'd freed us from beneath the bodies of the CorpSec agents they had probably just seen get blasted out. After a brief pause, they looked around quickly, as if checking for other watching eyes, then rushed forward.

I knew what happened next, because their feet were about to be in front of my face, their hands were about to lift a corpse off of me so that I could run. Though we'd already deleted any footage of that.

"Yeah, fuck it," I agreed. "I've had my fill of hostages."

Bryan nodded, knife already in hand again and extended to Riley. Riles shrugged, took the knife, and pulled up zir hood. Careful to keep zir face off camera, zie crouched down to cut the zip ties. I noticed zie seemed to be leaning a bit away from, I'd guess, the possibility of a venomous tongue.

The alien smiled, rubbing their wrists. "Thanks!" They could have been cheerfully thanking us for giving them a cookie.

I really hoped they weren't going to be one of those painfully chipper people.

We all sat back down, facing them, camera still running, and I sighed, "Let's try this again."

CHAPTER 2

"So, before I tell all...I want to point out that this could get me in big trouble. It could literally get me killed." The alien paused and took in our faces, making sure we took them seriously.

We must have looked sufficiently convinced, because they went on. "If I'm telling you about me, about my people, I want to know *something* about you."

We three conscious humans exchanged looks and acquiescing shrugs. Yeah, that was maybe fair. And, really, we could always lie, right?

"Okay," the alien went on, "let's start basic. Hello, my name is Zane."

"You're an alien called Zane?" Riles burst out, then took zir tone down a notch. "Sorry, that was insensitive. I was just expecting...something else." Zie leaned forward. "Is that your *real* name or one to make us humans feel better?"

"Mate!" I lightly punched zir arm. "You'd verbally eviscerate someone if they asked that sort of question of someone human who wasn't like them." I shook my head dramatically. "Disappointed."

Riles had the grace to look ashamed and mutter an apology.

Zane the alien (I was going to get used to that eventually) answered like they hadn't noticed our exchange. "Real name. I was born and raised here. There's every chance I'll live here the rest of my life. It makes sense to have a name that fits in...and that you can pronounce. Because," and now they leaned forward to mirror Rye, "you don't have the physiology necessary to pronounce my *second* name. Which I think you'll find satisfactorily alien." They sat back smiling and said...something. It was some sounds I could probably describe (s and sh and z and vowels...maybe l, m, and n?) and some I definitely couldn't. All sort of in a blended rush. "See?"

"That was your *name*?" Riles sounded delighted, at least to *my* ears.

The alien nodded with a smile.

With delight so unabashed that it must definitely be clear to even the alien who didn't know zir, zie exclaimed, "Cool! I now have total name envy."

I tried to quietly make some of the noises I couldn't even describe, and Zane laughed. "It's nice that you're trying, but I think you're proving my point. You could get close to some of the sounds, but you'd probably never manage to sound like more than...a struggling infant." They grinned. "And that's why our first names are always something you *can* say. So. Your turn." They looked at us expectantly.

Yeah. I was definitely not going to give them any name that actually had anything to do with me, especially not with the audio being recorded by the camera. But my head was full of other names, so I took over introductions and hoped everyone would just play along. I pointed to myself, "Kleene-star," to Bryan, "No-ce-bro—"

Bryan interrupted, playing the part. With a hint of self-satisfaction, he explained, "You know, kind of like nocebo, the opposite of placebo, but a bro." And he...he actually gave a kind of little douche-y wink, like he was letting us all in on something with his explanation. So gross.

I paused a beat to make sure he was done, trying not to laugh at his on-point interjection, then pointed to Riley, "Bossest-cossist," and finally to Jonny, "and Occam's laser."

Kl33n3*, n0cebro, BossestCossist, and 0ccamsLaZer were a few of our asshole peers who'd been bought out by (aka who'd sold out to) SWS. So, you know, fuck them if this guy went back and pointed fingers.

When Zane squinted, because those were clearly not normal names, Bryan shrugged. "For now, you get 'nyms. Those are a risk for us too."

I really hoped we all remembered which names I'd said for each of us...Good thing they were on camera, huh?

Zane nodded. "That...that makes sense. Okay. Hello. Nice to meet you all. Would...would you mind taking the masks off? I've already seen your faces, after all."

We looked at each other, as if we might psychically discuss this. I mean, it sounded reasonable, but I wasn't going to if Bry didn't. When he slowly pulled his mask down, shrugging because it had obviously been too little, too late, Riles and I followed suit.

Zane nodded, then shifted in their chair. "And here's the bit where it gets really dangerous for me. Where, on camera, I tell you that I'm an alien. That our ship showed up to Earth in the 1980s, intent on subjugating one more planet to my people's so-called peace. And, if those in charge decide we've failed, that Earth is too stubbornly non-peaceful, they'll order a...a cleansing instead. In fact, the only way I'll end up not living out my life and dying here is if that happens. In which case, as long as they don't find out that I'm a heretic, I'll get back onto the ship. And we'll leave a burning world in our wake." They paused, giving it a chance to sink in, then said grimly, "And that's not a future I'm okay with."

We all looked at each other, back to Zane, back to each other. This was the sort of thing that we happily bought into in our fiction, that we'd thought would be cool to live, but that, in reality...I was going to describe this as "terrifying" now, not "cool." Not at all cool. I didn't want to live in fiction anymore.

I cleared my throat, "So, you've been here 60, 70 years...How long until your people declare us failed and destroy the planet?" I tried to sound calm, just an adventure professional assessing the threat, but there was that mantra against fear from *Dune* swimming at the back of my thoughts again. *I must not fear. Fear is the mind-killer.*

Bryan added, "You said something, in that first alley we stopped in, about your people playing the long game. But 70 years sounds *really* long."

They nodded. "It is. And we've certainly, so the history says, played longer games. But those were with planets that showed clear progress. Which, uh, isn't really happening on Earth."

Riles suggested, "And, even though we thought we were just stopping a corrupt corporation from getting too much power and inflicting mind control on people, we were actually making a case for destroying our world."

"You were, unfortunately, doing both. I don't think I have anything much to add. But, for the camera, I'll confirm that SWS was established and run by my people. By, um, Peaceforgers.

Which is our religion and our primary identity. Even if some of us are heretics." Zane tilted their head. "*Technically* heretics. I'd argue that my beliefs are more in line with the original intent of our religion." They paused, and it looked like they'd caught themselves about to go off on a familiar tangent. "But I won't bore you with that."

Bryan snorted. "I suspect that you misunderstand what we'd find boring." He grinned. "I'd love to spend hours grilling you and satisfying my curiosity!"

With the sort of over-the-top delivery that told us they'd watched plenty of TV, Zane enthused, "Well, I'm here all night!"

Rye sat on the desk, then leaned forward, elbows on knees and chin on fists. Awe and curiosity tangled in zir tone. "Don't tempt us."

And that turned into a brief question and answer session, our brains trying to dredge up what might be useful to know. Zane didn't seem to hold back on anything. Didn't protest when Bryan insisted on getting prints (palms, individual fingertips, and eyes). And, though I knew it was just delaying things, it gave us a while where we seemed to be feeling okay.

I felt like, if we'd known we were going to have an alien to grill, we'd have had an organized list of questions. But, instead, we'd taken a couple hours to learn very little. None of which seemed actually useful.

But it was cool to know we *had* actually seen an underwater door with the little robot fishes and on the blueprints for SWS HQ. That, yeah, its purpose was to let them slip out into the Puget Sound...so their shuttle could get to their spaceship (!!).

Turned out Peaceforgers were amphibious and Earth wasn't the only planet where people found it easier to master land exploration than deep water exploration. So, they'd parked in water close to where they'd thought they might be able to blend in before they spread out: among the less-sundrenched populations along the upper part of the North American Pacific coast.

And, just to make blending easier, they'd taken advantage of, and tried to sway the trajectory of, emerging alternative scenes. They'd done what they could to keep those scenes aimed at fashions and aesthetic appreciations that had room for them. Felt lucky that humans were constantly mining alternative cultures for ways to spice up mainstream fashion. Even before the 2050s, Zane could have walked down the street with skin that wasn't typical and eyes that weren't typical and ridges on their head, and people would just have assumed it was some alternative kid really committing to being Alternative.

Though it sounded like they hadn't gotten off entirely easy. They had had to subject themselves and their children to some serious cosmetic surgery (things like ears and noses had to be added, and some larger head ridges had to be shaved down to fit under wigs or hair implants). 'Cause it was probably asking too much to create, for instance, a trend of humans removing their existing ears and noses.

So, basically, Zane didn't know anything strategically useful. Or wouldn't cop to it. Go fucking figure.

But they did know this: At the moment, there were a total of about 1000 Peaceforgers out and about in the world, with thousands more sleeping on the ship.

I was bone tired. I wanted to ask more, see if maybe we just needed the right question to get good info, but I could tell that *everyone* was flagging. Plus, my brain protested as I tried to scrape up possible questions.

Zane seemed to be especially struggling. They paused and apologized, "Sorry. I don't sleep the same way you do, and I'm overdue for a sleep period."

Rye stretched. "I could sleep. I have more questions, but I could sleep."

"One more—" Bryan stifled a yawn. "One more question. Then we should get you out of here." He looked around, verifying that sounded good. When everyone nodded, he asked, "What do *you* do in this plan?"

"Lucky for me, the answer is I don't actively do anything. Yet." Zane sounded a little relieved. "Um, we have this tradition, kind of like...Amish? I think that's right. Somewhere around late teens or very start of our 20s, after a sufficient time of learning and indoctrination into our culture, once it seems like we could be out on our own in whatever civilization we're in, we...well, we go out on our own. Not cut off, just not living with our parents or expected to really work. The hope, the expectation, is we'll experience the native culture, be horrified by the lack of peace, and begin our work for the cause with renewed vigor."

"Not working that way for you?" Bryan confirmed.

Zane responded with a cheerful, "Nope! You guys have problems, but not enough to deserve subjugation or extinction. And you've only confirmed my belief that true peace can't be forced."

Bryan stood. "Okay, I think we should make sure we know how to contact each other. And we should drop you off somewhere else. We all need sleep and...us humans have to decide what we're going to do."

The rest of us kind of dragged ourselves up, me from the couch arm near Jonny's head and Rye from the desk zie'd been sitting on.

Zane asked, "Any paper? I'll write down how to contact me. I...um...I hope you decide to stay. Because I guarantee that the Peaceforgers are about to consider you—your planet—a lost cause, and I'm pretty sure you're the only ones who even know about this. The only ones, then, who can probably figure out how to let other humans know." As they tapped their information into the mobile Bryan handed them instead of paper, they said, "No pressure. Just want you to keep in mind that this is a big deal."

Bryan pointed at the phone screen. "Last name too, please." Low key doing what he could to make it a little easier to look into Zane later, now that we'd have an address and full name.

I dug out one of the cards I'd put safe contact info on, like the one I'd given Dr. Scott, and handed it to Zane. "This should let you get in touch with us, but no guarantees we'll do what you want." I shrugged. "This seems like it should be somebody else's job. Like it's a war for someone with serious ordnance to fight."

"I understand. But, if you decide you want to try, you wouldn't be alone. You'd have an inside person." Zane gave me a reassuring smile, then clapped their hands. "Alright! Please get me the hell out of here."

We pulled our g/ap masks back on, and Bryan held up the blindfold. "For our safety, I have to insist on this."

"Of course you do. Just don't let me walk into anything." Zane closed their eyes. "Hope I see you all again sometime."

In spite of the sense of ease that had seemed to develop as we'd talked, we settled into grim silence in the car. We were all eager to get hidden away somewhere, but Bry was playing it smart and driving all over, taking a long while to make sure Zane couldn't easily trace the route back to where we'd questioned them. Who knew what DNA we might have left behind?

I used my mobile to scope out a place where we might safely drop them, close-ish to their home but not in the thick of police activity. I leaned forward and pointed it out to Bryan. He nodded and kept driving.

As we finally approached the streets I'd suggested, Bry said, "You can take off the blindfold now."

Zane reached up cautiously to remove it, blinking slowly in the glare of streetlights and taking in our location.

Bryan slowed down and pulled over.

I said, "We're not too far from your place, but we're outside the police investigation cordon."

"Alright. Okay." Zane nodded, and reached for the door handle. They paused as if giving us a chance to protest. "Okay, well, later?" And then they slipped out into the Seattle night.

We pulled away as quickly and immediately as we could without drawing attention to ourselves.

Now that the excitement and adrenaline had subsided, now that we were alone, the horrible realities of the day crashed down on us. Kitty killed. The deaths of the SWS executives that we'd been part of (because, good or evil, they were still lives...lives we'd taken...). The damage to Jonny and the chance he might not make it. My injuries. That *something* had gotten through before Rye had been able to shut down the satellite SWS was using, and we had no idea what that something was. Being stuck in Seattle with troubles still looming instead of victoriously fleeing to South Dakota to start our new, wonderfully boring lives. Our old lives basically off-limits. Oh, and the minor issue of maybe having accelerated an alien apocalypse. This on top of the shit in the previous two weeks, most notably the deaths of Huw (one of our brave remote comrades) and Bryan's girl 'Randa.

Bryan was breathing heavily, his eyes riveted on the road. Riles crawled into the back seat. We put our arms around each other, though I spared a hand for Bry's shoulder, and we wept. Our cries were initially muffled by our masks, but then we pulled them down as they got soaked with tears and snot. We pulled up each other's hoods, making sure we stayed slightly obscured from any cameras that might catch us through the vehicle windows.

Riles sobbed longer and louder, making me painfully aware just how much zie'd loved Kitty. Making me feel an extra helping of guilt. Reminding me that I had promised her I would root out my own internalized misogyny issues on the other side of the SWS thing. I held Rye and mentally swore to Kitty that I was going to stick to that. It was pretty shit, as legacies went, but my attempts at more enlightened behavior were all the legacy I could think to offer her.

As we quieted down, as we neared the same deserted edge of Seattle that we seemed to keep returning to, Bryan cleared his throat. "I know we're all wrecked and we have a choice to make, but there are also things we planned to take care of tonight. And...shit. I think I need to focus on that so I can keep it together."

Riley reached up a hand to squeeze Bry's arm. "We can do that. We can make a choice about what comes next after we finish what we can of the plan we made already." Zie laughed raggedly. "I'm *probably* not in great decision-making form right now. Probably."

We all laughed with zir, all sounded just as raw.

Bry nodded. "Now, if I find a building for us to stay the night in, will one of you get us electricity there?"

Riles perked up a bit. "Yep! You know I haven't paid for power in years. You give me the address, and, thanks be to computerized meters, I'll make sure it has power that seems to be going to other buildings. Easy!"

So we found an abandoned warehouse store. The thing about how Seattle had both grown in quantity and declined in quality was that the core had gotten denser and the edges had become something of a disreputable ghost land. And, whilst you'd think that wouldn't kill off all the big warehouse stores in the edges with their nice prices, the steadily decreasing quality of transportation (other than just walking), the ubiquitousness (is that a word?) of online shopping, and the shrinking average size of homes (and, thus, of closets and other storage spaces in them), pretty much did the job.

Which is to say that we had a number of options and no real neighbors. Plus, we had doors big enough to drive our vehicle into. Which, as soon as Bryan had broken a lock, was exactly what we did. Carefully, slowly inching in, looking for anyone dashing to get out of our headlights. We sat a moment, waiting to see if anyone would try to shoot us. When nobody did, Bryan hopped out to close the door behind us.

He climbed back in, pulling down his mask, and said, "Okay, we need to make sure this isn't already occupied." He considered the rest of us in the car. Took in everyone's injuries. Finally, he pointed to the forearm crutch I'd been given to lean on until my cracked kneecap healed. "Can you creep around, and do it quietly, or should I do this solo?"

Riley interjected, "Hey, I'm in the same shape *and* have had some healing time."

"Much as I'd like to not leave you and Jonny alone, in case there's someone here who moves on the car once we start creeping, I'm kind of feeling like you're not exactly in the best state to be cautious. And I'd rather leave you here than out there, a little too trigger happy, and maybe hitting someone I care about who's also creeping in the shadows. Like me." He softened the sentence with an apologetic smile, then turned his attention back to me.

I took a moment to consider how I felt. "I think I can creep, maybe even quietly. But you can't count on me to run. So my dodging is probably really shitty, and I better not have to chase anyone down. Me probably not shooting you accidentally might be the one reason I'd recommend me for this mission." I lifted my crutch. "Though I'm also prepared to use this as a bludgeoning weapon."

"Cool. So, you creep slowly along the far wall and I'll move quickly, starting on the closer wall, clearing the closed-in areas as I go. Yeah?" Without waiting for my reply, he turned the headlights on to their highest beams, because that and a couple little Maglights were all we had.

After we put our earbuds back in, Bryan gave me an "are you ready?" look, and I nodded. Even though I was pretty sure I wasn't. Good times.

As I started to scoot out, I looked at Jonny, still unconscious. I caught Riley's eye. "Keep him safe, yeah?"

Riles nodded, solemn. "We're not losing any more of us."

We slipped out of the vehicle and headed in our assigned directions. I tried to tell myself that my injury-slowed pace was just enforced stealth and a chance to be thorough. Yeah. That's what it was.

Abandoned warehouse stores would probably even be creepy if they were well-lit. Mostly empty, but with big, towering shelves. Shelves that threw spindly shadows in the headlights. I tried to creep quietly, concentrating on those shadows and hoping they were empty.

At some point, Rye's voice came through my earbud. "Please confirm silence means everything is fine and nobody has died."

"Slow but alive here," I quietly confirmed.

"Yeah. Alive here too," Bryan's voice hissed through.

"Maybe you could just mention that you're alive at regular intervals? You know, for those of us stuck in the car, waiting. Wondering. Looking for excuses to shoot someone."

I snickered, "Demanding! You'd think a lack of screaming in pain would be enough."

That and some sketchy shadows were about as exciting as it got. Though a rat briefly made me think someone was coming at me from the shadows. Given I was holding my gun in my *left* hand (with a cast on that forearm), I have never been so happy to see a rat. Though I have also never so much wanted a cat. I sent one of my non-prayers out to the air that, for the good of us all, Bryan would be the one who ran across any other people...Though, also, that we'd prefer no other people. Please and thank you, non-existent deities.

I didn't realize how slowly I was moving until someone stepped out of the shadows.

As I raised my gun, they said, "Dammit, Katja, you should have had that gun out in front of you the whole time. What the hell?" Bryan clearly hadn't realized that he was the only competent person at the moment.

"I'm pretty sure that me being shitty at this is why I didn't have time to shoot you before you let me know it was you." I tried to sound like I thought it was a solid defense.

"Sorry to break up the scolding session, but does this mean we're good?" asked Riles.

"Yeah," Bryan gently pushed my hand down. "You can turn off the headlights and I'll turn on some building lights, then head your way."

CHAPTER 3

We were lucky enough to find a long table in the employee area for Jonny to lie on. Whilst Rye got our portables and other gear plugged in and recharging on the other, smaller table in the room, and whilst Bryan held Jonny, I awkwardly pushed the long table against the wall, then rushed to try to put clothes from our packs on it (carefully avoiding pulling any clothing from Kitty's pack) before Bryan put Jonny down. Like I could somehow fake comfort. Like he didn't really belong in an actually comfortable hospital bed.

Bry stepped out as I was fussing with a hoodie under Jonny's head and came back with some sleeping bags. "Here. I put some stuff in the car the other day, just in case."

He held Jonny again as I unrolled a sleeping bag on the table. It wasn't much, but it felt more effective than our spare clothes.

I joked, "No pillows?" and immediately regretted it when Bryan, who took his responsibility for things that had to do with the meat world Very Seriously, looked ashamed. I laughed, trying to get him to see I was kidding, then said, "Joke, babe. Nobody expects pillows." I tried to make it sound soft, even though I felt like I was still all broken angles.

We shoved clothes back in bags and tried to set our other things up in a vaguely work-ready way, moving in grim silence, mumbling occasional half-phrases only as necessary.

I made sure Jonny's IV was okay, but I'd probably done a shitty job of it, because he gave a short moan and briefly stirred.

I could barely make it out as he whispered, "Did we get Kitty?"

He immediately fell back into the darkness, so he missed Riley and me crying again. We sank to the floor, leaned on the wall near the table on which Jonny lay. Bry clambered down to sit by us, his arm long enough, all of us sat close enough, that, if he put it around Riles, he could still put his hand on the back of my neck. He sat with us quietly until *we* could be quiet. Again.

We all leaned together a while without speaking.

I was dozing off when Bryan asked, "Do we stay? I know we said we'd talk later, but..."

Rye hung an "um..." in the air, but neither of us gave a useful reply.

Bryan sighed. "Because, on the one hand, we've done something that was kind of bigger than we thought. In a fucking ridiculous, impossible context we couldn't have imagined." His voice got higher as he exclaimed, "Holy shit, aliens!"

That got more reactions. We spent a number of moments being surprised and excited and impressed and maybe a little extra worried because, holy shit, aliens.

I noted, "We have to at least find a way to tell Gran. She'll go nuts over this!"

"Which brings us back to the question. And to my other hand." Bryan got serious. "Because, on the other hand, we may be the only humans who know about the threat. And even if we felt selfish or felt we'd done our part—"

Riley cut in heatedly, "Which we have! We *have* done our damned part."

"Granted. Yes. We've done our part. But, if we do nothing...The options are that the Peaceforgers win and, to my understanding, subjugate the human race. Because you *know* humanity won't actually find their better selves any time soon, if ever. So, subjugation or the destruction of all human lives on Earth. Which...how do we walk away from that?" Bryan knew he was talking sense.

But I was in no state for committing to a bigger war. Not right now. So, as calmly as I could, I suggested, "We said we'd table this until tomorrow. Until after we've taken care of all our other Friday night shit, and, you know, until we've had some sleep. Remember how important sleep is? Maybe we follow through on tabling it." I braced for Bryan to push, because that's Bryan.

To my relief, he just sighed and said, "You're right. I'm sorry. Let's stay on task." He gestured vaguely towards our gear. "We're set up to go, right?" When we nodded, he pushed to his feet and said, "Okay, then let's get going."

Riles and I hadn't planned how to get our hurt asses up from the floor, so we happily accepted as Bry carefully helped us to our feet. I hoped our hands and brains were more agile.

I limped over to the dingy plastic chair in front of the little table where my computer crowded with Rye's and Bryan's. I hesitated, didn't sit.

"Uh...can we...can we drag it over by the other table?" The table with Jonny. The table I was trying to think just enough about but not too much, because we still had work to do and distractions could be Problematic.

The others just nodded and helped me get things moved, kindly angling it so that it was my machine that ended up nearest the other table. I could hear Jonny breathe near me as I sat.

Time to see if my body was up to the one task it was actually usually prepared for.

I was relieved as my hands were, in fact, as capable as ever. Even if my fractured left forearm protested a bit. Machine booted, security checked, possible threats located, news channels opened to listen for attacks or danger from the offline masses. I *could* have moved faster, but I was slowed down by a constant awareness of Jonny there but...not.

A notification reminded me that I'd been ignoring my mobile since we left our hideout at Quinn's earlier in the day. (How had that been just today and not years ago?) I checked the logs. And there were no surprises. Family, friend who'd hidden us and would be disappointed we'd left him out (sorry, Quinn), and the law. "Did everyone else hear from Gran, Quinn, and Detective Engalls?"

They checked their own mobiles. I felt a little less absent-minded when the looks on their faces told me that they, too, had forgotten about all the calls they'd been ignoring. Both nodded and confirmed that, yeah, they'd gotten at least those same calls.

After confirming none of the calls actually needed immediate attention, we went back to our computers. I assumed they were doing similar security checks to mine. Nobody was freaking out, nobody was typing unusually frantically, so I figured that we were all okay so far. I put a note on my list, assuming Jonny hadn't changed his passwords since we made him give them to us, to check his security the best I could. Just in case someone online had connected him to us.

I made sure to cancel the auto-email that would have told Gran I was dead if I hadn't made it through the afternoon's explosion. Putting all my "make me untraceable" tricks into play, I carefully added an event—starting immediately—to Gran's calendar, making her phone ping a reminder. The event description was just three emoji: a heart, lips with a shushing finger in front of them, and a winky face. She couldn't reply, but I was spying on her phone, so I watched her try. I used the camera to see her go from confusion to relief and finally to a big grin. I watched her screen and saw her enter her own emoji on the event: a big grin, a heart, and a thumbs up.

Through her phone's mic, I heard her mumble "Newb." I watched as she rolled her eyes, presumably at herself, and saw her delete the emoji she'd added. She slipped her phone into her pocket, but I heard a quick snippet of conversation before I stopped spying.

An older lady's voice I didn't recognize, so it must be her mate Sarah, asked, "What's up?"

Gran casually replied, "I forgot to turn off a calendar notification." She laughed. "Guess my mind's finally going, huh?"

I laughed quietly, then got back to work.

As I was wrapping up my checks, finishing making my list of things to take care of based on them, and preparing to check Jonny's stuff, Riles cleared zir throat. Bry and I looked up, but zie appeared to be carefully avoiding our eyes.

"So, uh, not to make the night shittier, but I'm now at the part of my list where it says we kill MK." Zie looked up at me apologetically then. "You...you want to take lead on this?"

I groaned and let my head fall back. I considered the filthy ceiling tiles above us. I let myself worry that maybe this wasn't a clean enough place for Jonny to recuperate. I let myself contemplate doing the stupid thing, not killing MindKiller, not changing who I was on the 'Net. With a long, careful breath, I lifted my head and looked at Rye and Bryan. I nodded. I'd done enough stupid things recently. At least this death would be a bloodless one.

With quick key taps, trying to pretend I was all efficiency and business, I pulled up the death plan I'd written. "Heads up. Just a few steps and a timeline, but we might have to adjust because..." I had to stop and swallow. Why the hell was my brain getting so fucking dramatic over everything? This was just...fake. And... "Because I assumed Jonny would be able to post his own reaction. And, if he doesn't post, people are going to assume he was in on it and that could screw him over," (was I talking faster?) "and he probablychangedhispasswordsand—" (I was.) I stopped again. I took a breath. I started trying to at least log in as Jonny on Hashing Grounds, the forum people would be most likely to notice him *not* reacting on.

With my peripheral vision, I could see Rye was very studiously looking at zir screen and Bryan was calmly watching me. Watching me just like it was a normal break in conversation. Bless him.

I reached over to gently rest a hand on Jonny's shoulder. It was an awkward angle, but feeling his body heat under my palm was helpful. For some reason, my brain had expected him to be cold. I rolled my eyes at myself and tried to mentally shake off the shit.

"Okay." I heaved a little sigh, and Riles looked up, conversation back on. "Okay, I think if I concentrate on getting into Jonny's account on Hashing Grounds, I can have him reply on time. So..." I nodded, resigned. "Let's kill me." I stopped myself from crying by forcing a silly, exaggerated frown instead.

Whilst Riles returned the frown, Bryan reached over to give my shoulder a squeeze. Then they both went to work. I took my hand off Jonny and also went to work.

For a while, all I could hear was typing and Jonny's ragged breathing.

It didn't take long before there was a conversation on Hashing Grounds. apHellion was looking for MK, had anybody seen them? And, theoretically, variations of the "anybody seen MK" were going up on any forums apHellion thought MK might be on. It turned out that TesTur hadn't heard from MK in a while either. In fact, nobody had heard from MK, and some people were surprised that MK hadn't been part of the aggressive and public actions they'd been taking against hackers that had been outed as SWS lackeys (though relieved and not surprised that MK hadn't been on that list of lackeys).

Suddenly, everyone was in roll call mode. Maybe people who didn't respond quickly, who hadn't been seen in the last few hours, were part of what had just gone down. How they were presumed to be part of it varied based on who was voicing paranoid theories. Maybe they were hiding because they knew they'd be the next to be caught as traitors. Maybe they were too busy checking into the allegations. Blah blah blah.

Fortunately, my custom password cracker and some personal knowledge of Jonny and his tastes got me in just in time. Before anyone could ask where spaceGoddity was.

I did my best to sound like him as I posted the message that was him checking in, saying he hadn't heard from MK, and then saying he'd be ducking out to make sure no fucker was going to compromise him whilst all this shit was going down. Then, hoping to make room for when it was safe someday to let folks know Huw (aka Phrostbyte) had also been a hero, he (I) noted that Phrostbyte hadn't been around in a while either.

I was honestly pretty disappointed that nobody else had noticed, or at least mentioned, that Phrostbyte hadn't been seen lately. I let that feeling distract me from the task at hand for a moment.

"I've been holding my breath over here," Bryan mumbled, his fingers continuing the online fiction, "hoping you'd get signed in as him before anyone specifically called him out." He looked up and flashed me a grin. "Well done."

Before I could reply, Riles asked, "Are you going to make sure all his accounts are secure now?"

Guiltily, I shook my head. "It took just long enough to get this one, and there's no way he's using the same password everywhere."

Rye laughed, "Yeah, he's not quite that big a dumbass." Zie gave me a wink, then looked unsure, as if suddenly aware that my sense of humor over my injured boyfriend might be a little touchy.

I tried to sound light as I laughed in return. "Not quite. Just big enough to be with me." I gave a half-hearted smile. "Anyway, I have to finish other stuff on our to-do list. Then I'll secure his accounts." I cracked my knuckles. "I have auto-posting messages to fake now, poppet."

Soon enough, a post showed up on each of the forums where I'd been most active. *No, where* MK *had been most active*, I silently corrected myself. It wouldn't do any damned good thinking of us as the same person now.

So. The post. It was tweaked a little for each forum, but was basically made to look and sound like something that would auto-post if MK didn't stop it. MK asserted that some motherfucker here (on whatever forum) was probably involved in whatever was keeping her from posting. And then a few specific aspersions were cast, fingers pointed at a person or two who'd done bad shit. People who'd deserve the scrutiny and/or wrath that would follow after.

"Holy shit, Kot!" Riles whistled. "Your messages are making the forums go ape shit. Or more ape shit, given the whole SWS and traitors thing." Zie grinned. "I hope you planned time to read the drama and enjoy."

Bryan chuckled, not looking up from his screen. "Some of these people are moving a little too quickly posting custom 'rest in peace, MK' gifs. Like some of these bastards have been planning and preparing for you dying for a while."

I glared at Bryan's computer. "Assholes. I'll be sure to make them pay."

He looked up to give me a little snort of laughter.

I rolled my eyes and grinned, mumbled more vague threats, and got back to work. It was time to fake up another auto-send.

This one was an email to the comrades, the ones still alive, who'd helped us hack SWS, get their data, all that shit. It was written to a soundtrack of updates from Rye and Bryan, telling me about the chaos all over now that MK was probably dead and a lot of people were out to ruin the traitors in our midst.

I ended up with:

Hey. So, I don't want to worry you, but you getting this doesn't bode well for me. You should assume I'm fucked,

probably dead. Which means you need to know I had a silent
partner. Hopefully, they made it through. They'll use this secure
account but sign as D3AD_L1NX. I trusted them with all this
already. That we succeeded (shit, I hope we succeeded) is proof
to you they can be trusted, I hope. Either way, watch your six.
Thanks for kicking ass. -MK

Because, you know, a dead link is a link that goes to
something that doesn't exist anymore. You know, a broken link.
Like MK, who I'd been, was a dead link. And my whole life felt
like it was now dead links. Ugh. I suspected my brain wasn't at
its best, but this would do.

I just had to remember to choose an actual new 'nym for my
daily use. (Yeah, I should have done it days earlier, but I was
living in fucking denial. Seeing the mediocre one I'd thrown
onto the email motivated me to make sure I didn't get stuck with
it.) I sent it from the account we'd been using for all our
messages with the remote team.

"Oh, for fuck's sake," Bryan sighed. "Okay, it's time for
TesTur to pretend he's going to get together with apHellion in a
private conversation to investigate before it gets totally out of
hand. Let them focus on destroying each other a while."

"Seriously." Riles threw zir hands in the air. "These drama
bitches are worse than me."

Dryly, Bry noted, "I'm not going to disagree. Also, it will give
us a chance to work on other shit before we pretend to come
back with more info."

We all leaned back in our shitty plastic chairs. I put my hand
back on Jonny's arm and glanced to make sure his IV bag looked
okay.

It was like all the emotions needed was a pause, like that was
invitation enough. Suddenly, I felt crushed by them again. Shit.
They were heavier than the SWS CorpSec bloke who'd landed
on me after the explosion. I was crying, quietly, and I felt both
completely justified and stupid about it.

I used my free hand to wipe my face, then to cover it for a
breath. That had been my whole life we'd just killed there. That
had been every worthwhile thing I'd done, every proof that I
was capable, and at least 80% of my good memories. I'd been MK

for longer than I hadn't been her. Most the people I might say I knew actually just knew MK. (On the other hand, I wasn't actually dead like some people were, so get over it, Katja.)

The people in this room, all battered and exhausted, were almost all I had left now. Plus Gran and Quinn. That was it. And, whilst the ones left were the best, I had still...I'd killed off most of me. Also, there was my boyfriend mostly unconscious on a table, 'Randa and Kitty and Huw dead, Riles and I beaten up, the loss of all material possessions that weren't in our bags, probable threats to Gran's safety, having crossed a moral line when we blew up the HQ, and the big fucking weight of being the ones who knew about and had just ramped up the fucking alien invasion (a phrase that still felt too fictional to fully process).

I didn't say all that out loud, of course. What I did say was, "We just killed me and lost everything and some good people for...maybe not nothing, but for way less than we thought. For something that maybe was more harm than good. Fuck."

Riley's eyes were wet as zie tried to joke, "Listen, bitch, I'm in no shape to leap up and comfort you. Stop being sad until I'm healed."

Putting an arm around Riles and reaching a hand out to me, which I took, Bryan said, "It wasn't nothing. And it did plenty of good. We just, well, we just learned that what we saw was the tip of a nasty iceberg. And motherfuckers like us crack ice, right?"

We nodded.

"Good." Bryan nodded, satisfied. "So, now we stay on what's left of the plan I made for after demo day, okay? We make sure our accounts are safe, we check in on our comrades, we—"

"Sleep." Riles cut him off. "We should really, really get some damned sleep. Because I can't be the only one ready to crash."

"Can you finish up making sure your accounts are good?" Bry asked.

Zie nodded. "Yeah. But I don't trust myself to do much more. Not tonight."

Bryan looked at me. "Kot?"

"I can do my accounts...probably check in on everyone, including SWS." I took my hand back and started on that.

"Sounds good. Riles, get sorted then get sleep. Kot and I will make sure the rest is good before we call it a night." And then he too went to work.

As Rye got to work on zir stuff, zie said, "Actually, I'm also going to get nosy about Zane. Dig into their business. Because I think I'm due a little fun."

Nobody argued.

"Zane appears boring as fuck," Riles announced. "But in a harmless way. Sooooooo..." Zie stood up, closing zir computer and hobbling towards the pile of sleeping bags. "You'll now find you can easily snoop on their phone and their ridiculously basic computer and accounts." Zie unrolled zir sleeping bag with a snap of zir wrists. "Plus, I've got an algorithm that will ping if they say or type certain phrases." Zie carefully lowered zirself to the floor and into the bag. "Now, you beauties shut up. And don't stay up too late."

I didn't mention it, but I noticed zie held Kitty's bag, like a kid might hold a teddy bear for comfort, as zie slept.

We did shut up. But we didn't not stay up too late. We used a chat window to check in on each other as we discovered our comrades were safe, as we saw particularly good attacks made on the traitors, and as we parried attacks made on our own accounts.

It was just enough to keep us up. Just enough to keep me from getting to Jonny's accounts.

By the time we decided out automated security would have to do for a while because we were too fucking tired to go on, we only managed a few hours of shitty sleep on the cold tiles before Riles was up and we were back at it.

CHAPTER 4

Saturday morning didn't so much dawn, like some poetic types might say, as crawl into our bones with shivery fingers of "you might as well get up 'cause you're not really sleeping, are you?" and poke us to our feet. I don't know if I was awake before Riley moaned and muttered something unintelligible but clearly cranky, but sleep was such a hopeless cause that I didn't even pretend I was going to try to get more. Just sighed wearily and sat up.

The only light was the glow as we all turned on our mobiles to check the time. In that dim, we caught each others' eyes…Shit, we looked bad. Too much stress and too little sleep. And barely 06:00. Too damned early on top of everything else.

Bryan crawled out of his sleeping bag, but wrapped it around himself before he stumbled over to turn on the lights. I was suddenly aware that they were fluorescent, buzzing and yellow but at least not bright like sun would be.

Whilst Bry and Riles shifted over to sit in front of their computers, I checked on Jonny. He seemed to be breathing more normally, and I could see his eyes moving a little under the lids. Something like hope tried to put a warm spot in my chest.

Once he was sorted out, I booted my own machine. "I could do with more or bigger monitors," I mumbled.

"Well," Bryan cleared his throat, "we could throw news on Jonny's computer. Save our own for work."

I had a momentary knee-jerk reaction, like I was going to let every mention of anything to do with Jonny make me feel shitty and hopeless. I swallowed it, nodded. "Makes sense."

Jonny's bag was propped against the leg of the table he was on. I fished out his computer, booted it, and got a 24-hour news stream playing. We were at the point in the news cycle where they were still trying to make small or repeated bits carry the show whilst they waited for something new to happen. The new "news" at the moment was reporters theorizing about why the president and SWS hadn't said anything yet. The only real new news was that, among bodies they'd definitely been able to identify already, workers had found the body of CFO Jennifer Williams. If we were going to confirm one death...If there was one I might feel slightly less bad about, it was this bitch, who'd been involved in the deaths of at least some of our people. So, let's call this one a bright spot.

We were watching assorted agencies' and administrations' computers, so we could see, of course, that they were scrambling. The president had people drafting and researching and trying to make sure he didn't implicate himself, admit he'd been a big SWS supporter, or risk the ire of SWS just in case they weren't put out of business by this. Politics is a noble profession, so full of integrity...

Whereas SWS...Partly, they were trying to see if they could salvage anything from their computers, or at least from their backups now that the ones at their HQ were gone, to figure out who their actual enemy was. (We got some of our remote comrades to work on tracing where SWS was digging, trying to find those backups so we could copy and nuke them too.) And partly there were some very sparse messages flying between managers of big offices as they tried to sort out who should and could be interim CEO. There was one sender we couldn't nail down. It wasn't emails but some kind of chat messages. The user called Council did all their messages in...I mean I guess now we could say it was in Peaceforger-ese?

But also. Also, we had plenty to look through in terms of evidence that some assholes out there had spent our few sleeping hours trying to hack us. Oh, and *also* also publically talking a lot of shit on forums about MK and insisting that TesTur and apHellion must be problems as well. The main thread seemed to be that MK had called too much dangerous attention to our questionable community and might even be part of an SWS effort to destroy us.

I snorted. Those desperate, libelous fuckers.

The forums were war zones. Worse than the flame war of '47 when someone's homegrown AI had infiltrated and shown itself to be a bastard with no concern for security. This time, the sides were pretty clearly drawn. Not only had we made sure to release names of who'd been in SWS's pocket, but we'd found bank records and messages and plenty of other evidence. Those dicks were, even if just due to the paranoia—and not morals—of their peers, unwanted and facing more attacks than us.

Obviously, in between attacking us and trying to defend themselves, they were striking back. At least three forums had already been destroyed, infected, shredded to digital bits. Most the others were non-stop all caps shout-fests. NO LOWERCASE WOULD DO. My eyes were doing whatever the visual equivalent is of ears ringing.

I was glad for the break when the President of the U.S. finally showed up on the news with his prepared speech. Even if the speech was the usual drivel. You know "my fellow Americans, we'll be brave and we'll face this threat and we'll figure this out and we're investigating the allegations in the emails and we're taking steps to make sure there are no threats to us (but we're not going to specifically say those threats might come from SWS). No need to panic; the terrorists win if we do that. And blah blah blah." Social media was torn between declaring it too little and declaring it very presidential. The usual.

As he speechified at all of us watching, we three in the warehouse were checking in to see just how that investigating and figuring out was actually going. On both a federal and local level, we could see them doing just that, looking into the explosion and the allegations. Confirming that the email with the damning info had, indeed, come from SWS and was most likely legit. Bringing in their own doctors and engineers with clearance to confirm what ours already had. Trying to figure out just how dug into their own systems and lives SWS tech was. Discovering that the explosive used at HQ wasn't the common C-4 that took down the other (my) SWS building just a couple weeks before the HQ explosion. And so forth. Nothing that should lead to us. Yet. But plenty that should help them believe the truth we'd dropped on them.

There weren't more than a few minutes of the news anchors trying to summarize the speech back at us and introduce experts to tell us how we should react before they switched to a view from Seattle. A view of a raised platform with a podium, backdropped by the smoldering ruins of the SWS HQ building. It was clearly a hastily put together platform, but it looked like an interim CEO had been chosen and was ready to go.

Fortunately for SWS, there were already loads of press milling around as close as they could get to the HQ; it was really easy to get a crowd of cameras and mics there. To get anchors saying, "And it appears that SWS is also ready to issue a statement, so we'll send you to Brad. He's in Seattle covering the bombing and the allegations of criminal actions by SWS."

Before the chyron under Brad's face could set the stage for us, the tall, pale man at the podium cleared his throat.

He tapped at the tablet in front of him, then looked up with his jaw clenched and nostrils flared. The ragged edge to his voice was either a good bit of acting or some authentic mourning for his lost co-conspirators. "Good morning. Thank you all for finding the time to come hear what we at SWS have to say in response to this latest tragic bombing, coming too soon on the heels of the previous one, and the baseless allegations of criminal conspiracies."

He paused a moment, looked around at the assembled reporters, then went on. "I'm interim CEO Robert Trent. I'm both honored and overwhelmed to be given the responsibility of facing this grim moment in our company's history."

My heart sank a little as I realized that he was going to have the force of some serious emotional authenticity behind his words. The only thing he'd be lying about was if he mentioned their supposed innocence. But this had been a true and personal blow for him and his people. It had the added weight of his religious beliefs, of everything he believed in and had been raised to do as a duty to...I had to search my memory. Had Zane mentioned some particular deity? Well, anyway, his grief and righteous indignation were real and that was going to come through and give him an edge. Shit.

Trent delivered his short statement with careful gravity. "As you know, yesterday evening, Secure World Systems was the victim of yet another attack. This time, in addition to initiating an explosion that destroyed our headquarters and took many lives, including those of CEO Mary Johnson, COO James Smith, and CFO Jennifer Williams," the confirmation of those other two deaths set off some victorious fist pumps in our warehouse, "the perpetrator or perpetrators also falsified an email meant to do as much damage to our reputation and our ability to do good as they had done to our headquarters. But I'm here today to deliver these messages to you this morning."

Holding up the appropriate number of fingers as he went, Trent stared down the cameras and declared, "One: We will not be terrorized by these despicable actions. Two: We will continue to work to deliver peace through security and security through peace to all of you who have trusted us over the years. And, three: Our CorpSec will work, alone or with other authorities, to hunt down and bring to justice those who have murdered our employees, destroyed our property, and endeavored to ruin our reputation and shake your faith in us."

In a slightly less hard—but definitely nothing near soft—tone, he finished up. "We look forward to serving you today and tomorrow as we have always done." He gripped the podium a moment as he took a deep breath. He shifted his gaze from the cameras to the reporters, giving them a small, sad smile. "Keeping in mind that this is a time of loss for many, I ask you to consider we sit down for interviews if you have questions. However, I'm willing to take a question or two now."

The words were barely out of his mouth before the assembled press erupted. There was no way they were going to treat this...gently? Was that what Trent had hoped for? I saw a flash of annoyance on his face as he took in the clamor. He quickly smoothed his expression...and then he just waited. Stood with arms folded and face slightly stern and waited.

The clamor dulled down to a buzz, and then to something like an awkward silence that I could feel radiating from the screen. Damn. He'd played them like a school teacher with a rowdy class.

When, like good students, they raised their hands politely. Trent nodded. He pointed to someone, but an aid stepped in and whispered in his ear before the chosen reporter could even ask their question.

"I'm sorry. My assistant informs me that there are pressing matters I need to attend to immediately. I look forward to meeting with you, one-on-one, to answer your questions." Trent spared them another small smile and a nod, and then strode off.

Behind Brad, the reporter for the channel we had up, we could see other reporters stepping in front of their cameras. Like Brad, they must be doing that thing where they summarize what viewers had literally just seen. You know, mostly just padding out the non-stop news cycle.

I turned my attention back to my own screen, to see that another forum had fallen. This one had now been replaced by just one page, bold letters proclaiming all out war on SWS and their tech. Animated, fiery letters warning that any hackers who worked for or sympathized with SWS were also going down. Because I guess some people thought the non-stop shouting and shots fired since Friday night hadn't been clue enough.

We spent the morning in the digital trenches. We had about 5 minutes of notice before the next salvo, and only had that much because we were looking at SWS communications just right. Just happened to see that the orders for the hackers they owned had narrowed down. All other efforts should be scaled back to bare minimum in favor of finding and ruining me, with a massive bonus payment to anyone who could find proof—proof that would satisfy anyone—of MK's real identity.

"Kot," Bryan's fingers clattered across his keys, belying his calm tone, "tell me you backed everything up."

"Mate. Obviously." I tried not to sound annoyed (at least not annoyed at Bryan) as I pulled apart code that I feared might, in one way or another, allow people to trace my online stuff to my backups.

"So, we can immediately nuke all of MK's stuff? Like, now?" His fingers had stopped.

A quick glance told me he was poised to blow it all to smithereens. I nodded. "You can press the button." I gave him a half smile. "Thanks."

Riles was still typing as zie asked, "And did you include backing up and nuking private message logs?"

"Backed up," I confirmed.

"Shit," was Bryan's way of saying he'd forgotten those.

"No worries. I've got you covered, baby." Riles sounded pleased to have something to add (or, in this case, to destroy).

A few key presses later and the only thing left of MK online was people talking about her or people mentioning her in replies to posts that no longer existed. Fucking shame. I'd said some clever things. The only posts that still existed were private backups I'd made, because I can be a little sentimental, of threads that were also heavy on posts from Bry, Riles, or Jonny.

Of course, suddenly MK was mentioned in plenty of new posts, everybody noticing she was gone and wondering about it. Which is when things got extra shitty for TesTur, apHellion, spaceGoddity, and a few others I liked and had been known to work with frequently. Because the SWS toadies couldn't find a way to follow through on their orders, they turned their fire and libel at anyone who was known to be a close associate of MK.

I pretended to be spaceGoddity just enough to make sure nobody would notice he was gone. It felt kind of shitty, especially since I'd rather have been figuring out his other passwords and protecting him. I mean, I did that too. But having to be on forums slowed me down.

After a number of rounds of people rallying to defend MK and her known associates, Rye snapped. Zie snarled, and then lectured zir screen. "How the fuck are you all going to take down SWS and defend your shit if you're busy here with this bullshit?" A few extra-hard key taps later, zie posted:

Fuck this. I'm out. More important parties to crash, bitches.

Zie sighed loudly, then said to no one in particular, "I'm really glad people are defending us, you know. I'm more pissed off at the attacks and at how they're pulling people off target."

I just nodded in agreement and kept working.

Soon after, Bryan posted something similar to what Riles had posted, but making sure to include a little about how the attacks were waylaying our usefulness. And then, after a couple other people did, I posted like that for spaceGoddity. Those of our comrades who hadn't already posted their own "fuck this" tried to make it clear to those who slung accusations and criticisms that, no shit, of course people were going to ground after this all.

UGH.

It had somehow shifted from feeling like danger and being fighters for the right to being dumbass drama, and I was over that. So, okay, good. I'd still need to keep an eye on possible attacks, but I was basically out enough to be able to ignore the drama part. Thank fuck.

But, also, I guess now SWS had kind of blown up what I'd always thought of as *my* HQ. After driving me out of my home. Bastards.

I took a break to pretend I was just checking on Jonny. But I was also fighting back some sulky tears.

I massaged Jonny's hands and felt like it was some sort of recompense from the Universe when his eyes slightly opened. Fortunately, my brain wasn't too busy being sad or relieved to work. I leaned in, ear by his mouth and lips by his ear, and tried to be gentle and urgent when I said, "Baby, tell me passwords. I need to save you."

He mumbled some phrases, petering out halfway through one. I took a moment to kiss his forehead, to feel a pang of disappointment that this hadn't been him waking up for good, but then got to work. I knew a lot of ways those phrases might become passwords. I made a grid so I could track which of those ways I'd tried for each of his possible places to log in and then got cracking. (Haha! Hacker pun! Sorry...)

My grid-based work was done to the melodic sounds of SWS trying to hit back via one of those interviews Trent had suggested the reporters set up. It looked like Trent, without a scripted speech or the distance afforded by a crowd, was flailing as he tried to run the show. At the moment, that show appeared to be scrambling to salvage the company's reputation. And he wasn't giving up easily. Even after experts in other interview windows (all brought to one interview by the wonders of the 'Net) confirmed that the emails were legit and the docs all seemed legit and so forth (we high-fived over that win), he kept arguing.

In the end, he was left with disparaging *me*.

With a painfully obvious playacting of self-control he said, "But can we stop to talk about who put this information into the world?"

The experts all started to remind him that the emails had come from now-deceased CFO Williams, and interim CEO Trent raised a hand to quiet them.

When they stopped, he went on, an edge of disdain in his voice. "What we know, because many files from headquarters were backed up to a remote server, is that there was at least one—and we suspect more than one—hacker who was out to take us down. Surely, a hacker could have faked who that email came from."

"But, Mr. Trent," the news anchor broke in, and the network made the windows of experts smaller so we could see her, "isn't it true that the building was locked down for an event? If the experts are saying that the emails definitely came from inside the building, physically inside, how did that hacker get in?"

Trent blinked, but recovered, ignoring the question. "Rachel, the real question is whether we want to trust emails and documents built and sent by a hacker who goes by the infantile 'nym MindKiller? Does that sound like someone you would trust?"

Again, the clamor of the experts and the anchor, pressing the point of the locked-down building, some also asking how they knew the 'nym of the hacker. After a moment, Trent raised his hand again. I didn't know why people kept shutting up at that gesture, but they did.

"Now, SWS were investigating someone. I don't have all the details, because it was an investigation that was working out of our headquarters, looking into the bombing of our clinic two weeks ago, and not all details were backed up. And some evidence shouldn't be shared publicly. So, yes, we're asking you to trust us as you always have. But! We do have a possible name, someone that the professionals in our corporate security have been investigating since the initial, horrible incident."

I whispered, "Oh, fuck you. Don't you do it."

But the man on the TV, fucking Robert Trent, did it. "You may recall that there was one survivor from that bombing. And our corporate security, working with the police, have reason to believe that that survivor might be this so-called MindKiller."

A few things happened at once. Trent looked like he was taking a moment to pull my name up, the anchor covered her mic and had a whispered conversation with someone just off the screen, and I shouted, "Oh, suck a fuck!" at the screen.

Rye laughed. "Suck a fuck?"

I scowled. "Shut up, mate. I'm stressed. Don't you critique my swearing now."

Zie limped around the table and put an arm around me, still laughing. Bryan just mumbled "suck a fuck" under his breath, chuckling.

Trent didn't get a chance to name me. He didn't need to; they'd leaked my name to the press already. It was easy enough for the anchor to put it together.

"Mr. Trent, are you alleging that your employee, Katja Brennan, is this hacker MindKiller that you allege exists, and that she is responsible for what might arguably be considered whistleblowing, *as well as* blowing up SWS headquarters yesterday?"

I groaned. Though I didn't hate that our big email blast was being characterized as whistleblowing.

Looking up from the screen where he'd pretended he had to search for my name, clearly trying to pretend that he hadn't realized that everyone already knew who I was and had been talking about it on the news for days (he sucked at pretending), he replied, "We haven't concluded our investigation, but that's what we think." Trent nodded. He must have been pleased to put it on me and dodge the question about someone getting into the building.

"We actually have the detective in charge of the investigation of that first bombing with us now," the anchor said, and a new window was somehow squeezed into the screen. On a small portable screen, it was getting kind of hard to see the people in the smaller windows. I squinted and leaned in closer.

Engalls looked a bit disheveled. He clearly hadn't been on the schedule to show up today. He also looked plenty annoyed.

The anchor said, "Detective Engalls, thanks for being on the show. Can you say anything to us about the investigation into

Katja Brennan and these allegations that she is a hacker who goes by the 'nym MindKiller and might be behind yesterday's bombing?"

Engalls sighed, then went surly cop on them. "First, I want to say that this is irresponsible and verging on slander. Ms. Brennan was one of about a *dozen* people who worked in the smaller building who survived. Not only did my investigation lead me to believe that she is almost certainly *not* responsible for that, but SWS never brought any evidence to the contrary. Further, based on an open investigation that I'm not at liberty to discuss, we know that someone appeared to be targeting those who know Ms. Brennan in violent and deadly ways."

I reached across Riles to put my hand on Bryan's arm. Obviously, Engalls meant 'Randa's murder. It felt like forever, but it hadn't even quite been a week ago. Bryan's careful breathing made it clear that this was, as you'd expect, still a raw topic.

Engalls wasn't done. "And, obviously, I can't comment on details of yesterday's bombing. That's *clearly* an open case. But..." He clenched and unclenched his jaw, appeared to be struggling with some thought, and practically growled, "It would be irresponsible to let you all suggest Ms. Brennan did this when I haven't seen evidence that supports it." He looked briefly guilty, as if he knew he shouldn't be giving away even that much, then went on before anyone else could cut him off. "And I notice that Mr. Trent has failed to address the very important question about how exactly he thinks someone managed to sneak into SWS HQ yesterday evening during what we understand was a lockdown. As the experts have already said, those emails are legitimately from the network there, and there's absolutely no sign they were sent from outside the building. So, how exactly did someone unauthorized get in? Even if you're someone who doesn't believe that the emails are full of truth, shouldn't we be worried that this so-called 'security experts' company couldn't even keep their own network secure?" The slight lift of his eyebrow made me think he had enjoyed throwing some allegations back at Trent.

In his little square on the screen, they showed Trent, jaw clenched and failing to come up with a reply. I could see his eyes darting to the screen on the table in front of him. A quick peek at activity in SWS showed me that someone was trying to put talking points in front of him, but they appeared to have lost their best people in the explosion. It was amateur bollocks, and the writer kept deleting, rewriting. Nice.

As if it were damning evidence against me, the anchor earnestly asked, "But what about the fact that no one has managed to find her or make contact with her, Detective Engalls? Don't you think this means Katja Brennan is, well, possibly a fugitive? Fleeing after pulling off yet another bombing?"

"What I think," Engalls practically growled, "is that *someone*," he glared at what I assumed was the area of his monitor with Trent's face on it, "leaked her identity to the press, which was, at best, irresponsible. And what I think is that, once every news outlet with a reason to cover the bombing of her previous office had her name, she felt hounded and unsafe. In my *professional* opinion, she's an innocent woman just trying to avoid the unpleasantness of unwanted and unwarranted intrusions by the press into her life. That's what I think, ma'am." You could almost hear the sneer he was thinking but held back when he said "ma'am."

It momentarily disintegrated into noisy cross-talk from all the windows. But we were pleased to find Engalls being, basically, my defender.

After a few moments, the anchor finally got everyone quieted down, which appeared to have involved just plain muting some people. She tried to keep things going. (That's 75% of the job when you work a 24-hour news cycle.) Reading from her own monitor with notes, she said, "I want to come back to one point that's been brushed over a few times. Mr. Trent, while you've primarily mentioned this one hacker, MindKiller, as your main suspect, you've also suggested that there might be others who worked with them." She paused a beat, and now the screen was shared just by her window and Trent's. With concern that verged on being slightly too dramatic, she asked, "Mr. Trent, are there other hackers we need to worry about? Others whose identities we should be trying to figure out?"

In our warehouse, we froze. I quietly muttered, "No no no. You arseholes are supposed to keep your eyes on *me*. Just me."

Trent looked briefly surprised, and then pleased. Monitoring the notes being sent him, we saw that he was being told this was an opportunity to attack people I cared about, to take down any hackers not on their payroll, to make people feel more concerned and more in need of SWS. Someone was even typing up lists of hackers we knew they'd been investigating, hackers who'd turned them down, and even those who'd been blackmailed but now should be free.

Even as Trent put on his "serious and concerned" face, even as he opened his mouth to say, "Well, yes, actually. Rachel, we believe—" he was cut off by the anchor.

"What's this on my monitor?" She pointed, eyes a bit wide and worried, at the monitor in front of her from which she'd been reading notes. "Who wrote this?" She looked around at what was probably the rest of the news crew on the other side of the camera.

After a few seconds of fruitless, questioning looking around, Trent interrupted. "Is there a problem?"

And then we all saw it. Someone changed the view on our screen. It no longer showed us the anchor or the experts, but showed us the monitor. Showed the notes Rachel had been using. Showed that, in the middle, in all caps and bold, someone had typed:

MINDKILLER COULD DO IT WITHOUT HELP. RESPECT TO MINDKILLER!!!

I exchanged confused looks with Riles and Bryan. "Is this one of you?"

Both shook their heads, looking as uncertain as I felt.

I asked, "Is this a good thing?"

Bry and Riles looked at each other, shrugging.

"No fucking clue," Bryan replied. He sighed, "I could argue both ways."

Either way, the station ended the whole conversation abruptly by shutting down Rachel's monitor and feed and going to a commercial break. So at least the results weren't all bad.

"Oh!"

Bryan and I both stopped what we were doing to look over at Rye. Zie had zir delighted "new idea" face on.

When zie saw zie had our attention, zie grinned broadly. "You know what would be a nice gift to give Engalls for defending Kot's honor on the news?" Zie paused a split second, zir grin shifting into a smirk. "We make sure he can find the person who blew up Kot's building."

I narrowed my eyes at zir. I knew zie didn't mean give him Jonny, but I didn't see where zie was going yet. Bryan, on the other hand, was leaned towards Riles, looking intrigued.

With eyes wide, feigning innocent intent, Riles said, "I mean, surely there's a trail that can prove CFO Williams did it. Now that there's reason to look into her. Right?"

I gave a nasty chuckle, and felt less bad about it when Bryan joined me. Rye was somehow managing a hybrid grin-smirk. Yeah, okay, it was unanimous.

Bry asked, "Do you have a plan, or...?"

"I'm thinking you're our gear boy; you know who'd sell C-4 and things like the bugs, but make sure it's someone who also deserves to go down. And Katja is our bank girl, so she can easily set up the account side. The supposed source of payment." Riles chewed a nail contemplatively as zie noted the pieces.

Nodding, Bryan said, "Yeah, we just hide the trail enough so it looks like someone tried to be sneaky when they made their purchase."

"Can't make it too easy," I agreed. "That would look suspicious.

"If we do it quickly," Riley said, "I can kind of see how the Seattle PD's efforts looking into the HQ explosion are headed. They've got a note on the big group to-do list to look into Williams's financials. So..."

Bryan was already tapping away at his keys, eyes serious and thoughtful, but he was smiling slightly. "I've actually got some assholes I've been meaning to take down, but then the whole SWS thing happened." He looked up and over at Riles. "I'm going to send you info. I'll work on creating my side of the bug trail, you work on the C-4 trail, and," he looked at me, "Kot, you get the account set up. Try to make it look like it's supposed to be a secret account. And send the details our way once you do so we can make sure they match up at all ends."

I opened my messenger. "First, I'm going to have my sock puppet tell our remote team to lay off financials on SWS execs until I tell them otherwise. Don't want anyone fucking up the bank side of things before it gets found."

And we worked. The air was thick with vengeance. It wasn't going to bring back 'Randa, Huw, or anyone else that Williams had given orders to kill, but it sure felt good to keep ruining her. She might be dead, beyond our reach, but her reputation could still be obliterated. Even better if it helped keep *us* safe from accusations.

As a last touch, I implied a motive. I had the "hidden" account transfer the exact same not-quite-small amount, monthly for the last 5 months, into an account that had belonged to one of the head doctors at the clinic in my building. I'd overheard women in the bathroom complaining about him getting handsy, so, frankly, I didn't care what sort of story people made up about the money transfers. Didn't care which of them looked bad in the theories.

Once the pieces were laid out, we all gathered around my computer and they backseat drove as I made sure that Williams made one mistake, one less circuitous transfer of funds right at the start. I tried to make it look like a learning curve, like maybe she'd thought this was tricky enough, but then she'd gotten increasingly tricky over the next few times. Made sure that an account of hers that would be easily found had some transfers out that would almost not look suspicious and would match what investigators would find on the hidden account.

Then? We began the much-hated waiting game. Waiting and hoping, knowing we couldn't touch it more or push anyone without raising suspicion.

I really fucking hated waiting.

CHAPTER 5

A chat window popped up just as I was starting to make some serious headway with Jonny's accounts. I didn't read it, just glanced long enough to notice it was Zane using the contact info I'd given them. "Either of you done enough to chat with E.T.?"

Riles gave me a sort of frantic, overloaded look that turned to relief when Bry said, "Yeah. Toss them my way."

I got back to work, nailing down, doing backups (just in case Jonny had missed something), and doing plenty of deleting. Trying to make sure Jonny wouldn't wake up to his own 'nym and digital life in ruins. Well, no more so than literally everybody's now that the Great Hacker War of 2050 was in full swing.

A few minutes later, Bryan stood with a sigh. "Apparently, Zane's been trying to think of things to tell us that might be useful, but they feel nervous about doing it any way other than in person."

Rye kept working, but noted, "Could be a trap." Zie stopped and grabbed Bryan's hand. "We can't lose more of us."

Bry gave zir hand a squeeze. "I know, poppet. But...knowing is half the battle, right? We have to make sure we have all the info when we decide what we'll do. Don't we?" He looked questioningly at us both. "And we haven't seen anything pop up on their phone or computer that seems suspicious, right?"

"Did you spy through their phone just now?" I asked.

"Yep. And they didn't say anything like 'I think he bought it' or 'he's on his way; ready the chloroform and handcuffs.' So, I'm going, okay?" He managed to ask it in a way that suggested he would abide by our replies, even though I knew that was unlikely.

Riles nodded, looking defeated. I rubbed my forehead. Shit. I shrugged.

As Bryan grabbed his jacket and keys, I reminded him, "They think you're n0cebro. Don't slip and use wrong 'nyms."

"Damn. Right." Bryan squinted, trying to remember, then pointed at Riles. "0ccamsLaZer?"

I shook my head. "That's Jonny. Rye is BossestCossist."

"Which means you're Kl33n3*, yeah?"

I nodded. "Aye. That's me. Unfortunately." I laughed, thinking of what an asshole the real Kl33n3* was.

"Hey," Riles interjected, "at least the fucker whose name you're using is only a sexist prick. Mine's also racist."

Bryan snorted a laugh, walking out the break room door. He called back, "Yeah, well mine's almost definitely a pig fucker."

We sat and listened as he left. I held Jonny's hand and strained to hear the sound of the exterior door closing.

Riley must have been waiting to hear it too, 'cause as soon as it was closed, zie said, "When Jonny wakes up, let's not tell him at first whose 'nym we stuck him with. Don't want him to decide he was better off unconscious." Zie gave me a wink and went back to work.

I squeezed Jonny's hand before doing the same.

It seemed like no time at all before I'd gotten all Jonny's stuff that I could find sorted. If only I could so easily sort his health.

I glanced at what was playing on his computer's screen. The news channel was chaos, with hackers now fighting for control of which cameras were broadcast, filling the chyron with slogans and attacks, slipping graphics into and over the broadcast. The war was no longer just on our forums. I wondered if we'd have more casualties in the meat, not just in the digital world. After all, this was about more than ego now.

Casualties. My messy and paranoid brain wondered if we'd done enough to cover things related to Kitty and 'Randa. It gave me a little to-do list, cooked up in the background whilst I'd taken care of Jonny's shit.

First, I needed to find the footage of Kitty at SWS. I didn't think we'd taken care of that. I couldn't risk Engalls seeing it and connecting us to the explosion. Or, just as bad, her family somehow seeing it and thinking she'd been one of the villains in the story.

With the building and its computers gone, I had to hope one of our traces during the explosion had traced the path of security video feeds (if they were offsite and not destroyed). My logs showed there'd been one local copy and...it looked like one remote. Sadly, when I checked that out, it wasn't the full SWS remote backup we'd been hoping for, but it did have all the security camera video.

I figured deleting the footage would be suspicious, so I grabbed a copy for us to keep, and then I wrote an algorithm to do the work that needed doing. It would scrub through all the minutes that Kitty was on premises and would dirty the footage up just enough, add just enough noise and interference, that nobody could definitively ID her.

I messaged Bryan to check that all non-SWS Kitty footage had been scrubbed when the rest of the stuff related to us had been. I was relieved when he replied that it had. One less thing I needed to handle. I still had things on my to-do list of girlfriend-related actions.

Second, I had to try to confirm what happened to Kitty's body. As soon as I acknowledged that was my task, I felt sick. Punched in the gut by guilt. Guilt that we'd let her do this. That Jonny and I had failed to get her out at the last minute. That I'd been shitty to her before. I wanted to bury my head in my arms and sob. How the hell was Riles not doing that?

For the first time all day, I really looked at zir. Looked when zie wasn't expecting it, when I wasn't also half-watching something else. Finally saw that zie looked ill and haunted. That zir eyes were red and maybe even wet.

Zie looked up, feeling my eyes, and must have seen something that let zir know this was about Kitty. Zie hiccupped a little sob, and we reached across the table to hold hands a while.

I whispered, "I'm so, so sorry, poppet. Shit."

Zie just nodded and swallowed, trying to blink away the tears. "She was badass."

For once, I was entirely sincere as I agreed. "Hell yes she was. The baddest ass-est of us."

As if zie couldn't help zirself, Riles leered, "She did have a pretty bad ass. And, by 'bad,' I mean 'completely do-able'." Zie laughed, a short, surprised sound. "I guess my libido and my sense of humor are both entirely inappropriate." Zie shook zirself, like a cat shaking off rain. "Okay, back to the fucking endless crusade."

Zie went back to whatever and I started scrolling through footage from cameras that had a view of the SWS HQ after the explosion. I watched emergency vehicles move in, first responders assess bodies and dig through rubble, teams arrange and tag bodies before putting them in trucks. I felt sick at having had a hand in every one of those deaths, or at least a big percentage of them. I felt even sicker as I didn't see anything that looked like Kitty's body. Was she still buried in the rubble?

I'd seen some crews digging where I thought they should find her, seen more CorpSec bodies pulled out. But not Kitty. Actually...I'd seen them pull out the receptionist, but not Kitty and not any execs. That seemed...not right. Maybe I was just being impatient. Maybe...I froze, guilt and sorrow somehow increased exponentially by the only possible answer. Maybe hers had been one of the bodies so fucked up that they put it into a body bag before moving it out of the rubble, walking it through where people might see it on the way to the van that was filling up with corpses. We hadn't just killed her; we'd mangled her. I took a deep breath, held it, tried to think soothing vibes at myself, and then exhaled.

Okay, then, third, I needed to see if I could figure out what had happened with 'Randa's body. I checked police reports, hospital reports, news stories. It didn't seem like anyone had found it. Dammit.

I hit the cameras from in and around the club the night she'd been taken. They might not have seen the woman who took her leaving, but maybe I could find her showing up? Find her talking to 'Randa?

I set one of my image-search programs going, looking to see if anyone had taken selfies or vid in the club that night and caught 'Randa in the pic. Whilst it ran, I spent some time finding and bookmarking camera footage of "goth chicks" (to use Kitty's phrase from that weekend) who met Kitty's description of a generic goth woman, coming and going. Looking close to see if any of them seemed like they might be Peaceforgers.

When the hits came in, there was just one picture from that night that was at all useful. Normally, I think people who use flash on their pictures should be beaten, but...The club was dark, obviously, so it was only because some tosser had taken a picture with flash that I got this shot. In the corner, off and to the right of the people meant to be in the pic, there was 'Randa and a seriously unremarkable, very average goth woman. 'Randa looked really happy.

I breathed in a good, long breath. No use getting teary-eyed. I needed to see, to think. I went and found the woman in the camera footage I'd gone through. I followed her, using assorted traffic and business cameras, until I actually got to what I could reasonably assume was her home.

"Gotcha, fucker."

I must have sounded as hateful as I felt, because Riles said, "Shit, Kot. Who'd you find? I wouldn't want to be them."

I could feel the cold hate, coating my tongue in frost and giving the air in my nostrils a crispness, as I breathed in, then said, "I found the fucker who took 'Randa."

Rye's eyes went wide. "No shit?"

I nodded, picked up my computer to go sit by zir, and showed zir how and what I'd found. "We have enough to figure out who she is. To destroy her." I'd never thought of myself as bloodthirsty. Maybe for digital justice, but never for in-the-meat hurt. Nothing worse than wanting to punch the shits who messed with any of us when we were younger. But now...

"We have to let Bry decide what to do with this," Riley said, almost as if zie knew that I was ready to set repercussions into motion immediately.

"Yeah." I sighed. "Yeah, you're right. But this is solid, right?"

"Totally solid! You win the 'find of the day' award," zie confirmed.

I got up, scooted back around the table. "I'm going to wrap this up all neatly so Bryan can act on this however he wants. Going to see if I can find the picture source somewhere that we can point Engalls if we opt for legal actions."

Riles was typing as zie shook zir head sadly. "Giving it to the law? That would be such a waste."

When we heard the exterior door opening, Riley and I exchanged paranoid looks. I pulled out my gun, pointed it at the door, and Riles did the same.

"Should we move off to the side?" Riles asked.

I shrugged. "I can't get Jonny moved, and I'm not moving without him, so..."

So we both sat, waiting to see if we were fucked.

Bryan laughed when he opened the door to our room and saw us. "This is your plan?"

I repeated what I'd told Riley. "I can't move Jonny, so here's where I sit."

Bryan shrugged off his coat and settled back into his chair. "Well, as you can see, meeting up with Zane wasn't a trap. And, unless I was followed home, we're good."

"Did you get any good info?" Rye asked. "Because Kot got some...I don't even know what adjective to use. She got info you'll want."

Bry gave me a curious look. "What's up?"

I coughed, suddenly aware of how big this could be. "I feel like, when I tell you, that's it for the day. Maybe you should tell us what Zane told you."

Looking a bit confused and wary now, Bryan said, "Sure. Okay. I've got it on video, because I'm basically making a record of a new species. But I also want to know what the hell you found, so I'll just summarize while I check to make sure nobody fucked me while I was out."

He typed as he spoke. "At some point in the very distant past, having achieved peace on their own planet (though the details were vague and symbolic...very much a 'light of peace won out' sort of summary), tons of the Peaceforgers got into every ship possible and headed out to take their peace to the stars. They think they're saviors, helping other species to peace by any means necessary. Zane claims they honestly tried to do it in as non-traumatic (but non-resist-able) ways as they could conceive first. They totally believe they're the superior species with the superior cause, graciously lifting up and welcoming in other species that aren't too polluted to accept the gift they offer."

Bryan had to pause so that we could snort and call them assholes. Because, seriously, self-righteous, meddling assholes. Well, at least we now had insight into their motivations and mindset. Know thy enemy, etc.

When we quieted down, he went on. "Most the travelers on each ship—or at least in Zane's ship—spend their time in a sort of suspended animation. They know the universe is massive and that they'll need to spread out their resources. They sleep until the ship's computer detects, for instance, radio or TV waves, signs of a civilization, at which point three are woken to assess the planet and make initial plans."

"That's just...obnoxious," Riley said. "Just 'cause you can see my TV from outside my house doesn't mean I'm inviting you over to sit and watch with me."

"Yeah," Bryan nodded. "And they're playing the long game, like Zane said. Not just for this planet, but to make sure they maximize how many planets they can get their so-called 'peace' to. If possible, they breed the generations who'll execute the plan; they wake as few of their sleeping people as possible. Like Zane, most of them who're working to take over here were born here. And they expect to never see any others of their kind again. Never to see their home planet again or at all, depending on whether they were born there or on some planet they're 'helping.' Their whole plan is to bring peace to every possible planet or, when 'necessary,' to burn out so-called polluted planets."

There was a beat. I waited for Bryan to go on. When he didn't, I asked, "That's it? That's what they wouldn't tell you except in person?" That sounded suspicious and weird to me.

Bry gave a short laugh. "I know. Ridiculous. In fairness, it gives us a little context, but..." He rolled his eyes. "I think they're just super paranoid that anything we transmit will be intercepted and they'll get fucked."

"Is there some tech they have that justifies that paranoia?" Riley chewed zir lip. "I don't want us to assume that all our knowledge is enough when we don't actually know what the enemy have in terms of tech."

"Naw, mate, I don't think so." Bryan shook his head. "I just think that maybe there's a little hubris on that side, some assumption that they're so much more advanced than us that there's no way we could, well, do what we do. What we did."

He pushed back from his computer, giving me his full attention. "Now, what's this info *you* found?"

Dramatically, Riley reached over and took Bryan's gun from his holster. "I'm just gonna hold onto this while she tells you." Zie nodded at me as if I'd been waiting for zir to tell me it was okay.

I had to laugh at zir drama, but quickly sank back into the same "freezing hatred mixed with smug triumph" I'd felt when I found the information. I moved my chair around to sit by Bry, balancing my portable on my non-cracked knee as I pulled up pictures and footage. "I found the fucker who took 'Randa."

Bryan's voice was daggers and he gripped my shoulder like he thought I might disappear with his chance for revenge. "Show me."

After he'd seen what I'd found, Bryan stood up. Wordless. I could feel emotion boiling in him, coming off like steam. He paced in circles, his breathing getting heavier, until he suddenly veered towards a wall. With a snarl, he punched the wall, and then stood panting.

The wall was just sheetrock, so it got a hole and Bry only got some minor abrasions. He contemplated them a moment, and then came back to sit between Riles and me.

"Okay." His voice was husky with emotion. He cleared his throat and tried again. This time, it was clean and firm. "Okay. Now that I've been a walking trope of toxic masculinity, now we destroy the bitch."

But he didn't make any moves or offer any plans. I sat, fingers poised to call down any devastation he wanted. Feeling both ashamed and proud as I realized that I hoped he didn't want to kill her. I didn't want any more death.

Finally, wearily, he said, "We have to give her to the police."
What the hell?

I thought it, but Riles asked it. "What the hell? We're going to trust the fucking justice system to actually do its job? We're going to trust them to find the evidence? Are you fucking joking?" And then zie caught zirself. Quietly, zie apologized. "I'm sorry. You just...tell us what to do, and we'll do it."

"Maybe you're right." Bryan sounded defeated. "And, if I can't use this to hunt down evidence I think I can pass to Engalls that will stick...we'll take care of her ourselves then. But, for now, she's part of the bigger story, part of how we prove that we're innocent and SWS are the fucking monsters in this story. Not us."

"I think I know how you do it. Maybe. But it will probably involve seeing some shitty things." I felt bad that I hadn't already done what I was about to suggest.

"Yeah?" Bryan waited for me to go on.

"We'll have to figure out how to sell this to Engalls, how to get him to do the same, but..."

We scrolled through footage to find when the woman had come home Sunday, hoping that this was, as suspected, home and we wouldn't have to trace back further Saturday to find home. Anyway, it looked like this was home and she'd returned Sunday afternoon.

We followed her backwards, traced her to where she'd come from, to what appeared to be an abandoned office building with blacked out windows. We scrolled through footage to see her showing up in the wee hours with 'Randa.

We had to pause as Bryan hit the wall some more, and then we split the camera duties.

Bryan followed the two women back to the club, watching them travel in the goth woman's car. Trying to figure out how they'd left the club.

Riley stayed on the office building, scrolling forward, looking for any sign of anyone coming to remove the body. Zie saw people come and go, but didn't see anyone who seemed to leave with a body.

Me? I went looking for cameras inside the building. On the one hand, if it was where they did their dirty deeds, they might not want cameras. On the other hand, if they were going to broadcast more murders or keep an eye on prisoners (had they kidnapped others?), it made sense to have some cameras.

And they did. They had cameras. And tracing the data, it seemed like at least one copy of the footage stayed on site.

Footage that I didn't tell Bryan I'd found until after I'd made myself watch, made myself confirm that it had caught 'Randa's murder. I wouldn't have admitted that I'd found it at all, but I found myself sobbing as I watched.

When Bryan tried to come over and look, I shook my head and covered my screen. "You don't need to see this again, love. You don't."

Once we were all okay, as okay as we could be, we made our move. We made a fake account so we could send Engalls an anonymous tip. We claimed to be someone who'd gotten curious when he'd mentioned on the news that there was another open investigation around me. That they'd gone looking on social media and had found out about my friend's murdered girlfriend. Had then found a picture of her on social media. And then we suggested the footage he might want to get to follow the path of the woman in the picture and the girlfriend from that night through the next day. We suggested they get someone inside the office building quickly and quietly, before the murderers had a chance to destroy footage from internal cameras.

And, just in case, we also put a folder into one of his cloud drives with the relevant bits of video footage (I put it together), so he'd be certain what he was looking for.

We sent it. Yeah, it was Saturday, but he seemed like a guy with poor work/life balance.

We saw him check it. Saw him move it into a folder called Maybe a little too quickly.

So we sent it again.

And again.

And again.

Until he finally didn't move it. Until we saw him go check out the social media post we'd referenced. Until we saw him requisition some video, with a note to be very quiet about this.

"He's got it now," Bryan said.

"And you're good?" Riles didn't seem convinced.

Bry nodded. "He's got it. He's doing the right things. And I checked her accounts. They stupidly paid her as an SWS employee, including a bonus the Sunday she killed 'Randa. Other bonuses in there mean they'll probably nail her for other things *and* tie her easily to SWS."

I hesitated but suggested, "SWS aren't stupid. They've already got a story ready for all that."

"Sure, but that story was planned when they were still the public's darlings. Plus," and his voice got a vicious edge, "we can still go after her later if the cops and judges fail us. If it seems she should have more coming to her."

We ate, we got as cleaned up as we could (thank fuck for a city trying to be bike friendly, which had led a number of businesses to put in employee showers), and we kept an eye on the digital realm. Mostly, people had backed off of us, but we could see that SWS were still trying to find me both online and in the meat. Fun times...

Okay, actually fun times was seeing the reports the officers wrote up about taking that murderous goth chick and others at the torture building into custody. About finding and watching the videos that actually showed the goth chick killing 'Randa. I saw an email from Engalls that said:

If the video evidence doesn't result in maximum penalty, it will be a gross failure of our justice system. There's nothing left to the imagination here.

So, not everything was boring or full of our potential ruin.

I knew Bryan had some agenda when he asked, "So, has everybody loved sleeping on the concrete floor and eating the same shit for every 'meal,'" he made air quotes, "since we ran from HQ?"

Whilst I kept my face carefully neutral and my mouth shut, not wanting to walk into a conversation that might not be what it seemed, Riles took it as an invitation to complain. It might only have been a day, but it had been more than enough.

"I'm considering slitting my wrists before I have to do either again. We have to do better next time we go on the run. How the hell did we not pack sleeping mats at the very least? Or good road snacks? What the hell were we thinking?" Zie stopped abruptly. Had zie figured out what was really up? "Oh, Bry, look. I know last night you felt shitty that you hadn't packed pillows. But, honestly, none of us thought we'd be here, and this is really, really not your responsibility." Zie looked mortified.

Zie must be onto something. This was probably Bryan doing that thing where he blames himself for everything to do with the meat world that goes wrong.

"I'm actually over that." And Bry actually didn't sound guilty. "I had time to think while I drove to and from meeting Zane, trying to drive in ways that would make me hard to follow. Plenty of time..." He drifted off a moment, and I wondered what else he'd thought about. But then he refocused. "What I care about now is deciding what we *do* now."

I opened my mouth to make some kind of protest I hadn't even fully formulated, but he held up a hand to stop me.

"I don't need it to be a permanent commitment to what we're doing about the Peaceforgers. I mean more like the fact that it seems like a bad idea to run until Jonny is well enough for us to leave behind our one doctor, so what are we going to do *now*, until he's well?"

Oh. Huh. I'd been ramping up to argue the bigger question, the Peaceforger thing. But this was a sensible and less commitment-filled question. "I definitely agree that we can't go until Jonny is better." I looked at Riles, eyebrow up to ask what zie thought.

Zie nodded and allowed, "Yeah. I can see that. Plus, it's not like he's the only one hurt. Though the rest of us *could* hit the road and leave medical care behind. But, okay, we stay for now. For Jonny."

Helpfully, trying to show I was willing to not just dig my heels in on the Peaceforgers issue, I said, "And, whilst we can't even think we're the ones who can get them off our planet, we can at least do research or whatever. That's well within our wheelhouse."

Bryan must have been ready to argue too, because he looked slightly relieved at our response. "Cool. Then I'm going to keep trying to do my job of making sure the meat space shit doesn't suck. Because, comfort aside, nobody is going to heal well if we don't start sleeping and eating less poorly. You should see how rough you motherfuckers look." He grinned and started typing. "I'm going to make a list of what we need if we're camping out for...how long? Did Dr. Scott say?"

I shook my head. "She didn't want to even promise he'd be okay. But the instructions and meds she gave me for Jonny and my stuff make it sound like weeks. If we're waiting for bones to heal..." I did a quick search online. "Looks like bones are 6-10 weeks." I paused, then complained, "We're going to be stuck here at least through November, aren't we? Dammit!"

"I'll throw some things for entertainment on my list," Bryan said.

He probably thought he was being helpful.

"You know what you need?" Riley asked me.

"Do you want the whole list of what I need, or do you mean something specific?" I tried to make it sound like a joke. I didn't want to become that asshole who made a bad situation worse by constantly whining about it.

"Specific. I'm not drunk enough to listen to you complain that much," zie laughed.

"Don't keep me waiting, oh wise one. What the hell do I need?" Keeping it light. Keeping it a laugh. Haha. Remembering that my list was one item shorter than Riley's or Bryan's; I had my bae still.

"A new 'nym, obviously." Doing zir best impression of a wise guru, zie said, "My child, how can you find happiness if you don't know who you are?"

Zie giggled, and I couldn't help but join in. Even Bryan, who'd been quietly and seriously working on his plans for making this campout suck less, laughed a little.

"Oh, man. How did we do this last time?" I tried to pull up vague memories of what seemed an impossibly distant past.

This time, Bryan laughed less quietly. "Are you sure you want to come at it that way? Last time, you ended up with a stereotypically brash and ridiculous name that, when you stubbornly couldn't give it up, even people who liked you had to turn into initials to take you seriously."

I set my maturity aside to flail like an offended child and exclaim, "MindKiller is the coolest 'nym ever, mate! Bad. Ass."

If Rye had been near enough, zie would have patted me on the head. Zie had to settle for a tone that did that. "Of course it is, baby. Of course it is. So, sure, we can do it the exact same way as before."

Abashed, I said, "I'm actually serious. I can't think of another reasonable approach."

Rye's embarrassed cough and Bryan's silent shrug suggested they couldn't think of one either. So, we went at it old school (or what was old school for us), making a list of things I liked enough that I'd want that to be part of my name, crossing out any interests that might be too easily tied to MindKiller (that was a new step), and then making lists of all the possible 'nyms. And then just throwing in nerdy 'nyms that might work. Clever, funny, too serious, and all that.

I didn't want too funny or too serious (the latter is how you end up with MindKiller), so I crossed those out. I didn't want anything that was obviously gendered (because we can't seem to stop being extra shitty to people on the 'Net who aren't men, can we?). Anyway, yeah, strike 'nyms that would have extra shit baked into them. Anything that suggested I was anything other than a cis, het, able-bodied, neurotypical, white bloke. (Though maybe I'd make an alternate 'nym that was so totally not that and use it if I felt like I wanted to start fights over social issues.)

I had a short list of 'nyms left that I then agonized over. Did this one mean enough to me? How would it feel to be called by that one until I died? If I signed a threat or a "you've been meted out justice by me" note with it, would the recipient just laugh?

As we'd learned when we were kids, me choosing names for anything (pets, characters in games, that stupid egg I had to carry around and treat like a baby in high school) took long enough that even I got impatient with myself.

To help, or so zie claimed, Riles started calling me random things. Not just sticking to the list. Making up diminutives of them. And Bryan piled on, "helping" as well. Pausing to note which ones sounded like anyone that would be allowed to hang out with TesTur and apHellion, "because we have reps to uphold, bitch."

In the end, it was as I was trying (and failing...getting so close, but failing) to fall asleep. You know, that amazing creative space when you're drifting off and your brain can do its thing without you being in the way? Then.

"I've got it," I whispered, trying to do my quietest whisper in case everyone else was succeeding at the sleep thing. We were all smashed close in a vain attempt to have more warmth (and for emotional comfort, but we didn't mention that out loud, because everyone was still feeling a wee bit unstable).

"If you're talking in your sleep, I'm still going to hold you to it," Rye whispered back.

"Fuck that. I'm going to make up something horrible and then hold you to *that*," laughed Bryan.

"Nope. Pretty sure I'm awake. So, uh, I was thinking about what I actually want to do and have tried to do online and, I guess, in life lately. You know, as regards trying to help people see the bullshit and danger. Anyway, I'm thinking SecantSight. Like second sight, so that's a cool allusion. But also thinking how secants cut through things. And it's a straight line between two points on a curve or circle or whatever, so the shortest distance whilst everything else is taking the long way around. SecantSight cuts through the bullshit and lies. Rar!" I coughed. "So..."

"It doesn't suck too much," Bryan said.

"I'll think of ways to mock it in the morning," Riles promised.

I rolled my eyes in the darkness. I was never going to be not-annoyed that I'd lost my amazing, ridiculously aggressive 'nym. MindKiller forever, dammit.

CHAPTER 6

It felt like I'd only gotten about 5 minutes of sleep before my mobile buzzed. I tried to roll away quickly, headed towards the door, so the others wouldn't be woken as well. I whispered, "Hello?" as I trotted out into the big warehouse space.

"This is Dr. Scott. And I've already got someone who wants to talk to you."

My brain glitched, twitched, then fully woke from sleep mode, remembered where I was, what had happened, and who the person on the phone was. "Oh, cool! Someone who had a Peacemaker?"

"Yep. She was going to come in Monday, but the news yesterday had her begging to push up her appointment."

"Yeah, I can imagine." I cringed, thinking there must be plenty of that going on. "Thanks for hooking me up with someone, doc."

"After what you did? You're probably the one owed thanks."

Dr. Scott gave me the name and number of her patient, and I messaged the patient immediately. She must have been waiting, because she replied quickly. I knew it wasn't exactly safe, going out to meet a stranger, but I was kind of relieved at a chance for a little alone time.

I crept back in, just the light of my mobile to guide me. Bryan opened one eye as I crouched to look for keys in the jacket near his head, so I whispered, "I need the car. I'm going to meet some woman who just got a Peacemaker out and is willing to talk to me about it."

"I can go," he offered.

I tried not to laugh; it was kind of him, if not well-thought out. "Mate, imagine you're a woman who's just been a kind of techno-hostage, who's meeting someone secretly...And a fit, basically cis bloke showing up is just..." I smiled and shrugged, not sure he could see that in the glow of my mobile. "Thanks for being willing to get up, but I'm going to go and not scare her off."

He nodded. "Good point. So, where are you meeting?"

"Outside the old train station. Didn't want to go anywhere with people and risk them overhearing us. And I want to be able to get there first, see if I can see anyone else staked out or something."

Bryan grunted in a way that sounded like approval, then said, "Take your gun. And your g/ap mask. And don't forget that you should make it look like you showed up *after* her. That way, you can make it like you're probably farther from the station than her, whether or not that's true."

I nodded, and he easily found and handed me the keys.

He held onto my hand a moment and asked, "Do you at least want backup?" He did a shitty job hiding the worry as he noted, "You did get a little banged up the other night."

"Naw. I think I have this. Keep an eye on our battered babies." I pointed at where Riles and Jonny slept.

"Will do. I got 'em." He gave my hand a squeeze. "You be safe and come back without more injuries."

I returned the hand squeeze. Then I tried to get a good sense of how I felt as I grabbed clothes, struggled a little getting into them, and walked to the vehicle. A night on the floor had not helped. I was throbbing and stiff and definitely dead if this was a trap.

Even though going out was risky, I savored the aloneness of the drive. Short but silent, and free of other people. Look, I love all those assholes, but that didn't mean I suddenly stopped needing alone time.

I thought about how, whilst there was plenty about it that already did or probably would suck ass, being in hiding when it was cold out had some perks. We could hide behind outer layers and hats, wear gloves so we didn't leave prints, and keep our masks on.

Though the masks just had *more* reasons now that it was colder. Between shitty air since the EPA took blows back in the 2010s (never get Gran started on what went down in the U.S. in the last half of the 2010s) and the chill finally starting to really creep in (which meant everyone suddenly got paranoid about colds and the regular flu and other shit, like beat down flu, that—per Gran—were more dangerous than they used to be), we could totally wear our masks and not look weird. Most people were doing it. Bonus use? Helping foil facial recognition software. Just had to make sure you didn't always wear the same pattern if it was something interesting.

No joke. At least a handful of people got nailed every year because the poor bastards couldn't wear a bland mask even when they were doing a crime. It must be hard to be so fashionable...

At the train station, I did what I could, hoping that I'd learned enough from watching movies. (Because using movies to figure out how to lead the criminal life had done such a great job for Jonny...Ugh.) I didn't see anyone unexpected. Fortunately, the area had just enough office buildings that it was pretty quiet on a Sunday. And the train station wasn't inviting to...well, to anyone. It was run down and kind of creepy. I definitely wouldn't meet anyone *inside* it. Not on purpose.

When the time came to meet, I parked the vehicle a street over. As I was parking, I got a message from Bryan; the Seattle PD had issued an arrest warrant for the woman who'd grabbed 'Randa. Excellent! I looked forward to illegally following her downfall via Seattle PD's and the court's paperwork.

I got out, feeling more optimistic, and slowly walked to the meeting spot, keeping my hand near my gun and an eye out for watchers or snipers on rooftops and in empty windows. I tried to make it look more like a cool swagger than a cracked kneecap. But it was wrapped up tight, so I figured the lack of bending knee was probably going to give me away. *If the forearm crutch doesn't do it*, I snorted at myself.

Add in that my gun hand was currently my left hand, whilst my right one held that forearm crutch ('cause the left one was at the end of a fractured forearm that wasn't in any shape to take the weight...and probably wasn't going to handle gun recoil or even aiming well, if I was being honest)...I was *so* dead if this was a trap. Cool. Feeling awesome about that...

The woman standing in front of the station straightened up and watched warily as I approached. Even with her g/ap mask on, I could see that her jaw was set, and her hand was near a pocket where, if I were her, I'd have a gun. My own hand was ready to grab my own gun. I warned myself not to get so jumpy that I shot someone innocent. Or tried to shoot someone...Oh, man, I was going to die.

I took a breath and slowly dropped my hand from near my gun. She hesitated, but finally, slowly, also lowered her hand. Instead, I used my hand to reach out for a left-handed handshake, and I was relieved when she did the same. Also relieved I wasn't going to have to try to shoot anyone, what with me being even less capable aiming with my left hand than my mediocre right one. Fucking injuries.

"Did you leave your phone somewhere else?" I asked.

Even with part of her face covered, I recognized the look she struggled to suppress; she thought I was overly paranoid. But she didn't say it, just shrugged and said, "I did. But I don't get why I couldn't just turn it off."

I shook my head. We'd known better for decades, but people still thought that was enough. "It's easy enough to make it look like it's still off whilst secretly using the camera and mic."

"Huh." She narrowed her eyes, considering me. "I always thought that was some kind of paranoid bullshit." She shrugged again, shifted tone, ready to talk business. "Anyway, I'm Lex."

"Call me DL for now." I didn't want her to know my actual name or new 'nym. Or to be able to claim MK was still alive. Or to accidentally trust the asshole whose 'nym I was using when I talked to Zane. So, I was kind of putting D3AD_L1NX at risk a very wee bit as my compromise that I might remember. "Thanks for agreeing to talk."

"Yeah. I'm...the doctor said that you were someone who deserved at least that much."

"That's gracious of her. Uh..." I looked around and pointed to a half wall. "Do you mind if we sit?"

She took in my physical state. She could certainly tell my knee wasn't okay, could see part of my scratched up cheek and hands. The clothes I'd quickly and randomly grabbed (I suddenly realized with some embarrassment) were the ones I'd worn Friday, so they were scuffed, covered with random holes and dust. Plus, there was the light cast on my left forearm. Lest we forget what a mess I was on the other side of the explosion...

"Yeah." She led the way to the wall and sat, patiently waiting for me to get there. She tugged at the front of her dark hair.

I recognized the cut; I'd had a very similar one. It's one you got if you weren't normal but had to pretend you were to hold down an office job. It was almost cool.

Dammit, this was annoying, moving this slowly. At least she'd also pulled down her mask, a sign of trust. Also a chance to see that she had these amazing, lush lips. The kind that would have made me go full-on flirty if I were single. And suddenly even her office job hair looked really good.

Once we were seated, facing each other, I returned the gesture of trust and pulled down my own mask. Then I took out my mobile and asked, "Do you mind if I record this? I have some people back...where we're staying. They'll want to hear everything." I quickly reassured her, "I won't share it with anyone but the people I'm with. Not without your permission."

She narrowed her eyes. "You have your phone? Not to be a bitch, but can't someone just do all the same shit with yours as mine?" She scrambled to pull her mask back over her face as she realized the possible danger.

I quickly tried to put her at ease. "No, it's okay. I mean, yeah, spying through mobiles and web cams and whatever *has* been going on for decades, mate. But people like me mod our devices the instant we get them so no fucking person or company or agency can do that." I curled my upper lip a little in annoyance. "Especially people like me, 'cause other people like me might also be trying to find and spy through my devices. I can't have that." I held up my mobile. "This thing has been modded and tested by the best. I promise."

Lex slowly pulled down the mask, then took a long, considering breath. "What will you want me to say?"

"I want...everything. Anything you're willing to tell us about how it ended up in you, what it was like, how it feels now. Keep it short or tell me the whole damn story like we're old friends.

It's all really, really interesting to us. And, at this point, we don't always know what is and isn't relevant until we get other pieces."

"And you won't share it without my permission? Because this could straight fuck up my life."

"Mate, you have no idea. Your story is safe with us. We're a vault of..." and Zane came to mind, "of secrets you can't imagine. There are other lives counting on our discretion. I swear. It goes no further than us."

"Okay." She seemed to be nodding and taking deep breaths as a way to pump herself up. "Yeah. Okay. Let's do this! Because everyone knows the real villain here is SWS, right? Right! Okay. You recording?"

"Cool. Thank you!" I tapped my screen. "Recording now."

"The whole story?"

"Tell me a novel if you want. I've got plenty of memory and battery."

With another deep breath, Lex launched into her tale. I just shut up and held my mobile.

"I'll start at the SWS clinic." She paused. "Um. Sorry, just thinking what to tell. So...basically, I woke up in the clinic with no fucking idea where I was or whatever. Freaky enough. And then I completely freaked the fuck out when I touched the back of my head and there was something there, yeah?"

I nodded. I could imagine. I'd had nightmares about that scenario over the last couple weeks. A question occurred to me. "Sorry, before you go on, when did this happen?"

"It was...'bout 2 years ago, actually. Late in 2048."

"Oh. Wow. That's a long damned time to have shit in your head."

She nodded. "Truth. A long, long damned time."

"And did you ever get a clear answer about how you ended up there? 'Cause it sounds like maybe you didn't exactly expect it."

Lex gave a bitter little laugh. "I ended up remembering on my own. And I got no one but myself to blame. All I had to do was not run to Seattle when this Eastside business dude caught me lifting his wrist PC. But my dumb ass figured the best way to escape was to get to the water crossing. You know, because those lazy-ass legals will stop at the edge of their jurisdiction, just go back to their fucking donuts. But..." She rolled her eyes. "Not only did I pick the wrong fuckin' city for this story to end in, I also picked the wrong fuckin' dude to rob. Fucker chased me, and he was in good shape."

I sympathetically shook my head. "Bad fucking luck."

"So I actually end up on the motherfucking rooftops." She held her hands up defensively, anticipating my disbelief. "Totally fucking true. I figured only a lunatic would follow me up. That's why we head up a lot if things like this happen. And then I hit a spot where I had to jump and...and that's what put me in the clinic. Because the crowds had just seen some poor street drek jump from a building and hit the pavement...Instead of jump and make it to the roof of the next building, thanks to the constant drizzle and fucking slippery concrete ledges. Anyway..."

I gave her a second to stop looking so pissed at her luck.

She took a breath, let it out. "Anyway. That's how they got me. And it was weird. Like, I expected to be treated bad, the way you get treated bad if you land in jail. But they...I was definitely not free to go, but they were *aggressively* friendly and encouraging. They treated me like I was some good kid who'd just...I dunno...Like all I'd done was make a poor choice on the playground and they were just helping me grow up to be civilized. And bland. Like maximum vanilla, yeah?" Lex shrugged, like she was trying to play cool, as she said, "It made me think of when you read about creepy brainwashing shit that happens at a bigger level. You know, like with cults or whatever. Where you make someone think you're on their side and your way is the good way."

Because I knew who was behind the clinics, it kind of made me want to shudder, but I just nodded and said, "Yeah, that sounds pretty fucked up."

"Right? I mean, it shouldn't. If I just tell you some people got me healthy, set me up with a place to live and a job and whatever, that sounds nice. But..." She trailed off and looked into the distance past my head.

"But they put something in your head, and this wasn't your choice," I said.

"Yeah...But also...It was the cost. They made like it was no big deal, like it shouldn't freak me out. All I had to do was spend the rest of my life under the watchful eye of the bug in my head. For my own good, this little bundle of circuits and wires would monitor my brain and let a central headquarters know my basic emotional state." She finally stopped staring into the distance and looked at me, like she was making sure I was hearing her. Her tone vacillated between crankiness and sarcasm as she went on. "When my brain dove towards depression, the locator unit on my new little buddy would make sure SWS knew my location so that they could send someone over right away to talk to me and cheer me up. Seriously. No more frowns for me, because the Seattle do-gooders were on call twenty-four seven to help me buck up. And, just in case I wanted to try, in a moment of depression, to dig the bug out and get rid of it so that I could kill myself in peace, it was snugly inside and would somehow make my arms go numb if any of the wires that were around the healing part of my scalp were broken. Fucking terrific."

"I didn't know about the arm thing. It makes sense, but also...That thing was wired in deep, huh?" I'd known it was wired in deep, of course, but I'd also assumed that, if they put one of those in me, I'd dig the fucker out so I could at least die free.

"Deep. Yeah. And when I tried to explain what really happened, they were pretty happy to tell me that being a criminal would also have made this happen, so..." She looked tired as she said, "So, I just let it happen. I mean, I wasn't giving up, but I figured the best way out was through."

I interrupted Lex again. "Was this the first time you'd heard about the Peacemaker?"

Lex nodded. "Yeah. I think it was early on in the release phase. Not the very start, but right before they started putting out any advertising or anything."

I gave her a bit of a grin. "They were just waiting for you to come along and be their poster child."

She laughed a little, bitterly, and then went on. "So, I spent some weeks learning to get my emotions under control and shit. Let them remake me. Just went along. That was it."

"That was it?" I was confused.

"I mean, you just know it's there, in your head, but I couldn't feel it. I don't know what else it did, if it did anything else, yeah? Just told them where I was, somehow released counteractive chemicals if I tried to use derms, and let them know if I was feeling something negative. So, as I tried to figure shit out, I had to...learn to breathe and take yoga and whatever." She shook her head, still not over it. "Couldn't even just dope it away, dude."

I weakly suggested, "But figuring out how to handle your shit...silver lining?" Hoped she heard that I didn't think that lining was silver enough.

She snorted. "Like cheap brass with a thin silver coating." But she didn't look like she thought I was the asshole.

I tried to think of questions. "Uh, so, they decided you were rehabbed and they set you loose?"

"Kind of. More like put me in a bigger cage by giving me a shit job. Probably not how it goes if you're a rich kid. But, for street drek like me, you have to take the job they give you, and at first you live with someone who's been out longer. Like a sponsor, I guess. And, when they let you have your own place, they bug the hell out of it." She paused, then added, "Plus, I think the dude I shared my cubicle with was reporting back to them."

"Amped up surveillance state."

Lex nodded. "Amped up surveillance state."

"So, did they try to keep you guys apart? Those of you with the Peacemakers who hadn't proven you were totally fixed yet?" I guess I'd figured that's what I would have done, because I know that giving me people to scheme and work with was a foolish thing to do if you were trying to keep *me* under control.

"That was weird, right? Like they were so confident in their bugs—the ones in our heads and in our apartments—that they didn't care. Like their way was so obviously superior to our lives before that they couldn't imagine us rejecting it." She got a bit of a smile. "Not that I'm gonna complain about that. Getting to fraternize, yo."

Sensing a story, I lifted an eyebrow and encouraged, "Yeah? You maybe meet someone else with a bug that was...nice?" I let "nice" drip with innuendo.

"Yeah." Her smile grew and her voice got a little softer. "When I went to cash my pay check after a few months on my own...Normally, I didn't notice my teller, but this time...Girl at the credit union had a rainbow of track marks. Not like, you know, heroin marks where tracks are ugly little holes, like mouths opening to suck a needle again. But like rows of little derms stuck to her skin. This girl shouldn't have been at work." Lex used two fingers to trace a double line from her wrist to her elbow.

"Was she a mess?" I was trying to picture how many derms that must be, the variety, and just how useless it would leave someone.

"Naw," Lex laughed. "That's the thing. If I hadn't seen the derms, I wouldn't have suspected a thing. But this girl had this army of tiny, shiny, colorful dots marching up the inside of her right arm. They disappeared into her sleeve. There had to be at least 60."

"Shut the fuck up!" I exclaimed. "No fucking way." This was urban legend territory.

"Totally fucking way," she assured me. "So, obviously, I was in awe. You could tell she'd been junking a long time, too. Her movements were so smooth, laying out bills like underwater ballet, like she and the trip were one. It didn't even look like she was trying to hide anything. And somehow no one else had noticed the dots, or she would have been in a tiny cell, not handling cash." Lex smiled in a way that was both hungry and shy. "Maybe it was because there was plenty else to see. If I didn't instinctively scope for tracks, I would have been immediately sucked into those deep brown eyes just like the rest probably were."

"And she had a Peacemaker?" I didn't want her to feel like I was shrugging off her romantic trip down memory lane, but I felt like there was something at the edge of my memory that made this all seem weird.

"She did! I don't know why she could derm with one, but she had one."

Right. That was it. Lex herself had just said you couldn't get away with using drugs if you had a Peacemaker in. "You're sure she had one? You saw her outside the bank, where you'd see more than just her face?"

"Once I convinced her I wasn't trying to deal to her and that I didn't care that she was ace, uh, asexual."

I nodded. There might be pockets of people who still didn't know shortened forms like "ace," but I wasn't in those pockets.

"So, once she knew I wasn't just looking for a fuck, she let me take her to lunch. This weird, old-school diner, Sam's. Cheap food, but with actual servers like nice places. And that's where she told me, showed me, that she used all those derms to keep even so that the Peacemaker hiding under thick, black hair wouldn't sound the alarm."

"Huh. Interesting. Okay, well, I guess maybe she got lucky with the derm thing." I'd have to...I stopped my thought. I didn't have to do anything. I'd finished my job. I pulled my mind back to Lex. "So, it sounds like this woman was maybe your first...friend after?"

"She...Marleina. That's her name. Mina to her friends. Uh, yeah. She's the only one I've met that I trust is really okay. I mean, we had a...a rough moment where, uh, the clinic would have 'graduates' come in to talk sunshine and shit to people still not getting it or to, like, cheer on other graduates. Support group shit or whatever. And they used me a lot, because I was good at faking. And Mina was there one time, like at the start of knowing me. And I could see that, at first, she thought maybe I was...a company spy or whatever. But I guess the way I was talking, uh, describing how yoga is useful, she got that I was trying to help the others, not the company."

"Did you know she'd be there?" I was trying not to lean in and get too personal, but I was into this story.

"No fucking clue. And I didn't know what she'd do when I saw her there; I was worried she'd get the wrong idea. But, after, once everyone else cleared away, she was like, 'So, you help people with bugs learn yoga?' And I was like, 'Yeah, just trying to help them control neg spikes, keep emotions good.' And...she got it. She believed me."

Quietly, I said, "Cool."

"Cool. Yeah. After I said that, she just...reached out, smooth. And, like, her sleeve shifted and I saw derms. Derms! At the clinic! The fucking nerve of that girl." Lex grinned, proud and in awe still. "She put her hand on my neck, fingers lightly on that spot where I had a scar that matched hers. Felt like acknowledgement of a shared path. It felt like...like too intimate, but fuck the fear, right? So I put my hand on her scar, stood like that a breath..." She blushed and looked away.

I grinned. "That's fucking beautiful. Sounds like you found someone good."

Lex cleared her throat and tried to pull her cool back together. "Yeah."

"So, what happened with Marleina's Peacemaker?"

"Same as me. Dr. Scott. But she'd been saving longer, so she got hers out a few weeks ago."

"Nice. So, you're both free now?"

With a big grin, one that might have been kind of dopey, she said, "Yep! And with SWS falling apart, we can probably safely get a flat together. And...that's it." Lex shrugged. "Sorry there's no exciting ending. It's exciting to me, but not what I thought it would be."

I asked, "What did you think it would be?"

"I kind of assumed we wouldn't find someone here. We'd actually heard about some guy out of state and were thinking we'd have to plan a run. Then Mina's dealer said the guy, the out-of-state doc, had passed on his knowledge to some local doc. Running out of state would have been kinda exciting, I guess. Now, with the bug out pretty easily and normal doctors learning to take it out, if the rumors are true, my story isn't exceptional."

I winced a bit, thinking of the "exceptional" girl who'd been manipulated via her Peacemaker to kill those kids, then assured her, "Exceptional doesn't always mean better. I'm just glad to hear you made it through with yourself intact." I moved to stop recording. "Anything else you want to add or think we should know?"

She considered it. "Yeah. Two things. One, right before the SWS headquarters blew Friday night, I had...a flash. Like a snippet of vision or something. Like pale people, dressed in white. And Mina had the same thing. It was a split second, and it was just that. But, there you go. And, two...Look, I'm no genius, but it seems like maybe," and she gestured at my body, "you got into a scrape recently. Really recently. And that plus your interest in this and how Dr. Scott talked about you...I'm just assuming that maybe it's appropriate to thank you. So, thanks." She grabbed my hand and caught my eyes. "Seriously. Thank you. Fuck those assholes and their brainwashing."

I felt myself flushing and I looked away, but I gave her hand a squeeze. I took a breath to pull my head together. "If I'd done anything like you're implying, you'd be very welcome. I wonder...Would you mind if I got a pic of the back of your head? Most of us haven't actually seen someone who has or had a Peacemaker in."

Lex quietly turned to show me where, just like you'd think, a flap of her skin had been peeled back at the base of her skull. It was red around the edges, having been so recently re-opened. I wanted, as her friend Marleina had done, to gently touch that spot, but I resisted.

CHAPTER 7

As if maybe the Universe was on our side again, back at the warehouse, I found Jonny bleary but awake (awake!). I restrained my urge to smother him in my relief. I tried to be gentle as I put kisses on his face. Thank fuck he was awake. I felt like that was enough to keep me going for a while longer.

He weakly smiled and whispered, "Hi."

I rested a hand on his cheek, a big dumb grin on my face. "Hi." I was bloody well not going to cry, dammit. "Are you awake for real this time?"

He started to laugh, then coughed instead. When he was done coughing, he moaned and put a hand on his broken ribs, wryly noting, "Yeah. Unfortunately. I appear to be done with the bliss of unconsciousness."

"Well, shit. I guess now we have to try to make you comfortable." I rolled my eyes dramatically. "You were so much easier when you were out cold, you bastard."

He laughed, but more carefully. "Asshole." He looked over at Riles and Bryan, who were hovering. "Though maybe you can help me convince them that I'm allowed to sit up or even walk around now?"

I looked over and Riley shrugged."We were just being cautious, Kot. If you got home and heard how he was awake and we let him get fucked up again somehow..."

Bryan nodded. "Seriously. Can you imagine how much shit and pain you'd have rained down on us?"

"Right. Well, you lovely and well-intentioned bastards, I feel like none of us are doctors, and that means Jonny gets to be his own boss now." I shifted to get an arm under him, and pointed at the chairs. "Will one of you lot make sure there's a chair for him to fall into?"

Whilst Rye got a chair ready to help catch him, Bryan came over to help me get Jonny to standing. Gingerly standing. Somehow, he hadn't broken anything in his legs, but he had a turned ankle. Three of the four of us were pretty fucked if we had to literally run for our lives any time soon. At least Dr. Scott had made sure we had a spare crutch for Jonny.

As soon as his ass was in the chair, he said, "Okay, now get me back up. I need the bathroom." He grinned sheepishly. "And then...Is there food?" When he saw our faces, he said, "I will be happy with whatever you can feed me that isn't from an IV."

True to his word, after using the loo, he proceeded to enjoy the shit out of a protein bar, like I've never seen someone enjoy one of those things, as we caught him up.

We told him about the attacks online and in the media, trying to take us down or at least fuck up my reputation.

"I hope you're good to type," I said, "because trying to take care of your stuff and not fuck it up has had me more worried than nuking my own shit."

We told him about my new 'nym and that we'd used some assholes' 'nyms to hide behind when we had to give someone names.

We shared a look, and seemed to agree to save Zane for the end. So, instead, we caught him up on what little we'd seen and heard from SWS and from the government.

I showed them the video of Lex, glad that Riles also noticed her fucking beautiful lips, and I think we all felt a little better. Here was an actual, real, apparently not totally loathsome human we'd helped.

And then, we told him how some person had helped him and me out of the wreckage. Had climbed into the car with us, insisting they had info. But we didn't try to describe that info or what Zane was. Instead, we all (all! including Jonny!) watched the two recordings we had of Zane again. We had to pause the first one when Zane's tongue shot out.

"Holy shit!" Jonny looked at us, eyes wide. Looked at our excited grins. "They're not human?"

We kept grinning and shook our heads.

He barked out a laugh, managed not to cough, and exclaimed, "They're not human! You guys, the puzzle pieces are coming together." He grinned with the rest of us and murmured, "Holy shit."

When we'd watched both videos, Jonny looked a little down. "Dammit. I didn't get to meet the alien. That kind of sucks."

Helpfully, Riles suggested, "Maybe not *this* alien, but you go to clubs. You probably *have* met one at some point."

Glumly, Bry just said, "Yeah."

Oh.

Like 'Randa's goth chick at the club...The last time Kitty saw her...The night 'Randa was taken.

What little excitement we'd been feeling was squashed as we were reminded that 'Randa and Kitty were gone.

Shifting a little, clearly uncomfortable, Jonny cleared his throat. "I'm...I'm so sorry, Bryan. Riley. Just...so sorry."

There was silence a moment, then Bryan brushed it off. "Yeah. Yeah, it's a fucking bad scene. But," he coughed a little, his voice slightly rough, "we have a lot to do. We can't get lost in these feelings. Gotta make sure we're safe and shit. Uh..." He gestured at Jonny's computer. "You should check on your accounts. Make sure you're okay. If you're up for it."

Jonny looked at Riles, as if asking zir permission. When zie nodded, Jonny pulled his computer over. "Okay. Smart call. Kot, can you walk me through everything you did? Need to make sure you didn't besmirch my good name or some shit." He winked at me.

I nodded and sat to show him the moves I'd made whilst trying to lock down his accounts and pretend he was conscious. It was amazing to me how good this simple and quiet thing felt. Jonny awake and us just doing shit together online. Like we had for ages.

With all the bullshit going on online, and all the attacks aimed at us, the 'Net wasn't feeling much like our favorite place anymore. So it felt like a reminder of what had been good when we got word that one of our remote comrades had finally traced the SWS main backup servers and copied the whole damned mass for us before sending in every vicious bit of digital devastation they could find to wipe any and all SWS computers. Hell yeah! Try to rebuild when that's all gone, fuckers.

We were also pleased to find that, aside from mine, our online identities and our real-life identities still didn't appear to be in danger of getting connected. That no one had broken through the online defenses for our 'nyms. It didn't mean we'd use them or even be able to stay our real-life selves, but it was nice to know neither would be the worst option. Except for me. In fact, it seemed like our remote team had been helping keep us safe and covered, just in case we really were who everyone thought. It had only been a couple days, but the online war might be showing signs of at least having a few non-shit outcomes.

We were further pleased to find that one of our remote comrades had set up a site to curate and make widely available a good deal of the info we'd sent out. Nothing from the second email, which had dangerous info about how the tech worked, but everything from the first one. The one that explained the true story of SWS. And the site had been getting non-stop massive amounts of hits. We could see that the online conversation, in places frequented by normal humans, was starting to shift slowly and slightly in our favor. There were still plenty of them who thought SWS were just victims of the horrible MindKiller, but now there were just as many exploring the horrifying possibility that SWS were some kind of power-hungry cult. If only they knew...

And we were pleased to find that law enforcement at all levels and in all impacted countries were taking this seriously. Or they appeared to be. They'd all immediately started investigations. And as soon as SWS noticed their wiped servers and publically called out the big bad MindKiller for more crimes (and those bastards were on the news mere minutes after it was done), new notes got added onto those investigation files. To many, those computers all suddenly being wiped? Well, that sure looked like someone covering things up and trying to blame it on the hackers. Plus, some officers and agents were talking to doctors and engineers and confirming what we'd said.

We were...well, we weren't certain how we felt about it, but Seattle PD had released the names, where they could feel reasonably sure of the identities, of those who had died Friday. As soon as we saw that, we worried that people might get more sympathetic to SWS now that there were names and faces...Especially since that info included some of the human doctors and scientists who'd been dead even before the building was blown. We started trying to decide what we could put out to help keep public opinion pointed more in our direction.

Using the D3AD_L1NX 'nym, Bryan reached out to our person running the SWS leak site. He said he had some more docs and info to include relevant to that. Could he send that along?

We cleaned up the pictures we'd found of the previous execs in club gear. If they were going to try to take stabs at *my* reputation? Well, fuck them. Here's what those bastards looked like in their past. Not so squeaky clean, huh? I was suddenly really glad those assholes had hung out at the kind of clubs that we also liked. I knew that, whilst people were less and less judge-y over alternative lifestyles as the years passed, there was still plenty of deeply ingrained distaste for us freaks.

More likely to be damning, Jonny also trimmed and did some side-by-side of the footage from inside the building, from the cameras in the conference rooms. (And that, friends, is why you save all the shit you can; you never know what will be useful.) Because, you know what? Fuck SWS. Here's footage showing your fucking execs *smiling* whilst they watched as a whole other room full of people died. And it sure looks like they *expected* to see that, doesn't it? Suck it, bastards. (Fortunately, one camera angle made it easy to see that they were watching the same footage we were showing on the other half the screen.)

We included the communications we could to prove just how carefully CorpSec had combed the building before the meeting. Whoever set off the explosion hadn't been out for wanton damage. That's what we hoped they'd see.

Before we sent the whole lot off, I coughed. "Uh, can I suggest something? And I mean it in the most respectful way." When nobody replied, I took that as permission. "They've got...They've got Kitty's body. They'll identify her eventually." I choked, and paused a moment, then went on, my voice rough with grief and guilt. "I say we manufacture a memo, doing the best we can to make it look good, though we just send it to this site and not to anyone else...I say we say that SWS CorpSec and execs suspected this was MindKiller, and they'd brought her in. When the building was quiet. I already made it look like an account wipe was triggered for MK's stuff because MK wasn't around to stop it. People already know MK is gone. Is somewhere that stops her from stopping the trigger. So, let's give them an idea of where she might have gone."

Riley's voice was quiet. "Are we saying we let them think Kitty might have been MindKiller and that MK actually died?"

Bryan answered that with a question. "Would her parents be devastated if they thought Kitty was MindKiller?"

"Honestly? Her parents are cool. They'd probably be proud. Like, surprised that she was into computers that much, but proud." Riles sighed. "And it would let her have a little legend. She'd like that." Zie paused. "If you're willing to lose that bit of legend, Kot."

I shrugged. "I'm sure I'll survive without it. It's not like anyone but you lot actually know it's mine. But this maybe lets us make it look like, actually, there's no way it's MindKiller who did any of the shit Friday, because the person SWS actually suspected was in custody. Which sort of kills the legend for her in terms of the bombing, whilst also keeping my name, if not my 'nym, okay to use. Or okay-ish. But maybe not?" I shook my head. "I don't know anymore."

"And," Bryan noted, "once people realize that SWS are horrible and they're about destroyed, we—TesTur and apHellion, MK's known associates—can confirm that she'd actually hacked the system to send that memo to CorpSec, making it look like an exec wanted her picked up and brought in. That let her get on site and send the email even though the building was locked down, lets her keep being legendary. And we suggest that the self-destruct was SWS following through on their plan to burn it all once they were caught." He shrugged. "We've got the docs to prove that was their plan."

Rye didn't sound convinced. "It's a little convoluted."

Jonny finally spoke up. His voice was tinged with pain and a little floaty with medication. "But it's not. MK found documents while doing what hackers do. Their authenticity has been confirmed. She realized she had to be on site to send and get enough attention paid for law enforcement to take it seriously.

So, she faked a memo. That's great, because our faked memo can go ahead and be exposed as faked eventually. That got her dragged in for questions, and she just had to take a chance to plug in, make code go. It's a story. It makes sense."

"Well, if the guy who's high on pain meds says so..." Riles sighed, but zie said, "Okay, yeah. I see the story. It would have made a good backup plan if we hadn't known about the self-destruct and whatever." Zie smiled. "Plus, I think Kitty would like it."

I put an arm around zir shoulders. "Giving Kitty the gift of my reputation seems like the least I can do. Let's help people see that your bae was a fucking hero."

"Oh." We looked at Jonny, and he went on. "But doesn't this let Williams off the hook?"

Bryan grinned. "Naw, mate. It removes her status as a helpful whistleblower. Plus, we've got a scheme set up that should ruin her rep another way."

So, we faked a memo. And did what we could, looking for things we hadn't thought of Friday night, through the clamor of the warzone that was our part of the 'Net, to make sure everyone would believe that MK was really, truly dead and gone.

I watched carefully, both pleased and sad that everyone seemed to believe MK was actually dead. Time to move on. Time to fully embrace SecantSight. I am them. Them are I. Or something.

It didn't take long for people to notice the new things on the SWS leak site. Once they noticed, they reacted. Mostly, they reacted in ways we approved of.

In the case of photos proving the execs had, according to the normals, seedy pasts...Well, there was plenty of pearl clutching and shock over that from the mainstream. Those not in the mainstream simply gloated over yet another so-called spotless normal being outed as something other than perfect and posh. Experts in photo forgeries were all over the place with their analysis. This was news that was tasty to everyone, humans and tabloids and real news alike. And anyone who wanted to could include an expert in the conversation. A good 85% of those experts were plenty happy to note that, as far as they could tell, the pics were all real. People took more savage joy in tearing down the rich and famous than the joy they would have felt if they'd been told SWS hadn't actually invaded their privacy all these years.

In the case of the video...The same broad swath of humanity was all over it. Viewers were warned that this might be too much for children to watch. News anchors who hadn't gotten to preview it sat, open mouthed, in silence for a moment. Again, experts mostly agreed that this was real. That the image the execs appeared to be watching, the image of a room full of people dying, really was what they were watching.

Behind the scenes, any law enforcement who might have reason to care was scrambling and unhappy. The only people they could reasonably have brought in to hold accountable were already dead. Some of those unhappy cops and feds were brought in to be on the news, and they didn't bother to cover their grim hunger for justice, assuring everyone that, had anyone survived, there would have been a swift accounting.

Of course, my favorite part was watching CEO Trent squirm. He'd been sitting in an interview chair when it broke, so nobody got a chance to warn him. We got to watch him watching, though I suspect only a few of us knew that the real reason his face filled with horror was that he was watching his predecessors get caught. He got out of that interview as quickly as he gracefully could, and then he looked ill every time he had to shut down questions about the footage in subsequent interviews. I have never felt such an abundance of schadenfreude in my life.

And in the case of the fake memo...That caused a lot of heated discussion.

The news wanted Trent to explain why that memo showed that, actually, SWS had moved on from Katja Brennan. This was so much easier to address than the video that he almost looked relieved when it was *this* they asked about. Lucky for him, it made sense when he replied that he'd not been high up enough in management, so there was no reason he'd have heard that yet.

The police wanted the SWS leak site to at least tell them the name of the person from the memo, because the site had kindly blurred it out (wanting to spare the hero's family from any kind of assault). The site was run by hackers, so the police weren't going to get anywhere.

When an expert noted that the memo was faked, people on forums started demanding insight from TesTur and apHellion. They digitally shrugged and said that it seemed like a good way for MK to make sure she got on site, since we all know that there are times—thankfully very rare—you have to get on site to get at what you want. We weren't mad when some government hacker (we're assuming) or maybe some news-hired tourist saw the theory and made it part of the story.

The news didn't know how to handle their joy at the conflict; conflict fills more minutes in the non-stop news day than an easy truth. Had SWS brought in this person suspected of being MK, in a dastardly attempt to shut her down, or had clever MK gotten herself into the building to send emails as SWS claimed? (Either way, they were generally quick to note that the same experts who said that memo was a fake were saying the others, the ones with really damning stuff in the emails sent Friday, were real.)

This was all basically entertaining and satisfying for us. Plus, it kept SWS and the traitors in our hacking communities a little busy with things that weren't actually us.

Of course, it didn't take long for some misogynistic dickhole to bluster about how, duh, that memo had *obviously* been a fake because there was no way MK was a girl.

Sneer on, you thick wastoids. Lucky for you and the rest of the world, the real MK (aka me) had never been held back just because the gear in her pants wasn't like yours.

Nobody else was admitting to being "a girl" or otherwise, but it was gratifying to see how quickly and heavily people piled onto the dumbasses who held MK's sex against her. Maybe there were good people on the 'Net after all.

"Seriously?" Bryan was giving his computer questioning looks. When he saw us giving him the same kind of looks, he explained, "I guess Zane wants to meet again. Talk more."

Riles was looking back at zir machine, working on whatever, but zie said, "Somebody's sweet on you, big boy."

Bry snorted. "Naw. But...something's up."

Jonny (it kept pleasantly startling me to have an extra voice, his voice, back in the conversation) asked, "You guys really think we can trust them? Because, you're right; something's up. Unless you return with solid, helpful new info..."

With a sigh, Bryan stood. "I think they're probably not dangerous. So, I might as well go." He paused, then added, "You poor hobbling fuckers try not to get killed while I'm gone."

"Would it be horrible if I asked you to grab some groceries or fast food while you're out?" Jonny sounded hesitant. "I just...Right now, I'd punch a baby to get a real meal. Totally figuratively, of course."

I hadn't wanted to ask the same thing (I mean, I'd wanted it, but felt like I couldn't ask), but I figured Jonny had been in worse shape than me and could ask without Bryan thinking he was soft. I caught Rye's eyes and realized zie'd had the same thought.

"I can make a pizza happen. Maybe more. Definitely." He looked at me and Rye. "Any other requests?"

"Massive fucking list of them," admitted Riles. "But you should go and we can talk shopping later."

We definitely need to talk more than just shopping, I thought.

A few minutes after Bryan left, Riles stood. "Okay. My things are fine. I think I'm going to go take a usefully long shower." Zie gave Jonny and me a Very Meaningful Look.

"Thanks? But, y'know, I feel like Jonny's in no shape for fucking," I pointed out.

Zie clucked zir tongue at me and didn't change zir trajectory. In a kindly but long-suffering tone, zie said, "Oh, Kot. There's more to relationships than fucking. Even *I* know that." And then zir follow-up laughter grew fainter as zie continued to the showers.

I couldn't help but laugh as well, and Jonny carefully joined in.

We both stopped what we were doing on our computers and turned to face each other.

He said, "Sadly, I fear you're right. This body isn't in sex condition." He laughed a little at himself.

I took his hand. "How bad is it? How are you?"

He gave my hand a squeeze. "I think I feel about as bad as you'd expect for someone who got crushed under a pile of CorpSec beefcake. And I think my head broke my fall. So, not great. But awake. Mostly coherent. Which, I feel like that was a key component of your question?"

"Yeah," I nodded. "Your brain state was in question. Dr. Scott didn't want to promise anything. Not even that you'd wake up."

"Fortunately, she wasn't so hesitant when it came to sending me away with good painkillers." He closed his eyes and took a slow, deep breath. There was a hitch when he got to maximum inhale. All his broken bones, bruises, and battered organs protesting.

"I'm sorry you had to wake up on a table with a sleeping bag. Not the most comfortable."

He shook his head. "At least I haven't been on the cold floor. There's no way you guys have been sleeping great."

"Yeah..." I shrugged, and pushed away my mobile as it started buzzing, unwilling to be interrupted just now. "But it's hard to complain to you when I got less fucked up by the CorpSec meatbag who landed on *me*."

He stared a moment at my mobile, which seemed to have buzzed non-stop the last couple days. "You answer any of those calls?"

"Naw. It's all people I oughtn't talk to. Not until we know it's okay that I'm alive."

The screen told us it was Engalls I was ignoring this time. Jonny asked, "Who else has called?"

"Gran, Quinn, SWS, the press, random so-called friends. Nobody unexpected, I guess." I didn't love talking on the phone in general, but now I looked at my mobile with dread every time it made call-related sounds.

"You should probably quit SWS. They seem like an unsafe employer." He said it so seriously.

I laughed, feared for a moment that he'd actually been serious, that he maybe somehow didn't realize that I was obviously quitting, and then relaxed as he chuckled along. Okay, yeah, his brain wasn't in *that* bad of shape.

"But, in all seriousness, Kot...You did at least let Gran know you're alive, right? I'd be very surprised if she didn't worry."

I nodded. "Yeah, I slipped her a message. Figured that I owed her a little peace of mind." In a gentle tone, I asked, "Should we find a way to let *your* family know you're okay?"

He froze. I saw his throat working as he swallowed, saw his chest slowly move as he breathed. But, if not getting emotional had been the goal, he'd failed. It wasn't sobbing or anything, but his eyes were wet and red. "Not that they have any more reason to worry now than before, but...I don't know how I safely do that. Safely for me or for them."

I leaned carefully against his shoulder. "I'm the suspect. Or maybe Kitty is. Don't you think it's okay now?"

"Well, I guess that depends on what we do next. But, also...I'll never be sure they won't figure out it was us, all of us, who blew up HQ. And me who blew up *your* office. So...I don't think so." He got the words out, but then he had to do a lot more swallowing and blinking. "Sorry. You've seen me cry too much the last couple weeks."

"Pfft. Please. You've cried an entirely reasonable amount, especially given what's been going on. You can definitely feel free to cry more if you're inclined." I waved as if Bry and Riles were there for me to indicate. "We aren't exactly big supporters of gender norms or toxic masculinity bullshit here," I assured him.

"But...Bryan is so...even," Jonny noted with a little jealousy. "It's one thing to ignore aesthetics boundaries, right? Yay for counter-culture and men in makeup and all that. But Bryan wouldn't be crying right now."

"I'm going to spare you the lecture, though it would be a loving one, about what a bad idea it is to compare yourself to others. But, look, Bryan is Bryan. He's always been the most even of us. I always envied that. Like, he was one step closer to being a Vulcan or some kind of rational android than me. But, also, his parents were...brutally consistent about trying to make sure he conformed to the performative gender norms. Boys don't cry and all that bullshit. Even he knows it wasn't healthy. On some level, I suspect he wishes he could shake that off more."

"I hear you. I do. I'll...I'll do what I can to appreciate that I'm hanging out with people who are cool with me being me. That I didn't fall in with the sort of assholes who made it really suck to be a teenaged boy with emotions." He smiled a little. "Just sorry we're not hanging out in an actual home."

I shrugged. "Aren't we all?"

CHAPTER 8

When Riles came back in from zir long shower, Jonny and I were setting up a trail of interactions and cred for my new 'nym. SecantSight wouldn't be as known and trusted as MK had been, obviously, but we'd make it look like Sec wasn't a suspicious newb. Riles jumped in to help. We all appreciated that the explosion of the 'Net over the last few days would make it easier to plant new "old" things.

"Sec is stupid," Riles announced out of the blue.

"What? What the hell are you talking about?" I glared.

"I just mean that using Sec as your *diminutive* is stupid. I'll do it sometimes, but you deserve...better." Zie leaned back and stared thoughtfully at zir screen.

I was open to suggestions, and Riles had taste, so I was hopeful. And then I saw a slow smirk spread on zir face. I narrowed my eyes and braced for it.

"Hey, Jonny, check the suggestion I just sent you and tell me what you think," zie said.

Jonny made sure I couldn't see his screen, and I wasn't going to push in given his injuries (dammit), but I could definitely see when he got a matching smirk.

"Oh, that is *perfect*. You're a genius," he beamed at Riles.

"I know, baby. I know." Riles was preening and way too pleased with zirself.

I coughed a very clear "excuse me; I'm right here" cough. They ignored me and typed away, clearly chatting with each other. I heard Bryan pulling in, and I waited with squinty-eyed patience for him to come in from the car.

When he did, I immediately demanded, "Bryan, get in here and stop me before I beat these two with my crutch." I lifted the crutch and waved threateningly.

Jonny and Rye studiously ignored me, looking for all the world like innocent, diligent little worker bees who had no idea what my problem was.

Bryan gave me a little snort of laughter as he walked over to set down a bag of groceries and the promised pizza and then sit at his computer. "What did I miss...Oh." He grinned up at me. "Oh."

Bastards had obviously shared with him. "I think I hate you all," I sulked, treating each to their own instance of me sticking my tongue out at them. Nice to know that my immaturity had survived our mission and the shitty weekend.

Bry tsked and said, "Stop whining and eat yer pizza." As I moved for the pizza box, he added, "Sexy," like he was calling me that, not like he was saying me eating was sexy or that I should eat it in a sexy manner.

I paused, then slowly opened the box. The others were snickering and saying "sexy" as I grabbed a slice and settled back. Then Riles finally pushed a message to my laptop.

SECantSIght
SECSI
(SEXY)

I stopped in the middle of taking a bite, pulled the pizza back from my face. "Oh, hell no." I looked at their faces, at the over-the-top innocence on Riley's face, the too-pleased grin on Jonny's, and the slight smirk on Bryan's. "Ah, fuck." I sighed. "Just not in front of the other kids, okay?"

Bry gave me a wink, and Rye gave a horrified "I would never!"

Jonny patted my leg, and assured me, "Your diminutive is safe with us, Secs."

Oh, good. Another variation. I was clearly a master at choosing 'nyms.

As zie leaned in to grab a slice, Riles said, "I've never seen a sexier pizza."

Yes, everyone agreed, very sexy.

Bastards.

As we ate the sexy pizza, Bryan told us, "There's definitely something up with Zane. They didn't have anything at all important this time." He fiddled about so he could play video on his screen. "But you guys might still find it interesting. It solves one of the loose ends from...a few days ago." He paused. "How the hell has it only been a few days?"

Riley clapped a hand on his shoulder. "Mate, it has been *years*. We've been sleeping on this fucking floor for so long I barely remember what beds are like."

"I want to laugh, but..." Bryan pressed play.

On the screen, Zane looked a little nervous. "I hate being recorded." They held up a pale hand. "Don't worry. I know why you record. It's okay."

Off camera, Bryan asked, "So, what did you have for me today?"

Looking like a kid who'd prepared a report, Zane sat a little straighter and earnestly said, "Well, since they've now shown up on a web site, and since understanding our culture might help you decide best ways to deal with, uh, the rest of us. Of them. I wanted to tell you about the tattoos."

In the warehouse, as if on a cue, we three who hadn't already heard this whispered, "The tattoos!" and leaned forward. Yes! Wrap up this unimportant but super intriguing loose end, please.

Zane went on, "I was actually surprised anyone knew about the tattoos. Everyone was supposed to start covering those up years ago."

Video-Bryan said, "Yeah, but these are older pictures someone found. Maybe you're all covering them now, but you seem to have underestimated how much humans love taking pictures, especially when we're dressed up to go out."

Zane had an airy laugh. "Aha! That makes sense. Okay, so, the tattoos. Quite some time before peace overtook our planet, children of people in the religion started to be born with dark blue markings. Not the usual shimmers of barely-there blues and greens and purples you might have noticed on us," (we had not, actually) "but..." and they pulled aside their hoodie and the collar of their shirt to show a sprinkling of dark blue dots on their left clavicle. "Somehow, someone decided that this was a sign of the Divine. They became desirable and, fortunately, eventually became the norm for new children. More genetically common. Uh, most were born that way, I mean. Before that, those who didn't have Divine Marks got tattoos that symbolized specific principles they were ardently devoted to. It went from being a way to compensate for lack of Divine Marks to a traditional way to express extra devotion." Zane pulled up their right sleeve to show a tattoo on their forearm. They helpfully held it up so that the camera could see it. "This one's 'Truth'. That's my only one at the moment. But Truth is a principle I am...perhaps inordinately devoted to." Zane grinned. "Lucky for you!"

The rest of the video was Zane explaining what all the tattoos were that were visible in the pics we'd found of the execs. No surprise to any of us that none of them had Truth. Though we *were* surprised that the symbols generally meant things we could get behind. I think we just wanted to see nothing but villainy when it came to those fuckers.

When the video ended, Riley demanded, "That was it?"

Bry nodded.

Riley didn't let it go. "They made you come over just to tell you about tattoos?"

Bryan sighed. "Yeah, poppet. Like I said, not really useful. Just interesting and an answer to a previous question. But also—"

"Also totally suspicious," Jonny interjected.

"Yeah. Exactly," Bryan agreed.

I'd scrolled quickly through the video whilst they talked. "I'm going to have to agree with Riles."

Everyone looked at me, confused.

"Look, sexy, I appreciate you being on my team, but which tidbit of brilliance are you talking about?" Rye asked.

"Zane likes Bryan." I shrugged.

"Oh! Oh, yeah. Totally," Riles agreed. Zie looked very pleased with zirself.

I was just pleased that, for the first time in weeks, it wasn't *my* relationships that were the focus.

Jonny said, "Show me."

So I scrolled to a point where Zane had this sort of "small smile, looking away with abashed eyes" thing happening. I admitted, "They aren't human, so I could be wrong, but..."

"But they were socialized to be human-y. If they had hair, they'd be nervously tucking it behind their ear," Riles asserted.

Bryan looked to Jonny for dissent, but Jonny just nodded and shrugged. "I think they're right, Bryan. Sorry. Or...not sorry? I don't know how you feel about Zane."

"But why would they be into *me*?" Bryan asked us.

"Um, because you're a tall, handsome hero with pretty eyes and a sweet, crooked smile?" Jonny snorted in a way that said, "Obviously, dude."

"This fine ass group of humans is one game of spin the bottle away from having an excuse to be the sexiest orgy ever. And that includes you." Riles always offered the classiest reassurances.

"Yeah, I mean, my self-esteem is fine, but I kind of doubt the person whose people I just killed thinks I'm a good-looking hero," Bryan objected.

"Mate. Mate. Listen." Riley leaned forward. "First, someone can be handsome to you even when it seems like they've done things that are totally reprehensible." Zie gestured at Jonny and me, reminding Bryan that he'd recently seen that. "And, second, if Zane's not bullshitting about being against the way their people work, they really could see you as a hero. How many times have we watched movies where some asshole human is tormenting good aliens and we've cheered on the aliens as they've laid down justice and/or vengeance?"

Slowly, Bryan nodded, as if the truth was working its way in. But then he just said, "Huh."

CHAPTER 9

Bryan let us all have a little while to work, eat, and make sure Jonny was caught up. But, whilst the rest of us (or at least definitely Riles and I) were happy to procrastinate about certain things, our Bry was a man in need of an action plan. He did a very bad job of sounding casual when he said, "So..."

Jonny must have caught the wary look Riles and I exchanged, because it was clearly the two of us he looked at when he asked, "What?"

I just gestured at Bryan. I figured I'd let him take lead; I knew I probably wasn't the one with the right attitude here.

Bry nodded, accepting the job. "If everybody's accounts are good right now?" He took in our nods, then leaned back in his chair, sighing. "I think we should probably figure out what we're going to do. Now that we know about the Peaceforger thing." He grinned and too casually said, "Unless you're all enjoying this stalled out thing where we sleep on the floor..."

I scrunched my face in confusion. "I thought you said something about food and shit before this conversation."

"Yeah," he acknowledged, "but how nice the beds in this place should be, or if we should be somewhere else with nice beds, depends on the whole plan."

Rye perked up. "When you put it like that...You have my attention. Get me to a bed, baby!"

We all laughed, making it a little easier to engage. Which was good, because I was now only *mostly* dreading this discussion.

Jonny tried to put an arm around me, and I scooted closer to make it easier as he said, "Obviously, we finish what we started, right?"

Riles and I looked at each other again, possibly the only ones who realized there was nothing obvious here.

Jonny, confused, repeated, "Right? Am I missing something?"

I saw the way Riley's eyebrows went up and zir posture got a little straighter. A mini-rant was on its way, so I tried to pretend

I was being gracious. "I think that, maybe, it's just a little more complicated. That, uh, the first thing we probably need to decide is what it means to finish it." Out of the corner of my eye, I saw Riles sit back. Okay. Good. Rant momentarily defused. "And, once we know that, then we can figure out what part we four nerds can actually play. *Realistically and reasonably* play."

Zie didn't say anything, but Riles nodded emphatically at that. *Don't worry, poppet. We're still on the same page,* I thought, hoping zie might somehow pick up on that with the same psychic ability that let zir know when there was love or sex even maybe kind of in the air.

On the "let's run the fuck away" page, despite the fact we'd been raised on the sort of books and stories where bad shit happened and ordinary people—or people who didn't know they were extraordinary—had to step up and save the world. Sometimes literally the whole world. And they always sucked it up, pushed through injuries and shitty emotional or mental situations, and did the job.

I had never thought it was bullshit or that I'd fail to be like them in the wildly unlikely event some big thing happened to me. I knew (had thought I'd known) that I'd be as much a hero as I could be, or at least survive and keep what Gran would have called a stiff upper lip. But now, clearly, I was actually failing at that.

Of course, any time I'd contemplated apocalyptic events— you know, shit like a nuclear war or zombie outbreak or fucking machine uprising—I'd also quietly hoped I'd go in the first wave. Ground zero when the bomb hit, bitten before I knew about the undead, erased by the machine overlords in their secret first offensive, or whatever. 'Cause if I survived, I'd feel *obligated* to keep surviving. No matter what. Seriously, having to live even when you hated life? Fuck that.

In retrospect, I should have at least been ready for the possibility that I could end up a strong member of Team Run the Fuck Away. And I was kind of ashamed of that, but also not willing to let this decision be made without carefully getting Bry and Jonny to see that there were reasonable reasons to be on that team.

I expected Bryan to jump in, but he was just watching quietly. Probably happy to let someone else argue with me and Riles for once.

Fortunately for Bry, Jonny was consistently dedicated to fighting for what he thought was right, no matter how big or if it might require doing meat stuff. "Finished is when we've sent whichever of the aliens want to take over off into the void of space. Am I missing some other way we could consider it finished?" To his credit, he sounded more confused than confrontational.

Because something in me was rising up, ready to fight, I took a second where I was both trying to figure out other ways we could call the whole shit show finished and also realizing that there was some serious fear and exhaustion driving my fight instinct. I rolled my eyes (mentally; I wasn't so exhausted that I'd stupidly roll them for real) and felt annoyed (with a side of ashamed) that this whole "fight" thing was somehow aimed at my friends instead of at the fuckers who were trying to invade us. That it was only flight I actually felt in the face of the alien thing.

I looked at Riles. Zie barely raised a brow, but the question was clear. Had I thought of anything. When I gave a slight shake of my head, zie slumped.

I let my own slump lean me back into Jonny. "Yeah. I guess that's the only way we can think of that this alien thing would be finished." I fought not to sound sulky.

Bryan didn't smile. I'd assumed he would, at least a little, because this was something of a victory for Team Let's Kick Alien Ass. He just looked...grim and resigned.

I sat up a little so I could look at Jonny. He had that same look. Somewhere in the last couple days of quietly fearing we'd be stuck fighting, of quietly feeling sure that's what Bry and Jonny would want, I'd forgotten that none of us, *none of us*, had been thrilled to have to do more than hack our way out of a problem. I'd forgotten that, for all of us, other kinds of actions were no more than unwanted necessities. I took a deep breath, leaning back into Jonny, committing to myself to stop that whole "demonizing my own people" shit.

It had been silent a few moments before I realized we were probably all coming to terms with this fact, that this was the first time that we'd all admitted aloud that the end goal was something big. So big. Something that didn't even sound like a real thing, like a goal you'd have outside of fiction. Something we had no idea how to do and had every reason to think we couldn't do.

"Because it's us or them, right?" Riles asked suddenly, scanning our faces. "Like, we get them to fuck off or we accept that they're going to take over, right?"

I could feel that, like the rest of us, Jonny was nodding in response. He noted, "At best, take over. At worst, destroy our whole species, maybe the whole planet."

Riles breathed out a defeated little, "Fuck."

Finally, Bryan joined the conversation. He reluctantly stated the facts. "While it's bullshit that we'd think we're responsible for the whole of humanity—"

"Especially after we literally just went outside our norms and our comfort and our skills and all that in order to save their asses and let them know enough to save their own," I interjected, but with less rancor than I'd have expected.

Rye picked it up, a little edge to zir voice. "And especially since, overall, humanity has treated us shitty."

Bryan clenched his jaw, but didn't tell us off for interrupting, just picked the thread back up. "Okay. Yeah, it's bullshit on multiple levels to think of us as responsible for all of humanity." He shrugged. "And I'm not even saying we are or should be. But we might be the only ones who know. This time, there's not even some doctor in New Mexico who suspects more shit is up. It's us. If we do nothing, we're letting them win."

"Worse," Jonny said quietly, "we've stirred them up. It's not just that we're responsible because we know. But..." He sighed, frustrated. "We did the right thing with the info we had...and we did all we could to make sure our info was complete...But, the fact is that achieving our totally righteous original goal probably just put them into a more aggressive mode. And that's on us."

That hit us all. The air turned to concrete and landed on our chests. We'd been so bloody careful. We'd done all we could to make sure that there would be no unexpected consequences, no better ways to end what, just as recently as Friday, we'd had every reason to believe was just some human corporation getting away with murder (literally) and mind control and such shit. We'd all dreaded being wrong, doing more harm than good. And I still don't know what we could have done differently, not given they'd been kicking their plans into a dangerous gear Friday, but that didn't make this less bad. Even knowing the execs were probably all invading aliens, we'd still killed people. (And some of the CorpSec blokes must have been human; some of the aliens might have secretly been on our side.) And people had died for our efforts, people we knew and cared about. And that had been bad enough. But now...

"I fucking hate this," Riley muttered, and Bry put an arm around zir.

I wanted to complain. I wanted to whine that we should be in South Dakota, ignorant of the impending alien-enforced dystopia. I wanted to just fucking cry and quit. But I kept it in my head. I swallowed the bitching before it could get past my lips. That wasn't going to solve anything. And it wasn't who I wanted to be.

Instead, I joked, "This will teach me to idolize Diana instead of making sure I could kick alien ass like Juliet-fucking-Parrish."

Bryan and Riles started to chuckle appreciatively, but they stopped when Jonny asked, "Who?" They looked at me, and I must have had my "are you serious, motherfucker?" face on, because they shut their mouths and shook their heads. They had their "you sad motherfucker" faces on.

I leaned back and turned around to look at Jonny. "Holy shit. You've never seen *V*?"

He looked like he was a little afraid to admit it, but shook his head slowly. "Never even heard of it."

I shrieked and turned to pull up video, then stopped. "Shit. I don't think I can even tell you much without spoiling it."

"Yeah, if you say more than it was a limited series (but back when they called them mini-series) and a show in the 80s that starts with UFOs showing up..." Bryan shrugged.

"Please promise you'll let us watch you watch it," Riles begged. "Especially..." Zie trailed off, aware that the most important bit was a massive spoiler.

"So, all that," I gestured at Rye and Bryan. "But, uh, Juliet Parrish is this tiny, blonde woman who ends up kicking ass. And...I'm going to have to insist we start watching it ASAP." *Quickly*, I thought, *before one of us accidentally tells you who the aliens really are.*

"You can probably spoil it for me," Jonny offered. "It's over 60 years old. I think rules about spoilers no longer apply."

All of us shook our heads and noped at him.

Riles turned to zir computer. "Since he can't see anything on my screen, I'll get things queued up to start watching as soon as we're done with this."

"It will be inspirational," I promised. I took a breath and got back on track. "Right. So, even if I *were* Juliet-fucking-Parrish, I'd say we need more than us."

"More than us and our remote team," Jonny added. "Though even bringing them in...We'd have to prove that there are aliens, and do it without burning our one alien ally."

"Unless we can figure out how to hack their ship," Bryan suggested.

I snorted, "As if. This isn't *Independence Day*, mate."

But Jonny got this edge of...excitement? awe? to his voice and said, "Can you fucking imagine? That would be amazing."

He wasn't wrong. Especially given this was the real world and it was unlikely the aliens shared our programming languages or interfaces. It would just about be a miracle. One I'd love to be part of.

Rye looked up from zir computer, sat back, and viciously mused, "I'd fill every screen on their ship with the most violent videos I could find. On a loop. For fucking days. *Days*. Just really ruin their peace in every petty way I could."

I got an image in my head of a ship of Peaceforgers, half of them running in shrieking circles and the other half looking like malfunctioning androids from some old *Star Trek* episode. I let a little evil laugh out. Man, that would be beautiful.

Carefully, Bryan confirmed, "So, can we all at least agree that we have a responsibility to take action here?"

I hated to do it, but I nodded along with everyone else. Still, I suggested, "We could do whatever from South Dakota though, right? Somewhere with a little less heat on us?"

"That depends," Jonny sounded thoughtful. "If all our tasks are definitely things we can do online—"

"Like pull together info and evidence, figure out who to send it to, keep an eye on whatever SWS does next," Bryan ticked off each thing on his fingers.

Riles interjected, "Definitely figure out who to send things to! There's no way I'm trusting anyone else to decide who holds the fate of this big, dumb world in their hands. Now that I think of it."

"Right. If that's it, that stuff Bryan said, we can do it anywhere probably," Jonny said. "But..." He groaned at the thought as he said, "But if there's anything we need to physically do about the ship or the aliens..."

I could see in all our eyes that more things were coming to mind. I said, "Or if you're not actually well yet or any of us need a doctor we can trust, because who knows what would be available on the road or in South Dakota?"

"I was thinking that too, since we talked about it the other night," Riles said. "And I was thinking we just ask Doc." Zie sighed, acknowledging there was more to the thought. "But then there's someone who knows where we're headed. Plus, then we're asking him to tell us even more of his own people."

"And," Bryan laughed at the absurdity, "our only contact with the non-shitty faction of Peaceforgers, the only Peaceforger currently willing to tell us about their people, will only talk in person."

With feigned heaviness, I put my hand on his shoulder and said, "If only you'd been less sexy, mate."

Bry matched my tone, and lamented, "If only my ass weren't so fine!"

As we laughed, I had to feel grateful that we could at least still manage that. If we were all going to be stuck in this fight, in this warehouse, for however much longer, laughter was probably going to keep us from killing each other.

The tail end of our laughter was swept away as Riles softly, bitterly, said, "So. We stay here. In this miserable fucking warehouse. Until we drive off the aliens or they kill us."

"Or until we feel like we've handed off all our info to the right people? The people who have things like bomber jets and subs? And then we clear out to South Dakota whilst they finish things?" I suggested.

Nobody answered for a moment. From the looks on their faces, I could guess their current internal struggles. I'd guess Riles was trying to come to terms with having to agree to stay at all. And...I mean, obviously, Bryan and Jonny were both trying to squelch their irrational inner heroes, the dumbasses who still thought they'd suddenly turn into kick-ass superheroes and fling the ship back into space or something comic book-worthy like that. Finally, with much less drama than you'd expect for Heroes Committing to the Cause, we all sort of shrugged and nodded and approved that plan. This was the second time in a row we'd failed to be cinematic at such a point. *Please, let there not be a third*, I silently pleaded with the higher power I didn't believe in.

Jonny asked, "So, do we do this like the last one? Divide up research, email broadly?"

Bryan shook his head. "This time, I think we have to be more careful about who we send the info to. We don't want to cause some huge, general panic. I think we need..." He paused a moment to think. "I think we need to figure out who in government and the military, maybe of more countries than ours, maybe also including other law enforcement, can be trusted. If the Peaceforgers know they've been discovered, who knows what sort of shit they'll do?"

"But still research," Jonny pressed. "Research who to trust. Research...however the hell we're going to prove to them that the real threat is extraterrestrial. Then hand off."

"And still try to find a way to hack their ship," I added. When they all looked at me like I was crazy, I said, "Hey, I obviously know the odds on that. But how much arse would it kick if we managed that? If we could just take over their controls and make it so it's only the ones who aren't on the ship we need to worry about?"

"Sounds like Kot wants to hack the Gibson," Jonny teased.

"One, fuck you. Two, I love *Hackers* in spite of myself, so points to you for a perfect, ridiculous 1990s movie allusion. Three, fuck you." I grinned at Jonny and made a kissy face.

"While Katja hacks the planet," Bryan paused for us to snicker at his own allusion to the same film, "I can make this warehouse suck less."

Riley grabbed him by the shirt, hamming it up. "Don't you toy with me, mister. Are you going to get me a bed?" And then zie leaned in and batted zir eyes. "Cos if you do, I just might let you 'toy' with me after all."

Bry put a hand lightly on the small of Rye's back. "In that case, beds just became my highest priority."

They froze there a promising moment before both laughed and moved back.

I leaned in, "But, seriously, beds?"

"Um..." Bryan pulled his computer in front of him and started typing. "It might take me a few days, and we'll have to share as I get them all, but I can make mattresses happen. Yeah." He typed, examined something on his screen, and typed some more. "Okay. Here's the plan, just in case something happens to me. I'm going to place some orders to make this place more comfortable, so send me your lists of things we should have. I'll have things delivered to other buildings I know are empty or where I can have things delivered outside work hours or such. Not all near here. Then we'll just scrub footage of me grabbing our stuff and getting it here."

"Yes!" Jonny gave a victory pump with his arm. "I was prepared to just suck it up, but living on Katja's couch was as rough as I'd ever lived, so..."

Riley gave a short laugh. "Babe, the rest of us lived in a squat when we were teens, and I think none of us—well, maybe Bryan, because he's made of sterner stock or something like that—is enjoying doing this at this point in our lives."

I snorted and nodded. "Yeah, I don't remember floors sucking quite this much."

Quietly, still typing (ordering goods, I hoped), Bryan said, "Floors have definitely gotten much less ideal in the last few years. I *will* be getting a mattress for myself too."

We spent the next couple hours getting things set up. Bryan made his list of stuff to help us set up a more comfortable home base and started arranging initial deliveries. All of us started brainstorming lists of what kinds of things might count as proof that we had an alien problem, of who to start watching and investigating as possible recipients of that info, and of ways we might try to hack the Peaceforger ship. We readied ourselves for hacker action (hacktion?) and started working on gracefully resigning ourselves to not being done with the fight. Or at least I was doing that last thing. It seemed like Jonny and Bryan had already managed it. No idea if Riley was even going to bother pretending to be graceful or resigned, but I knew zie'd still work zir ass off to win either way.

We also started making a list of things for Bry to ask Zane the next time they asked him to come hang out. As interesting as the tattoo stuff had been, if Zane wanted to...flirt? with our boy, they were going to have to give us a little better info. Now that we knew we were staying and going to try to somehow fight, we could think of more useful things they could tell us about.

And, best of all, because his current efforts didn't take a full screen, we made Jonny watch *V* in the corner of his screen whilst we worked. We all managed not to pause and stare as we knew the big reveal was coming, the true nature of the Visitors, but we happily paused as Jonny exclaimed, "No fucking way! Badass!" at just the right part.

And then Bryan ducked out to pick up the first of his deliveries. I used the software I'd written to erase all traces of his actions, to watch as he drove over to another warehouse, pulled on a hat (in addition to his g/ap mask) so the driver just saw him as an anonymous working slob, and signed for a mattress. It looked like he and the delivery guy had a short conversation and some laughs before the guy just leaned it against the side of the warehouse and left.

Jonny leaned over my shoulder. "Is that a mattress he's struggling to smash into our car?"

I laughed. "Yeah. Bet he's wishing we'd gone for a full-sized SUV now."

"I don't know about you bitches," said Riles, "but I'm all for the four of us crowding onto that. Because I'm not interested in arguing about who gets to suffer. And I will cut the first person who suggests that *I* sleep on the damned floor."

"I fear none of your cooties. I'll share that mattress with any of you who can fit on if it spares me the floor," I said.

"Cool by me," Jonny agreed, then pointed at my screen and asked, "What are you using to track him?"

"Program I wrote to erase footage of us after we blew SWS HQ." I pulled up my code. "I've told it what things to look for, assuming it starts following us from when we leave the warehouse. It scans for any wireless cameras along the route, plus dips into networks of businesses that might have wired cameras, and it basically edits us out. Since we're probably moving, not standing still and being on minutes of frames, it can usually either edit just the space we're in or pull up the second before and make it glitch or duplicate it. Pretty basic. And then I have it go through and do some similar glitches or blurs or edits on other spots on the file that don't have us."

"So, we're feeling pretty pleased that even the cheapest businesses upgraded from film and hard media ages ago," Jonny noted.

"Definitely," I agreed. "If there's anyone using film, my plans are to burn their buildings or to distract their security with my tits whilst you guys sneak in and steal the tapes."

Jonny laughed. "We watch too much TV." Then his tone got serious again. "Can you show me what the footage looks like after you hit it?"

I could. I did. It didn't look obviously shitty, except for places where it was supposed to and where other footage on the same system had also been shit-i-fied.

"How are you getting such good accuracy on it targeting our car, even when he's driven past others like it?" Jonny was looking at a scene where other dark mini-SUVs hadn't been removed but ours had.

"Oh, well, we might have made sure the on-board systems can't connect to any other companies' computers, but I can connect. Means, for our car or for one of us if I set it up and it can use our mobiles, the program has an extra boost."

If only we could edit the Peaceforgers out so easily. Send in our own little alien, have the program select all but Zane, and delete delete delete!

Bryan didn't just return with a mattress. Even that would have been enough to make him a hero. No, he also brought burgers and booze.

"I know that one thing people were looking forward to was just getting drunk and relaxing on the other side of all this shit." He lined up bottles, putting some in the old fridge that, to our relief, hadn't been sold off and still seemed to work.

"My first toast will be to the slacker who did a shitty job stripping down and selling off the contents of this break room when the company failed," I said.

"To the slackers!" Riles agreed.

And then we drank. The burgers only helped so much in keeping us from getting too drunk too fast.

We drank and unspooled a little.

We drank and danced. (Or did the best dancing we could, given our fine assortment of injuries.)

We drank and cried.

We drank and talked about everything we'd rather be doing.

We drank and toasted Quinn, who'd taken us in.

Toasted Gran, who'd raised most of us right.

Toasted Huw, the first of us to fall.

Toasted 'Randa, who never should have gotten caught up in any of this shit.

Toasted Kitty, who also shouldn't have gotten caught up, but who stepped up and ended up being the big hero of demo day.

By that point, we were sloppy drunk. Sitting on the mattress and trying to make sure nobody's injuries were being jostled or held at a wrong angle.

And Riles started crying again. Not the big, ugly sobs from earlier in our weekend; these were just quiet streams of tears down zir face. And because zie was drunk, zie quickly went from crying over Kitty ("she was fucking beautiful and amazing and didn't deserve this") to crying over zir own loneliness. In spite of the tears, zir voice was dead steady when zie whispered, "I'll be alone forever now."

Suddenly, I realized Jonny was crying too.

"I'm so fucking sorry, Riley. I shouldn't have pushed the button. It's my fault." Jonny was quickly escalating to sobs. "I should have not pushed the destruct. Or I should have gotten her out. I was *right there.*"

Bryan put an arm around Riles and I put one around Jonny. But they kept going.

"No, you did the right thing. I don't blame you, mate," Riles sniffled and zir breathing got less even. "I'm to blame. I should have found another way; she should never have gone in." Zie got an edge of fire. "If anyone's to blame, it's fucking SWS and Peaceforgers. It's the fucking CorpSec meatsack who wouldn't keep his filthy fucking paws off her."

And then they were both just sobbing, with Jonny apologizing over and over and Riles holding his hand, telling him it wasn't his fault.

Bryan caught my eye, and I tried to figure out what he wanted. He quietly took Rye's hand off of Jonny's and got zir turned towards him instead. He wrapped zir in a hug and I could hear him whispering calming stuff.

Okay, good, yeah...I could do that. I wasn't bigger than Jonny, so I didn't do as good a job wrapping him in my hug the same way. But I tried. I whispered, "Baby. Baby, shhh. It's okay. We wouldn't have had another chance. You did the best thing. Nobody blames you." That sort of thing.

When Jonny got quieter, he whispered in my ear, "Do you think Riley hates me? I didn't mean to kill zir girlfriend."

And then he started crying again and I had to repeat the soothing. I just felt so awkward, clumsy. Both physically and emotionally. In my mind, the guilt demons were trying to prove that, actually, I was to blame. If I'd just kept the whole Jonny thing to myself somehow, Riles and Bryan and their girlfriends wouldn't have been involved. Everyone would be alive.

"It's SWS and the Peaceforgers." I didn't know I was going to say it until it was out. But it's what we'd kept coming back to over and over the last couple weeks. "They created this whole fucked up situation. Fuck them."

Quietly, everyone agreed. Yeah, fuck them. The tears seemed to ease up.

"Right. Music and happiness, bitches," proclaimed Rye as zie put on a playlist that, usually, would make for plenty of drunk dancing.

I sat quietly with Jonny, drinking (yes, still, because I never claimed that common sense was one of my strengths, especially not after I've already had a few), and watched as Bry and Riles sang the songs to each other.

Watched as, over a few songs, it suddenly became clear that Riles was unabashedly hitting on Bryan. And Bry wasn't exactly turning zir down. It had been a long while since more than one of us had been single at a time, but I recalled that drinking and fooling around hadn't been unheard of as a way to cope with hellish shit (or, sure, just to kill time back when we were 16 or so).

When Jonny caught on, he leaned in to ask quietly, "Are they going to fuck?"

I shrugged and kept my voice down. "No idea. But if they find some comfort in whatever this is, I feel like maybe they deserve it."

We crashed out on our side of the mattress, carefully arranged around our injuries, just about the time Riles and Bryan started making out.

CHAPTER 10

In the morning, as Bryan helped Riley stand up from the mattress (which had sucked way less than the floor, even if we'd had to lie on it the wrong way, with some of our feet or legs hanging off), Riley said, "Thanks for being kind to me last night."

Bryan kissed zir forehead. "You're one of my best friends. Even an asshole like me can be kind to friends."

"Yeah, well...You're fab. And I just...uh...I figured it was just us being sad and drunk. You know, still getting over what's happened. And, uh, you seem to be starting to like Zane, so, uh..."

Bryan looked a little surprised at the Zane comment but ignored it. "We're good. Same as when we were younger."

Riles grinned and looked relieved. "Exactly. Same as when we were younger."

I finally spoke up, teasing. "Just make sure we've got a few more mattresses in play before you invite Zane to hang out for some 'kindness.' Already a bit squished and not-private with just us four in the bed."

Bryan ignored that too. (I didn't have any evidence he was into Zane, but we all knew Riles just sensed things like that...)

Breakfast was scrounged and eaten to the soundtrack of Riley teasing Bryan and trying to figure out just what it was he felt for Zane. Because never quite growing up means that sometimes things *can* be the same as when we were younger.

Riles and I started our work weeks by sending emails to quit our respective jobs. Mine to SWS basically said that, yeah, the whole HQ bombing and my office being bombed made me think they weren't a safe employer so...When SWS replied, it was super smooth and professional and normal. Like they hadn't been talking shit about me on TV. Like they hadn't outed me to the press, killed people I knew, or bugged and invaded my home. Like they hadn't tried to slip a trace program into their reply to figure out where I was now. Yeah.

And then we checked out the state of the world. Funny how learning that the big company with its technological fingers in most homes and businesses was actually a bunch of super villains intent on world domination made people a little...reactive. Shit happened.

Shit like there'd been enough public outcry (and contacting of representatives) over the weekend, once we revealed SWS were dangerous bastards and called out that the Silver Standard Reassurance senior bill had a bit in it about putting a Peacemaker in every fucking senior citizen, that the bill was killed off. There was a big press conference where every rep who could squeeze into the camera shot nodded solemnly as the Speaker of the House and the majority and minority leaders took turns assuring us that they cared about our seniors and had had no idea and would never pass this sort of thing now that they did have an idea. That they would do some careful investigating before trying another bill for our valuable senior citizens. I had a cynical thought or two about how many of them might be relieved that this meant they could dodge paying for other things in the bill, things that were actually good and beneficial. I also couldn't help but notice that they hedged their language, spoke carefully as if not sure SWS was done being a donor. The cocks.

Shit like hospitals and doctors were swamped. Once people got the fear in them, and once the media had the weekend to stoke paranoia, anyone who had a Peacemaker, or anyone who'd ever thought maybe they'd felt a needle prick at a Secure World Systems clinic, rushed in to any facility or caregiver they thought could help verify they were clean or get the thing out. It was surreal to see the shots, the waiting rooms full of wide-eyed people. A lot of older people, given the door-to-door campaign and the push through senior homes and such. A lot of people our age and younger, weird kids like us, sometimes sitting beside parents who probably deserved the glares they were getting. And all quiet. No sniffles or coughs. Just terror. Even the more traditional waiting room visitors had caught the air of quiet fear.

Shit like the stock market going to hell. It wasn't just that SWS were big or whatever. But they had their fingers in so many other companies' security—including the security for the various stock exchanges—and people were, understandably, not feeling confident about that. And, with their global reach, it wasn't just the US stock market that was feeling the pain from the SWS thing. I did feel kind of bad about that. Don't get me wrong; Wall Street is full of money-hungry assholes who'd shiv their own doting grandmothers in the middle of Christmas dinner if they could make money off it. But I knew that the top 1% (hell, the top 10%) would be fine, would find a way to pass the pain on to everyone else. If I weren't busy trying to thwart an alien invasion (that still felt weird to acknowledge), I'd have plenty of douchebags to destroy.

Shit like news stations trying to go analog because the hackers who weren't us were still misbehaving and running rampant over their broadcasts. It had gotten to a point where the news mostly wasn't at all useful. But then we found a station where the person (or persons) who'd hacked them seemed to be reasonable. They had it locked down; we didn't see any competing shenanigans on the station all day. And their main thing was to expose or peel back the bullshit. A lot of fact checking done on the spot, with the truth put on the screen. Things like neon red "Lie! Crime has been slightly on decline in Chicago for 5 years." Or saying what the anchor was talking around. Neon green "By which she means they're cutting 500 jobs next quarter." Instead of going analog, every news station should get such reasonable hacker babysitters.

But also. I can't even think about this without wanting to fucking murder someone. But also. Shit like the discussion around SWS and Peacemakers getting more nuanced. And by "nuanced" I mean that some assholes who didn't like losing SWS as a "donor" were starting to point out how maybe we'd misunderstood SWS, maybe we were too quick to write them off or write off the good the Peacemakers could do. They started using bullshit tactics we'd seen historically, stuff like pulling out mug shots of people with Peacemakers and talking about them as criminals (even the ones who weren't, like some old lady who'd been given a ticket 40 years ago for indecent exposure when she streaked as part of a sorority hazing), whilst only showing the polished pics of SWS people. They even found people who had, or claimed they'd had, Peacemakers in and were willing to talk about how much SWS and the Peacemakers had helped them be better people. Because, you know, someone decided there were two sides to an argument where one side was "I'd rather my planet didn't get taken over by a corporation and I didn't get mind controlled by them." Obviously, CEO Trent ate this shit up and lauded those who didn't let themselves be fooled by hacker lies. He even made sure to point out that all their CorpSec had Peacemakers (what??) and here are some of our more attractive CorpSec officers to tell you why it's better that way.

And, (seen whilst digging in, trying to research and decide who to hand info off to), shit like there were quiet emails flying between all sorts of government and law enforcement types. Not everyone seemed 100% bought in to SWS being the bad guys, or at least bad enough to risk them as donors. (The donors thing was going to be our ruin, wasn't it?) There was a whole discussion going on about whether those who'd had Peacemakers put into their family or themselves (looking at you, Mr. President) could quietly have them removed without SWS seeing it as a betrayal. You know, just in case.

Yeah. Not all wins.

We also saw some new people fucking around in the war zone that was the hackers' part of the 'Net. It didn't take much digging to figure out it was government hackers. This was...It was good and bad. Bad, obviously, because they didn't seem to discriminate between taking out the assholes or the white hats. And some of them had, clearly, not just gone government due to lack of sufficient skills to play with us big kids. But, on the other hand, they were clearly researching to confirm that the things in the emails we'd sent a million years ago (aka just a few days ago) were true. And there wasn't much for them to find, but we did our best to point their efforts at things (without them actually realizing anyone was doing that), to help them find bits and pieces. Not enough, but not nothing.

The other group to enter the fray, though not on the 'Net, was other corporations and citizens trying to either figure out the truth or trying to use this chance to knock over SWS and take their pieces of the pie. And SWS had...not just its fingers, but its whole hands in so many pies...There was a lot of potential pie action for people to pick up. Just like you'd expect.

And, of course, just like you'd expect, there was a continuation, if scaled down a bit, of the attacks on us and our accounts. That was already feeling routine. Cool...

At this point, it seemed like maybe we could settle into a little digital defense, some digital preparation for offense, and healing (in the meat, not digitally...not yet).

In less global and less routine news, Lex messaged me late in the morning. Squee! Heart eyes! (I didn't feel too bad about my wee crush because we had consensus on the fact, FACT, that Lex was hot-tastic.)

"Message from Lex, kids. 'Let us buy you thank you drinks tonight. Bring your friends if you want!'" I looked up from my mobile. "I guess we probably can't, huh?"

Riles and Jonny looked disappointed, because obviously we couldn't. But Bryan stared at his computer screen a moment, clearly considering.

"We really shouldn't..." Bryan's tone told us that wasn't his final answer. He sighed. "But I've been wondering if we shouldn't make more local allies. Especially some who aren't just hackers. More people used to living in the meat."

I exchanged looks with Jonny and Rye; both looked as surprised as I felt (though Rye got distracted by zir buzzing mobile). Was a hangover making Bry as foolish about meat stuff as the rest of us?

"Are you sure?" I wanted to pretend, for even just an hour or so, that things were normal, but shouldn't we be massively paranoid?

Bry nodded. "We have to be careful, but...Let's check out whether Lex can be useful." He paused and cringed. "Damn. That made me sound like a horrible person." He shook his head. "Sorry, I'm having a hard time balancing freaking out over all the things we need to do in the meat with being a decent human."

Riles put a reassuring hand—the one that wasn't typing on zir mobile—on Bryan's shoulder. Zie drily said, "Don't worry, babe. We all know exactly how big a monster you are."

The research, looking for info to prove there were aliens, wasn't exactly going as great as it had when planning for demo day. Not as quickly and easily as expected. (Which made sense, given Jonny had come to us with a mass of research done already. But we'd kind of hoped we'd get magically lucky.) We had so many different places we had to dig, a lot of undefined parameters, shit like that. Even when we found interesting stuff, like the fact that none of the SWS execs had social security numbers, it just wasn't conclusive enough for what we needed to prove.

(We might have done more, but Riles seemed tied to zir mobile non-stop. I'd have given zir plenty of shit, but I wasn't the one who'd just lost my partner, and it seemed to have taken the place of hugging Kitty's bag like some kind of beloved stuffed animal, so...)

Our exciting day of information hunting, news watching, and online account protecting was punctuated by guidelines from Bryan for the night. Any time he came back from picking up supplies he'd ordered and had delivered other places (including mattresses!), he had a new thought.

"No heavy drinking."

"Keep your mask on or your back to a window at all times."

"Wait, no backs to windows. Backs to walls but, somehow, no faces to windows."

"I know it will be hard for you limpers, but remember gait recognition is a thing. So, try to mix up how you walk."

Blah blah blah. (I pretended to wave him off, but I was definitely taking paranoid notes.)

I was also looking into Lex and Marleina. And wondering who the hell Riles was messaging all day. And happily leaning against Jonny.

About an hour before we were supposed to go, out of the blue, Bryan grumbled, "Why the hell didn't Lex suggest drinks in a week." He looked at me. "Is it too late to suggest we do this in a week? When it's Halloween and we can also use costumes to hide behind?"

I tried not to make it obvious that I froze; I'm really not great with spontaneity. Less okay the closer to go time things got. Fortunately, Riles was in prime psychic mode. And also probably even hungrier than I was for some normal-ish going out.

"It's kind of a little too unplanned and last minute. And rude. Even if you aren't Katja. Don't you think?" Zie put on zir best "disappointed parent" face.

Bry took in Rye's face, then glanced at me, and must have remembered how I felt about last-minute changes. He nodded. "Point taken. Okay. Plan still in effect."

"So, while we're asking last minute questions that we should have asked earlier...Can we trust Lex and Marleina?" Jonny asked.

I shrugged. "I looked into them, obviously. They're the right kind of 'not squeaky clean,' so I wouldn't call them *huge* risks."

"I looked too," Bryan said.

Riles said, "Same."

Jonny nodded. "Okay, then. I can't ask for more. Yeah, let's grab that drink."

We were meeting Lex and Marleina at Sam's, the same place they'd first grabbed a meal together. Fortunately, Sam's wasn't too popular; we didn't have to park too far away or push through any crowds inside. Always a bonus when there were still some messed up arms in our group.

We found Lex and Marleina in a corner booth, one with big sides and no window exposure. Lex was gorgeous, but Marleina...Lex hadn't been exaggerating. Fucking impossibly beautiful. The sort of person who, when they look you in the eyes, you want to get naked right then and there...or maybe just never move so the eye contact never ended. My last girlfriend had been like that. Dangerous.

We slid into the booth, Bryan on the outside. I got to slide in right next to the women because I was the least stranger to them. Lucky me!

Before I could make introductions, Marleina leaned in and whispered, "Are you really MK?"

I flushed. With my face getting flashed somewhat regularly on the news, I was so much less incognito than I wanted. Of course Lex had realized. And of course she'd told Marleina. But I didn't have to confirm their (totally correct) guesses. "No. That's just SWS trying to cover their asses—"

"Too bad your face got splashed all over the news, huh?" interrupted Lex. "Rough that."

I shook my head, frustrated. "Yeah, not ideal. Way fucking not ideal."

Marleina leaned against Lex and smiled. "No troubles, pretties. We do secrets here, yeah?"

Lex waved at my three friends. "No need for names if you don't want. Don't need names for just chilling, right?"

Well, thank fuck for that, because I was suddenly having a hard time remembering what I was supposed to call everyone when other people were around. There was no way I wouldn't fumble introductions.

The server came to take our orders then. I hadn't looked at a menu, so I just randomly ordered beer and fries.

Lex said, "You gonna beat yourself later if you don't also get cheeseburger, yo."

So, I did that. And Bryan copied me, because he was too busy being vigilant to read a menu, especially now that it had been made painfully clear that Lex and Marleina knew I was Katja. Jonny and Riles exchanged a look, shrugged, and ordered the same. We could blame our lack of originality on Lex's enthusiasm for the burger.

Something about the interruption of the server sort of reset the conversation, or maybe it was just that Marleina was less socially awkward than me. She swung things towards what I guess is normal talk. It felt like it had been ages since I did that.

Music and plans and did you see that story, with a touch of flirting. It was really weird to talk to people who didn't want to discuss aliens or whether SWS had gotten closer to finding us or if the warehouse was going to be warm enough in the impending winter.

It was weird to talk to people outside my little group who weren't hiding personal details. I walked out knowing about some of their past crimes, their holiday plans, that Marleina was half Filipino ("Got my mom's coloring and my dad's height, so I spend a lot of time fending off drunk assholes who think I'm 'so exotic'."), and that Lex was creeped out by roaches but not rats. Was this normal? I didn't know anymore. But it all just came up naturally in conversation, so maybe?

At some point, I remembered to try to look for derms on Marleina. There was one line, a rainbow track up the inside of her arm, but I didn't see others. Still, a hell of a lot, even if not as many as Lex had claimed. As the meal wound down and got the feel of people going separate ways, I figured I should ask my questions.

"So, out of...let's call it professional curiosity...You guys been okay since you got the bugs out of your heads?" I was leaned in, trying not to make it easy for any eavesdroppers.

They both nodded.

Lex said, "Yeah. 100% old me."

Marleina nodded. "Perfect."

I indicated the arm with the derms, pops of color behind the netting sleeves of her top, against the light brown of her inner arm. "You using fewer of those?"

She grinned the sort of lazy grin you'd expect from a very pleased cat. "Oh, now I'm just on bliss and maintenance." She tapped the back of her head, where I knew she'd have a scar that matched Lex's. "No more uninvited guests to hold at bay. Lower dosage does the job. Easy times, miss."

When we were heading back to our vehicle, so we could get back to our "cozy" warehouse, Bryan said, "Holy shit. Marleina."

I gave a sort of dramatic, lovelorn sigh. "Yeah. That chick is...something else."

Jonny just grinned in agreement and gave my hand a squeeze. (Well, at least we were probably safe to point out attractive people to each other. Good taste!)

Bryan nodded. "But also? Lex! At least, if they accidentally out us, we'll know we were betrayed by *those* lips. Either of them. Lush lips, amazing eyes." And then he shook off the lust.

"But I think they're probably okay. Maybe connected to some slightly useful people. Probably totally good at secrets."

Which was great, because I wanted to cross one worry off my list. Bryan is the one who excels at shit in the meat, so, yeah, let's go with his assessment.

On the walk to the car, some dickhead catcalled Riles. Yay.

Riles stopped and turned, shouting in reply, "Shut your filthy mouth, asshole, or my boys will fuck you up!"

The guy stopped walking and turned. I noticed I wasn't the only one who suddenly tried to stand taller, tried to look possibly physically intimidating.

"Your 'boys'?" He sneered and pointed at me. "Is she a boy too? Or maybe she'd just want to join you in fucking me."

Riles waved zir arms as zie started lecturing. "You need to watch your sexist bullshit. She's probably twice the man you are. You and your fucking patriarchal gender boxes. I'll burn them and you to the ground!" Zie leaned like zie was going to lunge forward.

I managed not to laugh as the guy backed away slowly. I saw Riley take a breath, and I quietly hissed, "Leave it." We didn't need an actual fight. I put a hand on zir arm like I was holding zir back, just in case.

So zie just stood and glared, pretending like I was the reason zie didn't do more, until he turned and hurried off. Then zie turned to grin at us. "Well, this outing has been all kinds of fun."

Guess Riles really did need this night out more than I did.

We didn't make it even halfway home (home? ugh...I hated that the warehouse was that now) before Bry got a message from Zane. We all giggled like school kids. Tee hee. Bryan and Zane, sitting in a tree. Etc.

Bryan grinned, flipped us off, and asked, "Can we meet up with Zane? They say they've got something important to tell us."

I wanted to make a snarky comment about what Zane seemed to think was important, but I held back. Whatever. Let

Bryan and Zane keep having their weird flirtation. "Do you want us there? In all seriousness, if you like them, I don't want to cramp your style."

Jonny noted, "You *are* looking pretty sexy, all cleaned up for leaving the lair."

"Just something in the way they phrased the message...I think we should meet up now. Just..." We were at a light, so he turned to make sure we were all paying attention. "Just spare Zane the teasing, okay?"

We all nodded and mumbled assorted promises to behave.

Bryan sent a quick message and turned the car back towards the heart of the city. At Zane's building, he pulled up at a loading zone, and Zane came out from the lobby.

Riley popped out to let Zane have the front seat, and zie climbed in the back to sit with Jonny and I. Zane looked a little surprised. They must have thought they were going to have Bryan to themselves.

"Hello...everyone. I'm sorry to interrupt your night." They pulled their hoodie more tightly around their torso, as if they felt awkward being around us.

"You're totally fine," Bryan assured them. He pulled back onto the road. "I'm going to drive as we talk; more than two people in a vehicle that's parked would seem kind of suspicious."

"It is likely to be a short drive, because I have fewer details than you'll all want, but..." Zane turned in their seat so that they were addressing all of us. "They're building a new control machine. Like the one destroyed in the explosion. But this time on the ship, so that no humans can get to it."

All the air went out of the vehicle and my mouth was suddenly dry. Another machine. Shit. "How long?" I asked, trying to play cooler than I felt.

"Until it's done?"

I nodded, and bit back the freaked out and mean "obviously; duh" response.

"I don't know. There is a delay, because there'd been errors recently with the automated data backups to the ship for...I'm not clear on how long. But someone had neglected to take care of that. Which means some final information is missing. Thank the Divine!" Zane actually sounded relieved.

I don't know why I found that surprising. Maybe because I hadn't been the one interacting with them the last couple days, so I still had a hard time really believing they were on our side.

"Can you get any more information? Pictures or updates or even get us ship access?" Jonny asked, the hard edge on his voice suggesting he was trying to play cool too.

"I...I don't know." Zane furrowed their brow. "I only know that little bit because I overheard the end of a conversation when I arrived at my parents' home."

That threw me. I hadn't thought about that. If they'd been born and raised here, obviously they'd have parents here.

"Can you ask your parents about it without them getting suspicious?" Bryan asked.

Zane shook their head. "No. We are pretty strict about, uh, security clearances. We are raised to not ask about projects that we aren't on. If I ask...At best, I will get a lecture. At worst, they might become concerned about me and look into how I spend my time, and maybe look into my associations. None of us want that."

"A new machine means they're probably planning or already manufacturing and distributing more Peacemakers. I'm guessing you probably don't know how they're planning to do that?" asked Riley. Zie sounded a little weary, like maybe zie was too tired of this stuff to be freaked out.

"I don't. I would have told n0cebro if I did."

I had to pause a moment. N0cebro? Oh, right, our stolen 'nyms.

"Well, thanks for getting us what you could, Zane." Bryan put a hand briefly on Zane's shoulder.

Zane definitely blushed blue. The streetlights made that clear. I bit my tongue, but my inner child was giggling and pointing. I quietly shooed her away. No more teasing. Let them have this.

I did try to catch Riley's eye, to share the moment of pleasure zie was surely getting from this, but zie was on zir mobile. Again. I didn't know what zie was working on, but I hoped zie was at least kicking ass at some stupid game given how much time zie had been spending on that all day.

After we dropped Zane at their place, I waited only a moment before I said, "So, demo day. That was basically a waste." I tried not to sound bitter. Really, I mostly felt tired.

"No." Bryan's voice was firm. In the streetlights, I could see that his jaw was set. "Not a waste. Maybe not the win we thought, but..." He took a breath, then listed our wins. "We slowed them down. We took out the architects of the plan, or at least the ones running it, the ones with all the info and experience or whatever. We made a contact, Zane, who might help us sort this all out. Who let us know the extent of what's going on, the real stakes. We did what we set out to do, we just didn't realize it was the tip of the iceberg."

"Yeah. Okay." I wasn't sure I agreed, but I heard him. I wanted to agree.

Jonny caught that I wasn't sure. "No, seriously, babe. We met our goals, plus got more information. In war, if you just destroy the part of the enemy's force that they use in one battle, you've still won that battle. That they have more troops doesn't change that."

I nodded, wishing my brain wasn't so eager to cling to the negative feelings. I knew Bryan and Jonny were right. When my irritation didn't disappear, I looked for a target. And there was Rye with zir face in zir mobile still.

"Mate, what the hell is with you and your mobile today?" When zie didn't look up, I snapped, "Hey! Riles. I'm talking to you, bitch." I felt bad about my aggressive tone as soon as the words were out.

Riley blinked. "What the hell, Katja? What's your problem, mate?"

I took a breath, let it go. "Sorry. I'm sorry, poppet. You didn't deserve that. I'm clearly just out of line lately."

"I mean, yeah, but..." Bryan shrugged. "Riles, you *have* been on your mobile way more than usual today. Even when you've got your computer in front of you. What's up?"

Jonny leaned forward, as if hoping for a glimpse. "What're you working on?"

"Um...Nothing. It's nothing. Just...nothing..." Rye clutched zir mobile with both hands, ensuring nobody might accidentally see the screen.

"Not real convincing, babe," Bryan pointed out.

Riles scrunched up, as if zie could cram zirself into the corner of zir seat, pressed against the window, and somehow disappear. As if zie could wait long enough and the curiosity would lumber by, like a dread beast, and not notice zir.

"I know I was just a bitch, but you know you can tell us anything. I'm sorry I was a dick, poppet." I reached forward to put a hand on zir arm kindly.

Zie jerked zir arm back, as if afraid I'd grab zir mobile.

Casually, as if saying he'd have the soup, not the salad, Bryan noted, "Yeah, that didn't make me feel any better about whatever you're doing."

In tones that sounded like he was trying too hard to be kind, Jonny said, "I know you're a badass, paranoid hacker like the rest of us, but this kind of thing makes me worried about what you might be doing, Riles."

So quietly I could barely hear zir over the car and the road noise, Rye said, "You wouldn't believe me."

"We're fighting aliens," I pointed out.

"And Katja found a person she seems to be having more than a one-night stand with," Bryan helpfully added. Bastard.

"And there was a building with an underwater escape hatch and mind control tech," Jonny noted.

Rye shifted uncertainly. "Yeah, but nothing that seemed...supernatural."

Jonny and I shared a confused look.

"Supernatural?" Bryan asked. "Like...vampires and werewolves?"

Zir voice still unnaturally small, Riley said, "Like ghosts."

We were quiet for a beat, as if we were all searching for the right way to reply.

Jonny got there first. "Whose ghost?" He sounded ready to believe whatever answer Riley gave.

"You definitely won't believe me. You'll say it's grief." Riley was less quiet, and now sounded a little stubborn.

"Are you...Are you talking to Kitty's ghost, Riles?" Bryan didn't sound at all patronizing, not even the gentle kind of tone when you're humoring someone and you don't want them to feel bad about it. It just sounded like a normal question. Like "Do you have the salt?"

Rye looked down at zir screen, nodding. "It kind of seems that way."

Bryan informed us, "I'm going to take us home anyway. If someone has hacked zir mobile, this has been going on for long enough that they'd have found us by now if they were tracing the signal." He took a breath, let it go. "Okay, tell us about it."

"So. Uh..." Riles inhaled deeply, and it was like zie relit zir fire. Zir personality was back. "This morning, my messenger started pinging. At first, it wasn't anything coherent. Random letters, not even words. So, at that point, I was looking at my mobile to try to troubleshoot. But it was words by...noon or so, just not in any sort of useful order."

"Did you reply?" Bryan asked.

At the same time, Jonny asked, "Who did it say the sender was?"

"No, I didn't reply. And, that's the thing, there was no sender. Which my messenger shouldn't allow. I have it programmed so that *some kind* of identifying info is mandatory." Zie shrugged. "That's why I assumed it was a malfunction. I even turned off its 'Net connectivity, so I didn't accidentally send anything and shouldn't have been getting the messages. But it was still happening."

"Not to sound like I think I'm in charge, but, for future reference, I'll gut any of you who has this happen and doesn't say something immediately," Bryan sighed. "This sort of thing could indicate we've been found or hacked."

"Yeah, I know. I'm sorry. I just, you know, got so sucked into troubleshooting. And then realized you'd be upset I hadn't said something right away, so I really wanted to fix it without you knowing...Anyway." Riles was now turned toward zir audience, no longer crushed into the corner of zir seat. "Anyway, within another hour or so, the whole screen just said 'Kitty' over and over."

"Holy shit, Rye!" I exclaimed. "How the hell does that horror movie shit happen and you don't at least grab one of us to freak out?"

"I almost did. I swear. But then it cleared, which it also shouldn't be able to do on its own, and it started to be stuff strung together. Mostly just 'I Kitty' for a while. But then it got coherent. It was trying to talk to me. It sounded like her. Like someone who'd at least analyzed her messages to me from...before. Just trying to get me to answer. So...I did."

"Shit, mate..." Bryan sounded frustrated and confused. He sighed. "Okay. I get it. You have a chance to maybe not really lose her. I still think you should have told us, but...I get it."

"Is it her?" I asked.

Riles sort of shook zir head and gave a helpless half-shrug. "I still don't know. It *seems* like it's really her I'm chatting with."

Gently, Jonny asked, "What have you guys been talking about?"

"Don't worry. I'm sad, not stupid," Rye gave us a sly little grin. "Nothing about what we did or where we are or anything. More...reminiscing and talking about what's on the news, current events, that sort of thing. I've been trying to let her take the lead, not volunteering things, keeping it vague until she gives details I can confirm."

"Any slip ups in the reminiscing?" I didn't want to sound like I was interrogating, but...

"I've totally been watching for that," zie said, "but nothing so far." Then zie tilted zir head and confessed, "Though it's hard to tell with how, uh, kind of surface we've kept it and with...she's still not totally clear all the time."

Nobody said anything, just exchanged looks. It seemed like maybe I wasn't the only one who didn't know where to go with this.

"Can I keep messaging her or do I need to stop?" Riley begged us with zir eyes to choose the former.

Jonny shook his head and admitted, "No idea, Riles."

"Yeah, this is a new one, poppet." Bryan rubbed his jaw. "As long as you keep it at the same level...My only concern is that someone might be slowly working their way into your mobile."

"Well, whoever it is? They're...they're managing to ping my messenger even when I've got all normal connectivity turned off. Airplane mode, no Wi-Fi." Zie looked ashamed.

And that was appropriate. That seemed kind of important to know. Maybe a problem, but also maybe a clue.

I got excited as I realized the implications. "You guys don't think that's maybe...alien? That the messages are coming from the ship?" I barely held back a squeal of glee. "If it is, if we can figure out what sort of protocol or wavelength or whatever, maybe this is how *we* get to *them*."

"Can we maybe get her back?" Riley's voice sounded small again. Small and vulnerable.

Jonny reached up to put his hand on zir arm, and zie didn't dodge it this time. "We can't know, but..." He looked at Bryan and me. "But, we can see. We can try."

Riles nodded in gratitude.

"I *am* kind of worried about some kind of connection frequency we don't know about." Bryan sighed. "So, we add figuring that out and figuring Kitty out to our list." Even from the backseat, I could see he was mentally building a list of things to do.

At least we'd have plenty to work on. And we had people who were better at hardware, especially hardware beyond just standard computers and mobiles, than me. Nobody would be bored, and maybe...Maybe Kitty was still alive somehow. And, if she was, nobody in this vehicle could deny that she deserved saving. Or that, if the Peaceforgers had her and had caught onto our whole "Kitty is MK" thing, we might have inadvertently caused them to treat her shittier than she deserved. I was going to worry about that, feel guilty for suggesting we make her MK, for a long time.

During the drive home, I flipped through a folder of random images on my mobile, no real goal in mind. There was so much going on, so much to figure out. Sometimes, if I just looked at my collection of memes and shit, my brain sparked, got clever. I really needed some sparks, or something to get me going. All the things we had to sort out were...big. Too big. I was listing towards being a whiner again. Inclined to order t-shirts for Riles and I that said "Team Run the Fuck Away."

And then my eyes caught on a quote. Somebody had used nice font and put it on a pretty background, but that was all secondary. It was the words that got me. They said:

"It is not your responsibility to finish the work of perfecting the world, but you are not free to desist from it either."
- Rabbi Tarfon, Pirke Avot 2:21

That made me pause. I wasn't religious, but it still resonated. It was just...common decency, wasn't it? It was just being a good member of the human race. It was choosing not to join those who lived in selfish entitlement, taking and never worrying about what they cost the world. Behind our digital crimes, we had always been idealists. We didn't want to burn the world or steal everyone blind; we wanted to make it better...whilst we freed ourselves from the bullshit chains of day jobs, of course.

But we didn't make it better, we didn't get it closer to perfect, by running. By just letting it implode or get taken over.

Okay. I was going to suck it up. I was going to try to shut my fucking whine-hole and keep working. The rabbi was right; I wasn't free to desist, and I knew it.

CHAPTER 11

Back at our warehouse, we started with such purpose. We strode (limped) intently to our seats. We booted our machines and cracked our knuckles. We narrowed our eyes in concentration and took deep breaths, ready to dive into it. To solve the Kitty mystery! To stop the machine on the ship! Yeah! Team!

And then there was throat clearing and shifting in our seats and...nothing. I might have laughed if it wasn't all so potentially world-fucking.

Jonny sadly noted, "I have absolutely no clue about any transmission stuff aside from Wi-Fi or Bluetooth, just what I need to connect."

The sighing that answered him from the rest of us confirmed my suspicion that none of us had been hiding a Transmission Stuff skill. Well shit.

And then Riley laughed. When all eyes turned to zir, zie looked abashed. "Sorry. Just testing Kitty's memory or, you know, whether this is actually Kitty."

Bry asked, "Can I look at your message history? See if anything strikes me?"

Zie paused, but then Riles nodded and passed over the phone. "The last one is what I was laughing at." With a grin, zie said, "I casually mentioned a fake memory of camping in the Cascades over the summer."

Bryan laughed and reported, "And her reply was 'Camping? WTF? Who this? Rye and Kitty don't camp, bitch'."

I snorted a little laugh and admitted, "Whoever it is, the delivery is on point."

"Right?" Riles sighed. "Like I said, it's totally not clear." Then zie changed to a sensible tone. "Okay, we don't know about transmissions, but we know how to research. So, I'm going to go educate myself on the topic."

"I'll join you," Bryan said, handing back zir phone. "It seems like that's going to be key to figuring out Kitty and to getting at things on the ship. Unless we find a way on physically."

The thought of doing that terrified and thrilled me. I wondered if there were other underwater doors for us to find. If there were shuttles zipping back and forth right now...I had a thought. "Rye, can you send me any notes on hacking that satellite we used before or satellites in general?"

Beside me, Jonny nodded. "Good idea. Probably get us access to all sorts of equipment or different kinds of transmissions."

"And," I held up crossed fingers, "maybe get us a look into the ocean. Maybe even figure out if they've got other shuttles on land."

"Nice." Bryan paused a moment in his typing. "I would love to even just take a joyride in one of their shuttles."

With a dramatic final keystroke, Riley proclaimed, "Done! Go git you some satellites, girl."

"Me too?" asked Jonny.

"Yep." I quickly forwarded the info I'd just received. "I'm guessing we might need different satellites, so more than one of us on that sounds smart." I had a thought. "Also, if nobody objects, I'm going to tell our remote folks that we learned there's still at least one plant making Peacemakers. Get some extra eyes looking for that."

Nobody objected.

So, we settled into our research and our hacking. Bryan had bought a bigger screen for us all to share, so we kept lists of things. Successes, failures, possible tools and vocabulary to use with researching that transmission stuff. And we punctuated it with attempts to get Riles to message Kitty increasingly ridiculous memories of shit they would never have done. Entering competitive eating contests, queuing all day for a boy band, driving at monster truck rallies, winning weightlifting competitions. That sort of thing. An appropriate use of our time...

Bryan looked up from his screen. "Okay, I think I've ordered any gear that isn't huge or military only or whatever that might sense signals." He looked up at Riles, who was looking over his shoulder, and zie nodded to confirm it looked about right. "Not to be your mother, but it's morning so, I think we should probably wrap up for the 'night' now."

I groaned as I stretched my arms, my back cracking. "Yeah. My brain isn't going to get more successful at this satellite thing as it gets more tired."

"Kind of what I was thinking." Bryan rubbed at his face as he yawned. Then he asked, "Any thoughts on what we can do about the machine on the ship?"

We all shifted uncomfortably. Guess I wasn't the only one with no fucking clue. I tensed up when he sighed, disappointed. I was feeling paranoid from the whole bloody situation and from being beyond tired.

But then he said, "Yeah, me neither. Fuck. Okay, we'll all keep thinking. Maybe see if I can get Zane to help us get on the ship."

"I wouldn't hate hacking an offensive satellite and blasting the shit out of the ship," mumbled Riles.

I actually held my breath for a moment; I didn't know how I felt. If this were a movie, I'd be entirely in with this plan. Blast them out of the water for a flashy finale! But this was real life and I'd had my fill of killing. Even if it was bad guys. Fortunately, everyone looked conflicted.

Riles looked briefly ashamed. "I'll keep that one on the back burner. Just in case. Last resort."

Bry put his hand on Riley's shoulder. "It might not be our ideal answer, but it's the only idea we have for now. So...Gold star for making sure we at least have an option, poppet."

"I think I might have a good bedtime story for us," Jonny looked up from his screen. Seeing overly hopeful faces, he clarified, "Not a great story. Just a good one. Here." He tapped some keys and shared his screen with the big communal screen.

As we stood and got close to the screen, he told us what we were looking at. "Unless I'm totally off, this is a NOAA satellite, one doing fish counts in the Pacific." He pointed at a spot on the screen. "It's not exactly a glowing beacon, but..." He paused, giving us a moment to see what he saw.

"Fishes, bitches!" Riley exclaimed, laughing. Then noted, "And...they're swimming around something aren't they?"

Bryan and I leaned in even closer. And, yeah, there was something out there in the Pacific Ocean. We couldn't really see it, but we could see—because we were looking—how fish swam around it. I might have gotten a wee bit over-excited when one of the "fish" that swam in a really clean curve to avoid hitting the ship was a giant squid. I was still entirely against using satellites for surveillance and whatever, but bless them if they let me watch giant squid TV. (Watch it and try not to think too much about the level of detail and magnification, about the ability to use assorted wavelengths of light and such to see even down into the depths of the ocean. I had heard and believed allegations, and seen alleged pictures that proved the government could use their satellites to read over your shoulder as you typed in your password. But seeing it yourself, in real time, was something else.)

"Now I'm kind of amped," Bryan grinned. "This is why they say no screen time before bed."

Really, I think it was the worry, the paranoia, the sense of certain failure that kept me from falling asleep easily. But, yeah, let's blame the screen time...

Tuesday afternoon, as we were having our first coffees and preparing to get back to work, only a few days after we'd planted it, we watched online as Seattle PD found the bank account we'd carefully manufactured. The one that would lead them to the conclusion that CFO Williams had purchased both C-4 and little bug robots, much like what was used to blow up my building. We high-fived (carefully...fucking injuries) as they found it and as they drew the conclusions we'd hoped (as evidenced by notes they made in files).

It was so clear and yet hadn't been too easy. Just like we wanted. It wasn't long before Engalls was writing up the final report. The one that said it definitely wasn't me who'd blown up my building. The one that suggested, given the things SWS had been saying about me to anyone who'd listen, that these findings be made public. After all, not only would it help clear my name, it also couldn't really do much harm to CFO Williams (and she didn't seem to have a family around to protest). Nice!

I liked that the public, those who still didn't think it was MK who'd done the good stuff, would also stop thinking that Williams was some sort of hero. Now that we'd decided to let the world believe that Kitty had been MK and had maybe saved them all, I was delighted to let all the shit come back down on the person who had, as far as we could tell, given the orders that left 'Randa and Huw dead. Suck it, bitch.

This also put Bryan in a good mood; along with taking down the goth chick who'd lured her in, this was as close as he'd get to avenging his girlfriend's murder. Sure, we'd blown up the building and killed Williams, but that was more an attack on their whole group. This was personal. This was pointed at just her.

It somehow made it easier to get to the business at hand. We divided up the work: Jonny on proof there were aliens, Riles on vetting who should get the info, Bryan on "transmissions stuff" and Kitty (because we needed his objectivity on that, not Rye's deep desire to have her be real), and me on satellites.

Technically, we were all on the problem of the machine on the ship, but we were all also continuing to fail to have an idea how to handle that. I kind of hoped, if we left the questions floating in our subconscious minds, one of us would miraculously come up with something totally new. As it was, our hope was to figure out how to interface with the ship (insert hysterical laughter here) or to physically get there (more hysterical laughter, though slightly less impossible...but also freakier because it would be meat stuff).

And, of course, this was all done to the soundtrack of news channel bullshit, regularly fending off online attacks, and reports from our remote comrades that they were so far failing to find the new Peacemaker plants. Ah, the new normal. Non-stop party time.

"What if we go old school? Really, really old school?" My own brain might have come up with something to do about the machine on the ship.

Bryan's brow only slightly wrinkled with confusion as he asked, "Context?"

"Sorry. Right. Machine on ship."

Now I had everyone's attention. I suddenly wished even more desperately that my idea was stronger.

I cleared my throat, then thought out loud, "If this is war, um, sometimes you get blockades, right? Stop supplies from getting through? So, maybe we see if that NOAA satellite can help us figure out where shuttles are coming from, and...we find a way to stop them, in case they have supplies. We, uh..." I trailed off, then admitted, "I hadn't gotten much of anywhere. Just kind of the initial idea."

"If they can't just manufacture on the ship itself," Bryan gestured over his shoulder at the 3D printer he'd gotten for us, as if to give an example of how that might work, "and if we can find a way to do it that doesn't let them know that we know they're there..."

"Ugh. Right." I grimaced. "Sorry. Weak idea."

Ever the cheerleader, Rye piped up, "Hey, at least you're having ideas. Plus, we don't *know* that we can't do anything with it. So, yay! Go you!" Zie gave me a big, silly grin, mouth open and eyes wide.

I had to laugh. "Okay. Well, I'll keep trying to come up with new anyway. But, there you go."

"I can ask Zane about on-ship manufacturing next time they call me over," Bryan said, making a note on his phone.

"How did you figure out which satellite they'd use, Riley?" Jonny asked out of the blue.

We all turned to him.

It took Rye a second to sort out context. When zie did, zie blinked and nodded. "Right. The satellite for the machine in HQ?"

Jonny nodded. "I feel like maybe we should figure out which one they'll use for the machine on the ship, just in case we don't kick their asses before."

"It was actually more Bry for figuring out which," Riles said. "He had some kind of model of working satellites and whatever."

Bryan started typing. "Black market, obviously. You'll need to update its database. But this can help you figure out which satellites might do that job." He looked at me. "Since you're doing satellites, and since I guess you won't mind if Jonny looks over your shoulder, I'm sending it your way. Let me know if you have questions."

When I saw the model, I was glad Jonny had asked. I'd known our planet was practically encased in space debris and in satellites, working and defunct, but I hadn't really grasped the scope of it. My most careful and well-calculated guess would be that there were approximately a bajillion satellites out there. That Jonny had found that one, useful NOAA satellite had been more luck than we deserved. And I was going to use the hell out of the model. Which was fine; I preferred games that could be won by logic or research, where it wasn't at all about luck. Plus, I had a sneaking suspicion that the code and databases that made this model work might also give me some clues for more easily hacking them.

But, just in case, I pleaded with that deity I wasn't sure I believed in. *Please let the agencies behind these be as lazy as private humans and reuse passwords.* That, I reckoned, would have been the loveliest miracle.

Even if the stakes were higher (machine on ship) and weirder (maybe-Kitty), it at least felt like what I'd assumed it would be as we worked. You know, just normal hacking shit that might have been fun if not for the impetus. It felt like that, except...

For some reason, I felt like every 5 minutes they found an excuse to flash my face on the screen. We'd given them Kitty as MK. The news had quickly been leaked of the forthcoming results from the Seattle PD investigation, the one that showed CFO Williams was actually murder-y. They should have been off me, so maybe that's why I was feeling particularly sensitive to it.

I started wondering what was going on behind the scenes to keep them finding excuses. What had the news been made to believe about me now that they weren't saying yet? (Yeah, paranoia. I know.) How many people who'd seen me at Sam's during dinner had known who I was? How many hackers had seen my face, heard my name, and decided to look into me? Was I going to have any chance of a normal life again, even if we made it to South Dakota? SWS must be very pleased with themselves.

Fucking news. Fucking SWS. And fucking me for making it so neither I nor those with me could actually stay under the radar.

"I need to take my newsworthy face for a walk," I grumbled, and I limped out into the warehouse main floor.

Jonny's ankle seemed to be healing more swiftly than my kneecap (lucky bastard), so he easily caught up with me. "Hey."

I didn't answer. I was too busy being mad at myself.

"Kot? What's up?" He was in no-nonsense mode.

I wasn't sure I could coherently explain. I could feel that my head was spooled up to a point where I might not manage that. But, for Jonny, I'd try. I took a breath and launched into what was at the front of my brain. "The news is keeping my face in rotation, like there's something new they have coming up on me. And I introduced myself to three people after the explosion. *Three.* One of those is someone on the other team. At least by birth. Which sounds racist or something when I say it out loud, but you know what I mean. Right?" I looked over at him slightly, trying to keep an eye on the floor I was hobbling over as well. It was not spotless in this warehouse, and I didn't feel like tripping.

He shrugged. "I know what you mean. But, if you think Zane is a problem, we should probably deal with that. And you guys didn't use real names or 'nyms."

I gave a frustrated little growl. "I don't know. That's the problem. I used to know who I definitely could trust, and then who I might be able to trust. And I just treated all those 'maybes' and everyone else like they couldn't be trusted. But I feel like...the stakes are higher and I have less control here. *Anyway.*" I took a breath, trying to inhale calm and exhale the bad or some shit like that. "The other people I told, kind of, are some random chicks I don't even know. Who the hell knows what Lex has said and who she's said it to? What Marleina will say?"

"So, let's go do what we do and poke into people's shit even more. Lex's and Marleina's, since I know Riles is keeping as much an eye on Zane as zie can." For all that the way he'd approached me the very first night had been naïve and cinematic, Jonny was turning out to be Mr. Sensible. "Though, again, you didn't tell any of them your 'nym or name. The news did that. At most, all they could reasonably infer, if they're believing you're MK like SWS claims, is that MK didn't work alone. Or that it wasn't MK."

"And if Lex and Marleina aren't online enough for us to really do that? I mean, I bet money they're, at most, rarely online." Man, I really hated everything and also wished that nobody I wanted or would want to dig into was allowed to have offline lives. I'm a person of simple desires...

"We do what we can, we peep through web cams if we have to. We sort it out. And maybe you hang out with the hot chicks, build enough rapport to make sure they won't talk, if you think that will help. Hell, we know they can keep a secret if they want, right?" He put an arm around me.

I sighed. "Yeah. I just really—and I can't believe I'm saying this—I want to be in South-fucking-Dakota right now." The pain and the non-stop stress had me in a constant state of discontent and borderline sulkiness. I tried to fight it, but kept feeling I was losing that battle.

"Me too, baby. But..." He sighed. "But here we are. We'll just get through this. We'll heal and lay low while we build our case. And it will be okay." He almost sounded like he believed it.

"I guess we should go back so we don't miss anything." I paused a moment, standing still, watching moths fly around near the lights, then turned back towards the office.

Later that night, when I was just feeling cranky and unlikely to do anything worthwhile (I hadn't made any real progress that day, so my feelings seemed justified), I was sitting in the corner of the warehouse where we'd had Bryan put the mattresses (yes, plural, because "I wanted you to have the option to have your own, especially with your injuries") he'd gotten for Jonny and me. And I was trying to explain to Jonny why I was constantly fighting a sulk, even though I'd agreed we should stay.

I'd resolved not to complain to the others, but every time I'd woken up and I was in a fucking warehouse, still at war and still nursing injuries, instead of in some cheap home starting a new life...every time I'd been trapped in layers of ugly weather-resistant clothing because heating a warehouse that's supposed to be abandoned wasn't exactly resulting in the same level of comfort as heating a flat or a house...yeah, well, I had a lot of moments where I felt a mix of "the Universe is unjust and fuck this shit" and "we're going to die and our last days will have been...this." So, yeah, Jonny might just have noticed I was struggling with an attitude problem. And only a few days into this little camping trip...I felt so ashamed that I hadn't shaken this yet, or that I'd so easily reached this point. I wasn't sure which it was.

I tried not to sound whiny, even though I was *feeling* whiny. "I...I don't know what to say. I know why we're staying. I agreed; it's the right thing to do. But...But that doesn't make this awesome. And..." I mentally flailed, looking for something new to say. I knew it was weak, but I said it anyway. "Look, I made it through the two weeks before demo day by telling myself that demo day would be it. I started counting down as soon as we knew. Telling myself 'I can do this for 4 more days' or whatever, and then we can get on to lives with more regularity and routines, even if they weren't going to be the same ones as before. I feel like...Like I barely held it together and lived with how we needed to live. And I hate changes to plans, especially big ones...and here we fucking are with a massive, unplanned change." I sighed.

"Right. Because you're on the spectrum. I should have been more thoughtful about that." He said it like it was obvious, like it was no big deal.

But people rarely caught on that I was Autistic. Even after decades of people being told that women and girls often display it differently than the male-based stereotype, it seemed like it was still too subtle too often or...something. "Uh. Yeah. I am.

How did you know?" I narrowed my eyes. "Did you look at my juvenile eval records?"

He laughed lightly. "No. For once, I'm not guilty." He shrugged. "You're just a lot like my one sister who's on the spectrum. And your focus when you're working is intense in a way that's...amazing. And just enough different from the focus of the neurotypical kids in the room. Little stuff."

"Oh. Cool. Okay. So, yeah, big changes to plans, which I'm not really hardwired to deal with well, and some sensory stuff. I'm trying not to make that everyone else's problem, but..." I waved my hands uselessly. "I'm sorry. I wish I could be more graceful about all this."

Jonny leaned against me, put an arm around me. "I know you're trying. This whole thing just...It's not what any of us planned or expected. I'm sorry I dragged you into it."

I barked out a laugh. "Given the alternative was for you to let me die?"

He shrugged. "I could have not contacted you after. I could have done it solo. Then you wouldn't be here. Kitty and 'Randa and Huw would be alive." I could hear the guilt crawling up his throat.

I turned to face him, to make sure I had his eyes and his attention. My voice was, I hoped, kind as I said, "You're a badass, but you'd also never have managed it alone. And then we'd all be more fucked. So maybe you just embrace the old 'blame SWS' thing, yeah?"

Before he could object, I leaned in to kiss him. I tried to be mindful of our injuries as I pulled him to meet me, as I pressed my mouth to his, parting my lips to invite him in. Kissing him aggressively until he winced in pain.

"Shit. Sorry. I was pressing my least healed ribs against you," he said.

I laughed. "Yeah, it might be a while before we manage anything epic. But, look." I put my hand on his cheek, making him look at me again. "Did that kiss feel like someone, does this face look like someone, who holds you to blame? 'Cause, if so, your brain still isn't healed enough. I might have to restrict your 'Net access until it's healed enough that you're not going to be foolish online."

"Like when Riley was on zir pain pills."

"Exactly like that. You'll have nothing but daytime TV."

He chuckled and said, "Yeah, I'm suddenly feeling much better. I'm opting to believe you. Just don't put me on a diet of daytime TV."

"Good to know your brain's not completely gone."

CHAPTER 12

Wednesday started out well enough. We woke to find that Seattle PD had officially released a statement, exonerating me from the bombing of my building. They used very careful language, of course, but they did include that all evidence pointed to CFO Williams. We might have celebrated that with some victory dancing and crude shouting at the expense of said CFO.

If I believed in omens, I'd have said this boded well.

And our quick peek in on everything suggested it was a true omen. Whilst the public still weren't as solidly opposed to SWS as we'd have liked (because, whilst we scrambled to make plans, SWS acted...and they had a kick-ass PR budget and had had adverts out as early as Monday), they still mostly believed that the company was shady as hell, that CFO Williams was probably guilty, and that the person who'd leaked the documents had probably saved them from subjugation and ruin. Okay. Cool. Not entirely ruining my omen.

And we were delighted to see private citizens and corporations had already started bringing lawsuits against SWS. Usually, I'd roll my eyes at the litigious nature of Americans. But, in this case? I'd allow it. Hell, I'd look for ways to support it. Your honor, I definitely don't object.

Riley reported that, so far, as zie researched leaders at assorted levels, of assorted types, throughout the world, they *also* seemed to believe the CFO Williams ruse. They hoped it was true, because that meant there was no one alive to be a threat to them. Though they were pretty damned relieved to have been saved from the dangers of SWS. With no camera footage to show anyone else had been involved and no real leads to make it appear otherwise, their only planned actions seemed to be to double down on screening other contractors more carefully. I mean, most of them, that we could tell, felt that way.

Fortunately, the less legal and corporate citizens were continuing to attack SWS in other ways. 'Cause in any country where SWS had warehouses or factories that hadn't been bombed once news of their schemes broke, whoever went in to clear that shit out—always some kind of law enforcement who reported back to superiors, so we could find their reports on computers—found that inventory was missing. Or at least there was less than the logs and reports we'd made sure they could get their hands on reported. Some machinery missing. Some units of both the Peacemaker vI and vII short. Not huge numbers, except in our area, where it seemed like somebody had cleared out loads of that shit. Maybe that was their current "manufacturing" plan?

Our theory was that some criminal—possibly some U.S. law enforcement agency (just another kind of criminal)—had decided to see if they couldn't engineer their own mind control. We did what we could, poking at things on terrorist web forums or even just in anarchist ones, to aim other people towards blowing up what was left. After that, all we could do was keep an eye out for the sort of shit that would let us know somebody else was trying to pick up where SWS had left off.

We saw nothing. But we didn't really trust that.

Whilst we tried to keep ourselves on track with our research assignments, our remote team were doing all they could to keep SWS from rebuilding their computers. With that, with any buildings left being blown by domestic terrorists, and with employees quitting in droves, SWS rarely got more than one or two computers up and going, probably in some off-the-books hidden location, before they were found and kicked back to nothing. People were reacting to them with respectable speed.

So. That had us in good spirits even as we spent the day failing to find a way to connect to the ship. Failing to figure out the Kitty thing. Failing to detect whatever protocol was letting her connect to Rye's mobile. Failing to find any good proof to email people to convince them there were aliens on our planet. Failing to feel solid about the people we were considering sending that proof to. Failing like we hadn't failed at our last goal. And the contrast made it suck more. We felt like we'd kicked serious ass in the two weeks leading up to demo day...and now we were failing to do more than not get me outed as an actual criminal (aka vigilante hero).

And we were all feeling it. We were frustrated. We'd committed. We'd come straight off a moderately successful operation. We had a responsibility. We were living in a bloody warehouse and...and we didn't appear to be getting anywhere. Not as quickly as we almost always did.

Even just over the course of the day, it was clear: We were getting cagey. Cranky. Increasingly paranoid. In short, we were a delight.

Later in the evening, my mobile buzzed.

"Yeah?"

Lex's voice was rough. "It's Lex. You got a sec?"

"Sure. What's up?"

"I think there's some shit going down, and I think maybe I need your help. 'Cause it turns out that 2 years with the bug in my head left me less connected. Not so many different kinds of allies, yeah?"

I swallowed disappointment as the hope that Lex might have a street army to help us faded a bit. But I was also kind of hopeful in a slightly selfish way. Maybe she had a problem that I *could* actually solve, get us some kind of victory that we'd actually made happen. "Do you mind if I put you on speaker so my people can hear you?" They, "my people," gave me curious looks, but I put a finger to my lips to keep them quiet.

"Um...Okay. If you think you should."

I touched the button that toggled the speaker on. "Okay, Lex, go ahead and tell us what's wrong."

"So, both me and Mina have been ignoring...glitches. You know, like I described before. That flash of white people or whatever right before the explosion. Like something still sparking in our brains. We figured maybe there was something that had actually been done to our brains and it was just a remnant we'd always live with."

I asked, "Why didn't you mention this when we saw you?"

"Dude, we just figured brains be normalizing." She sounded impatient with my question.

Bryan put a screen in front of me with another question for Lex, so I asked, "Is it the same glitch? The people in white?"

"Yeah. The same thing. Tall, pale people in white with a sort of white light and, like, a presence of...assertive peace. Which, to me, obviously makes sense with that whole Peaceforger thing that came out. If that's what SWS is about, yeah? But Mina wasn't totally sure. I guess...well, she thought maybe it was from her derms at first and thought I was just saying it was happening to me too so she'd feel better. She was even gonna stop with the derms, just in case. Then she got sick with that thing that's going around."

The "thing" in question was a nasty bug. Fever, vomit, diarrhea, massive sinus swelling that caused ridiculous amounts of mucus production, and large purple welts. It had some official name, of course, but people were just calling it the beat down flu. You know, because those welts made people look like they'd gotten a beat down, and anyone who had it sure as shit felt like they had. Even the news preferred that name, obviously, because it was more interesting. Though they always had to pretend they were doing it just to connect to us common slobs. They'd say something like "the so-called 'beat down flu'" when they talked about it.

I was confused. "Wait, don't you guys live together now? Because I heard beat down flu was super communicable."

"I should totally have gotten sick. I guess I'm one of the lucky, rare ones who dodges the bullet. But not Mina. She got really sick. Came on Friday morning, so we got into a clinic before things got crazy from SWS shit. And then we heard that that church, Divine Community, had a cure."

I hadn't heard about that; it must be new. I did a search on my computer as we talked.

"Is the cure thing new?" I asked. Seeing the first note about it was from the Friday evening, which kind of explained how we'd missed it. What with just having blown up a building and all.

As Lex confirmed that it was and that their clinic doc had just heard about it Thursday night via some professional grapevine, I skimmed the first article I found about it.

Some local-grown megachurch had a doctor in the congregation who'd been brought onto their philanthropy branch and found a cure. Which was kind of cool, because they were actually living up to their professed values and offering the cure for free to anyone who wanted it. They were working to set up mass production. No companies felt like being that kind of generous, so Divine Community Church was setting up their own facility for that. Basically, they were renewing my faith in humanity. That story and the lady who was rescuing and reforming feral cats were all I needed to feel good about the world some days. It was making me think that maybe, just maybe, I might want to save this damned planet. Maybe *don't* just fuck humanity, Fate.

"So, she got the cure?" Riles picked up the conversation just as I noticed Lex was done talking.

"Yeah. And it totally worked. She was well within a couple days like they said she'd be. You saw her Monday. Fully charged. And they didn't ask for anything, not contact info or a donation, which I totally thought they'd do. Didn't care what her religion was or anything. I guess Mina was even more impressed than me, 'cause she started volunteering with the church to help get the cure out, or at least get word of the cure out, right off. I guess I'm a bitch, 'cause I resisted getting involved. I...I felt like I had to resist being nice in order to reclaim being Lex instead of the drone SWS tried to make me." She sighed. "Shit. That sounds stupid when I say it out loud."

"I've been guilty of similarly stupid actions; you're good," I reassured her. Though my paranoia was kicking up and now I was thinking the cure thing maybe sounded too good.

"As long as I'm not alone in being stupid...Anyway, so she's been going around with the church to do this do-gooder thing every day the last few days. She was even off the derms Tuesday. She seemed happier, but not in a way where she was unhappy with me, if that makes sense."

"Yep."

"Basically, things seemed good. I got kind of worried Monday night when she told me that her visions had been getting more intense, lasting longer. That's what she called them, 'visions.' And she told me that she believed now they were angels. That she was thinking the church had more to offer than just the cure for beat down flu. But I wasn't going to be a jerk about it, 'cause she wasn't treating me differently or asking me to act differently."

Lex took a breath. "Tuesday evening, she took off to join a group who were working all night to set up for some hokey-ass harvest festival meal or whatever today, and she never came home."

"You think she took off or maybe got hurt on the way home?" I flinched. "Sorry, those are both shitty options."

"I don't think she took off. I assumed it was her getting hurt. So, I called hospitals and walked the path to the nearest church building, asking questions along the way, but nothing came of it. Obviously, I also asked at the church. And that's when I thought maybe I needed you. Or who I think you are. 'Cause the people at the church office, where she would have checked in for volunteer shifts, claimed they'd never heard of her. Like, not at all. And you know, you've seen her; Mina isn't someone you don't notice."

In the warehouse, we shared a round of dreamy-eyed, appreciative nods. That was too true.

I asked, "Think Marleina might have been lying to you?"

"No. I mean, I would, but she'd talked about this way that the lady there was always patting at her hair...sort of, gingerly, with just her middle finger. And the lady did that while we talked. And it was just like the impression that Mina did. So, yeah, maybe Mina just met her once and had been lying. But I don't think so. I think the lady is lying."

"You think the lady knows something?"

"Yeah. But I can't figure out why anyone would...do anything to Mina. So, maybe it's nothing, but it seems like a weird coincidence that the visions increased when she started hanging around the church. Like, um...I was thinking maybe there's some side effect with the cure or something in the juice there, and what if Mina figured it out or suspected or was talking about the visions so that people might find out, and so they did something to shut her up? I mean, they've probably had more people join since they started doing this, right? They wouldn't want word out if there were problems."

Everyone in the warehouse with me nodded and made "yeah, sure, that could happen" faces.

I translated their body language into actual language. "Yeah, Lex, we think that's a reasonable option to consider. Um...gimme one second..."

I turned to quickly tap a question on Bryan's screen.

Do we help?

There was a very brief moment as people considered, looked at each other...Bryan was the first to solemnly nod, and Jonny quickly nodded as well. Riles and I looked at each other, weary. But zie nodded too. Right, well, it was something to do, and the women seemed cool and this church sounded shady (even if partly because they were too nice), so...

"Okay, we'll help. Um...do you have email access? Can you send us a recent pic of Mina and the church lady's name? Send to the account I gave you and...try to cover your face when you go out to do it. Put on a mask, go to a library, set up a throw-away account to send. Unless you have a computer of your own that you feel okay using?" I knew the answers to some of this already, but no need to tell her we'd already hacked their computer.

"We just got one! And took all the SWS software off. Does that help?"

I talked her through getting me her IP address, keeping up the ruse of not knowing, and then I set up a secure chat connection so she could get us the name and the picture.

"With this, we should be able to at least see if there's anything questionable on the church's computers or the lady's computer. Plus, we can look for Marleina on cameras to see where she went after she left your place Tuesday evening. Get some software doing facial recognition shit."

"Thank you! I owe you, man. You just...if there's anything you need...I just have to find Mina."

When we hung up, Bryan said, "It's a quick poke through data. We'll get what info there is and get to our own plans tonight or early tomorrow. Another fun, little adventure to tell...somebody's grandkids when we're old."

We were definitely on the hacker-to-hero transformation plan, weren't we? At least this one should be easy-ish and was for people who we kind of knew and liked.

It was easy enough to follow Marleina on cameras. She wasn't trying to duck anyone and Tuesday evening had only been typical Seattle misty, so she hadn't bothered with an umbrella. And, just like she'd told Lex she was doing, she walked straight from their flat to the church building. Divine Community's own lobby camera showed her enter the building, greeted by a woman who, our research showed, was the very same person who'd lied to Lex in the office earlier. Interesting.

I didn't like the look of the woman, so I tossed out an initial theory. "My money's on that bitch doing human trafficking. She figures Marleina is both sexy and unlikely to be missed by much of anyone."

Everyone hmm-ed or grunted in what sounded like "that could be" ways. I glared at the lying lady, already enjoying how it would feel to take her down.

What we didn't find was any footage of Marleina leaving the building. We set up some facial recognition software to see if we could find her anywhere in the neighborhood on any footage we could get our hands on. It was nice that we had fewer than 30 hours of footage to cover.

Whilst the computer handled the camera search, we humans decided to divide and conquer the church's computers and any information we could find about the lady or the church outside their computers. Easy enough.

The lady, one Ms. Karen Cartwright, just looked like some average church lady. Early 50s, few social media posts but all about church stuff, modest bank account. She made her pennies as the church's admin and receptionist. There wasn't much we could find on her. If she was doing sketchy shit, she was doing a great job hiding it, or at least a great job keeping her head down so nobody would notice.

And the Divine Community Church was, really, just like any other megachurch. You know, charismatic preacher tweaks his message just enough to welcome in the masses (we're inclusive!) whilst also making the masses feel like they're special and better for being welcomed (but we're also somehow exclusive!). Church slowly, steadily grows, and then suddenly booms and becomes mega. In Seattle alone, this sort of thing had happened a few times every decade. Unlike those other times, Divine Community had, so far, managed not to implode. I guess that, eventually, someone not-horrible had to start a megachurch, right?

This longer-than-usual lifespan of the megachurch seemed to me to be due to there being enough power to go around. The longer the church went on, the more buildings it could open for its services and its non-Sunday outreach stuff, the more nights per week it could have services, the more positions there were to fill, etc. It looked like the growth rate had out-paced the usual power-grabbing that seemed to have taken out a few other such churches. Plus, their philanthropic branch opened up plenty of leadership opportunities, so they didn't even have to wait until there were enough new members to justify opening a new building. Just set up a new philanthropic mission and put some long-term board member or other promising person at the head of it.

The doctrine was basic enough. Christianity kind of, with a wide open door for things they deemed good in other religions. They were all about welcoming in anyone who was willing to walk through the door and then working to keep them in. Forgiveness, generosity, compassion. Even the way they let their members get the sense of exclusivity was more along the lines of making them feel special for having this church in their lives and for being the ones who could share it with others, save their fellow humans.

It was all pretty basic and mild and available online or in person (your community, your way!) for maximum accessibility. And if that's not enough to get you on their side, their original preacher? The one who started it and was still helming things? Yeah, he was called Justin Michaelson, and he had charisma to spare. I wasn't at all religious, but his warm tones were so full of love and earnestness, with a frosting of intensity and sparkle (or some shit like that), they made even me wonder if opening my heart to the message wouldn't help.

There were no negative stories about him. He tipped his servers well and was kind to everyone. Even those who criticized or attacked him were met with understanding and forgiveness. If, in the name of defending him, his followers attacked back on his behalf, he was quick to call them off. At a certain point, he started to tend to include preemptively calling them off in whatever response he made. The guy might actually be good. Huh. Maybe the lying Ms. Cartwright ran her human trafficking ring without him knowing.

(Also, I noted that he wasn't pale, and that he appeared to have pores. So, not an alien. Because that was now always on my mind.)

Not that he hadn't said an objectionable thing or two. I ran across assorted interviews, like you do when someone is or wants to be in the spotlight. One was from right after we blew up SWS HQ. When asked about that particular current event, he said, "The Bible says 'blessed are the peacemakers,' and I don't mean to imply that God is endorsing SWS's product," he chuckled and the reporter joined him, "but I can tell you that God *would* likely join me in refusing to endorse murderers and terrorists." Somehow, he sounded both resolute and like he regretted having to take a stand against anyone.

I mumbled, "Fucker," but it didn't mean I'd changed my opinion about his possible basic goodness. After all, even a voice in my own head had wondered more than once if we'd really and truly done the right and necessary thing.

(Though, okay, if not an alien, still maybe a collaborator. I was open to distrusting anyone not standing in the room with me.)

Of course, then there were the Divine Community computers.

Protected by SWS firewall software. (Why the hell hadn't they taken it off like the rest the paranoid world? Maybe they were religion smart and tech stupid...) We might have done assorted kinds of laughing (snickering, giggling, snorting, chortling) when we discovered that. We, obviously, had no problem getting through their firewalls. And they didn't appear to pay their IT department to set up any extra security measures on their system. Easiest hack of non-personal computers that we'd done in ages.

The biggest drag was the time it took to find anything other than what you might expect on a church's computers. Membership records, financial stuff, programs for in-person services and scripts for broadcast ones. A whole directory of all Shepherd Michaelson's sermons. And look, here are photos of youth and the elderly having a dinner together to learn perspective from each other! And pics of a night they staffed a soup kitchen. That sort of shit.

This was actually the least fun part of any job, sorting through all the useless data, looking for the good stuff. With no real info to go on (not even whether the church was involved in what happened to Marleina, whether they were up to something untoward, or what they might be doing if so), we really did have to look at most everything. But, with four of us working, it was easier than just one of us alone.

Part of the problem, we soon realized, was that this wasn't a normal corporation. (In my opinion, they were big enough that they really should have had more corporate structure and procedure to have made it this far without falling apart, but they weren't paying me to advise them, so...) There didn't need to be loads of memos or super-formal letters, or they didn't seem to think so based on what we found. There were bare minimum records for all their employees, and no records of those who just volunteered. Marleina's name wasn't in anything we found, which wasn't massively surprising. Even appointments on people's calendars had informal titles that didn't really give us clues. And, because Shepherd Michaelson and Marleina were both local, whatever happened there could certainly have gone down via quiet, in-person conversations. If anything *had* happened. If the church had been involved in it. I kind of just wanted to physically corner that lady who'd lied to Lex, 'cause we knew she was at least lying about knowing Marleina, and just beat some truth out of her.

Fortunately, Divine Community was big enough that some corporate sensibilities had necessarily crept in. So the philanthropic branch had their own servers, and that section of things was nicely organized. And there were solid enough financial records for all the branches of the church. Nobody wanted to fuck with the IRS; they were one of the few pieces of the country's government that hadn't been made mostly toothless over the years. As the person who'd gotten us this "job," I got the least boring task; I got to go straight into the sections on fighting beat down flu. I'd revised my prediction to include drugging Marleina when they gave her the cure, and using that to make her more pliable and easier to steal for their human trafficking. I didn't necessarily think the church was behind it, but my hate for Ms. Cartwright was making it easy to see her as the sort of person who pretends to be "righteous" but is hiding a rotten core made, in her case, of selling other humans. (Yeah, I was really leaning into my human trafficking thing.)

I made sure to grab files that I could pass on to Jonny's doctor friend in New Mexico. I didn't know that we'd need Doc to help, but it seemed like something that, if I were a doctor, I'd find intriguing. I sent him a quick note, letting him know that, and then started plowing through. I noted aloud anything that seemed worth mention.

"Looks like their cure is legit."

"Looks like they're pulling together an information packet to share so others can manufacture the cure."

"Looks like...um...huh."

Jonny leaned over to look at my screen. "Um huh?"

"Doesn't this look like maybe they *made* beat down flu?" There went my faith in humanity and in Shepherd Michaelson's honey voice. Fuckers.

With that, Riles and Bryan also crowded in to see my screen.

Bryan asked, "Where was this?"

"Well, that's part of what's suspect. It wasn't on a normal harddrive. I had to grab this quickly when someone plugged in an external drive. And first I had to get through some extra security on that external drive. So..."

So, what I had was some quick reports, one liners, on what appeared to be the progress of building a disease. There appeared to have been a few tries, because they were numbered, and the end of the notes on a numbered try was always heralded by something like "Unable to find cure for #H62; abort and move to next attempt."

With the possibility in mind, I looked for more info. And, damn, I definitely found some. There were docs that outlined how each attempt was built and what they'd tried to cure it. There were notes about the best options for fast rate of contagion, for contained contagion, for minimizing deaths as they did this. One document mapped how many units of cure they'd need to have on hand to keep up with likely infection rates for various scenarios.

There was only one hint about *why* they did it. One note from Shepherd Michaelson, reminding them (it wasn't clear who "them" was) that the optimum situation would scare people enough to open their hearts and homes without killing them, give Divine Community a chance to shine their light. "At the end of the day, we want to save everyone possible, bring them into our community."

We still didn't know what had happened to Marleina, but we could now feel pretty good about considering Divine Community a possible threat, a target for our brand of righteous, vigilante justice.

Jonny asked, "What do we want to do with this?"

I shrugged. "Let's shift medical files to Doc. Otherwise, right now, my mission is to find Marleina...and then to get back to the Peaceforgers thing. Until that's done, much as they are surely dodgy bastards I want to destroy, this has to be a side quest. You know, alien apocalypse trumps evil religion." I almost meant it. I really wanted to focus on the bigger thing, the Peaceforgers and SWS. These assholes were, well, assholes, but they were just trying to grow their congregation by super messed up means and weren't trying to actually subjugate or destroy the whole human race. They'd be a fun dessert after the main meal, something to take down after we kicked the aliens out.

Bryan made a surprised sound. "I hear you, but don't you think this is kind of big? Don't you think we should at least get this information out?" As if he were replying to the objection he thought I had, he went on. "The thing is, I think that precisely because this isn't even a big deal like SWS. I mean, there's nothing served by us doing anything more than just releasing this. Old school. And everyone is so paranoid after SWS that we could tip off the cops or the feds and let them handle this. They'd probably act on it quickly now, as opposed to the past when tips clearly from hackers were mostly given side-eye."

Huh. Okay. Clearly the smallness-in-comparison thing was having a different effect on Bry. And he wasn't wrong.

I gave something like a grunt of annoyance, aimed more at the part that was less easy than at Bryan. "Except that this is on a removable drive. We can't point them at the specific computer. We can't even point them at the specific building to raid, because this drive could be in anyone's bag or home or...whatever. It would end up being our word against Divine Community. Unless we can figure out where some solid proof is for the law to get their hands on in the meat." I thought Bryan was letting his frustration at our lack of other success drive him thoughtlessly towards the easy win.

"And, honestly, Bryan," Rye piped up, "it might be shitty but they're not actually doing anything huge, not given the new bar for 'huge' set by aliens invading. I mean, yes, getting people sick, but also giving them the cure. It's just another fucked up ploy for a church to get followers." Zie leaned against me. "I think we could wait on this one."

"Yes!" I pointed at Riles. "That! I'm not saying never; I'm just saying that I'd love to get Mina found and the alien threat shit taken care of first. We haven't even figured out where they're manufacturing or how they're delivering their Peacemakers, much less how to stop the new control machine. After we do that, let's definitely get info out and fuck up this church. Pretend it's simpler times again. I want this like I want dessert, but only after I've taken care of the big hunger with a real meal." (I think the dietary compromises we were making living in the warehouse were having an impact on my metaphors.)

Bryan was clearly begging for backup when he prompted, "Jonny? Mate?"

Jonny slowly exhaled, his brows pulled together in thought, then took a breath and said, "I want to do the hero thing here. I really do. But...We have two people here who are burnt out and, no offense, not exactly as excited to play hero as you and I are. If I'm going to help you try to keep us all motivated to take on something bigger than looking for Marleina, I'm going to save that up for convincing them to keep fighting the planet-destroying threat." Jonny coughed nervously. "Yeah. Sorry. I mean, if you come up with a plan and you just need an extra set of hands, count me in. But I don't think I can vote to push for all of us to go gung-ho on it. Not until, like they've said, we fix the Peaceforger thing."

Bryan stood, paced, grunted. "Right. Well. I hear you and...I know you're probably right. But I hate to not do something now. I'm disappointed. I think I need to go run a few laps."

I kept my eyes turned away from him as he left. I didn't like to disappoint Bryan. I wished, kind of, that I were the sort of person who could jump at this threat, at any threat, and save the world. But...I was pretty sure I wasn't and never would be.

No amount of looking seemed to narrow down a reason or exact location. All we could confirm was that Marleina had gone into the Divine Community building on Tuesday and hadn't come out. Not that we could see. So, as far as we could tell, she was still in there. Somewhere. (We couldn't find any internal cameras to look around with beyond the lobby ones. Which seemed weird, but maybe we were too used to "real" businesses? And the church was only spottily that.) Hopefully she was alive, but we couldn't guarantee that.

I called Lex to let her know what we'd found in terms of Marleina. Confirmed that, in my opinion, it might be that they were worried her visions had been a side effect of the cure. I didn't mention my alternate human trafficking theory for why they'd taken her. I apologized that most of us were in no shape to come help her look inside, but offered our able-bodied person (because Bryan was dying for a win, and he looked super pleased when I offered him) to help.

Lex snorted, but there was an edge of kindness. "What? Leave you without a fighter if Johnny Law gets news of you while we out? Can't do that to you." When Bryan tried to protest, she cut him off. "I be enterprising. Remember, street drek. But thank you. I feel your kindness."

We made sure to find her the public plans for the building and passed them along, warning her that sometimes people made changes after. I hoped she could find people who *could* help see this through. I hated to leave it at this.

We better get a breakthrough on Peaceforger things soon. I don't think we were in a good place for continued failure.

We checked in with each other before bed a few hours later. We were running low on ideas, but our only options were to give up or to keep plugging away. So, no real action plan. Damn. I'd hoped that maybe others had come up with something I hadn't.

Quietly, I was starting to worry I'd lost my skills. I was either completely sucking at getting satellites under our power, or something was wrong with the satellites. I knew satellites were tough, so I was waiting to confirm it wasn't me—spare myself a well-intentioned lesson from Riles (who *had* done some satellite hacking) or Jonny (who also had and who I didn't want to drive away by revealing a way in which he was better than me)— before I said anything.

I mean, to be fair, there was a little progress. Rye did feel like we could start building the list of people to send our "they're here!" email to. Zie had done some serious work on that in just a couple days. Gotten to a point where zie at least felt zie'd narrowed the pool significantly.

And Bry said he'd found a way to hack into some of NASA's more experimental things, and he thought he could probably find new kinds of readings to take of the ship, maybe find something to help find a way to hack in or to help prove they were there or...something.

"New readings might lead to figuring out how Kitty's talking to me?" Rye asked hopefully. "It's sounding more like her now that she's figured out how to watch TV and wants to talk about shows."

"But where the hell is she? How is she watching?" I pressed. One thing that had me suspicious at this Kitty thing was that she never gave straight answers to concrete shit like that.

Riles shrugged. "You know what I know. It's dark, she can't understand the language on things, and she doesn't understand how we're talking." Zie squished up zir face in an uncertain frown. "She's got to be in the ship or in some secret facility that's just for the Peaceforgers."

It was fishy as hell. I was sure there was some Peaceforger trick behind it. But it had been going on for days and they hadn't come for us, so...I dropped it.

Jonny handed out game controllers as he confirmed, "So, in conclusion, we can't make a plan because we don't have enough to go on? Meeting over? Play time? A little necessary R&R?"

We realized too late that Bryan was replying by picking the most coveted character before anyone else had a chance. The bastard.

I scrambled to make a selection before I was left playing someone who sucked. To get the game going before someone (Bryan) decided that we had to be heroes every waking moment and pushed us into setting the fun aside.

Yeah, I'm a much better hero when it's vidgames or all in my head.

Before we could press play, Bryan said, "Actually." When some of us failed to not groan slightly, he assured us, "Don't worry; I totally think we could use some group unwinding and shit. But the controller made me think...Look, just in case...You know how most fighter planes are unmanned? There are tactical subs that are the same. Plus, obviously, tactical drones. I don't want to mess up the real fighters taking action or anything like that, but let's figure out how to hack those. I mean, I already know some...And we should all work through the associated training programs for them. Just in case. Keep that option in mind." He turned his eyes back to the game. "It will take me a little while to get what we need, and I think we need to nail down our other shit first, but plan to add that to your fun in...a week or so, I think."

And then he started the game, and I barely had my controller in the right position before we were blasting aliens. Maybe Bry's idea would let us treat the real ones just like these digital baddies?

CHAPTER 13

I figured that, if Riley could have zir girlfriend on messenger (or maybe it was a Peaceforger bot, which was even worse) and Bry could hang out and flirt with an unverified alien ally, I could set up a secure messenger with Gran. Dammit. Besides, I'd thought she was staying a couple weeks with Sarah, but (according to my snooping) she'd come back after just a week. So. Yeah, I set up a messenger on her computer. And I actually meant to wait until Halloween to make it a holiday thing, but Thursday would have to be an event enough.

I kept an eye out all day for her to be on her computer. It was late afternoon when she finally logged on. I took a quick peek through her webcam to verify she was alone, and then I opened a window on her computer.

Katja: Heya!

Gran: Hey yourself. Hadn't expected to hear from you. Like, maybe not ever. Did you put this program on my machine?

Katja: It's the holidays, kind of…almost, so I'm pretending to be a good person. This is your present. Ha!

Gran: Pretty sure you're too late if you're trying to fool Santa into giving you anything.

Katja: Yeah, pretty sure I've already made it too hard for him to deliver this year as it is…Even if I still have almost 2 months to prove my innocence. Anyway, pleasantries aside…How are you? Aren't you back from Sarah's early.

Gran: Doing okay. Just needed my own space and home, you know? Same boring old person life.

Katja: Boring is underrated. I'm all for it!

Gran: I'd mock your envy, but I was about your age when I decided I preferred a little boredom in my real life.

Katja: Can I make one suggestion to keep your life boring?

Gran: Is it cutting you out? Because that would clear up
      more time for reading... ;-)
Katja: Pfft. As if! No, in all seriousness...You've heard about
      beat down flu, no doubt.
Gran: More than heard about it!
Katja: ??
Gran: Came down with it Tuesday when I got back to town
      and ran straight to my doctor. I knew you'd hate to lose
      me. You're welcome.
Katja: So, you're sick? Oh no!
Gran: Nope. That church who has a cure has staff on call.
      My doctor just called them and they had me sorted. I
      slept most of Tuesday and Wednesday, and I feel so
      much better now! So, don't you worry. I'm totally fine.

"Those motherfuckers," I growled.

Jonny stopped what he was working on. "What's up?"

"Gran had fucking beat down flu this weekend." I just let that
hang, angrily, in the air.

"Is she okay?" worried Riles.

"Yeah. Because she also had their fucking cure," I snarled.
Then I sighed, "She's fine. Just, y'know, they fucked with my
family."

Katja: I suppose this means you've found religion now? Will I
      have to get a more reputable career to avoid lectures
      about hellfire.
Gran: Heh! I'm pretty sure you're safe on that front. Can you
      even imagine me doing that? 'Oh, thanks for using
      science to cure me. Do tell me about yer god.' Haha!
Katja: Good. Because that would have thrown off my whole
      Satan-themed Halloween gift basket idea.

Well. At least Gran hadn't fallen for their bullshit.

Even if we'd stopped actively looking into them for the time
being, we were all still interested in Divine Community Church.
We knew they broadcast their services, so we threw the evening

service on. In the broadcast listings, this one had been called Thursday Evening Music and Miracles. We figured, sure, show us your miracles, you deceptive assholes.

We all paused for a luxurious dinner of cheap ramen packets whilst we watched. This was interesting. But bad-interesting. I mean, at least from our perspective. Because, if we were going to take the bastards down later, it wasn't helpful if Shepherd Michaelson was even appearing to do miracle healings. Not everyone had read essays on how old-fashioned tent revivals and Christian churches that believed in signs and miracles actually made things happen (or appear to happen). I couldn't approve of things that helped Divine Community's reputation remain ridiculously solid and shiny.

Normally, I am totally pro-healing, pro-miracles, and pro-things that make life better for people. Not that I really believed in miracles in the church-y way. But, you know, in a theoretical sense. Especially if it wasn't actually some conniving group trying to find a new way to soften up people and suck them into their power. Michaelson was clearly running into my exception.

There was nothing miraculous at first, just choirs and soloists singing church songs, shots of people in the audience looking moved, whatever. (I know it's a congregation when it's a church, but these megachurches always seemed more like big theater crowds to me.) They started throwing in shots of people in the front row, the poor people who were about to go through the revival tent sham that passed for miraculous healing. I was disgusted to note that they were all the right kind of attractive. Cute kids, good-looking adults, adorable or kind of humbly elegant seniors. This only confirmed my suspicion that this was at least as much about PR as actually doing good.

About a half hour in, when we'd finished our food and were distracted by other things on other screens, Shepherd Michaelson finally took the stage. But, of course, he didn't get right to the main event.

From a logistical perspective, I got it. It's like the news; you keep promising the big thing everyone came for, which gives you time to pull in more viewers and pitch them your other stuff first. You couldn't do much after the big event, because it would seem like a let-down. You end on a high if you're smart, right? Still didn't mean I wanted to sit through that.

So, he did some preaching. And he was definitely good at what he did. Charismatic, just handsome enough in a normal way, engaging. I might not buy what he said, but he seemed to have a good writer (or be a good writer...whatever).

Finally, he thanked everyone for listening and being there and sharing their faith and prayers, and then he announced it was time to begin the evening's healings.

Helpers in suits and dresses ushered everyone who'd theoretically be getting healed up onto the stage. They didn't rush. Everyone watching got a chance to see their faces, to feel sad at such nice-looking people being in not-entirely-perfect condition. The quiet music the organist played let me know I was supposed to feel Very Sad for them. And I did. Both because it sucks to be unwell or not match up to what this society expects you to be and because it really sucks to have hope in something that's going to let you down.

Once everyone was settled comfortably on stage in a sort of semi-circle behind him, Shepherd Michaelson started to...I guess it was praying? His words were addressing God, but he was working the stage, directing his words at the audience.

"Now, God, we know You give us imperfect bodies for many reasons. Sometimes we have things to learn, and sometimes we have things to teach. But we're grateful, on behalf of these beautiful souls standing behind me tonight, that sometimes You give us our imperfections so that You can show Your power. We are grateful that You have condescended to put Your power into my hands. And we ask You now to use my hands for healing. Not just for healing these bodies, but also for healing the hearts and souls of all who watch. Let Your Light find its way into their lives."

Riles folded zir arms tightly across zir chest and muttered, "You leave my fucking dark heart out of this, bitch."

We all chuckled at zir, but our eyes were on the screen. We wanted to catch the tricks.

"We're recording? So we can rewind and figure it out later?" I confirmed.

"Yep." Brian sounded hard. "When we finally come to take them down, we're hitting them with everything. Shining our own light on all their 'sins.' Including giving false hope to these people."

"Seriously," Jonny joined in, angry. "Do you know how many people stop seeing doctors or give all their money to churches like this on the vague promise of a cure? It's a damned crime."

As Michaelson walked up and down the line of people hoping to be healed, he touched their heads or their cheeks, and he promised, "And I feel moved to tell you all tonight that God has told me this power to heal, this Light of the Divine, will soon spread to other righteous church leaders, to allow them to do what I'm about to do." He paused and turned, ostensibly towards the audience, but he ended up looking almost straight into a camera. "If they will allow us, the Light will spread, and we will heal the world."

The audience lost their shit over the promise. If I were another one of the church *leaders*, I'd also be losing my shit, but more out of worry that I'd get outed as unrighteous if I failed to fake the same miracles. I guess that was one more way to make sure the power-hungry in his flock were kept in check.

Michaelson stopped in front of an older woman. She just looked older, bent over. Nothing dramatic. He helped her stand, and then she hobbled along with him to center stage. I rolled my eyes. This was classic.

"He's gonna make her stand straight," I announced.

Nobody replied, but I saw nodding heads in my peripheral vision.

Kindly, Michaelson asked, "What's your name, my friend?"

They must have had plenty of mics over the stage, because we could easily hear as she replied, her voice shaky, "I'm Jennifer Nelson, Shepherd."

"Hello, my friend Jennifer." His voice was so warm that I almost believed she was his friend. "Are you ready for the Light to touch your life and make you whole?"

"Oh, yes, Shepherd! I know God can make my back straight again." The conviction in her voice broke my heart. How crushed was she going to be in a few hours or so when her back, which he would surely force straight, curled back down?

Michaelson gestured, and two of his helpers moved in silently. They each took Jennifer by an elbow and smiled at her like she was about to get the greatest gift and they were so excited for her.

With his hands aloft, Michaelson stood behind Jennifer and invoked, "God, light my hands that I might straighten Jennifer's spine on Your behalf!" The camera was too far out for us to see what sort of tech made it possible, but his palms lit up with a bright, white light.

The audience, who'd gone quiet as he spoke to the lady, screamed and roared at that sight.

"Probably sub-dermal implant," Bryan noted. "That way, there's nothing external for people to notice if they shake his hand or whatever. No gloves to pull on that the cameras might catch."

And then, predictably, he ran his hand down her back, pushing it straight. It took a few passes, but it got the job done.

Where it had been dead quiet again whilst he worked his "miracle," it suddenly got very noisy. Again. The audience cheered and shouted praise, the organ played something that was kind of triumphant, and Jennifer made a sort of incoherent but happy sound.

Yeah.

In the warehouse, we all snorted.

Jonny said, "No need to watch that one back to figure it out. That sort of 'healing' is already well-documented."

But after Jennifer, it actually got...I don't know if "impressive" is the right word. He just brought out people who were less likely to be tricked. They had to be actors, in on the trick and playing their parts well. Though how they were removing contacts, makeup, and prosthetics live and in front of us? Well, *that* was impressive.

"Nice trick with the subtle hue changes to the light," Jonny pointed out. "See how it's like his hand has a few settings?"

"That's almost taking it too far, though, isn't it?" replied Riley, who knew a thing or two about taking the theatrics too far.

As it went on, Bryan pulled his portable onto his lap and worked whilst he watched.

"Stop making the rest of us feel like slackers, mate," I teased him.

He gave me a half grin, and said, "I just figure now is a fair time for me to keep digging into these assholes."

The last person Michaelson brought out wasn't alone. Some kid in a wheelchair, sallow and hairless and looking like she was a step from death. The actor playing her mum wept as she explained that this was their last hope. That the doctors had said that her little girl wasn't responding to treatment for leukemia and she was unlikely to make it to Christmas. I really hoped this was acting. What a shitty situation. Even knowing it must be fake, I could feel my throat getting tight with grief for the kid.

Michaelson did his thing, and his hand light actually shifted hues a few times. He didn't seem to touch the girl, just skimmed his hands over her. But he was thorough, had his assistants help the girl stand so he could skim her back. Had her lift her feet when she sat back down so he could skim the soles. He made this look like serious work, not bullshit theater. The light might be a bit much, but there were no flourishes with his hands, and the look of concentration on his face seemed real.

He paused, closed his eyes as he held his hand on her head. The light got dimmer and reminded me a little of the wan look of ultraviolet lights if you used them in a room that wasn't dark enough. Then he opened his eyes and did the skimming thing over a few specific areas, as if those hadn't gotten enough light.

The thing was...I'd been watching, trying to figure out how they'd make the kid look better. She could obviously just sit up straighter. I'd figured they were maybe using the lighting to make her look sallow, some kind of focused spot, but Michaelson and his hand—which would definitely have been in the same light—didn't look sallow at all. And, when he was done, neither did she. Her eyes looked less sunken. She literally had spots of healthy color in her cheeks, like some recovering romantic heroine.

She spoke, and it was more than the wheeze with which she'd told him her name was Tiffany. "Shepherd, my head is buzzing."

"That, my young friend, is all your hair follicles waking up and getting ready to make sure your hair comes back quickly!"

He sounded pretty damned pleased. "I can't wait to get pictures of you with your beautiful new head of hair to share with everyone."

My heart broke for the kid. At best, she was an actor who was learning some shitty lessons about morality. At worst, she was a kid who was about to die, who now believed she wasn't. Shit.

So, that was the Music and Miracles show. I hadn't expected to feel so angry on the other side. I was more and more eager to take them out. Looking for ideas to somehow justify continuing to spend energy on these particular assholes. "Hey, just an idea here...But what if we see if beat down flu hits Peaceforgers worse?" I didn't know why we hadn't thought of it before. It was a classic sci-fi answer to invading aliens.

Everyone sat back, thinking.

"Are you suggesting we find a way to get our hands on the disease, purposefully infect a Peaceforger, and...see what happens?" Bryan's tone was weird.

I shrugged. "I mean, I know that's basically biological warfare, which is generally dirty. But how many times in stories have we cheered on the resistance fighters or whatever as they found that something like a cold, or some other biological agent they engineered that didn't kill humans, could take care of the alien problem?"

"Fair point." Bryan chewed his lip a moment. "Do we also test the cure? Because everyone knows Divine Community has it. The Peaceforgers would surely run to get some."

"I don't think I object. Morally. Except that I'd want us to not accidentally also kill Peaceforgers who seem to be on our side," noted Jonny. "Not that I want to kill anyone, but I guess I don't have any solid moral ground to stand on anymore when it comes to that." He had never sounded more defeated. He took a stabilizing breath and added, "Plus, invading aliens and us being at war changes things, right?"

"That," agreed Bryan. "All of that."

"It sounds like there are probably a million complicated parts to it." Riles started counting parts on zir fingers. "Testing, manufacturing, delivering, etc." Zie shrugged. "But, yeah, as long as we don't accidentally kill any good guys..."

I nodded. "I'll ponder this. Just trying to use one problem to solve another...Before we kick the shit out of the church."

CHAPTER 14

Friday started quietly enough. Routine, by our standards. Look for ways to prove there are aliens invading. Look for who we can trust to take that info and run with it (where "run with it" = save the world). Look for how Kitty is managing to contact Riles. Look for proof it is (or isn't) Kitty. Try to figure out my scheme to test beat down flu on Peaceforgers. Try to get us access to satellites and maybe the Peaceforger ship and its control machine. At least that's what I thought we were all working on.

I overheard Riles as zie tried to quietly ask Bryan, "Do they have a clinic or a medical facility?"

I looked up and they looked like they were trying to keep something quiet. "You know, if you two are actually trying to do something on the down-low, you should message, not talk."

Bry gave Riley a look. "I think zie wanted you to catch us. Zie felt bad that I convinced zir to take a break and look at Divine Community stuff with me and that we didn't tell you." He gave me an apologetic smile. "With how slowly everything else is going, I'm just impatient to nail these fuckers. Get a win."

I rolled my eyes, but I tried to do it at my screen so maybe they wouldn't notice ('cause I actually understood). "The things you can get someone to do with a little pillow talk." I shrugged and half-smiled. "It's okay. You work on whatever. Maybe a change of topic will give us new perspective for solving the bigger one."

I pulled up the files I'd snagged from the church's computers, as I replied, "I didn't notice them having a clinic. Nothing beyond whatever they'd use for philanthropic stuff." I started flipping through the files to see if I'd just not paid attention to mentions of something like that. "I'm not seeing anything like that...except some clinics in impoverished countries."

"But they had to have something," Riles insisted. "They had to have had human trials before they started infecting people out in...in the wild, as it were."

"Pass around some of those files, Kot," Jonny suggested. "Let's get all of us looking. Digging deeper. They had to have done those trials and had to have documented it. At least from the way those notes about building it sounded. There were actual scientists involved, which should mean methodical work and tracking."

Bryan had been watching our conversation with increasing confusion. "Uh, you guys do know that clinics in impoverished countries are used for quasi-legal medical and drug tests all the time, right?" Bryan sounded sincerely surprised. "How have none of you run into that before?"

I blinked. I was as shocked as Bryan was. "Huh. Okay, then there really should be something." I pushed a chunk of files to each of them. "Files are in your hands, kids."

After a few quiet moments, I nudged Riles with my foot. "How did Bry convince you to get back on this?" I asked. "Didn't you also think that Marleina was the only side quest we'd look into as we worked the alien problem, not this disease?" I tried not to sound cranky. Logically, I knew that it was unreasonable to get cranky just 'cause zie'd changed zir mind. And now that Gran had been sick and this was personal, I really had been using a good deal of discipline to make sure I didn't focus on the church yet. Just, y'know, I was doing worse than usual with plans changing.

Rye assured me, "I'm with you on this. But...what if there *is* a connection between Marleina getting sick and cured and having more visions—like the one we're pretty sure was really something from the Peacemaker—and then her disappearing? Lex thought so, didn't she? Even if Divine Community is just trying to figure out why their cure set off visions, they'd maybe tuck her away in a clinic, right?"

"Okay...I can see that..." I mused aloud, "What if the changes from the Peacemaker, whatever it is that clearly happened in both Lex's and Marleina's brains, are exacerbated by something in the cure? So, Marleina has this exacerbation, and she probably mentions her visions to someone at church. Probably the timing of it too, right, because to her it's significant that it happened when she was cured. She maybe even sees it as spiritual, so she thinks she's witnessing or whatever. And the question becomes whether *they* think to connect it to her having had a Peacemaker in her head at one point. If they even know that she had one."

Jonny nodded. "Yeah, that seems on track. I'm just going to search the files for SWS or Peacemaker. See if it's actually that easy. If they made notes about her visions before we got lucky and grabbed files." He paused then said, "Also, sending Doc a quick note to ask about changes to the brain or other physiology that might persist after the Peacemaker is out."

Sounded like a good, quick idea. So, what the hell? I saw that Riley was also searching that way...Too easy, but let's follow the logic and hope they knew the Peacemaker was the factor they'd missed. I returned to my own search for a clinic.

"I can answer your clinic question," I reported within seconds. "Looks like most of their infection and cure tests were done in..." I hesitated, but pushed on, "in the clinic attached to the building I worked in. Maybe even built the disease there."

"No fucking way..." Jonny swiveled my portable to see for himself. And he went a little white. "Oh. It looks like it *was* done there, but the destruction of that building caused them to set up their own small clinic just when they would have launched their bug."

Jonny's portable pinged, and he looked over at it. "Doc is looking at my question, but says that it's at least *possible* there could be small changes he didn't notice. Brains are super complicated things."

I grabbed my portable back, skimming the document I'd been looking at before Jonny grabbed it. "So, yep, their own clinic is in the lower levels of the very building into which our Marleina disappeared. Which means that might be where she is now. If Rye's story about what could have happened is right." I typed quickly. "Just sending Lex a quick note so she has that info."

"No." It wasn't the victorious response I'd expected from Rye. "No!" zie wailed. "Oh, fuck fuck fuck!"

"Should I not?" I looked up, saw Riles was looking at zir screen, not me.

Looking dejected, zie said, "Send it. Then come here."

I sent, then got up and moved behind zir as quickly as I could, looking over zir shoulder. "What have you go—" I didn't even finish my word...The missing T just hung in the air. It would never be "got." Because, more important than some unfinished word, was the evidence on Riley's screen. I put my hands to my head, trying to press back the despair.

There was an actual memo on the screen, on SWS letterhead. From (now deceased) CEO Mary Johnson. It outlined how many units of the Peacemaker vII they could have to Divine Community before the church started infecting people (though it didn't say 'infecting people' but just the date that we had already learned infections had been scheduled to start). It also warned them that there'd been no testing done about the effects of multiple Peacemakers in a single individual's head. It recommended either testing on people before they started dispensing "the shots" (so, still not clear if SWS knew what Divine Community was up to) or training those giving the shots to look for signs or ask questions that would indicate a person likely already had a Peacemaker in them. "In which case," the memo instructed, "you'll want to have clean doses of the shot, without vIIs in them, to use on people who are likely already implanted."

Oh.

Jonny had been reading over our shoulders. "Oh, come fucking on! Isn't this shit sorted already?"

Bryan, leaning over in his chair to see the screen, just growled his frustration. "Motherfucker."

I put my arm around Rye and we leaned our heads together.

Zie mournfully asked, "We're going to be stuck handling this alone now, aren't we? 'Cause we know the government is slow to fuck with SWS ventures even now."

"I hope not, poppet. Dammit. I hope not." I pulled a little away and turned to face zir. "Look, we're all going to vote. You and I can still vote to not do more than leaking evidence like usual. It's not over yet. There's nothing that says we have to go blow up a building again."

I looked over at Bryan, expecting nothing but anger. He looked both concerned and tired. And there was this faraway thing in his eyes that told me he was working something else out. Finally he said, "I think we saw that SWS made contributions to Divine Community. You know, the thing where a corp tries to seem good by making donations to orgs doing good shit. Maybe their donation came with a price...We might need to dig into *everyone* SWS made contributions to."

I groaned. This thing kept ballooning and not being dead. "I've rarely so badly wanted you to be wrong. For all we know, Divine Community was into the SWS public mission and benefits of the Peacemaker and reached out to see if they could get the benefits—the publicly stated ones—into more lives. We don't know that Michaelson or his crew knew what was really up with the vIIs. It's still shady as hell and illegal and whatever, but maybe not everyone is part of the conspiracy?"

Bryan considered me, considered Riles leaned up against me, and seemed to reconsider what he was going to say. Shook his head. "Okay. I hear you. But you can see that our SWS job isn't done if this is the case, right? If the vII might still be in play?"

I nodded. "Yeah. But, this seems like a safe task to see if our remote comrades can dig things up, right? It isn't about aliens; it's about finding hidden SWS influence. Same as they've been doing."

Jonny suggested, "Can we also call Zane and see what they know about this? We're all thinking this is Peaceforger Plan B, right?"

"If it is," Riles noted, "even if they're just being used, now we have one more place to look for where they're manufacturing."

"And we know at least part of their distribution plan," I added. Okay, maybe this was horrible but also helpful.

"I'll message Zane," Bryan said, picking up his mobile.

"And I'll shoot a message to the remote crew." I was already composing something careful, not wanting them to take action against anyone until we had the full picture.

Soon enough, I was getting confirmations that our people were up for it. Everyone remained hungry for this, intent on grinding SWS into the dust. I knew we were lucky that the company's crimes were exactly the sort that spoke to us. I quickly sent out my replies, messages where I'd already assumed everyone was in and had divided up the list of donation recipients so our people didn't overlap each other's work.

Bryan's phone pinged and he read it. "Okay, I'm off to run this by Zane. Back soon as I can be."

"Ask them about Michaelson and the healing too," suggested Riles.

"Will do." Bryan stood and pulled on his coat. "Message me if you have more questions. Oh, and can somebody send some vid or screencaps of the healing for me to show them?"

"I'm on it." Jonny turned back to his computer. What a clusterfuck this was becoming.

I'd started working on finding a list of buildings belonging to Divine Community, trying to figure out where they might be manufacturing the vII (if they were part of that...still part of it, after the revelations we'd blasted out to everyone mid-October). Then I froze, my mouth wide with horror. Oh fuck...

I pushed into Gran's computer, made it play a silly sound file that I knew she'd respond to. Might as well get her attention with an old joke, because shit was about to get serious. I watched through her webcam to see if she was coming, to make sure it was just her. When she leaned forward to give the screen a puzzled look, I opened a chat window and stopped watching through her cam.

> Katja: Gran, when you went to the church, when you were sick, did they give you a shot?
> Gran: They did. And my doctor says that, so far, the cure has had 100% effectiveness. So you'll be stuck with me for years more.
> Katja: Okay. Hang on a sec. Please.
> Gran: Sure...

"I need advice. Like, stat." I tried to breathe myself calm. It didn't work. "Because remember how Gran had beat down flu? *Had*? Until she got the cure?" The room went still. "A shot. Delivered right to her doctor's office by Divine Community." I was freaked out and mad at myself for not immediately thinking of this when we'd discovered the info about vIIs in the cure. I'd been so sucked into the bigger picture that I'd forgotten the smaller, way more important to me, picture. Dammit.

Jonny was first to react, moving closer and taking my hand. "Oh, Kot. Oh, shit."

Riles, intense and concerned, asked, "Did you tell her about the vII yet?"

I shook my head. "I...I don't know what to do. I mean, do I tell her?"

I got a chorus of yes, and Jonny added, "I'll contact Dr. Scott right away. We'll get Gran in and get it out immediately." He gave me a reassuring smile. "Remember, we made sure the doc has the specs to deal with it. It's going to be okay, babe."

My next attempt at calming breath was a little more successful.

> Katja: I'm really glad you're okay, but...I've got some bad news.
> Gran: Are you sick too? Sick but can't see anyone due to your current situation?
> Katja: I so wish that were the case. Because...Listen, did you pay attention to the news after SWS went down?
> Gran: Much as I usually avoid news, that seemed like something I should pay attention to.
> Katja: Well, remember how there were the shots we told you not to let them give you because they had one of the Peacemaker vIIs in?
> Gran: I don't like where I think this is going.
> Katja: The good news is that one of the big emails that went out and blew the lid off things included information about how to take the vII out. *And* we know a doctor who can definitely do it. I'm just waiting for confirmation of when.
> Gran: Well, shit. I am now definitely with you on wanting things to be more boring. What should I do?

I looked over at Jonny, just hanging up his mobile. "What should I tell Gran?"

"Okay, according to Dr. Scott, we should wait until Sunday, because she wants to make sure that Gran is actually cured and back up at full health. She says, from what she's seen, people are usually at a point she'd consider cured about 48 hours after they get the shot. But then she wants another few days, especially since Gran is older, for her to stabilize and be what she'd consider 'healthy enough' before she'd want to risk surgery like that. And, given what we did, she's willing to come in on a Sunday to work. We should show up at 13:00."

"Thank you!"

> Katja: We're going to pick you up Sunday just after noon. Not sure if you'll need after care, so pack a little bag in case we need to keep you with us for the night. Head out at noon, and meet us at the park where we used to play.
> Gran: You mean the one that got covered with a convenience store?
> Katja: Yeah...that's the one.
> Gran: Just do that and you'll take care of it?
> Katja: Yes. I will always, always take care of you. I might even be less of a smartass until this is sorted.
> Gran: I guess you actually do love me ;-)

We chatted a little, but I got the sense we were both just trying to make sure the other was okay. After I signed off, all the emotion came flooding in. I quietly stood and headed out into the warehouse to rage. I was so afraid for Gran, and really pissed off at Peaceforgers and SWS and Divine Community and the fucking Universe that would make or let this shit happen. And mad at myself for failing to protect one of the few people I felt personally responsible for.

I must have been at it a while, kicking the walls (and hitting them with my crutch, which was sturdier than my legs) and shouting and then "running" (aka carefully hobbling) laps to try to work off the energy, because Bryan was back when I finally returned to the break room. He'd obviously been briefed about the situation; he looked as worried as everyone else.

Gran is one of the few things in my life that is too precious. Technically, she's a weak spot. But, as all the strength I have was learned growing up in her home, I didn't see her that way. She was the foundation on which the best of me had been built. And I would do whatever it took for her to be okay.

I didn't bother with preface. "You guys shouldn't come with me Sunday. You shouldn't risk it." I really wanted company, mind you, but I wasn't entirely lacking in judgment. Just in case they all felt like saving the world, I shouldn't put them at risk.

"I don't want to come off like some kind of stubborn prick, but you're wrong." Jonny regarded me calmly. "You see, I'm coming with you to back you up. You can decide whether I'm doing that because of how I feel about you or because I want to give your gran more reasons to like me." He tossed me a hint of a smile and a wink.

"Backup is a smart idea," Bryan agreed. "I'll come too, if you want. But I also think that some of us hanging back would be wise."

"You are totally the boss of me, love," replied Rye.

I nodded. "Okay, two stay here; two go. And until Sunday..."

Jonny turned back to his portable. "Until Sunday, in addition to other stuff, I'm working with Doc and Engie to see if they can finish up a project they've been working on that could be...mildly useful in situations like this." He looked at Bryan. "You seem to be the supply pro here. Is our 3D printer good to go?"

"I'm confident in my abilities to make it good to go for whatever we need." Bryan began tapping quickly at his own portable.

I could see that Jonny had a chat window open on his screen. Must be Doc and Engie, the awesome doctor and engineer who'd helped make sense of the Peacemaker specs when we were prepping to take down SWS. "What exactly are they working on?"

"They enjoyed working together, and they saw a need for something that could detect that tiny vII, whether in people's heads or in a shot. So, they've been sorting that out. Hoping to get it into as many hands as possible. Once we build a story or way for them to put it out that doesn't aim any Peaceforger bullets at them."

"Solid idea," Rye said. "And I bet we could make good use of one here."

Bryan noted, "They can just anonymously sell a 3D printing design. Keep it all online. Accounts and shit like that are easy enough for any of us to fix up in our sleep."

Jonny grunted agreement and typed quickly. "Telling them about your gran, though not mentioning she's related. They're wondering, if it's okay with everyone, if they could have Dr. Scott set up a camera so they can watch the removal. Doc hasn't had anyone in with a vII, and both Engie and he would like to actually see the thing and how it builds out into the brain." He turned to look at me. "Is that a weird request? Should I have asked differently?"

"No, that makes sense. I think it's a great idea. And I'm just going to go ahead and answer for Gran. She can yell at me if I'm wrong. But it seems like hands-on experience—or observation of it—can only help, right?"

Riley's voice was low, taut, as zie said, "Of course, there's another way to confirm the vII in Gran, without waiting for the device."

All eyes were on zir, and I felt my own voice tighten. "What other way?"

"I was specifically looking for proof of Marleina, just in case we could give Lex better info. And I found her name in two lists, both in an encrypted folder with what might easily be passed off as membership info by someone else. There are two key differences between the two lists. One of them is quite a bit longer and also has a field for a unit code. If I had to guess, the unit code is a vII identifier, so they can target specific people. And...and that longer list has been updated as recently as today." Zie let that hang in the air.

I rushed over to look at zir screen, where zie grimly pointed to the entry on the list that was Gran's name.

"I will kill these motherfuckers." I stood, eyes blazing. "I'll burn *them* to the ground and put something in *their* heads. Preferably a bullet or a knife."

Riles quietly noted, "I'll grab updated copies of this list throughout the day. Just in case someone misses it when we get the info out, I'd like to make sure everyone affected gets a personal note about what's been done to them."

Bryan opened a video window on our shared monitor. "So, now seems like the right time to let Zane answer our questions."

It was cued right up to Bryan's voice asking, "What do you know about how Divine Community fits into your people's plans?"

Zane paused and made what I assumed was a thinking sound. "I...I don't think I've heard anything. I'm sorry. I'm still not committed, so still don't have a job. And, even if I did, they keep things segregated."

"Which is to say that you don't know anything."

"Sorry. No. I don't. But now that I know it might matter, I'll pay attention and let you know if I hear something."

Bryan asked, "But it wouldn't be strange for your people to have had a Plan B?"

"Definitely not! At this point, there have been many plans quietly built and fallen apart. Plus...plus religions are another area that has a lot of influence on people and *could* help turn people to peace, but without the same level of scrutiny of leaders that you get with politics. So, yeah, in that way it makes sense."

"And can I show you some pictures? Some video?"

Zane leaned forward.

In the room with us, Bryan said, "I was showing them footage of the 'miraculous' healings."

Zane nodded slowly. "That definitely looks like it could be a, uh, a piece of our tech. I haven't had anything serious enough happen to me to actually see any of our medtech in action, but, from what I know, yeah. That could be from us." They looked up, probably right at Bryan. "I think it would be safe to assume that this man is involved with my people. Or *is* one of my people."

Bryan paused the vid.

Voice full of awe, Riles asked, "They have tech that can do *that*? I mean...Hell, if their people had come in, offering this stuff in exchange for humans behaving themselves, we wouldn't have stood a chance."

"Naw," Bryan countered, but kindly. "Human greed would have come into play. Worried Earth medtech companies would have freaked out. This sort of thing avoids that *and* avoids xenophobia."

"Fucking humans," muttered Riley, returning to zir portable.

Though he was theoretically talking to us all, Bryan looked at me as he said, "Can we agree that our side quest isn't looking so side-ish? That an info release is warranted? Nothing as big a mission as SWS or the Peaceforgers. Just leak it to a number of doctors in the area, let them push it out once they confirm...Or maybe at least leak the SWS memo, the one that ties it to the vII, to all the same sorts of authorities who got the SWS emails we sent? Let them get the stink of the SWS scandal on them?"

"Dammit," I hissed. "So, do you think we can thwart this sickness ruse and expose this church without having to blow things up or get physical? Do you think we can do it with just our usual skills? On the computer?" I was directing this at Bryan, trying not to make it sound like I was begging.

He didn't reply immediately. He looked at Jonny, and I looked in time to see Jonny return a considering look and, finally, a small nod. He took my hand.

Bryan looked at Rye next, but it was a different look, because he knew that Rye had been mostly agreeing with me about staying on focus with the Peaceforger thing. Zie didn't meet his eyes a moment, and I watched as zie fought with zirself. It was clear on zir face that zie both wanted to reject any action but that zie also wanted to join in. Zie covered zir eyes, briefly, with zir hand. When zie dropped zir hand, zie nodded at me and took my other hand.

"Yeah," Bryan said. "I think we can do this all via our computers and with no deaths. Just a straight info leak. Carefully built, sent to just the right people. Old school us. And, if we're lucky, we can let our remote crew deal with anything they find like this with other benefactors of SWS 'philanthropy'."

I exchanged a look with Rye, making sure we were of the same mind. We shrugged and nodded, and I said, "Yeah. Sure. Though I'll still be coming back after we beat the Peaceforgers so that I can destroy anything left of them."

"Excellent. So, I'll plan that, and maybe you can keep at the Marleina angle? See if we can give Lex some better intel to use?" Bryan surveyed our faces.

We nodded and went back to work. Not that I was doing great work with the gnawing pit of worry and anger that had moved into my stomach.

Since our attack on SWS in October, I hadn't really done any aggressive hacking; no financial institution had felt my fury. I'd been focused more on my own safety and the alien thing. So this return to infiltrating someone else's computers with explicit intent to take them down or extract reparations for their wrongs was welcome and comfortable. Or it was that as long as I didn't think about the bigger picture and who was actually behind or working with this particular organization.

It was comfortable to return to this activity, and it was nice to do it with these same three people with whom I'd often taken such actions in the past. Aiming our time towards this had also seemed to take more of the edge off our sense of failure. What with having felt pretty hellish both physically and mentally the last week or so, not actually being settled into a new life, and not having success sorting out what to do next, we'd all been straining not to be general assholes or complainers. This was just what we needed. Even better than vidgames or drunk dancing.

By the time we went to bed Friday night, we were at ease with each other again in a way we hadn't been in a while, feeling like we were accomplishing something, our anger and frustration pointed at Divine Community. We were...well, there's a fine line between confidence and cockiness. But a plan that simply involved "pull together documents that prove an organization's guilt and release them to the people who will best use those docs to finish the takedown" was so old hat that the cockiness seemed reasonable.

Saturday, we just kept at it. We'd never minded working the same thing multiple days if it felt like we were getting somewhere. And we felt that now.

The church might be "mega," but it wasn't the behemoth you'd find in a business that might merit being considered mega. And there were four of us. And we'd already found damning documents. So, yeah. Suck it, Divine Community bastards!

<h1 style="text-align:center">CHAPTER 15</h1>

Bryan woke us in the middle of the night. "Hey, you two decent?"

I groaned. "Bastard, the only indecent thing right now is you waking us up."

Jonny laughed in agreement, but did have the sense to ask, "What's up?"

"Zane messaged. You should probably come see what's on the news. And they think it's serious enough that they're hoping they can come talk."

I coughed. "Uh, so, this is the first time they've asked to come talk, right? Which means, if this is a trap, this would be a good time for them to drop it on us."

In the pitch dark of the warehouse, Bryan sounded hesitant. "Yeah...I...I'd thought of that too. But I've also seen the news, and I think we'd probably like to hear whatever important things Zane says they should tell us."

I gave myself a moment to wake up, felt Jonny rolling over to grab the boots he kept by the bed. "Can you hand me my boots too, babe?" I might as well take a look at the news. Which I could do on my mobile, but I was reading the room. I'd get up and do it with everyone else.

Jonny handed me my boots and warned, "Going to turn on a light."

"Go for it." I put on my boots and closed my eyes part way against the incoming glare.

The lights flared into life in the little walled off section we slept in. It looked like it had been a refrigerated section, and the lighting was exactly as lurid as you'd expect.

Bryan held up a flashlight. Jonny nodded and found ours under some jackets on the mattress we didn't sleep on. I grabbed blankets, because I wasn't ready to let go of them, and followed as they turned off the light and used the flashlights to guide us across the open (but not litter-free) expanse. I could see the lights on in the break room, could hear the low voice of what sounded like a reporter. Riles greeted us with a nod and some pretty glorious bed head.

We all slumped into our chairs and pulled up our news feeds, though the news channel playing on the shared screen told the general story well enough.

My news aggregator had a number of stories at the top about beat down flu. And the headlines were...problematic. "Small Illinois Town Infected with Beat Down Flu" and "First Cases of Beat Down Flu Found in U.K." for example. I softly swore.

I scrolled and found just too many. Too many first cases all over the U.S. (though, I noted, none in South Dakota...go figure) and in a shit load of other countries.

Jonny swore less softly.

Riley just added a miserable, "Yeah," confirming things looked the same on zir feed.

Bryan gave a helpless shrug. "I feel like, maybe, this is demanding our attention first. That's..." he sighed, "a whole lot of new people about to be implanted with Peacemakers."

"Yeah. Yeah, there's clearly something we've missed. If we're right about Divine Community as a Peaceforger plot. No more SWS should mean no spread of their excuse to inject the vII. 'Cause there shouldn't be enough vIIs around to do all this. So..." Jonny trailed off.

"We need to know what Zane knows," Rye said, by way of agreement.

"Let's just set up a much smaller fake camp in another empty place, okay?" I didn't see a reason to risk our real home, such as it was.

We got cleaned up enough, gathered together just enough of our stuff, and Bryan dropped us in another empty building. Whilst he went to get Zane, we set up our computers, the shared screen, and some snacks. We made sure we had some power routing through so things would run. We read the news with no small amount of discouragement. Oh, but because it was a smaller space, we also got the heater going. And it worked. So, we were unhappy but properly warm for the first time in over a week. (Had it really only been a week? Fuck.)

Bryan must have driven around a bit to make it harder for Zane to guess our location, because it was an hour before they returned. The rest of us had started a list of all the places beat down flu was now being reported. We'd also made sure that there was a chair for Zane, almost like we were good hosts.

Everyone crowded around our portables. I indicated with my hand that Riles should go ahead.

Zie pulled up the list of infected places. "As you can see, it looks like they've gone ahead and released the plague broadly. I'd like to map this against places where they have established congregations, but some of these *are* in places that aren't super Christian. So, I'm guessing they hope the cure will let them reach people in spite of religion."

Jonny leaned back. "But SWS are basically on their way out. The factories where they'd been manufacturing the Peacemakers were some of the first buildings that other groups destroyed. How the hell are they planning to contaminate all the cure doses? Unless we think that Divine Community is distinct enough a group from SWS and this is going to happen just to grow the church, even if it doesn't grow the Peaceforger zombie army?"

I really hoped the latter was true.

We all looked at Zane.

Jonny pleaded with them, "Please tell us you have real answers."

Zane stood, pushed their hood back. They hadn't bothered with anything to hide the ridges on their head or their non-human eyes. Even so, possibly because they'd been born and raised on Earth by parents who had been as well, their mannerisms seemed human. And they looked agitated, conflicted.

"I've been given permission to tell you a little more." Zane was pacing and wringing their hands. "Again, this is placing...immense trust in you." They stopped to regard us. "I need to know that you understand that and that you won't expose us."

We nodded, and I asked, "Us?"

"Um...yeah...so, I'm not the only heretic. And...we aren't an army or anything, but there's some organization. There's...leadership. I think that's all I should say about that. Even just that information would be enough to start...I guess it would be a witch hunt." Zane took a deep breath through their mouth, exhaled heavily. "Okay, so...some of the others are already sorted into the work. Already done with their time out in the world. They hear stuff. And...I learned today that those who were working on the SWS effort are being moved into the Divine Community effort."

Bryan interrupted, "So this is confirmation that the church *is* a Peaceforger plan? Not just Peaceforgers taking advantage of the church?"

Zane nodded. "Probably. At this point, at least, taken over enough so the church is theirs. Or, uh, I guess, ours. In the case of Earth, the best general approach was to infiltrate the areas or set up presence in the areas of great influence. Like...clearly powerful corporations have...arguably an unreasonably large amount of influence in the world. We, avoided politics, like I said before, because that *always* leads to people digging aggressively into your past. But religion was deemed another influential entry point. Apparently. So, yeah, Divine Community was probably created by my people. I think. I'm...I didn't get a straight answer on that. But created or taken over by."

I had pulled up and was staring at a picture of Shepherd Michaelson. "Is this guy, the leader of the church, is he a Peaceforger?"

Everyone leaned in to evaluate. Our usual tell-tale signs were pale, too-smooth skin and quite big hair. He didn't seem to have either.

Zane had also leaned in. "That hair is just big enough for someone with smaller ridges. And...they...rather, he...that's what his identity is now...*he* might well have made the sacrifice of letting them shave his ridges down. That's also an option. Um...The hair is thick. And it's blonde, so you wouldn't really notice the pale scalp so much through it." They shook their head.

"I don't know why we're not going blonde on everyone's hair implants, just to be safe. Anyway..." They indicated the skin with a finger. "And that's all makeup and photo manipulation. Probably. Could be."

"Yeah," I pushed, "but what about in person? He gives sermons and does 'miracles' in person and meets with people."

"He does, but...on stage...his congregations are big and he preaches from stage, so you wouldn't really see the makeup that way...And, in person...I don't know if any of you wear makeup..."

I thought, *Not when you wake me at 3 A.M., bastard*, but nodded along with everyone else.

"Okay, so you know how you can do very natural looking makeup? Well, then you just get someone who can add pores...pore-looking bits. Right? Or you at least do enough to look like they're just one of those people who seem almost pore-less with makeup."

I was kind of annoyed. How the hell was I supposed to know the enemy now? Be homogenous, damn you! Aloud I said, "So, our previous ideas about telling which people are humans and which are Peaceforgers aren't always right?"

"Sorry. Yeah. Not reliable." Zane paused, as if waiting for more questions. When none came, they went on. "The other thing is that, after so long, and after...um...after how the SWS thing ended...it's possible that Divine Community is a final attempt. I'm getting that sense. You, uh, you could say that the Peaceforger leaders are sick of your shit. Sick of humanity's shit and dogged clinging to violence, hatred, and all the things they see as tied up with that. Which for the record, includes some things that I like. Like individuality and strong passions. So, this is the leaders and their followers, not me. Not my group." They flushed a little, a tinge of blue on their cheeks. "I wanted to say that in person, because I need you to understand that this is at least as serious as you think."

Bryan asked, "So, in terms of the bigger picture, what does that mean?"

"Um...bigger picture...I haven't, obviously, been around for things like this on other planets...and this hasn't filtered to a level where my group could be *sure* what, if anything, the plan is. But...Okay, based on history, what I think, what we all think, is that...If you just let this happen, they'll just keep spreading and probably manage to get a vII into almost every head. And then...I mean, they could fill brains with visions or happy emotions or eliminate the ones who resist too much. But, as long as they keep rolling forward, they'll probably just press on. They'll consider the situation here hopeful."

"And if they don't keep rolling forward?" asked Rye.

Zane hummed a bit, seeming to contemplate the question. "So...okay, if you slow them down somehow...well, at some point they'll realize. They track every vII put into a head. They might think a temporary slowdown is just that, but it just pushes the decision out. Pushes out one of the two likely endings."

I asked, "And the other option? The one where we take down Divine Community in a definitive way?"

"Well, in that case..." Zane rubbed the back of their neck. "At best, you get a last chance of, uh, of them revealing that we're here and why we're here and offering an ultimatum. And...when the pride that seems normal in human leaders wins out, I'm pretty sure they'll call us all back to the ship, get off planet, and destroy you all."

"Just like that?" asked Bryan.

"Yeah. Because, at that point, you'll have proven—in their eyes—that you have too much corruption to ever be won. And, if you aren't taken out of existence, then maybe you will make it off the planet and infect others." They nervously held up their hands. "Again, that's how the others think, not us."

Bryan considered his fingers. "How will they do it?"

"They...I mean, it has varied. Depending on who's in charge. Sometimes they just bomb the world until it's lifeless. Or sometimes they let loose a sickness that kills all the people. Let the planet and animals live. Which, obviously, they've already got a head start on, you know, figuring out here. Though they'd infect you and stay near enough to check in and make sure everyone actually died."

I interrupted, "So, on that note, is it safe to assume that Peaceforgers were involved in creating beat down flu? And that your species wouldn't be in danger from it?"

They nodded. "That would be very safe to assume. Both parts. And, in the event that the flu was something conceived of by humans before we got involved, my people would have made sure it was changed not to affect us." With a sneer, they said, "Our so-called altruism rarely drives us to actually risk our own lives."

"Got it." I tried to keep it all matter-of-fact. No need to let our one Peaceforger ally know that I'd been quietly wondering if I'd be forced to "accidentally" infect them in order to test my idea about beat down flu being worse for their species than mine.

Zane picked up where I'd cut them off. "Anyway, in terms of how they're likely to end things here, for you. Um...not often, but sometimes...sometimes they see if they can just kill all the older people, just leave the children and babies...Leave behind Peaceforgers to raise the...the remaining people. But figuring out doing that last one, it's difficult. I wouldn't count on it."

"And then some third option where we figure out how to get your people, or at least the ones who aren't heretics, off our planet?" Bryan asked. "Is that something you and your group would support?"

Zane looked surprised. "You'd consider that? Instead of just...killing everyone?" They quickly said, "Not that you don't seem brave and willing to save your people, but...It has seemed like you were not necessarily inclined toward war, and doing it selectively would be harder."

I kept my face carefully neutral, but Jonny and Bryan both nodded enthusiastically. Shit. I was going to have to hero-up after all.

"Well, yeah, that's something we would like. If...if there's a way to do that, I think we'd consider that a best case scenario," Zane said.

"Not that now is the time for exact plans," I clarified, "but, if we did somehow get them off the planet, is there any way to be sure they wouldn't just turn right around and bomb us?" I leaned forward, directing my question at Zane. "Aren't we actually talking about needing to kill any of your people who are awake?" I leaned back. "You don't need to answer at this point, but I just want that possibility in our heads as people consider which path they want to pursue. That the one path that doesn't lead to humanity being subjugated or dead leads to us having to kill...What did you estimate? Maybe a thousand people?" As Zane nodded to confirm those numbers, I went on, "And without probably having the luxury of confirming which of them, other than Zane, are innocent, unless Zane can be right there to point out who's on our side. Because there's every chance that there are people who *aren't* in their group who also disagree but are afraid to speak up."

It was probably a shitty thing for me to poke at the still oozing guilt in all our souls. But, if anyone was going to use guilt over leaving humanity to the mercy of the Peaceforgers as a motivator (which, let's be clear, is kind of bullshit...I am not responsible for others' horrible actions or choices), then I wanted to make sure they understood that *all* paths led to deaths in which we were, arguably, complicit.

Very evenly, too evenly, Bryan picked up the conversation and turned it away from that. "Zane, was there anything else you thought we should know?"

Suddenly, Zane became the poster child for nervous mannerisms. Ah, so here was the real meat, in Zane's mind, of what they wanted us to know. I couldn't imagine what would be more that than confirming the Peaceforger connection to Divine Community.

They planted themselves and faced us. "First, I, uh, I should probably tell you about how we're...born and raised."

What the hell? I was kind of getting tired of the weird excuses to see Bryan, the useless info. But I held my tongue. Whatever.

"Does this mean there's finally an appropriate time for me to indulge my curiosity about how you have sex?" For such a cheeky question, Riles sounded quite serious. When Jonny gave zir a look, zie retorted, "Fuck you. We all have special interests."

"Uh, actually, that's kind of where I was going to start." Zane smiled at Rye. "Though...not the pleasurable act you're thinking of. I mean, we have that. But it's different from procreation. So, don't be too disappointed." They laughed a little and Riley gave them a smile.

"Thanks for the warning! Do go on," zie encouraged.

"Okay. So. Peaceforger families aren't...it's not two parents and their offspring. And procreation isn't like...it's not genetic material from two parental donors. Not an egg and sperm situation, as it were. Not brought together in the way that's, uh, most common for humans."

Riley didn't interrupt, but zie was leaned forward, chin propped on hands. This was, to zir mind, the good stuff. This and the art, the culture. For all that zie loved tech, learning about the tech would never win out if zie had to prioritize which things zie learned about people who weren't like zir.

"For us, well...I guess one of the relevant facts is that we have five biological sexes."

From the looks on our faces, I'd say we were all impressed by that. Not sure why more sounded better, but, wow. Five.

"At some point in the far, uncivilized past, you might have just two parents. But it's now considered, well, uncivilized. Maybe because it limits the children's chances in terms of which sexes they might end up. And also it's seen as selfish for that reason, but also because it results in children with only two parents to love and care for them. So, at least three parents. And all a unit. So they can raise the offspring together. And, I guess, I mean, surely, in the past..." Zane faltered, gave Riley something of an apologetic look, then went on. "In the past, it must surely have been a...purely biological process. But procreation and gestation is, well, it's all genetic deposits and machinery now. Incubation pod. Not...not sexy or romantic. But it's done with intent. So, I think, it's beautiful. A...a mindful choice to have offspring. Everyone is wanted, even before they exist." They shrugged. "Plus, absolutely no risk to the health of the parent who carries the child if nobody's doing that."

They started pacing. "Every...um...we call it a 'brood'...every brood is...well, it can be as few as one child, but that's really, really rare. Usually, there are three to five children. Broodmates. Which, from what I've seen...In Earth media, twins or other multiple births are usually portrayed as being closer. And...and, for us, broodmates are definitely closer than siblings seem to be for humans."

"Holy shit. Three to five per brood and some families have multiple broods?" As soon as the words were out, Riles looked abashed. Zie coughed. "Sorry. That was...culturally insensitive and totally inappropriate."

Zane waved away the apology. "No. It's okay. And, yes, some families have two or three broods, depending on how many children they can support healthily. Anyway, so, we're close. And we don't really leave the house the first few years. They have to...well, it's partly to make sure we don't accidentally give away that we're alien. But it's also partly to make sure that...that we are adequately educated and bought into the Peaceforger culture and ways before we meet humans in a way where they could...infect our spirits." They looked embarrassed. "Sorry."

Riley assured them, "Oh, humans have plenty of shitty attributes. Completely understandable."

With a grateful nod, Zane went on. "So, that's all to say that families in general are close, and broodmates are *really* close. And, at least in my brood...we adored the hell out of each other. We stuck near each other all through childhood. We didn't start to really make space between us until this," they waved their hand in a circle like they were including everything, "this free period. That's, well...we started exploring more. And...and it can look sort of odd if too many of us are in a group, trying to get a home. Too much possible weirdness for the humans we're trying to fit in with. So...I took advantage of that to have my own space. To be able to be alone with my...my heretical leanings."

"Sorry, I know it's probably off track," Jonny acknowledged, "but how do you decide you're a heretic in a situation like that?"

Zane shrugged. "Honestly? It actually started from devotion. I was making a deep study of sacred texts and the like. And...and I realized that I didn't...I didn't understand them the way that everyone else did. I couldn't find answers for my concerns. So...yeah. That's how it happens. Or how it happened for me." They looked at Jonny to see if that had been enough.

Jonny nodded and just said, "Got it."

"That's all the background you need." They looked abashed. "Which seems like a lot of information now that I've said it all out loud. Anyway, now you'll understand the problem. My problem."

"Problem?" Bryan's tone was tinged with wariness.

"I didn't know...I didn't know because I was afraid they would figure out I was a heretic. I was afraid, so I didn't keep in as much contact with my broodmates." Zane's voice suddenly got soft. "I missed them. But I was afraid. And so made them believe I was immersed in study, which I kind of was, and...Anyway, I didn't know how the other four were doing. Didn't know *what* they were doing. Until tonight."

Zane walked over to Rye's portable and asked, "Would you open a news feed? Please."

Rye did as asked, and then opened the article to which Zane pointed. It was a story about how, in light of the spread of beat down flu, Divine Community was expanding and had some new leadership positions to fill. In the group photo of the new leaders, Zane indicated a smiling woman with dark hair. I could see the similarities; I saw the problem.

"That's Shay." They sounded glum. "And, according to the article, they're...she's now leading the Divine Community Seattle Cure Outreach. And that complicates things for me."

I saw Bryan and Jonny stiffen and inch their hands nearer their guns. Bryan asked, "Complicates how?"

I mentally gave myself a high five for seeing it when they didn't. Guess all these years of over-studying people in an effort to seem neurotypical enough (because I like me, but the world is full of bias) was letting me see Shay's face in more detail.

"Don't...I mean, you know, I'm still a heretic. And I still think we need to see if we can stop what's happening. But...I don't think I can...I can't hurt my broodmate. Or make plans that do. So, no physical violence when you take care of Divine Community. And preferably no solutions to the issue of my people invading your planet that are a definite death sentence for my family. Please." The last word was truly pleading.

I gave Zane a reassuring smile. "I can promise you that our current plans absolutely don't involve us doing anything like that. We aren't actually fans of physical violence either." I flushed, guilty. "Even if the bombing in October makes it look otherwise. We really, really don't want to hurt anyone." I sighed. "My fucking soul can't take more of that."

With a sigh of relief, Zane said, "Good. Okay. Good. Thank you."

"I actually think there's a question that's been forgotten whilst we've talked." I figured we should see if Zane had neglected to mention an important thing that might save us work if they had more info. "We've been assuming that SWS were supplying the Peacemakers to Divine Community, which should have meant they couldn't push out the cure, or at least not with Peacemakers in. But SWS are gone and the whole cure scam just ramped up, so the cures must still have Peacemakers in. Instead of keeping it local, they've pushed out, infecting the world, as if they've got a supplier. Did we miss a Peacemaker factory?"

"Oh. Right. We aren't *sure*, but it seems like the cure scam was supposed to start a month earlier. And so we think... well, they had a stockpile, but also they set up the, uh, the cure factory to also produce more Peacemakers. We're pretty sure about that part. Nobody burns down the factory where a cure is being made."

The conversation kind of petered out then. To Rye's delight, Zane offered to answer any and all questions zie had about Peaceforgers, including ones about "biology." I had meant to stick around, working and eavesdropping, and I did for a while.

Riles started with innocent questions, got innocent and not-tactically-useful answers. The Peaceforgers were amphibious and slightly endothermic. They had sorted out immunizations so they were safe against known Earth diseases and sicknesses (dammit). They had two 3-hour sleep periods per day; kids had three of them, during which they were in some kind of sleep educating pod. ("A necessity when your people know enough that you'd never learn it in a normal life.") One good aspect of their culture was that they hadn't fallen into the bullshit gender trap, which was an aspect of Earth cultures they found hard to deal with. Especially when they became adults and had to choose what sort of gender presentation they would live with as so-called human adults. Like I said, innocent, interesting, but not likely useful.

However, gender talk gave Riley an opening to ask about sex ("and I mean the pleasure part"). I'm not exactly prudish, but I wasn't in the mood, so I took my portable and went to sit in another room with it. I made sure to give Riles a wink on my way out.

It didn't take Jonny long to join me. He laughed as he sat down. "I have no idea where that conversation is going, but I suspect I'm not old enough to hear it. Riley definitely isn't sticking to mundane biological facts."

I laughed too. "Our Rye has questionable boundaries when it comes to satisfying zir curiosity about sex. And the unique nature of what Zane can tell zir has got to make it even better."

"I guess we count this as a silver lining for Riles to the whole mess."

"Aye. And, really, I can't begrudge zir that. So I hope the details are so titillating that we hear the moans from here." I kind of meant it. Anything to heal up zir heart...any of our hearts...

Bryan finally ducked out, but he didn't seem to be fleeing. He had something in his hands that he was holding out to show us. We set our laptops aside and stood.

Jonny asked, "What have you got?"

With a grin, Bryan replied, "This beauty should detect Peacemakers!"

He handed me the disc, and I wondered if Doc and Engie had purposefully designed it to mirror the shape of the Peacemaker vI.

"Freshly 3D printed before I woke you up about this beat down flu shit. Got too distracted by that and forgot to show you. Verified to work on the vI by Doc. And it looks like tomorrow, or later today really, we'll be testing it on the vII." His grin faded a little. Thinking of a vII in Gran's head could take the shine off any good news.

Jonny gave me a squeeze. "Don't worry. Within minutes of this detecting the one in Gran, Dr. Scott will have it out. It's going to be fine."

Bryan reclaimed his grin, encouragingly. "It *is*, Kot. This time tomorrow, Gran's head will be clean. She'll be dreaming her own dreams, not the pasty bastards'."

CHAPTER 16

The next morning, as Jonny and I made sure we had guns and knew how to work the Peacemaker detector, the mood seemed carefully light. It almost seemed reasonable to hope all would be fine in time for supper. Of course, all it takes is one "huh" to skew the mood.

Riley said, "Huh."

We all stopped what we were doing to look at zir. Zie was, as usual, staring at zir mobile screen.

Casually, Bryan asked, "What's up, poppet?"

By way of answer, zie turned zir mobile towards us, and we all moved in to read it. "It's from Kitty, by the way," zie clarified.

After not asking for almost a week, this was the sort of question we'd been worried about:

Did we take out SWS?

"She hasn't asked about it at all before?" Jonny confirmed.

"Not once. So I'm torn between asking why she's asking now and telling her...something ambiguous. Like, what's going on with SWS but not saying we did it." Riles chewed on a nail.

Bryan shrugged. "I'd do both."

"Tell me," Riles directed, mobile turned back so zie could tap out what Bry said.

"Say that SWS seems to be struggling to exist after the explosion last week. Then just ask why she's asking now. Simple." Bryan moved to watch over Rye's shoulder.

Just standing and waiting, it felt like minutes, but it was probably just seconds before Riles reported, "Says it's taking time for her brain to come back together. Says she just remembered everything from the last few days before she ended up in the dark." Zie looked up at us. "Where she is now. That's all we know about it. She's in the dark."

"I know you don't want to lie, just in case it's really her, but try to dodge questions about that whole thing, okay?" Bryan asked.

"Sure thing. Though, listen, somebody has to tell me when I can tell her the alien thing. If it's her, she'll kick my ass for not letting her in on that tasty bit of info sooner." Riles grinned at the thought of Kitty's future excitement at the alien news.

"Will do." And then Bryan was back to his own work.

When it was time to pick up Gran, I collected some "good luck" hugs, and Jonny and I headed out.

"While you're gone, we'll finish prepping for the Divine Community info release. We should be good to go tonight. Definitely in time to hit inboxes Monday morning," Bryan promised.

"Give Gran our love!" called Riles.

And off we went. We took a circuitous route, with me at the wheel and Jonny making a (probably vain) attempt to keep an eye out for anyone following us. At least Sunday traffic was slightly lighter, so he had more chance of noticing.

As we drove, Jonny said, "I wanted to run this by you first, but I'm pretty sure that, unless there's some secret Peaceforger record, it's safe for us to be us. To stay. To not run or change names."

"Huh." I was too sure that that was incorrect to be excited.

Misinterpreting my lack of enthusiasm, Jonny said, "No, listen. This isn't me trying to convince you to stay and physically fight or anything like that. In fact, if we *do* fight, we probably can't take advantage of this until everything's over. This is about...normality. About understanding our options. Maybe getting back the domesticated life we've been missing after we fight. Or settling back into it ASAP if we're not fighting. Or after a brief stint in South Dakota to make sure the heat is off us."

It didn't seem possible to me. "Are you sure? That we can just be us?"

"Obviously, I can't be 100% positive, but my personal project the last week or so has been trying to dig deeper *specifically* to verify that neither the cops nor the Peaceforgers know who we are. Not just that our 'nyms aren't connected to our names, but that we covered our tracks sufficiently."

"And we did? Even though the Peaceforgers thought I was MK? And told everyone I was?"

"It appears to be the Universe trying to balance out the loss and hurt and...everything. Yeah, I think we did. I dug deep. And, the last couple days, I focused on making sure there were no traces of us on Divine Community's computers either. I mean," he shifted in his seat, "it's possible that they've got all sorts of information on us on some hidden, centralized Peaceforger computers. Or that they totally don't believe that Kitty was MK. And I've been looking, just in case. But, from what I can find, we're good. The humans definitely have no problem with us, and the SWS people pretty much...I found a conversation between Trent and the thing that we think is the ship's address. They admitted to each other that it's entirely possible Kitty was MK and you were just the victim of some unfortunate coincidences."

"How do we confirm? Do we send one of us back into one of our flats as bait?"

"That's a meat space question. I figure we should get Bryan in on this plan. But...I'm up for trying. If you are." He put a hand on my leg. "I know we're not in total agreement about what we should do after we get info to send to people with real power, but I want you to know...This particular disagreement? It's just one issue. One decision. When possible, I want to back you up or be on the exact same side. So, I won't even bring this up unless you want to try."

I kept my eyes mostly on the road, trying to be a safe driver, but I reached out a hand towards his face, and he kindly helped me land it on his cheek. "We don't have to agree on everything to be okay. But I appreciate this. And, yeah, let's bring this up. I want nothing more than to sit around our flat watching vids and to go have suppers with Gran regularly. Like normal people. Normal-ish." I grinned and put my hand back on the wheel.

Jonny turned his attention back to watching the road. "So, 'our flat,' huh? Think we should keep living together, even when we have a choice?"

"You don't have a lot of extra furniture for me to fit in. So, yeah, I could probably handle that. If that's okay with you." Pretending to be breezy and cool was easier when I could keep my eyes on the road.

"Yeah," I could hear the grin in his voice. "I could probably handle that too."

I wondered if the door on my old flat had gotten closed and locked, if the flat had been looted, if the automatic rent pay that I hadn't bothered to cancel had been enough to keep it mine. And I wondered if I could ever feel safe there again, even if there was a locked door and all my stuff was intact.

Gran was exactly on time, walking up to the convenience store that had replaced my childhood park just as we pulled up. She barely missed a beat as we paused at the curb, Jonny hopped out to get her into the front seat, and we pulled away.

She squeezed my hand and said, "I expect a hug as soon as this car has stopped."

"Absolutely!" I grinned and squeezed back. "Now, if you'll let Jonny have a look at your head, we'll have you to the doctor in no time."

Uncertainly, she consented. "Okay...Do I just sit here?"

Jonny scooted around in his seat, the detector in his hand, and said, "If you'd lean forward just a bit, please. I need to pass something around your head, a bit of a detector that some brilliant friends of ours cooked up. You're our first chance to confirm it works on the kind of Peacemaker we think is in your head."

"Yay?" was all Gran said as she leaned forward.

As he ran the detector around her skull, it emitted clicking sounds. It was only supposed to do that in close proximity to a Peacemaker. (It hadn't clicked on any of our heads or on Zane's. That was as much testing as we'd managed with our particular unit.)

"Is the clicking good or bad?" she asked.

"I'm afraid the only good news here," Jonny answered, "is that your granddaughter knows the sort of genius people who can make this gadget, as well as get that bug out of your head. Sorry." He gave her a smile that was both apologetic and reassuring.

"Did you know I never even had a broken bone? No surgeries? I figured I was going to make it through life without any major medical issues." Gran sighed dramatically and settled back into her seat. "I guess I was saving up all my medical luck for having brain surgery to take a bug out of my brain. Hope I saved up enough."

I said, "Just think what a story you'll have to tell at whatever passes for parties when you're old. Everyone else losing their heads and you telling a story about finally cleaning yours out." I laughed.

She snorted. "I'm about to put something upside *your* head." Then, gleefully, she reported, "And, for your information, Sarah is moving back to Seattle. There will be plenty of parties. So get ready to answer when I call to tell you we've broken our hips dancing, smartarse."

It was clear that Dr. Scott wasn't doing her off-the-books work out of any lack of professionalism. I knew that both from researching her carefully and from watching how she worked. Her operating room was spotless, her demeanor was cordial, and there was an actual normal entry with a very normal waiting room if you bothered to come in via the street instead of the alley.

"I want you all to know that I've got plenty of experience successfully removing the Peacemaker vI, and that I've spent the last week plus making sure that I understood those plans that went out about how to take out a vII, preparing for when someone realized they had one and needed me." She squeezed Gran's hand. "This is going to be just fine."

She got Gran's permission to record the operation and share it with "the people who figured out all the SWS stuff." Got Gran prepped and settled, ready to administer sedation.

Jonny and I had scrubbed and were going to be allowed to sit in the room, out of sight of the camera (which would be a closeup of Gran's brain anyway) but where Gran could watch us. We hoped that it would be comforting for her.

Before Dr. Scott started the camera, I gave Gran a quick kiss on the cheek. "You be brave and we'll get you some ice cream after. Or some of those shitty hard candies old people like."

She laughed. Just what I was going for.

We all settled into our places as the sedation took effect on Gran. Dr. Scott confirmed that Doc and Engie were online and watching, able to talk to her just in case they saw something. The machines gleamed, Dr. Scott took a deep breath, and, ever so carefully, a laser cut into Gran's skull, opening just enough skin and bone for what needed to be done. Just like she'd programmed it to do. And then tiny metal arms took up their part of the program, carefully placing something around Gran's open skull.

Behind my mask, I did a mediocre job of playing it cool. I'm not squeamish, but this wasn't exactly any random skull, was it?

"We'll wait a second for your grandmother's sedation to wear off." Before I could freak out, but not before my face told her it was coming, she assured me, "Doing awake brain surgery isn't uncommon. I put her out during the incision, because I find people usually freak out otherwise. And I used localized pain blockers, so she won't feel anything. But brain surgery can be complicated, and being able to talk to your grandmother while I work is actually helpful for knowing how things are going."

"Are you trying to talk about me behind my back?" Gran asked with a laugh, sedation clearly worn off.

The mood lightened the littlest bit, and the doctor returned to the task at hand.

Dr. Scott talked as she worked, telling us—and the camera—which step she was on from the plans she'd gotten, walking us all through with her. She'd say the step, pause for confirmation from Doc and Engie, and then proceed. Every step. Calm and easy. Occasionally, she checked in with Gran, had her answer a question or share some mundane piece of information just to make sure she wasn't fucking up something in Gran's brain.

My eyes went from Dr. Scott to Gran's face, back and forth. Always giving Gran smiles and encouraging nods. I held onto Jonny's hand, but only because it was pleasant. This was going to be okay. It was going well. Calm and easy.

It didn't seem like too much forever before Dr. Scott finally said, "Alright, we've got just one last connection to sever, and then I can start carefully extracting everything and close you back up."

But then...I tried to sound cool as I asked, "Gran, are you okay?" Her eyes were wide and her mouth open, but she wasn't making any sound. She *should* be able to reply.

She didn't.

"Gran? Can you just blink for me, please?" I was now feeling anything but calm. Fuck.

At the same time, the machines monitoring her vitals went...jagged. They shrieked and pinged.

Dr. Scott firmly asked, "Is this as expected? Guys, did I miss something?"

"Shit, hang on." I could hear in Doc's voice that it wasn't as expected.

Sticking to a tone that was still firm but now somehow reassuring, Dr. Scott said, "No need to worry. This is just new territory. We'll get on top of this." But she clicked a switch to make sure that now only she could hear Doc and Engie. And she turned off the sound on the monitors. Which just meant Gran couldn't hear them, but the rest of us could see the flashing visual indicators. Something was undeniably very wrong.

Now it wasn't just something pleasant; I was holding Jonny's hand so that I could channel my worry into that, hide it from Gran. I didn't want to talk, because I didn't want to risk Dr. Scott not being able to hear Doc and Engie. She was talking just loudly enough for the two of them to hear her clearly. But, like the machines, lack of sound couldn't hide the flashing visual indicators. Something was undeniably very wrong.

I tried to give Gran my most sincere and reassuring look. Just in case she could still see me.

I tried to press all my worry into my fingers, wrapped around Jonny's, and smash them all out so Gran wouldn't see it.

Dr. Scott was moving quickly, but she didn't look as confident. She flicked glances up to monitors. Nothing got better.

And then...there was no light in Gran's eyes. I couldn't say what I meant by that; there was no clear physical change. Just...the light was gone. She wasn't there anymore.

I was on my feet, silently and desperately pleading with Dr. Scott to fix it.

Silently and desperately pleading with any possibility of a higher power to fix it. Swearing to believe in any of them, even the Peaceforger's Divine, if they'd fix this.

And then...Gran's open mouth was slack.

No.

No no no!

Fuck.

Fuck!

Jonny was holding me. And Dr. Scott had frozen. And I could feel tears sliding down my cheek. A scream was trying to crawl up my throat, but it was just coming out as air.

My brain was a buzz of emotions, of static and shrieking. It was the wail that my own voice was failing to make.

Dr. Scott pulled the camera in closer, moving it, apparently, as directed by Doc and Engie. After a moment, she said, "Just a minute," and she looked at me. For all that she was a hardass doctor who made plenty off illegal work and fixing those who did illegal work, she still looked stricken.

"I am..." She had to pause, to swallow. "I am incredibly sorry. It appears..." She seemed to be listening to the people in her ear. "There was a kill switch. Something that wasn't clear or wasn't included in the specs your people had. It's like...like something sent a message to tell her autonomic nervous system to just stop..." And then she looked embarrassed. "I hate to ask this." (I believed her.) "We'd appreciate your permission to continue on, to examine what's going on here so that we can update the information and save lives."

Why did it keep coming back to me saving lives, me endangering lives, me taking lives? I nodded, in enough shock that I was starting to feel numb. "Gran would want to do some final good in the world."

I suddenly felt unstuck for a moment. "And I'm also going to start looking at your machine, if I may, to make sure it wasn't hacked. That there are no remote hands pushing yours off course."

She looked down at her hands a moment. "I understand what you're asking, but I'm right here. The movements are all what they should have been. Not like, well, not like I've seen when surgical units are hacked."

Oh. I felt useless again. Helpless. My brain scrambled, needing something to do to somehow add good, try to balance out a death that couldn't be balanced. "What about...can I maybe come back some time to set up, basically, a firewall to make sure nobody *can* hack it in the future? Something better than what came stock?"

Dr. Scott seemed to understand my need. She nodded. "Sure. We can set up some evening when you have time and I don't have clients. I can do paperwork and you can do that. Okay?"

It wasn't enough, but I eagerly nodded. "And...um...what do we do with Gran? I mean, she wasn't a criminal..." I was trying to be sensible. Fighting the urge to dissolve into emotion and never come back.

"I'm legally a doctor, and she's just been ill. I'll...I'll fix her scalp as soon as we're done, and I'll report that she came in with complications from beat down flu. And it will be treated like a normal death." She gave me an apologetic look as she said, "You'll probably want to leave. And, if you're her next of kin, expect a call."

I mutely nodded. As I moved towards Gran, Dr. Scott advised, "Take a moment to make sure she's got no valuables. You won't want them disappearing if you get a dishonest person involved before she's safely at the coroner's."

I took a peek through her bag, taking the few things of monetary or sentimental value. She traveled light; there was just a little cash, her favorite ring, and a coin purse with stars on it that she'd let me use as a child when I had pennies to spend on treats.

Finally, I ducked in to give Gran one last kiss on the cheek. I whispered in her ear, "I failed you." I choked and swallowed hard. "I failed you. We should have done better. I'm sorry. I'm so sorry. I love you. I love you forever."

It got fuzzy from there, but I know that Jonny maneuvered me out of the room, held me a moment, and then helped me into the car. He took his time driving back, didn't take a direct route, both to make sure we weren't too easily followed and to let me get through the first, brutal wave of sobbing before I had to face anyone else.

Bryan and Riley met us with guns out, but they quickly holstered them.

Bryan said, "Sorry for the reception; we weren't expecting you yet." Even as he said that, he put the pieces together. It was an easy enough puzzle...our early return and my bloodshot eyes. "Oh, Kot..."

I was enveloped in my friends' arms, and Jonny tried to calmly and quietly recount what happened.

He finished with, "Dr. Scott says one of them will get to us with updated information as they have it."

I hadn't heard her say that, but that was no surprise.

I could feel the rumble of words in his chest as Bryan spoke. "We need to send out word to everyone who got the email the night we blew the headquarters. We need to warn them not to try to remove a vII until we revise." He took a step back, held my face in his hands. "You okay?"

I nodded, shook my head, started crying again.

"We're going to make them pay. I fucking promise you that." Bryan's eyes were red and I only remembered then that Gran had mothered him too. Had mothered all of us. Not just me.

With that realization, I could feel the soft shaking that was Riles crying silently beside us. I reached over to pull zir into the huddle of emotion. Fuck all of this. Fuck Peaceforgers and Peacemakers. Fuck SWS and Divine Community. Fuck their disease and fuck their so-called cures. And especially fuck their false peace.

I had always, on some level, assumed Gran was immortal. That she would at least last as long as me. Even if just because she was stubborn and I did stupid shit. It had never truly occurred to me that she was entirely human. Mortal. Dammit.

I wailed.

My brain started laying out the pieces. A part of me had held back on buying into taking down the Peaceforgers because I figured the doctors could stall things a while by taking out Peacemakers. A part of me had held back because I had already given too much, but it turned out that there was a certain line in my head where far too much became having not enough to live for that would hold me back from action. A part of me had held back because I didn't care enough about humanity, fucked up and horrible creatures who were inhumane to each other and animals and the planet, to take on more for *them*. But now that lack of care had grown into a mass that consumed me. That consumed the guilt and the conscience.

I wouldn't fully buy into staying for the sake of humanity. I *would* fully buy in for the sake of ruining Peaceforgers until they filled the gnawing hole where my soul had been. I would fucking burn myself out to grind those motherfuckers into nothingness. That thought pushed me into the eye of my emotional storm.

Jonny stood behind me in our huddle, arms around my shoulders, just above Bryan's arm and Rye's arm. He held tight and promised me, "I'm right here. You're going to be okay."

Could he hear how flat and devoid of believing my voice was as I told him, "I know"? Could he hear the wind that shrieked through the vacuum where my heart had been? Because, me, I was deafened by the sound.

I lay on Rye's mattress in the break room whilst everyone else worked. On what? I didn't really know and didn't much care. I only noticed the quick reports they called out.

"Email sent. Everyone should know to hold off on removing vIIs." (Bryan)

"Doc says they've definitively confirmed there was an undocumented kill switch." (Jonny)

"Engie says they have enough info that they'll be able to figure it out. Eventually." (Riles, reading through the D3AD_L1NX account.)

"Map of countries hit by beat down flu is getting dense." (Bryan)

"Doc says that vII is more invasive than the vI. Even more than they'd realized." (Jonny)

"Engie says...shit...she says that she's 90% sure the vI was built in a way that it deposits what we now know as the vII, so you could take out the vI but still have a Peacemaker in." (Riles)

"Email sent warning people that vI deposited something like a vII. With reminder not to attempt removal." (Jonny)

"Divine Community has announced they're partnering with established aid organizations and the CDC to distribute the doses of cure that already exist far and wide while everyone sets up to make more." (Bryan)

"We can't send out the Divine Community email. If they're wrapped up with Peaceforgers, it will tip them off that we know." (Jonny)

I finally sat up. Through gritted teeth I commanded, "Just motherfucking stop." I was staring into the empty air in front of me, the wall across from me, but my peripheral vision told me they had all frozen. "Enough." I stood and aimed myself out the door, towards my own mattress. The day was piling on too heavily, too much shit and failure.

I could hear them behind me, talking quietly as soon as I was out the break room door. Bryan explaining that Divine Community was also "generously" providing a representative to oversee every individual manufacturer of the cure, almost certainly letting them get the vII into every damned dose somehow. And their voices, brainstorming solutions, blended and swirled in my wake.

It was one thing to fight a corporation. Even if the law was in their favor, most people instinctively longed to see corporations taken down a peg. But a church that was distributing a much needed cure for free? A church that had kept its reputation as sterling as a church could? Not so easy.

Even if we had solid enough proof to get people to consider it...*Would* they consider it, given that the company that was supposed to be the source of the Peacemakers had been thoroughly smashed, was in what appeared to be death throes?

Cops wouldn't want to risk public opinion...Again, did we have enough proof to get them to take action?

And that's before we even had to try to bring in the whole alien thing. Fuck.

My head was a thick swirl, like tar and mud. Doubts and pain. It hadn't hurt like this when my mum died. It had never hurt like this.

I collapsed on my mattress and sunk into the sticky, sludgy blackout that had replaced everything else in me.

I woke to Jonny petting my hair as he tapped away on his mobile, the room lit only by the screen. My mind felt slightly less consumed by the maelstrom in my heart. I lay for a while, eyes closed, enjoying the feel of his fingers, trying to pull myself back. Back from the compelling violence, back into being the person that some part of me vaguely remembered I wanted to be. Back into being the person *Gran* would want me to be.

With that thought, I sighed.

Jonny didn't stop petting my hair, but softly asked, "Did sleep help at all?"

I opened my eyes to see him looking down at me, worried. "It took a very small edge off. But nothing is...fixed."

"Is there anything, anything at all, that I can do? I'll bring you food, fuck you any way you want, shoot a Peaceforger, dance a silly jig. *Anything.*"

I smiled a little. "Naw. I'll let you know. But, no. I can't think of anything that would help. Not even taking down the aliens and the church. She'd still be gone."

"Okay. Consider it a standing offer though." He gestured towards the light switch. "Do you mind?" When I shook my head, he moved from where he'd been sitting on the edge of the mattress, turned on the lights, then turned to sit with legs stretch out right beside me. "Are you hungry? I can at least grab you something from our paltry kitchen."

"Um...that depends. What time is it?" I didn't find my mobile in my pocket.

Jonny leaned over to pick it up from the floor by the mattress and hand it to me. "I fished it out of your pocket and silenced it so it wouldn't wake you. You needed sleep."

According to my mobile, it was 02:00. "Why are you still awake?"

"We were trying to dig up info, help Doc and Engie, keep an eye on things. The usual. Besides," he reminded me, "02:00 isn't that late in computer time."

"I know I told you guys to stop, but is there anything new I should know?"

"Nothing important. Just progress inching forward, as it does when we stay on top of an issue. But..." His tone shifted, now careful and serious. "I did some different looking because it's probably going to become relevant."

"What's up?"

"You know I respect your privacy."

"You mean aside from that time you basically stalked me and broke into my accounts?" I made sure to laugh so he wouldn't think I was still mad about that.

His laugh was a little forced. "Yeah, aside from that. Sorry. Seriously."

I waved away the apology; in that particular case, he'd been right to break into my accounts. "And aside from what else?"

"Aside from seeing who was calling while I was silencing your mobile and taking that as a cue to go dig into someone."

I tapped my mobile to see what I'd missed. Looked like just two calls, both to my public number. Both were from numbers already in my mobile. The first came from Detective Engalls's Seattle Police Department number. The second, a few minutes later, was from his mobile number. It looked like both had left voicemail.

The last time I'd talked to Detective Engalls, I'd called him because Gran thought someone was trying to get her whilst she waited to grab a flight. I'd made him promise to help her, and then I'd hung up. I hadn't answered any of his calls since then.

But Gran had told me what happened at the airport during her recounting of her last couple weeks as we'd driven to Dr. Scott's.

According to Gran, Engalls had shown up so quickly that there was no doubt he'd used sirens and one of the department's flying-capable cars to avoid traffic and other impediments. They'd met previously, when he'd brought her in as they investigated me whilst hunting for the person who'd blown up my building. In that meeting, he'd been cordial but professional and Gran had kept her side of the conversation to answering his questions as minimally as possible. At the airport, he'd shown nothing but calm concern for her situation.

He'd made sure to really visibly flash his badge, trying to scare off anyone there to harass Gran. He'd made sure to stare down the couple that Gran thought were there for that purpose (and they'd hustled off, not to be seen again). And, instead of leaving it at that, he'd sat by her until she'd boarded. Not just silently, either. He'd managed to at least come across as friendly and genuinely concerned with her safety.

Gran had taken advantage of the time to tell him stories about me.

When I was very young and very small, some of the bigger boys in the neighborhood were pulling wings and legs off bugs. I have never liked most bugs, but I still wasn't standing for it. I shouted at them to stop, but they laughed and ignored me. So, like a wee ball of fury, I attacked them. I didn't ask my friends to help. I just went for it, shouting at them to stop hurting the bugs. Lecturing, as best I could, about the value of all life, as I tried to beat the shit out of them.

When I was less young, we had to stop watching news because I cried at every story of humans or animals or even the environment being hurt. I pleaded with Gran to help me understand why people did this and why we couldn't stop them.

And so forth.

Story after embarrassing story that showed that, down to my core, I just wanted everyone to live in peace and equality.

Well, maybe not loads of stories. But my embarrassment at the things she'd told him made it feel like she'd surely cornered him for hours, unfolding my every soft spot. And, to his credit, she'd said he'd listened kindly and had seemed to believe her. She'd said he had seemed thoughtful.

And, of course, we couldn't know what went on in his head, but our last check on his files for the original case (the one in which my building was blown up and I had been a suspect) showed that, on that same day he'd sat with Gran, he'd finished a report where he'd made it clear that it was his professional opinion that I was not guilty. He'd urged his superiors to support him in looking for a different answer. And, as far as we could tell at the time, he hadn't revisited my files after that, not even as he continued to work the case.

"So, you went digging into Engalls?" I asked Jonny.

"He didn't try to make you a suspect again after you sent him to the airport, even though he's surely smart enough to at least wonder if you were involved in what happened to SWS HQ. He's basically stopped trying to contact you the last week. Even though he has to wonder if you're the one who handed him the bitch who kidnapped and killed 'Randa. And now, the evening after you lose Gran, he tries you from both his numbers." To his credit, he didn't explain more about his reasons than that, didn't drive his point into the ground. Yep, I got it.

"We didn't really dig before. Should we have? Is he more than just another fascist pig?"

"I don't know that it would have mattered. But there are some items of interest, at least to my eyes. If you want to hear." He hesitated. "I can just write it in an email for later or wait until morning, if you prefer."

I pulled myself up to sitting. "Only if you're tired. I've just had some sleep. And this will help me decide what I'm doing about these calls come morning."

"I think you should return the calls. At least one of them is an official call to...to let you know about your gran." He wrapped his arm around me a little tighter. "Basically, because he'd so recently been on two cases with your name attached—"

I broke in, confused. "Two?"

"The bombing investigation and 'Randa's murder."

"Oh. Right. I was only thinking of the case in which I was considered a suspect."

"Because he'd been lead on those two, and had headed the really brief investigation when a shot was fired at your place—"

"A *warning* shot," I reminded us both scornfully.

"That very shot. Anyway, it looks like the officers who would normally have had the responsibility of contacting you took this to higher ups, having seen your name on the news when SWS was still regularly insisting you were the one who bombed HQ. Their superiors contacted Engalls. The first message they sent him was to check with him and see if he had any read on whether you could or should be contacted, whether maybe they should use this to lure you in."

"The bastards!"

"Seriously. But Engalls reminded them that there was no need to lure you, that you'd officially been cleared of charges and are in no way an active suspect or person of interest in any case. That there was no law against hiding from the world when the press was making your life hell. Then he said that, given you already knew him and had trusted him enough to call when we got the pic of 'Randa, it might be slightly easier to hear the bad news from him than some random other officer."

"Wait, where was this?" I wasn't sure if he'd said yet and my brain had failed to grasp it.

"It was their internal messaging system."

"So, his official line remains that there's no reason for Seattle PD to be trying to get its hands on me?"

"Sure sounds that way." Jonny sounded cautious.

"That's cool." A part of me (a very paranoid part) had been quietly wondering if the public press release saying I was innocent of blowing up my previous SWS office building had all been a scheme. I'm healthy that way...

"Yeah. And weird. Not to cling to stereotypes, but I don't expect anything cool or reasonable from a cop. Which is why I dug a little."

"And did you find that this was some kind of trap? That they assumed we'd be looking at their messages?" My paranoia perked up, ready to "I told you so" at me.

"Not that I can tell. What I *actually* found explains more." He sounded slightly excited.

"Which was?"

"Engalls is divorced. One kid. A daughter who has a Peacemaker in her head because her mom and stepdad had no patience with minor teenage shenanigans or depression."

"Oh...So he might have his own misunderstood girl-child, plus a reason to be really upset over Peacemakers." I liked the possibilities there.

I saw Jonny's nod in my peripheral vision. "That's what I'm thinking. And it was a vI, so, if he's made the guesses he might have made, he might see you as the reason a doctor was able to take that thing out of her."

"Maybe we should hold off telling him about the vII that's probably in there...I feel like it could be useful to have a cop who is...if not on our side, at least not entirely against us." Ugh. Was I a horrible person for suggesting that? For even thinking it?

I didn't wait for him to reply or judge. I asked, "Did you guys get the warning out about not removing the vII until there are updated specs?"

"We did. While you were there."

Enough cobwebs fell out of my brain to confirm that. I sighed at myself. "Right. You did. Then I guess there's nothing else we need to do before morning." I slid back down in the bed, hoping that more sleep would pull me a little farther out of my grief and hate. We still had work to do, and I needed my brain to be fully functional.

I reached out for Jonny, pulled him down with me. I found his mouth with mine, wrapped his legs with mine. Hoping our injuries wouldn't get in the way. Maybe he could bring me a little comfort...or release...or even just distraction after all.

<h1 style="text-align:center">CHAPTER 17</h1>

The next morning, I made sure to lead off with an apology. I entered the break room with, "Sorry I lost my shit yesterday."

Riles gave me a hug and a "perfectly understandable." Bryan waved away the apology and handed me a doughnut. I was grateful they were being so forgiving. I was so heavy with guilt that I wasn't sure I could manage more apologizing or handle them being upset.

I took a deep breath. "Okay, so, what's up today? What can I do?"

Bryan finished what he was doing on his portable and turned to report. "Okay, at this point, we've distributed the new info that the vII isn't safe to remove yet and that the vI might have left behind a vII, so nobody who's had a Peacemaker should assume it's over."

Jonny said, "We've also now released the detector schematics into the wild with an anonymous donation link. Doc and Engie didn't want to delay anyone getting this, and I figured I could just use some of my digital magic to make sure people could throw money their way without them getting caught."

Our own detector sat on the table, probably not moved since Jonny and I returned the afternoon before. I asked, "They're small...Would it make sense to have one for each of us? Just in case?"

Riles pointed at the busy 3D printer. "In progress. Plus we'll keep some in the vehicle so we can distribute. And we're trying to sort out how to make sure that these get into everyone's hands." Zie noted, with an air of mischief, "You know, if all the libraries' 3D printers—and any other 3D printers I could find on networks—suddenly churning them out non-stop since last night doesn't do the job."

I grinned, appreciating zir style. "Nice! But we haven't told people the truth about the cure or Divine Community?" I asked.

Bryan shook his head. "Their reputation is just too sterling. We—"

"Well, shit." Jonny interrupted. He looked up from his screen. "Sorry. But it's...kind of good news."

Everyone else looked like I felt, faces filled with desperation for *something* good. Something that didn't just make this whole thing feel shittier and more tangled.

"Doc and Engie have been beating themselves up since yesterday, going through every Peacemaker schematic with even more care. The problem, where they missed something, seems to be due to labeling." He held up his portable, and we could see two new Peaceforger symbols. "These were small and, as you can see, look almost more like someone testing out a pen. But," he turned the portable back so he could skim the message he'd gotten again, "they now think these are marks that mean something like beta version and release version. So, they found two versions each of the vI and the vII. Which is probably why, for instance, Marleina had an older vI that didn't stop her taking drugs, but Lex's did. And also how they ended up just looking at a schematic for the version of the vII that didn't have a kill switch." He looked up at me with pained eyes. "They feel fucking horrible and can't imagine you'll forgive them."

I chewed the inside of my cheek. I didn't know, for a brief moment, if I *could* forgive them. But then it rose up in me, my hatred for the Peaceforgers. My understanding that all this shit was on them. I asked, "It would have been a very small detail? On the plans? They would have looked at them, side-by-side, and not had a reason to think that they were two different models?"

As if he'd known I'd ask, Jonny had pulled up both specs, and he pushed them to the communal monitor. I got close, and even when Jonny circled where the difference was, I could barely see it.

"Plus, in going through the written specs, where things are described with words, adding the kill switch was a last minute addendum. One line in a memo." Jonny kept his tone and face neutral, like he was giving me permission to feel whatever I needed to feel.

Everyone was looking at me that way, willing to take their cues from me on this one.

I nodded. "Tell them this shit, like everything else, is on the Peaceforgers. Besides," and I sighed, "we sent them so much stuff and they didn't have enough time to go through it all as carefully as they'd have liked. Let's just...let's get past this. Let's get out amended instructions as soon as they find a way to deal with the kill switch."

"On it." And Jonny went back to the conversation on his screen.

After a pause to make sure that that conversation was wrapped up, Bryan opened his mouth to pick up the thread of the conversation we'd been having.

My mobile buzzed, cutting him off again. "It's Lex. Hang on."

Lex was breathless. "I got her!"

"You what now?"

"I motherfucking got Mina!"

It took me a second, brain still shaking off fuzziness. Right, Mina was what Marleina's friends got to call her. "Holy shit. Congrats! How did you manage that?"

"I reconnected with an old friend. We broke in, crept around like badass raiders, found her in the clinic in the basement, like you thought, and got her out." Lex's voice was shot through with elation.

"Wow! That's great. Is she okay?"

"Yeah..."

"Yeah, but?"

"Because of how she'd been, we stole the IV that was in her arm. The dude who helped says it's dripping in the drug that's keeping her under. And we're going to find more or something until we can figure out what to do. Because it seems like the church must have given her something that gave her visions, and I'm worried they're in her head or something."

"Okay. That sounds smart. Um...I want to make sure you've seen some things on the news. It just hit."

"The news? What?" She sounded distracted.

I figured nothing on the news could seem as interesting to her as the fact she'd just gotten Marleina back.

"I need to make sure you're listening and hearing me. Yeah?"

"Yeah. Yes. Listening."

"First, new evidence has come to light. You guys may have had your Peacemaker vI removed, but there's a *really* good chance it planted a vII in your heads. At least yours probably did. Not sure about Marleina's."

"Are you fucking kidding me? No!" She shouted loudly enough that I jerked my mobile momentarily from my ear.

After a moment, I put the mobile back and said, "Sorry. It's true."

"Can we make sure?"

"Do you guys have access to a 3D printer?"

"Yeah."

I made sure Bryan was paying attention. "Okay, at that email you gave me, you're going to get a spec. Feed that into your 3D printer. There are directions along with that."

Bryan typed quickly, then looked at me and nodded.

"Cool. Thank you. So, we confirm that and then we see a doctor?" Lex was definitely giving me her full attention now.

I managed not to cry. "No. At the moment...a doctor discovered that there's an undocumented kill," I tripped on the word, swallowed, tried again, "kill switch. You can't take out a vII, or at least some of them, without...without dying. Not yet. And we don't yet know how to tell which ones you *can* take out. So..."

"Dammit! What are we supposed to do?"

"I'd say that you live carefully, not going anywhere you wouldn't want to be tracked, just in case some hidden SWS team or other group has enough computer left to track you. And you watch for news that the problem has been solved." *And my friends and I thank our lucky fucking stars that we never had you here.* I was just clear enough to know I should think that, not say it. But, yeah, shit, definitely glad we hadn't even had Zane over, one of the few people who was probably safe from having that metal piece of shit in their head.

"Got it. Okay." It sounded like she was going to hang up.

"Quick question."

"Sure."

"What can you tell me about their building?"

"Um...Nothing really stands out. Seemed normal except for the tiny clinic room in one corner."

"What can you tell me about the room?"

"Had five beds and equipment that looked...I guess I'd say like stuff I saw at our mutual doctor friend's clinic. But the only person there was Mina."

"And you guys wore masks? Covered her face as soon as you could?"

"We did. And we aren't staying at our place for now. Just in case. We're...we're hoping that someone will take out Divine Community so we can go home." She cleared her throat. "If you hear about anyone like that and you think they could use help from someone like me...Well, I figure I owe you."

"Oh shit!' Riles sounded distressed. Which was becoming one of our few default emotions.

All heads whipped around to look at zir. Zie looked as distressed as zie sounded.

"You guys, with all this bullshit, we almost forgot that it's Halloween!" Zie looked ready to cry at the near disastrous loss of a chance to celebrate zir favorite holiday.

I barely managed not to laugh. It was so...ridiculous and on brand and normal. I exchanged glances with the guys, and they were apparently also holding back laughs.

Rye didn't notice, just seriously talked to zirself (or maybe it was for us too?) as zie typed. "Okay. We can salvage this. Even if we're trapped here. So." Zie hit a key, and a classic Riley Halloween playlist started playing. Zie looked up at Bryan. "Can you intercept or pick up an order? Just some appropriately themed and colored treats, and some easy costume bits we can wear as we work. Though," and zie sounded Very Serious as zie spoke, "I'm also hoping you understand that a small Halloween party at the end of our work day is necessary."

I had pulled my scarf up to hide my mouth, because I was no longer holding back some serious giggles. This. This was why I loved Riles. This was perfect.

Anything that put Halloween-themed cupcakes in my mouth was a win.

I was trying to work myself up to talking to Engalls. In reality, I wasn't even feeling up to listening to his voicemails yet. Instead, with a liberal coat of black lipstick and a black cat mask adorning my face (Halloween, bitches), I continued my frustrating attempts to acquire more satellites. Mostly, I ignored the news in the background.

"Sorry to interrupt you, Hillary, but we've got some breaking news here. We're going to go ahead and go live to Brad at the interim SWS headquarters." The anchor sounded like he was about to wet himself with excitement.

That got my attention.

The image switched over to Brad, standing in a cluster of reporters, in front of a polished metal podium. Behind the podium, the SWS logo loomed. A simple globe wrapped in the company name, it had become a sinister image for me in the past month or so.

With a too-chummy smile, Brad said, "Sorry to cut you off, Hillary. Can't wait to hear more about the new bridge tolls! But we've just been told..." He got distracted by noise and movement.

CEO Trent was stepping up to the podium, so Brad stopped talking and pointed for the camera to focus on that instead.

Usually, Trent looked dour. He was a man futilely scrambling to save an empire. But not now. He was beaming. Glowing. That couldn't be good for us.

I noticed we'd all stopped working (or stuffing Riley's snacks into our faces) to warily watch whatever this was. Bryan had frozen in the middle of adjusting the rainbow boa (that matched his rainbow striped eyes; Halloween, bitches), and it floated lazily down as he leaned towards the screen.

In a downright jovial tone, Trent said, "It seems you keep doing us the favor of showing up with no real notice. Thank you for doing it once more! Today, I'm thrilled to share amazing news." He took a moment to check on the tablet he held in his hands, then smiled back up at the cameras. "As you all know, SWS have long had a bit of a foot in the medical game. If nothing else, our work to build Peacemakers, to help ensure that you and your loved ones could monitor and maintain your best health, necessitated some pretty intense and illuminating medical research. So, it should be no surprise to you that we have amazing doctors on the payroll. We've always been quite proud of them and considered them the best. And, while we've always viewed that as our way to do our best for *you,* they've now done something incredible for *us.*" He paused, his grin somehow looking uncomfortably triumphant. "As honored as I have felt to be CEO, I hope you'll join me in enthusiastically welcoming back CEO Mary Johnson and COO James Smith."

He clapped vigorously as the cameras swiveled, trying to catch the two executives entering from behind a screen. The reporters lagged a moment, but joined in the clapping.

What. The. Actual. Fuck.

It was them. Looking alive and barely battered.

My hatred rose up, like acid bile inside me. It was joined by a stabbing despair. I choked out, "But we killed those bastards." I looked around, aware there were tears in my eyes. I needed someone in the room to tell me this wasn't real.

Bryan was jumping up to get close to the screen, even as all the cameras zoomed in on the smiling—smugly smiling, I thought—faces of the two execs whose deaths had, it appeared, not been more than a rumor. He softly exclaimed, "Son of a bitch!"

Riles took off zir glittery devil horns headband, as if acknowledging that this was exactly the sort of news that could ruin zir beloved holiday. I saw zir shoot the heavens a sort of "why me?" look, before sulking, "I didn't think I could hate them more. Assholes."

Irrationally, I thought it was as if they knew it had been Gran who'd gotten killed by their piece of shit Peacemaker (which was possible, since every one had its own identifying code), and as if they wanted to pour salt on my wounds. I fucking hated them. I wanted to burn everything. I could barely hear them through the sound of drums in my ears, my own blood beating out marching orders.

CEO Johnson held up her hands, and the clapping petered out. Her smile also faded out, and she addressed the assembled reporters and all of us watching at home. "Thank you. We want to acknowledge our grief that our CFO and friend Jennifer Williams was beyond saving. We also want to note that hiding that we were still alive...The blame for that falls squarely on us. The information was kept from all but our personal doctors the first few days, as they worked to make sure we'd pull through. We thank our loyal employees," she smiled beatifically at now-ex-interim CEO Trent, "for obeying our orders and keeping us a secret. We will happily take all responsibility for that. I can only say that, after what happened, we feared for our lives and wanted to be back on our feet before someone tried, again, to kill us. And, as you can see, we are now ready to stand up both to those who would physically attack us, as well as to those who would attack our reputation."

As the reporters tried to start asking questions, she smiled again and said, "I'm sorry. We won't be taking any questions at this point. We just felt it was time to assure you all that SWS, like us, is still alive and well. As we have always done, COO Smith and I will give our all to help ensure that you have peace through security and security through peace. Thank you."

And, with that, she and her fucking smile exited stage right.

In our break room, all eyes turned to me. My rage and hate must be shining out, because everyone looked Very Concerned.

I clenched my teeth, took a deep breath through my nose (nostrils flaring, because that's anger, right?), and carefully informed them, "I'm going to go 'run' some laps. And beat the shit out of...something."

After I found some shelving that I could demolish, I felt...if not better, at least cold and clear. Like my hate was clean fuel. I felt somehow untouchable, like anything that tried to hurt me would be burned away in that flame. It was time to see what Engalls had said. I felt like the hate would help me survive that now.

Before I got to voicemails, there was a message from Jonny:

SPD dispatched officers to pick up Johnson and Smith. To question them about the Conf Rm Beta deaths and about why they had goth chick and her torture bldg on payroll. Whee?

Okay. That was something. I knew it wouldn't last long (they hadn't lost any lawyers in the explosions), but at least SPD were trying. I was still pure hate, but hate with a wee side of hope that not everything was shite.

The voicemails Engalls had left were really basic. Both almost the exact same phrases, as if he'd had to say similar things too often in the past. "This is Detective Engalls of Seattle PD. I have some bad news and would appreciate a return call." Though, on the call from his mobile, he'd added, "If it helps, in case you didn't see the news, you should know that I determined you weren't a viable suspect for what happened with your building. You've been totally acquitted. You're not in any trouble." I kind of doubted that.

I used a throw-away number and called his mobile. I appreciated his guarded tone when he answered. "Hello?"

"It's Katja."

"Oh, man." I heard relief. "Thank you for calling back."

"Sure. I figure you did me a solid last time I called you, so..."

"I'm sorry that the reason I'm calling today is that...I'm sorry to tell you that your grandmother went to a doctor yesterday due to complications from beat down flu and...I'm afraid she's passed away."

Even knowing that was where he was headed, it was still a blow. It turned out that, in fact, something *could* make it through my cold hate and stab me right in my fucking guts. I exhaled sharply and dropped to the floor. "I...Shit. I mean, crap. Sorry. Language."

"No worries. This is an appropriate time for that. I'm very sorry for your loss. She seemed like a good woman."

"What do I need to do?"

"Well, we didn't have confirmed contact information for you, so I've been asked to verify a number. You'll need to...well, it depends. If she didn't do it already, you'll have to make funeral arrangements. And, because you're next of kin, unless she's directed otherwise in a will, you should expect to be responsible for her belongings. That's all I can tell you from my end." I heard him shift in his chair. "Is this an okay number for someone to contact you about all that?"

I paused. I hadn't thought of that. I didn't know if, in this case, I should be hiding, or if I could take care of my gran's things. But Jonny had said it was okay for me to still exist, so...

He must have taken my pause for worry that this could be a trap, because he lowered his voice, and I could hear him get up from his chair and walk...somewhere. "If you're worried that...that there are any legal dangers for you for...well, for any reason...I know you don't have a reason to believe me, but you are not, to the best of my knowledge, in any way wanted or under investigation or suspicion. Certainly not by us. And the...the other corporation that might disagree, well, you've probably noticed that they don't really seem to be thriving. Kind of in some hot legal water themselves this very moment. And *someone* did a good job of making sure that said corporation no longer has much standing or clout." It sounded like he had walked outside. I could hear rain hitting something and there was a breeze that tossed his words. "If anything, what I suspect you of now is something more likely to get you praise than prison. At least from me. Unofficially."

"That's good to hear." I had a thought. "Detective, whilst I have you...If you got a notification that some well-respected organization was actually really dangerous and up to no good, what should be included in that notification for the SPD to take it seriously and act on it immediately and quietly?"

He chuckled. "Unless we've just gone back in time a few weeks, aren't you asking this question a little late?"

"I wish. But, let's say that someone had the misfortune of finding an even better-respected organization was up to possibly equally devious shit and, before they retired from anything other than just watching TV, they needed to get authorities into action..."

"Seriously?" Engalls sounded totally confused. "I can't decide if it's weirder that certain people would let the law handle a thing or that they found another big thing."

"Mate, some people find skeletons in closets regularly. Especially when it turns out that it's, I don't know, that one skeleton was actually holding hands with the other maybe? Sorry, I was struggling with the metaphor. Anyway...It's just the authorities getting invited to take over that's actually new."

"Okay, well, if this organization is truly well-respected, your theoretical person would want something that was hard evidence. It's no secret that actual law enforcement is less respected than CorpSec officers. So, if a department or office incorrectly or on weak evidence went against some company the public liked, it would be financially devastating and yet another blow to their reputation and ability to get things done. And if you have any information about how whatever authorities your theoretical person contacts could avoid tipping off the organization that it was about to be taken down, so that the org didn't have time to destroy evidence of...whatever their misdeeds are, that would also be good."

"Got it."

"Bonus points if you can help make sure that, just in case there's a trial, you don't ruin possible evidence. And you don't make any of it entrapment. If you obtain something illegally, make sure to tell whoever you contact how they can find it legally. Like which computer and a file path or something, to give a random and theoretical example. Make sense?"

"It does. In such a theoretical situation, would you be a good point of contact, or would you just want to be Bcc-ed on an email to see what's up?"

"Oh, I'm really curious. If I could see the information without anyone being able to find out, I wouldn't say no. But you want to have your theoretical person contact someone higher up than me. And...put on your most suspicious mindset as you look into who you contact. If there's anyone where you get the vibe they might fuck it up over a power grab or fear of public opinion, you're probably right."

"Thank you. And, I never got the chance before, but thank you for getting my gran safely on her plane. I won't forget that."

"One more point of curiosity. A request for truth instead of just thanks." His voice sounded a little less friendly.

Cautiously I replied, "Sure."

"It *was* you then, with your building, wasn't it?"

Ah, no wonder he sounded less friendly. He thought I'd been lying and making a fool of him. "No. Absolutely not me. But that was what got me digging. What changed everything."

He sounded relieved. "Good. Because I'd hate to be wrong about you."

"I'm just saying that, given the kill switch makes it more important that we keep them from even getting the Peacemakers in, *and* that this is one branch of the Peaceforger effort we can take out without tipping our hand and letting them know we know what they are...I vote we annihilate Divine Community." I didn't think anyone was arguing against me. They were just trying to make sure it was me saying things that involved thought, instead of me being driven by pure rage.

"We can even, in our tip off email, say that we were messing around with that Peacemaker detector everyone's printing and we found one in the head of someone who'd had the cure. Or were even playing with it while getting the cure and found it in the shot itself. Something like that, so they have a story to point to about why someone found it or why they suspected," Riles suggested. "Always important to have a story beyond 'because we are mad and paranoid' if we can."

Bryan shrugged. "Sure. Let's chip away at them. Try to limit our problem."

Jonny nodded. "Yeah. Let's do it."

Which is why we were quietly working on our Divine Community take down instead of the stuff we'd been doing before. And our to-do list was pretty basic. Make an email list of the right people to send our info to, make sure that we had docs that didn't need our narration to make them see the situation, toss in the Peacemaker detector specs in case they'd missed that bit of news, and send the email. No running around, no bombs, just computers. Let actual law enforcement handle this. Simple enough, if they could be convinced to move, to confirm the vII in the cure and in the heads of the cured now that the detector existed. Easy.

Because we'd already done most the work on the documents from Divine Community, Riles was finishing that solo, and the rest of us were making sure our list of people to send to was solid. The hardest part was having to pause occasionally to consult and decide whether or not someone ought to get the email. Again, not actually hard. Easy.

And then Rye shouted, "Oh fuck!" and quickly popped zir battery and power cord from zir portable without shutting it down first. That was always a really bad sign, so all eyes were wide and on zir.

"Riley?" I let zir name stand in for all the questions that suddenly crowded the air.

As zie replied, zie was connecting a spare burner mobile to zir laptop. I knew what was going on before zie said it. "It appears that, probably due to paranoia after Lex freed her friend, someone decided to attach a virus to the list of people with vIIs in their heads. The one and only doc that they had that was actually on a drive we were getting to without," zie waved zir hand about, like doing magic, "luckily being looking at the right computer just when they plugged in an external drive. And the only doc that I was grabbing one last, most updated copy of. Just in case there was some name on there that would be important to hook in one of our email recipients."

"Fuck." Jonny was on his feet, as if he was looking for some action to take. "What can we do to help?"

"And how the hell did they get a virus past you?" asked Bryan.

"They must have woken up some hacker prodigy of their own, because it was a tricky bit of code. If I weren't used to watching for shit like that, I'd be more worried. But," and zie booted zir portable to a safe mode, navigating it via zir mobile, "I think I was quick enough to prevent real damage. If one of you can check the shared drive, I'll clean the shit from my machine."

"I'm already on it," my fingers raced over the keys. And then I stopped still.

"Dammit, what is it?" Jonny, quick to pick up on my body language, sounded like a man on the edge of despair.

"You will want to confirm on your own portables, but the good news is that, thanks to our habit of partitioning and keeping everything in discrete chunks, only the particular shared location that had our Divine Community files seems to have been impacted." My fingers flew as I finished confirming my portable was fine and I sent a little code of my own out to check on the health of other remote locations.

"The bad news," and I cringed as I said it, "is that their little nasty appears to have devoured *all* of those files. All the Divine Community stuff we have is gone." I turned to face them. Their jaws were tight with frustration, eyes narrowed in anger. "We're going to have to find them again somehow."

I would never, ever again jinx us by thinking something would be easy. Fuck.

After that...let's call it a setback but acknowledge that "setback" is a damned weak word for what had happened, we shifted the work balance. Jonny took over finishing the list of email recipients, and the rest of us set about trying to figure out how to get our hands on the evidence we needed. Again.

I headed straight for Shepherd Michaelson's email, where I quickly found the message that shut down our current approach. "You guys probably want to hear this email that Michaelson sent very early this morning before you waste any more time."

"Oh, for fuck's sake," Bryan glared. "What now?"

I read the email aloud:

Please drop by my office ASAP. After last night's incident, we need to make sure all relevant materials—including documents—are kept at the plant. Let's make sure we both agree on the steps and make it happen *immediately*.

I looked up. "So, we need to figure out where 'the plant' is before we waste more time digging anywhere else." I hopefully added, "Unless one of you is already in the plant?"

"Yeah, I started searching as soon as you said 'the plant,' and..." Riley turned to face us, looking pretty annoyed. "Remember how this was going to be an old school, purely digital mission?"

"If you say we have to break into somewhere," I was warning and pleading, "I will put a fucking bullet in my head. Come *on!*" I directed that last bit towards the ceiling and the higher power who, if they existed, clearly didn't much like me.

"Unless there's another plant, this is the location where they've been manufacturing the cure. It looks like..." zie examined whatever was on zir screen, "the location used to be part of the Divine Community network, but all machines there were cut off from 'Net access..." zie sighed. "Of fucking course." Zie looked at us with a face full of annoyance. "They took them off 'Net access the day after *someone* blew up the SWS HQ."

Bryan exclaimed, "Dammit!" and bolted from his chair, as if his fight or flight instinct had kicked in and directed him towards fight. He was breathing heavily, fists curling and uncurling. "This is like some never-ending shit show." He growled as he turned to punch a wall. If we didn't get him a break from wall punch-inducing news and stress and living on the run, he was going to become nothing more than a trope. (At least he was managing his mounting frustration by punching walls, not people, right?)

I didn't bother to react. I could have said the same things, but my tone would have been pure despondence. I didn't expect or need an easy life, but this new trend of problems that required us to take exceptional action in the meat, not just online, was too much.

I looked over to see that Jonny had stopped working and was just looking straight ahead, nostrils flaring and mouth set in an angry line. He'd taken off the silly headband with boppers that were supposed to look like alien antennae, and I could see him carefully not breaking the cheap plastic as he clenched and unclenched his fists.

"Okay." Jonny's voice was low and even. "I suggest one of you dig up info on the location in case..." He gave me an apologetic look. "In case we have no choice but to go in." He lifted his hands as if asking me to let him finish. "But I also think that the other two of you should see what you can find in the SWS files. Because there were two parties involved in this bullshit scheme."

It was a ray of hope! We'd been so focused on finding *Divine Community* files that we'd forgotten that SWS involvement meant we had more we could look through for info. We had all their files, and we knew that at least one should be a memo to Divine Community; we'd seen that memo already in the now-deleted Divine Community stash.

Bryan returned to his portable. "I should probably be the one to look into the plant and options for that. You two," and he pointed a finger at Riles and another at me, "search SWS. Yeah?"

CHAPTER 18

I had thought (hoped) I was done with the files from Secure World Systems. Going back into them now felt like failure, even though we'd kind of mostly achieved what we intended in terms of taking them down.

Rye was searching the files for obvious things, using variations on "Divine Community" as zir search string. None of us recalled seeing the church mentioned back when we were all about these files, but that was back when we had no reason to pay attention to the church. The files could be full of meaty stuff and we wouldn't necessarily have found it significant.

Fortunately, Riles and I were the ones who'd spent the most time in the files once Jonny brought us in on the situation, which meant we weren't just bumbling around. It was, however, nice to do this with all the files on a drive we owned instead of trying to sneak around the SWS servers. It let us do a little sorting and tagging of our own to make any future searches (please, spare us future searches) easier.

The tag I was adding now, as I dove in, was just to indicate to myself that I'd been in the files before. I also added a tag to the folders they'd named Trash that totally weren't. I'd get back to them. It's not that I knew these weren't useful (they'd been super useful in planning and prepping for demo day), but I'd seen some things flash by, back when I'd been doing a panicked mass download of their files the day we blew the SWS HQ. I knew there were files we had missed (or, rather, not gotten to...SWS had a *lot* of files), and I wanted to find those first.

Sporadically since our attack on HQ, in spare minutes or when I needed a quick break, I'd been building a digital keypad and list (that I hoped would become a glossary) with what symbols we had—thanks to photos and the edges of a few SWS documents—from the Peaceforger language. I didn't know if they were more like what we'd consider words or more like letters, but they were all I had.

I'd seen at least one file named with Peaceforger characters in that download, so I figured finding that file location would be a good bet for finding other files I hadn't seen before. I tried searching on one character at a time, slow going, keeping an eye on our TV as I worked. If I had to compare the pace of how beat down flu was spreading (according to the news) to the pace at which we were getting results, beat down flu would be winning. Riley found the memo we'd seen before, but that was it for a while. At least for us.

The remote comrades were starting to report in on other orgs to which SWS had made donations. So far, it seemed we'd gotten lucky. It seemed they were all...if not clean, at least not obviously secretly involved in yet another plot to spread the vIIs. Cool. We could keep our focus on the church.

I rubbed my temples. "What would you lot think about asking Zane for translation help?"

"Like, give them a list of symbols to translate so we can apply that to all our docs?" Riles asked.

"If we're lucky. If it's not a language where the meaning changes dramatically based on the other symbols around each symbol," I noted.

Bryan looked up from his work. "Do you have a document you need done?"

Waving at my screen, I said, "I've got no results for all my searching, but I do have a folder full of docs in their script. Plus, all the bits we keep finding on other docs. And I don't know if the folder is in their script because it's, I don't know, someone's journal, or if it's because they want to make sure no admin accidentally stumbles across their partnership with the church."

"We should ask," Jonny said. "And prep for showing them single symbols and groups of symbols."

"I'll see if Zane's up for it." Bryan reached for his phone.

"I don't know. This seems like it could take a while. You better plan to take an overnight bag." Riley kept zir tone aimed more towards innuendo than towards teasing. But only slightly more.

"Sorry, Rye, did you have some thoughts on this?" Bry grinned. "Maybe Zane said something about me the other night? Or was it all just nothing-to-do-with-me sex talk?" He capped his question with a cheeky wink.

"They did not. But, if you wanted to see Zane again, I'm sure they'd be into it." Rye was doing a pretty shabby job playing cool.

Amused, Bryan asked, "Is there something I should know about?"

"I don't know. Um...Do you guys think Peaceforgers are attractive?"

It was an unexpected question, but I had a relevant reply coming out of my mouth before I thought about it. "Ugh. Riles, that's kind of...specist, implying they all look the same. That's like asking if someone likes guys or women of a specific race. Shame!" Before zie could reply, because zir blushing face was enough to let me know zie got my point, I said, "But, to answer your question, at least for myself, I think that *some* Peaceforgers are attractive, or could be, even without all the human costumes. However," I grinned, "I suspect that my answer isn't the one you *actually* care about." I would have nudged Bryan with my elbow, but I had zero idea what he might be thinking.

To my surprise, Bryan kind of stammered. Very un-Bryan. "Well, I...I don't know. I mean...I mean, you know that my attraction is person-specific. So, sure, I could be attracted to a Peaceforger. Sure."

With feigned innocence and wide eyes (something he'd probably picked up from Rye), Jonny asked, "Golly, could that include Zane?"

Bryan coughed and stared at his portable.

"Riles, you're doing a shit job of...well, you're either trying to play matchmaker or Zane already mentioned they're interested in Bryan." I tried to stare Riles down, psychically willing zir to tell me which it was.

But, with painfully playacted attention to zir portable, zie said, "I'm just making small talk while we work. However! If we did want to ask Zane, I could open a secure chat with them right now."

I put a hand on Bryan's shoulder. "I swear this is not me trying to push you one way or another. I fully respect your right to be interested in—or not interested in—anyone you want." I fixed Rye with a look. "I also believe that Riles can do a better job at playing it cool and that zie won't forget to put your interests before Zane's." I waited until zie nodded solemnly. "But I would sincerely love to get help from Zane with some of these SWS docs. Maybe they could translate enough to know if it's important. Maybe build us a dictionary from all the Peaceforger characters we can find. Randomized, of course, so they can't make anything of it."

Bryan kept his eyes fixed on footage on our shared monitor of what *appeared* to be Shepherd Michaelson running a glowing hand over blind eyes, restoring lost sight, but said, "I think Zane could definitely be useful. And, as far as I can tell from keeping an eye on their computer and comings and goings at their flat, they're probably at least a little trustworthy. And..." He sighed, but the edge of his mouth lifted the slightest bit, a smile that wanted out. "I'm with Katja on this. Some Peaceforgers are definitely attractive. But I'd probably want to know them better and take it slowly, because we aren't exactly in settled lives. And, horrible as it sounds, I wouldn't want some kind of relationship tiff to interfere with our one inside person."

The slight bouncing out of the corner of my eyes was a sign of a happy Riles. "Cool. Got it. So, with no ulterior motives or suggestive phrases, what about bringing Zane over ASAP to help?"

"Here?" Jonny looked surprised.

"I was just thinking how much easier it would be, for once. Unless Bryan wants the excuse to go over to their place alone. In which case, we'll make it work. I'm just...Can we go faster and be done soon, please?" Riles just managed to not whine.

Jonny asked Bryan, "You trust them?"

Bryan considered the question, rubbing his head thoughtfully. "At this point, I agree that it would be easier to bring them here. And it's been enough days, over a week. They could have captured us all easily by now if they wanted. If they're waiting to get us, I don't know *why* they're waiting."

"And you like them," I added.

"I might just." Then Bryan's eyes lit up. "Oh! Plus, if your intuition said they were bad news, you'd have said something already, right?"

I nodded.

"So, there you go. I'm with Riles on this. As long as you two are too." Bryan raised his eyebrows, a question for me and Jonny.

"Okay. You're right about my intuition. I'm fine with it," I agreed.

"Sure. I guess it's okay then," Jonny said.

"Alright. I'll ask Zane over. For translations." Bryan smirked a little, shaking his head. He was much too sensible for matchmaking silliness, obviously.

To Rye's credit, zie didn't exactly squeal.

Just like you'd expect based on their name, Will File was one of those digital repositories of official wills. When someone died, Will File was one of the parties notified. If the deceased had bothered to file their will with Will File, the company reached out to appropriate parties to set things in motion. A very sweet representative called me as Bryan was heading out to pick up Zane.

It started a little rough, because one of the first things he had to do was try to pronounce her legal name. Niamh Oonagh O'Shiel isn't exactly an average American name.

"I'm calling on behalf of..." I could hear in the pause that he'd read Gran's name in advance, maybe even gone on the 'Net to see how to pronounce it, maybe practiced it. But now that he had to say it out loud to someone who loved this woman and who probably knew how to pronounce it, he wasn't sure. And he was mortified.

A mean part of me considered delighting in his discomfort, but I'd been working to be better, so I did what I'd often heard Gran do. Kindly, I said, "It's '*nee*-uv,' kind of run together so it almost sounds like one syllable. But you can just call her Neve. Like that old actress Neve Campbell." I tried to use a reassuring tone, because I'd never seen Gran want anyone to feel bad about this. "She always told people that was close enough."

He thanked me and apologized and got back to doing his thing. It was a short, kind conversation, in which he confirmed that I was the person in Gran's will and that he had accurate contact information to digitally send me the will and information for finalizing things with one of their lawyers.

He sent it all immediately after we hung up, and I curled on my mattress to read the will. It was very simple. Gran had even already taken care of her "burial" arrangements, and the only thing she wanted me to do, per the letter included with her will, was to spend a night *happily* reminiscing about her with Bryan and Riles. She listed a few friends that she wanted me to send brief notes to, but she really didn't like the idea of me sobbing with a room full of strangers, staring at her corpse. Not that there would be a corpse. She'd made sure she had enough life insurance that she could pay to have her ashes delivered to space by one of the companies that did such things. Classic!

Burial arrangements aside, Gran had carefully made sure there were no debts to pay. Not even the house. But that might have had something to do with me changing her mortgage files on the bank computers...And the house, along with everything else, was mine. If we could live normal lives, we could live there—or Jonny and I could; I wasn't going to live with everyone—in the house in which I'd grown up. Surrounded by all the things I'd loved. (And hopefully some of my own abandoned things, if my flat hadn't been looted.) Aided by a little remaining life insurance that, even ignoring the secret accounts I'd already built with my illegal exploits online, was a pretty nice cushion.

I wept.

And it wasn't the bitter or angry tears from before. No raging. Just love for the amazing woman who, even in dying, gave me everything she had. And, in dying, saved the life of whoever would, otherwise, have been the first to have a vII removed. Maybe more than one person, since others might not have gotten the word out like we did. Or have figured out the cause was a kill switch like our people had. She was as close to a saint as I'd ever known.

I curled into a ball on my mattress, soaking my pillow with tears.

I must have fallen asleep, because I went from weeping to being gently shaken awake by Jonny. That seemed to be happening regularly now.

"Hey, pretty, Bryan's back with Zane. You want to come make use of Zane's brain or not yet?"

I stretched and considered. "I guess I should at least get working on my list of Peaceforger symbols for them to go through."

He flipped on the lights and sat down by me as I sat up. "Riles and I started working on that when we realized you might not be heading back in soon. We wanted to make sure that we made best use of Zane's time."

"Yeah, but did you guys see the documents that were all in those symbols that I had just been digging out?"

"Ah. No. No we didn't. But we *did* build a little program you can use to scan them and add the symbols, randomized, to the list. If you think that might be useful." His tone told me he already knew the answer to that.

I leaned against him. "You guys are pretty okay."

"We really are. And how are you?"

"I'm...I'm okay-ish." I sighed. "My heart is broken, but I feel less...nasty." I considered my toes. "She left me everything. And she's having her ashes sent into space."

"Wow. That's cool. Two different kinds of cool." I could tell he was struggling to sound pleased and impressed but suitably restrained, given the situation.

"We should make sure the house is okay. Because I...I think I might want to live there. If we get to stay in Seattle and not permanently on the run." For some reason, I mentally braced, expecting an argument.

"Okay." No argument in his voice, no hesitation.

I quietly exhaled in relief. "Thanks." And then I stood at last. "Let's go get those new docs into the list for Zane. And see if we can detect any flirting."

"I'm pretty sure that Bryan was coming across a little shy when they got back." Jonny grinned. "It was pretty fucking lovely to see. Makes me hope his heart will heal from losing 'Randa sooner rather than later. At least enough to try to be happy again."

We shut up as we walked into the break room. No need to make anyone feel awkward.

Riles noticed us in the doorway and gave me a wink. "Ready to get back to it?"

"Aye." I nodded. "I've got some things to add to your list. Plus, we should do word groups." I pulled up the directory I'd found, finally, with the many docs all in Peaceforger symbols and leaned back to let Jonny set the code running on them.

"N0cebro said something about me translating a list of characters?" Zane focused in on the three of us at my portable.

Why did I keep forgetting we'd only told Zane those douchebags' 'nyms instead of our own? Even if we'd told them our actual 'nyms, it would have been weird. We'd never had a situation where someone we knew in person only knew us by our 'nyms. (And I suddenly realized, given how often my face had been on the news, that Zane was just being polite when they didn't use my real name.)

Ever a fan of love (or lust), Rye said, "We're just finishing pulling it together. I'm afraid n0cebro will have to entertain you for a few minutes."

Zane definitely blushed blue at that. But it was slight and quick, and I don't think Bryan saw it.

He certainly sounded like he didn't know Zane liked him as he awkwardly suggested, "We can kill time seeing how much of my music collection you hate."

"Hang on." My head was clearing up from the sleep and emotional haze. "I did have a question."

Bryan and Zane both looked a little disappointed to be delayed, but whatever.

"Of course," Zane said, tone totally belying the clear desire to go huddle up with Bryan.

"Did you know that Johnson and Smith, the SWS execs, were still alive?" I didn't mean to come off as suspicious, but who knows how it sounded.

Zane shook their head. "I think a cliché like 'above my pay grade' or 'I don't have clearance' is my best explanation. And I don't think much of anyone knew, based on how many people were using them as, you know, saints to drive us on in our 'holy' task."

I considered that. "So, someone decided it was more important to have them be out, being the faces of SWS, than to have them be inspirational saints?"

"I suppose so. Though, uh, they're still being seen as saints in a way. People are saying—and it's all just rumors—that they really were basically dead, and only by the Light of the Divine were they saved to finish leading the effort to bring the Earth to peace." Embarrassed, they said, "They're now something like saints *and* heroic leaders. And I suspect the hope is that their hunger for revenge on behalf of Williams will drive them."

"And have you heard about what that revenge will look like?" *Sorry to harass your date, Bryan*, I thought.

"All I'm hearing is that it's a miracle and that they're now just working hard to try to save their company from ruin."

I couldn't think of more questions, so, after a second, I just nodded and turned back to my work.

As soon as they were distracted by Bryan's music, I whispered, "It doesn't take three of us to prep the word list, does it?"

"Of course not," Rye confirmed. "But it *definitely* doesn't take a single one of the three of us to help Bryan decide how cool Zane is."

"I'm really just fine with an excuse to do nothing for a moment," confessed Jonny. "I finished my list of email recipients for the Divine Community stuff, and that means that we're all now just on the hunt for proof in the SWS files."

"My concern with that, now that I've had a nap," I said, "is that these are files they, the authorities, won't be able to confirm came from SWS servers. We're on less firm ground. And that's if we find anything more than that one memo that we can actually use."

"You know I'm as loath as you to take any actions in the meat, but I'm worried this won't be enough." Rye leaned in so that there was no chance Zane could overhear zir. "The problem is that we only have the one document from SWS to Divine Community. Anything on the SWS side appears to be...well, must be using a codename or something. And I haven't found anything to let me know what that is, much less to convince someone else that's the case."

Glumly, I added, "And even if the docs Zane's translations help us read are blatant and clear, we still have to convince the authorities that the translations are correct. So, those are no good either." I slumped in my chair. "Fuck."

"If it helps," offered Jonny, "I'm only grudgingly willing to do non-computer stuff. And only because I feel like we have to. I'm not at all happy that it seems like, once fucking again, we might be stuck getting physically involved."

If only our unhappiness actually seemed to fucking matter...

Whilst their program built the word list, Jonny and Riles watched me do something I hadn't considered doing before. Why would I hack my flat, the one I'd abandoned? Not until Jonny said I might be able to stay myself had I thought about it as anything more than a fond memory. Suddenly, I was okay with having forgotten to stop my autopay on my rent. Because maybe my stuff was still safe.

We'd had to wipe the system there, but that didn't mean I couldn't still get myself in. Build enough new code in the old drives that I could confirm they were still there and still empty. That I could...Well, I couldn't confirm my door was locked. Someone would have had to activate my digital lock for the sensors to tell me that. But, thanks to my own cameras and sensors that Bryan had installed, I could check out plenty.

I could tell that all doors and windows were closed. I could see that, by some miracle, there was no obvious damage or theft. I mean, maybe some investigating officer or nosey landlord had picked up something small...But nothing *obvious*. I used my old controls, glad for the time I'd put into building my home system (and making sure that nobody but me was likely to be able to access it), to turn on all lights as bright as possible. To get a good look.

Riles pointed at the screen, whispering excitedly, "Zoom in! I think your door is locked."

"Can you rebuild the code and engage your digital lock?" Jonny asked in a similarly quiet voice.

I nodded. Yeah. Yeah, actually, I could. I didn't know that I would or could live here again, but there was now hope that I could rescue the pieces. Dig in and even extract my old home controls and system pieces, the ones I'd added. Make Gran's old house a little cooler and safer using pieces from mine.

It was just stuff, but, damn, it put a glow in me that it was still there. It was still mine. I'd have preferred all our people make it through, if I'd had a choice of prizes in this fight, but I wasn't in a state where turning down the consolation prize made sense.

Before I moved back from securing my old flat to working on the whole alien mess, I hacked into Dr. Scott's office. I didn't know when I could handle being there again, and I didn't want anyone else at risk whilst I was short on time and emotional capacity. Because, whilst I'm a badass, it was clear that someone less badass could have hacked her.

I took a look at machine logs and confirmed what I already had reason to believe, that my Gran's death couldn't be blamed on someone hacking Scott's equipment. So, there was that.

Then I set up the most kick-ass firewall and security I could manage for her. I left Scott a (digital) note, letting her know what I'd done, and why I'd done it the shitty way (hacking her) instead of showing up in person. I hoped she'd forgive me. But, mostly, I hoped she'd be able to take out loads of Peacemakers soon, with no fear of interference.

As the day wore on, Zane was still busy helping affix meanings to the Peaceforger characters we had in our list (I was super pleased that they could do single characters and didn't need whole phrases), whilst Bryan continued to hunt down information on "the plant." We other three kept at the slog through SWS files, with little luck.

Mindful of our limited trust for Zane, we were forced to communicate things about our tasks via a chat window. Mostly, it was unimportant bitching about failure or Riles sharing something funny Kitty had messaged zir. But we also had conversations like:

> Jonny: I think we need to regroup.
> Bryan: ??
> Jonny: We're just spinning our wheels on…so many topics, dude. It's not great for us to keep doing that.
> Riley: I am feeling kinda perma-shitty from also seeming to be perma-fail-y.
> Katja: Same
> Bryan: Ok. Maybe we make it through another 24 hours or so of trying this, and we try to work out what the hell we're doing tomorrow evening?

Nobody typed a reply, just looked at each other and nodded. It probably wouldn't be a fun conversation, but we had to do something about the current situation (aka the lack of any real success).

The cherry on top of this shit sundae came from Bryan, who'd apparently been researching bits because Zane didn't actually need his help to just put shit on a list.

> Bryan: The plant isn't documented anywhere at all other than its address. Nothing. Nowhere. Cameras near its location and the street view on the map app show nothing. Big brick block, really small grimy windows up high, metal doors. Nothing useful about who comes and goes. NOTHING. Dammit. I think we're going to have to go in and go in *blind*. Fuuuuuuuu!

"Alright." I stood up, closing my portable. I was pretty fucking done for the moment. Time to switch gears. "Listen up, assholes, my gran only made one request of us in her will, and tonight's the night." I went to where we had a stash of alcohol and started pulling out drinks. "She wanted us to spend a night *happily* reminiscing about her. And, as long as it doesn't ruin anyone's Halloween plans, that's what we're going to fucking do. And I plan to do it whilst consuming a sizable portion of this stash." I faced them. "No real names (sorry, Zane) and no sad stories. Those are the rules." I stood with hands on my hips, not sure whether they'd protest.

"Oh, *hell* yes." Riles closed zir portable. "I'm done spinning my wheels for the day. And having a party for the recently dearly departed seems like totally appropriate Halloween action." Zie grabbed some crisps from our food stash and put them in a pile by the drinks. "Don't want to do this on an empty stomach."

Bryan looked at Zane and suggested, "I could drop you near home if you want to escape the impending wake."

"The wake?" Zane looked confused.

Jonny put a gentle, protective arm around me. "Her grandmother just died due to...complications from some Peaceforger schemes."

"Oh." Zane flushed blue, from what looked like shame, not shyness. They awkwardly offered me, "I'm sorry beyond words. I don't..." They swallowed and looked at all of us, down at the portable they were working on, and said, "I'm almost done with this. I'd like to finish so you can use it. I'm okay to be here. If that's actually okay."

With an astonishing lack of innuendo in zir tone, Riles warned, "You might get stuck here overnight due to people being too drunk to drive you home and us not being ready for you to know where this is."

I almost laughed at the awkwardness as Zane and Bryan tried to nonchalantly turn their faces from each other. One face with a slight red flush, another with a similar blue flush.

Zane managed to sound normal as they said, "That's okay with me. If it's okay with you."

A bit too quickly, Bryan closed his portable and said, "It's okay." He looked at me. "Yeah?"

I hadn't seen him like this since...since he'd first met 'Randa. Bryan interested but not yet involved was not the confident and solid person he was the rest of the time. I was just pleased to see this sign of healing. After 'Randa's shocking murder, I'd wondered if he'd keep himself apart to keep himself (or the people he liked) safe. Yay for that not happening! So I nodded. Sure. I was working hard to remember that Zane wasn't responsible for what others of their species did.

Jonny didn't bother to say anything, just closed his portable and squeezed me tighter.

It seemed like mere minutes later that we were all drunk (or the humans were...I had no clue about inebriation and Peaceforgers) and roaring with laughter over tales of Gran at her finest. Bryan and Zane had completely randomly (riiiight...) ended up sitting side-by-side on his mattress, with the other three of us on Rye's mattress. The crisps were gone and the alcohol was dwindling. I was going to feel like shit in the morning, but this had been the right answer. I dozed off with Jonny leaning on my right side and Riles on my left. As my eyes closed, I was pretty sure I saw a first, tentative kiss between Bryan and Zane. *Gran would be pleased that her wake led to that*, I thought, and settled into fuzzy darkness.

CHAPTER 19

The next day dawned groggy and hellish. Which is to say that hangovers were all the rage...Or raging in us all? Welcome to another glorious day, worker bees!

Fortunately, it meant that nobody was actually annoyingly cheerful or loud or really moving much at all. (Go fuck yourself, well-wishing types. That shit is too bright for me.) Those of us on Rye's mattress quietly noted that, on Bryan's mattress, there had been kissing but, as far as we could tell, nothing more. On that mattress, Bryan and Zane were softly talking and smiling at each with dopey eyes.

Bryan got up quietly, grabbing bottles of water. He tiptoed over to hand us some bottles. "Hey. You guys feel like ass too?" His smile didn't look very ass-feeling-like to me.

"I wish I'd meant it the last time I swore I'd never drink again," moaned Jonny.

I couldn't keep my curiosity at bay. "Hey, lover boy, did Zane get drunk too?"

"Yeah. Apparently, plant-based things from Earth metabolize for them much like for us. It's animal products that make them feel unwell. So, for all intents and purposes, they're extraterrestrial vegans. And alcohol works for them."

Rye shook zir head in exaggerated disgust. "*That's* what you're asking about? Have you learned nothing from me?"

"Let me stop you there," Bryan laughed. "There was a kiss. One. And it was nice. But there are not currently any salacious details for you, nosy. Or reasons for me to apply your dirty mindset to my life." He turned to go with a wink.

"I hate to delay you from your mattress, but..." Jonny waited for Bryan to come back so he could speak quietly. "Am I right that we're dead-ended, or nearly so, and today is still about deciding what's next?"

"Yeah, anything other than the discussion about how far we're taking things in the meat?" I asked.

"Actually," Rye spoke up (quietly), "I have one more thing. Well, aside from also talking about next steps with this church mess. I think we should take advantage of the Dia de Muertos night street crowds and occasional people in cultural appropriation-y masks and makeup to do a walk-by on the plant. Maybe drop off one of Jonny's bugs? If any made it out with us."

We all nodded. It was a good idea. No matter that it annoyed the hell out of me that, in the spirit of finding any excuse to drink too much, people had stolen the "fun" bits from other cultures' holidays to extend their own carnival of bullshit. No matter that I'd spent my life loving the aesthetic but playing it safe by never using it as an excuse to join the crowds...Ugh.

Bryan suggested, "Let's get ourselves together, combine dropping off Zane with looking like the other assholes and walking by the plant before the sun sets and we lose the light, and then come back for plans and arguments."

"And I do have a bug. I think. I should. I'll check and bring it if I do," Jonny said.

"I don't want to make you waste time you could spend with Zane, so," Riles hooked zir arm through mine, "I volunteer Kot and I to 3D print masks and cover them with glitter."

"You stocked up on glitter?" Bryan sounded incredulous.

I snorted. "Duh. We aren't uncivilized drones! Do you even *know* us?" I laughed.

Riles joined me. "Come on, Bry. Being on the run is no excuse for being bland. As if."

Laughing was hurting my head, but I couldn't resist a bit of silliness.

"Yeah, yeah. Fair enough. I guess I *shouldn't* be surprised. Not with you two. Just...keep it on the down-low; make sure Zane doesn't see what you're making." He turned towards his mattress again, saying, "Now, I'm going to deliver some water and pretend I'm just as awesome sober."

Bryan grabbed me, briefly, when Zane was in the loo. "Am I an asshole?"

He seemed so serious that I didn't even pretend to consider it for comic effect. "Of course not. Why?"

"I kissed Zane."

"Yeah?" I was trying to figure out if he maybe thought he was hurting Riles by doing that. Hadn't he and Riles made it clear that anything between them recently was just comfort?

"I just...It's only been two weeks." He was forlorn.

I had to think a moment; the hangover was doing its best to slow down my brain. Two weeks? Oh. 'Randa.

I put my hand on his cheek. "You are not an asshole. If you don't feel good about doing something, then don't. But if you've been lucky enough to meet someone you like before you have a chance to decide to be alone forever? Go for it. Whether you're just looking for snogging or...more. You're not doing anything wrong." I didn't bother to remind him that, also, when she was alive and they were definitely together and theoretically monogamous, 'Randa flirted shamelessly—and perhaps more than was innocent—with all sorts of people.

He was searching my eyes like he was looking for some sign I was just being nice. Fortunately, there's rarely any chance of someone seeing that in *my* eyes. Heh!

Finally, he nodded. "Thanks, Kot." He took a deep breath and seemed to...if not let go, at least put some distance between himself and the guilt he'd been feeling.

"Anytime. Fuck knows the lot of us are carrying too much guilt these days. I'm not going to let you carry unnecessary extras."

Our little field trip was not spectacular. We started by driving in meandering circles to make sure the blindfolded Zane would have a hard time figuring out where they'd been. We finally pulled over in an alley somewhat near the plant, where Bryan kissed Zane goodbye. Once they were out of sight, instead of our g/ap masks, we put on the painted skull masks (that made me feel dirty, even though I knew our intent was disguise and not cultural appropriation, and let us blend with all the rest of the skull-faced crowd) and a little bit of a drunken stagger, like we'd gotten an early start on our Dia de Muertos celebrating.

As humans are wont to do, the people of Seattle were out in patchy but growing crowds, taking advantage of an excuse for drink and partying. We were neither the least dignified nor most drunk looking group. Excellent.

There was only so much we could do without feeling like we were conspicuous. And, unfortunately, there was nothing interesting about the building that we thought was the plant, nothing that would justify needing a picture or paying attention. Even in person, it remained just a block of bricks with metal doors.

In the end, we settled for Jonny faking a stumble to cover dropping one little bug, a tiny remote-controlled bit of metal that would be hard to see after the sun finished setting. For now, we hoped it would look like trash for the seconds it took Jonny to walk it, using his mobile, into a shadow and out of the way. I then pretended to realize I'd forgotten my mobile in the vehicle (just in case anyone was paying attention to us), and we all staggered back.

Whilst we drove back to our warehouse, Jonny aimed his bug towards a vent. It was grabbing video, and we hoped it could see enough to make things suck less when (if...*if*, dammit) we broke in. Until Jonny groaned.

"Well, this is more proof they worked with SWS." He showed me his screen. "When SWS installed mesh over all openings to make sure I didn't get more bugs into their buildings, looks like Divine Community gave this building the same treatment." His voice was heavy with disappointment. "I'm sorry, guys. I think we're going to be stuck going in blind."

Riley and I slowed down our return to the warehouse, and agreeing to difficult plans of action, by insisting we needed groceries. And a warm meal, even if it was just grabbed from a drive-through. And it wouldn't hurt to bulk up our first aid kit, given the way things looked. And bleach to remove traces of us from the warehouse if and when (and for whatever reason) we finally left for...well, whatever destination. And...Bryan didn't call us on it, but he looked a little relieved when we ran out of errands.

Back in our current HQ, no one really talked as we put away purchases, checked messages, ate dinner. I think none of us were eager to have the expected conversation. And, for my part, I was worried that there was no way out of this that I wouldn't hate.

I'd said I would stay until we handed off the Peaceforger info, passed on the job of physical fighting to the military or cops or whatever. I'd said I was in for taking down the church, which we'd also specified we'd do by purely digital means. No physical shit. And, though I was working hard to make sure my mind and heart were still aimed at doing my part to fix things, I *wanted* to leave. I *wanted* to be done and let the rest of humanity just deal with it; I wasn't sure most of us deserved to be saved. I *wanted* to cut off my losses and my guilt; both had already been too big. I was not feeling my most cooperative or heroic.

But I also wanted to be a good person. I wanted to be like the heroes I'd grown up watching and reading, willing to give whatever it took to save their people. I wanted Gran to be proud of me. Not that she was around to be proud...Which also led to the fact that I wanted some revenge for Gran. I'd heard, from those same heroes of my youth, that revenge wasn't actually satisfying 99.9% of the time, that it was just as likely to make me feel shittier. But there was no denying that my desire for revenge coated all my intentions. My desire to burn the fuckers and their so-called "peace fire" to ashes. To stomp their bugs, those bloody Peacemakers, and make sure that humans were at least doing the rotten shit they did of their own free will.

I wanted to refuse to raid the plant, but I was pretty sure that I should do it. Fuck.

I ate very slowly.

I checked messages very slowly.

I tried to slink out unseen so that I could sit in a corner and will some kind of resolution out of myself.

I was no clearer when Bryan hunted me down and asked me to come back to the break room.

"I know you don't want to have these conversations; I don't think any of us do. But...we have to, don't we?"

I sighed and stood. "Yeah. We have to. Dammit."

He put his arm around me as we walked. "I'm sorry everything is shitty. I promise to buy you a solid VR rig and make it totally safe when this is done so that you can escape like a boss from *everything*. I'll even switch my focus to writing you kick-ass VR programs. Something no hackers but us can get to."

"I'm going to want that in writing, please!" I teased as we entered the unhappy silence of our common space.

We sat around our table, staring at each other uncomfortably for a few moments until Bryan said, "So."

He cleared his throat and poked at an errant crisp on the tabletop. "I was going to suggest we cover the easy issue first, but the Divine Community issue is no longer so easy." He paused and, when no one spoke, kept going. "I'm still going to suggest we discuss that first, because I *think* we all at least agree that we have to take them out. Right?"

"Are they even separate issues anymore?" Jonny queried. "As I understand it, this is the Peaceforgers' last play, short of the ultimatum that might come next and will surely go poorly. If Zane knows what they're talking about."

"Or maybe their last play is the resurrected SWS execs saving their doomed company," I interjected with a snort that should indicate what I thought of their chances.

Jonny snorted with me, and then went on. "Humans are...brave, egotistical, ill-disposed toward a loss of freedom that isn't dressed up as safety." He shifted and gave Bryan an apologetic shrug. "Choosing to take out Divine Community is choosing to put the Peaceforgers into kill mode, which means we *have* to stay to the end or accept all pursuant deaths. Choosing not to take out Divine Community is probably choosing to let them win."

"If we're going to go there," Rye was trying not to sound defensive, but I could hear it on the edges of zir voice, "then let's also note that choosing not to take out Divine Community gives us more time. Lets us sneak around and try to take them all out at once. Maybe even gives us a chance to find a way to take out them or the whole alien thing without us having to go in physically." Zie leaned forward, pressing the point. "That said, if we think that, in the ultimatum scenario where *all* of humanity, not just us, is involved in kicking their arses off this planet...If we think *humanity* loses in that scenario, how is it you think *we* alone win?"

Wearily I asked, "Is there any scenario where we see ourselves winning? Because, as much as my inner hero knows we should sacrifice everything and do what it takes to fight for our planet, or some fictional bullshit like that, my inner realist isn't exactly seeing the point in doing anything other than a lot of drinking. At most, just passing on what little info we have now and *then* doing a lot of drinking."

"Didn't Zane say that, if they establish peace, they leave?" Jonny suggested. "Can we confirm that? Work *that* angle?"

Bryan and Riley both grabbed their portables and laughed when they realized they had the same idea.

Riles put zirs aside and gracefully said, "I won't take away an excuse for you to talk to your crush."

I folded my arms on the table and laid my head on them. This was so fucking beyond me, just so big. And I felt the size and the weight of it. I briefly wondered if I'd be better off ignorant of the situation, with a vII in my head. Obviously not, but, you know, passing moment of angst.

For a few minutes, the only sound was Bryan's typing. Then he reported back. "Okay, the deal there is that, if they feel they've succeeded, those who want to leave and are willing to either be stuck on the ship for the rest of their lives or to potentially have to undergo surgery again to fit into another civilization get on the ship, and they pretend to leave. They watch for a number of years to make sure the peace is real, and then they take off. *But.* Any who already live among us may well choose to stay and grow a new offshoot of their people on the new planet. In many cases, part of peace is entrenching some of their own in leadership positions. And, in all cases, some kind of weapon or technology is left behind that, should something go awry and seem unfixable, the Peaceforgers still on the planet can kill the other species."

"Damn." Jonny sounded as deflated as I was struggling not to feel. "I was hoping maybe we could let them think they'd won and then clean up when they left."

"Even in that scenario," Riley pointed out, "seems like we'd be left with a vII or something like it in every head and having to slowly reclaim our people. Like, all the people on Earth. And they'd have built all their machines up by then. Turn us all into puppets."

"Well, we can't just not do anything!" growled Bryan. "There's not a one of us who could actually let the world burn, literally or metaphorically."

My mind was creaking, struggling to come up with a solution. "Maybe...So, our big plan has been to convince the authorities of the bigger picture, right?" When Bryan leaned forward, I took that as encouragement to go on. "So, we are clearly in way over our heads already, and also have been failing to find a way to get at the machine on the ship or to dig up things that prove that what's going on is, uh, what's going on. But, in theory, the cops or the feds or military or whatever, if they go in smart, are at least better suited to handle this, right?" Nods all around. Good. Keep going, brain. "All we have to cover is getting evidence, compelling evidence, of what's happening. Of the tainted cures and of the fact that, basically, there's been an alien invasion underway for 60 or 70 years. And make sure that it's also clear from the evidence that a frontal assault is a bad idea. And, really, the only thing we don't have is the alien invasion part, right? Because we've been trying to just stick to existing and actual evidence, right? Even though we've never before, except for the whole release of info on demo day, thought it was cheating to fake evidence if we knew we were right. To create things that, whilst faked in themselves, point people at seeing the real truth."

"So, we just do enough to make that happen? Is that what you're suggesting?" Bryan confirmed.

"It is. I know that means we have to get Zane to agree to help with the proof of them being aliens probably. Or at least for the ideas coming to mind right off. And, worst of all, we have to get into the plant to get documents and samples and...whatever else we can. But Zane can also be part of the proof, or can sort of witness against their people, that the authorities have to deal with it secret mission style." I sighed. "I don't think that path guarantees success. But I don't think any path does." I shrugged weakly. "But this should at least stop them from getting a vII into every head. And then should give humanity a better chance than if we have to do it alone because we couldn't find memos that said, 'Hello. We are aliens. We are here to eat you. No, for reals.' After all, it's just one ship. Not a fleet. Right?"

Jonny was mulling it over. I could tell he was trying to push through his own lack of relevant experience to try to be useful. "I think one of the issues, at least for me, has also been that not everyone in government or law enforcement has been as strongly, clearly anti-SWS as I'd like. And we now know that Peaceforgers can look pretty much like humans. Can we make sure that this doesn't go to some Peaceforger mole right off the bat? Get us caught before the actual...let's call them 'good guys' in this case...the actual good guys get a chance to take action."

"Oh, I know this one. Kind of." Bryan was pleased; this was finally something in his wheelhouse. "All applications for law enforcement involve DNA tests to make sure the person is who they say they are, not someone in the criminal database, and to scan for the genetic markers that would indicate certain mental health stuff. If nothing else, we can feel pretty sure they're human. That, plus we check to make sure they haven't had beat down flu, and so shouldn't have a Peacemaker in their head. It's not perfect, but it's a start."

"Mate, at this point, I'm glad for *anything* that helps us." Jonny gave a forced laugh.

My brain was trying hard to be a helper. "And, Bry, did you end up figuring out the unmanned drones and planes and subs thing? Because...Maybe we use a sub to get footage that's from their own cameras? Or, worst case, we have a few shots we can take. Physically."

Bryan nodded. "I'm about there. I'm building docs and a database, so everyone can guide themselves through training and whatever. That, plus I'm close to figuring out how to make sure we have gear on hand that actually lets us drive or fly things." He grinned at me, probably relieved I wasn't dodging all meat action. "I'm glad you remembered that. I hope it gives us an option that won't be too ruinous to our psyches if we fail to find another way."

"But how do we bust in? To the plant? Sorry to shift back to the nearer issue," Riles said. "I'm...this is the least bad idea, all things considered. But we still have to physically break into a building that we know nothing about. Nothing. Not its security or layout or even what's in it. We have to break in, find the things we hope are there, and get out without getting caught. *Us.*"

"If you guys are willing to risk it, I have an idea for kind of helping. Maybe," Jonny offered. When we all gave him questioning looks, he said, "I can have my bug wait by a door and hope I can slip it in without being noticed when someone opens that door. Then, I can do some recon." He smiled a little. "And, in a rare case of randomly doing something right, because I didn't need to put C4 on it, I put a mic on it. We've got a crawling audio/video bug. We can see and hear for as long as its battery lasts *or* as long as we feel like we can wait."

"Do it!" I encouraged.

"Yeah, definitely." Riles agreed.

"Just be really careful; we don't want to tip them off that we're actively looking into the plant," cautioned Bryan.

"As careful as if the world depended on it," Jonny promised. "I just hope Divine Community doesn't take evenings off from world domination. I'd like to get looking immediately, so somebody has to come or go."

"Given the rate they're letting beat down flu spread, we don't have time for them to do any of that 'work/life balance' stuff," Bryan agreed. "Every day we take is...Riles, before they boobytrapped the list, how many new people were they adding per day?"

"Hmm...They were adding hundreds per day. But it was a higher number each day. I'd bet money it's in the thousands by now." Rye looked grumpy. "I don't want to encourage any of this meat stuff. But, yeah, we are currently looking at thousands, many of whom appear to be in underprivileged populations, which makes me even madder. They may not even have an option for getting the Peacemaker out once we get this sorted. And, not to be classist, but I'd feel a bit less anxious if I knew they were in the heads of entitled, rich assholes who could afford to see a doctor."

None of us were going to argue with that. We might have helped ourselves to some money and changed our situation, but we remembered too well the extra hell of being poor. The impossibility of something like voluntary brain surgery.

"Jonny, how long will the bug's battery last?" Bryan was tapping his face thoughtfully.

"We'll get maybe two days out of the bug that's video and movement, depending on how much we have it move or use its camera. The audio bug on its back will last for weeks, months maybe. Haven't really had to test duration beyond that." Jonny pulled out his mobile and opened his portable. "I'll use the camera on the building across the street to keep an eye, try to move it in ASAP. So, you'll all forgive me if I'm distracted until this is over."

"Okay, you slip it in and let us know when you do," Bryan said.

"That's what she said," Rye snickered.

I didn't even try not to laugh. Shit, I needed our Riles and zir inappropriate sense of humor. Fuck this serious world-saving shit.

Bryan didn't laugh, just paused a beat, smiled the tiniest bit, and then went on. "We'll save the video, poke around, try to have it die somewhere it would at least be interesting to listen. Sound good?" Bryan surveyed the group. Nods all around. "And, while Jonny does that...we need to talk about whether we get help on the break-in."

"Quinn." I figured that was obvious enough. "He's not an online boy, and we know he's good in a fight. And that we can trust him."

"What about Lex?" asked Riley. "Someone helped her break into the other Divine Community building. Maybe she could make some suggestions or introductions?"

I nodded, and added, "I think we'll also need Zane." I put a hand on Bryan's arm. "I know we don't want them to get hurt and that they have possible conflicts. But what if we show up and there are signs, documents, computer keyboards, or whatever that are in their language, not ours? I mean, we can document and grab things like crazy...But if we don't know which door to go in or can't use the computers..."

Jonny helpfully suggested, "Why don't we make sure to check out as much of that stuff as we can with the bug? If we bring in anyone who might, as they say, be a lover, not a fighter, let's make sure it's totally necessary."

"What about Kitty?" Riles asked.

Right. We'd forgotten that piece. At this point, there were so many pieces I wasn't surprised to forget things.

Bryan shrugged and shook his head. "I don't know, mate. You're the one who's been talking and looking for anything to figure out how she's talking to you or if it's really her. I think we have to go with whatever you think."

"I've been trying to think what else it could be," I added helpfully. "But she hasn't pushed you to tell her where we are or what our plans are. She didn't even push you to flat out admit we're the ones who blew up the HQ. And you're the one of us who actually can do a good job of playing careful conversation games. It seems like...I guess, to me, if you said it was her, I'd cautiously believe you."

"They did save Johnson and Smith, so it's possible the Peaceforgers saved Kitty," Jonny pointed out. "Though that would be both good and bad."

Rye breathed out a soft, "Yeah," then said, "I guess I'm still hesitantly believing it's her, but being careful not to give her info she could use against us. Just trying to figure out where she is and what the deal is." Zie grunted, annoyed. "It's been over a week, and she's either dodging or she literally only knows that she's somewhere dark where she can sometimes watch TV. She just gets...weird sounding when she tries to answer questions about that."

"So, we just keep trying to figure out, maybe let people know that the Peaceforgers have some human hostages when we hand off the info?" Jonny suggested.

"Fair," Riles said, though zir tone let us know that "fair" and "ideal" weren't the same thing.

There was a long pause.

I asked, "Is that it? Did we actually make our choices?" I groaned, "Shit. I can't believe we fucking chose to break in." I put my head back on the table. Bloody hell.

I could hear the grin in Bryan's voice, "At least we made these choices, had this discussion, without anyone getting maimed or even scratched. Go team!"

"And in time to not end our day fighting with each other. *Amazing*," Rye praised us all. Then added less cheerily, "Probably our last days. Fuck my life."

I half-raised my head. "I'd suggest we drink to that," I laughed (a little hysterically, if I'm being honest), "but I remember too well that I swore this morning I'd never drink again."

"Maybe tomorrow," Rye offered.

"Sure. Maybe tomorrow." Suddenly, my head was full of some dumbass song from a really old musical. Gran hated musicals in general, and even she didn't know why this one didn't make her want to stab, but it didn't. So my brain was belting out, "The sun'll come out tomorrow!"

Someone get my brain a sedative...

The preparation for getting what we needed from the Divine Community location known only as "the plant" separated nicely into four chunks. And we four humans dove right in. Though not all the diving was as exciting.

Bryan set off, hoping that extra activity on the streets for Dia de Muertos wouldn't just make traffic worse. In theory, it should also give anyone keeping an eye on the comings and goings of people enough to look at that one very average vehicle driving about wouldn't catch attention. With any luck, he'd return with Quinn. Not just one more body, but a body that had done its share of breaking into places and getting into fights. Actual *physical* breaking in and fights, not digital capers.

Riley took on the task of reviewing email recipients. Again. Given the updates to our general plan, zie needed to confirm that these weren't just legal authorities in Seattle who might swiftly raid Divine Community. No, we now needed to expand to the old scope, to make sure the recipients were the sort of humans who might be willing and able to carefully and discreetly work to root out an alien threat all over the world. Sadly, such information wasn't standard in bios. (*Captain Harris has experience in domestic and foreign terrorist investigations, as well as in discreetly working to root out alien threats. In her spare time, she enjoys hiking with her dog Buddy.*) Which meant Riles would have to look at how they'd behaved in past initiatives and whether they seemed more motivated by personal power than by actually taking care of the people they were being paid to take care of. Things that weren't black and white, that would take trying to remotely read a person's character. Better zir then me.

Jonny was babysitting his bug, hoping that the Divine Community cause didn't keep reasonable work hours. It would take as little as a quickly cracked door and he'd get to do more than just stare uselessly at a screen.

I called Lex, hunting for criminal manpower. It took me a couple tries to get her to answer. She explained, "I'm distracted by paranoia and by staring at Mina, wondering when I get to let her wake up."

"We'll make sure you hear as soon as there's an answer," I promised.

"Thanks, man. But I'm guessing you don't have the luxury of time for social calls. So, what can I do for the cause?"

"It looks like our brains won't be enough to handle things. We're wondering if you know bodies who are up for a ninja-style building raid. People who know how to do that shit and are probably in better shape than us." Really, I wondered if she knew an elite squad of operatives, but fit criminals would have to do.

"You'd think so, wouldn't you, what with the prison break we just pulled. But...You want discretion? Do you mind some violence and destruction?"

"It's definitely a violence-free mission. Hopefully, making it in and out without being seen."

"Yeah...My contacts are more interested in explosions, or at least graffiti and vandalism. I had to spend half my time the other night keeping the dude who helped me get Mina from leaving signs we were there." She sounded disgusted, and I couldn't blame her.

"Ugh. Because you needed that stress on top of the stress inherent in getting your girl back. Plus, whilst they couldn't call cops to report someone taking the woman they'd kidnapped, they could totally report vandalism and trace vandals back to *you*."

"Exactly. So, I'm more than happy to do you a solid, set you up. But you'd be out for my blood as soon as you got out of whatever building my connections ruined," Lex said apologetically.

"I think I like not wanting to kill you. I want you to keep your blood in your body." I sighed. "But thanks for your willingness."

"Oh, yeah, dude. Consider me down for you and blood," Lex laughed.

"Right, I'd better get back to investigating my options. But here's to our lives being Peacemaker-free for the holidays!"

"You stay cool, hero. If you can get this out of my head before Thanksgiving, I'll steal a baby just so I can name it after you."

When we hung up, I turned to report, "Lex's contacts will only turn this into exactly the mess we want to avoid. So, my efforts are failed. Rye, need help?"

Zie drily replied, "You're always welcome at this party."

Man, our parties were getting really sad.

"Door!" exclaimed Jonny.

Fortunately, we all knew what he was up to, so that was enough to get our attention. Rye and I leaned in to see Jonny's screen, and he laughed at us.

"Why don't you guys get this up on the TV? Give me a little space." He sounded too victorious to actually be annoyed with us. Too victorious and too busy concentrating on not dropping the ball. (Dropping the bug?)

I worked around Jonny to get the feed from the bug onto our TV. He was scrambling to get our little critter in the door and into a shadow.

"I never thought I'd be a fan of people working late," said Riles. "But, good for you, guy. Hope you're off to a party. November isn't going to be a great month for your organization."

"Okay...We're in the door...Now, how to make the best use of our battery life." Jonny considered the image on the screen as he tapped to record everything the bug picked up. In the silence, we could hear that the bug was also in a quiet place. At the moment, the bug was still facing down the wall with the door that had let it in.

Fortunately, in the silence, we heard Bryan return.

Jonny let out a sigh of relief. "Good. Because he's the one most likely to have strong ideas about what I do with this recon."

So we all waited, staring at the door, until Bryan walked through with (oh, hell yes!) Quinn.

Riles spoke for us all when zie threw zir arms in the air like we'd scored a goal, and shouted, "Thank fuck! A win!"

I hurried over to give Quinn a hug and to gracefully accept his loving, "Fuck you for leaving me out of the fun in October. Glad you're alive."

Bryan stopped, still caught on Riley's greeting. "Do we have losses?" He was a man trying to sound cool but clearly worrying.

I rushed to reassure him. "Nothing major. Just that our hope for a criminal army is in vain. Apparently, our mate's friends don't really go in for things they can't blow up or vandalize. So," I gestured to the room, "this may be the extent of our army." I shrugged apologetically. "Sorry."

Quinn's answering shrug was casual. "Guess we'll just have to plan well." He grabbed a chair. "Plus, now there are fewer people to make noise and get us caught."

Jonny pointed at the screen. "Okay, then. You tell me where to move our camera. This is our one shot at recon. Tell me how to not waste it."

Quinn settled in and kept his eyes on the screen as he said, "First, I want you all to apologize for cutting me out of the SWS action. For not really bringing me into it. You bastards." There was no rancor in his voice, but it didn't sound entirely like a joke either.

I stared at my feet and mumbled, "Sorry, mate."

"Yeah, Quinn, sorry. We were just trying to keep you out of the mess of it," Riles added.

Quinn snorted. "You lot are idiots. But you're forgiven. And you've clearly realized the error of your ways." He grinned. "I'm glad you've all come to your senses." He stood and walked closer to the TV. "Do we have *any* info at all on what's in here?"

We left a gap so that Jonny could see the TV, just in case he wanted that bigger view, and gathered in front of it.

When we shook our heads, Quinn asked, "What all do we *think* is going on in here?"

"Near as we can tell," I answered, "they're making a cure to beat down flu, as well as Peacemaker vIIs to put in the cure. And there's probably an office or desk with computers. Maybe even the equipment for manufacturing whatever they're using to spread the flu in the first place."

"And we want to get pictures of things in here, of the manufacture of the vII and of it getting put in the cure. Plus, obviously, we want to grab files off the computer. Or computers. Documents that lay it all out, hopefully," said Jonny.

"Okay. So, we have our objectives for the bug. Get footage of the manufacturing, of machinery that puts the vII into the cure, and of the layout in terms of getting us to the computers and getting our hands on the cure. Plus, keep an eye out for security measures." Quinn sounded confident. He seemed to think this was all very do-able.

Good. We were all resting on his confidence here.

"And, since the audio bug will outlive the rest, I'd suggest we find a good place in the office area for our bug to die. That way we can at least keep ears on the situation," Bryan suggested.

"How quickly do we need to move?" asked Quinn.

"This is definitely an 'as soon as possible' situation," said Riles. "Especially since beat down flu is just spreading faster and faster."

"Recon tonight. If we don't see anything I think's a real issue, liberate our proof tomorrow night. A productive work day." Quinn looked back at Jonny. "Ready to drive?"

Jonny nodded, and Quinn started directing. Go, bug, go!

Whilst the rest of the city raged and drank and pretended that they were just really into Dia de Muertos ("no, like, I'm not religious, but I'm spiritual, so I totally feel the whole ancestor thing, you know?"), we caffeinated and we plotted and we moved a tiny bug around.

The plant was a pretty basic space. There was an office area along one wall, a stock area full of "finished" product (cure doses, maybe some infection method) on the other end, and three groupings of equipment between (one each for manufacturing the cure, manufacturing the vII and putting it in the cure, and maybe a smaller one that was for manufacturing the infection vector from the looks of it). It looked like the machinery mainly ran itself, which meant few people. Unfortunately, it did appear to need some people as monitors, *and* the whole thing appeared to be a 24-hour operation. No union had yet saved machines from working without breaks or weekends.

In addition to a few people, it looked like our main security hurdles were locked doors and hardwired cameras. The doors and cameras could be handled by Quinn's skills for breaking in and by all of us wearing masks and nondescript clothing. Quinn kept reassuring us that, even if we couldn't find files to wipe, the cameras would be a non-issue. But the people...

"There are people there. Which means someone could get hurt." I hoped those simple sentences carried the paragraphs I was thinking. That I couldn't stand anyone else getting hurt, including the people who worked there.

For all we knew, they'd been tricked or misled. They might be good people with families who thought they were saving the world and who fed the homeless people they walked past going to and from work. We didn't know that they knew what was being made there. I couldn't condone hurting them, and I couldn't condone risking us. My ideals and emotions weren't helping here.

"Does this footage," Rye waved zir hand around at the screen, "seem like proof enough of what the machines do? Do we need to get actual physical samples?"

"I think," mused Jonny, "that there's room to accuse us of fakery if we deliver a sample of any of that. There's no way to prove that it's real."

Bless him.

And he went on. "Even if we have documents that say that's the case, I don't think the sample we could steal from there actually helps. I think they'd need to go in and see it themselves."

"'They' being the authorities?" clarified Quinn.

"Yeah. And I agree." Bryan nodded. "No benefit in grabbing a sample. Just files. Minimal time and actions necessary in there."

"Okay, that makes it a simple-ish plan." Quinn sounded pleased. "We go in the door off the alley, so we don't get seen cracking the lock. If we head to the left, hug the walls, scurry quietly to avoid being seen by the staff...That part has a lot of variables; we'll have to play by ear, see where people are and where they're looking, but it's not that bad. Duck into the office and, well, whatever you guys do with the computers. Then track back and go out the alley door."

"And we go in armed," Bryan clarified. "We plan *not* to have to use them; but we'd be fucking stupid not to carry guns everywhere these days. Okay?" He put the question to the room, but he was just looking at me.

I grudgingly nodded. I didn't love it, but I didn't think we'd do better than this plan. At least not with what we knew. "We're always armed now. We'd have to be a special kind of stupid to choose that night to not carry."

I changed my focus to the computer part. "There are three computers in the office. Looks like a shelf with a few external drives as well. So, we go in prepared to carefully hack and copy whilst Quinn keeps watch. That way, we don't have to grab machines. Nobody there gets tipped off we were in the computers, and all the computers and drives are still there when the cops raid."

Fortunately, we hadn't seen anything in Peaceforger symbols, so we wouldn't have to drag Zane into the action. Which was good. Not only because we still hadn't reached the point where I felt like they should know our real names or actions, but also because it was one less life in the crosshairs if things got fucked up. No more deaths *No more deaths.*

"Are we done with the bug?" Jonny asked. When we all nodded, he drove it into a dark corner under a shelf in the office at the plant. With the bug secreted away, he stood. "I'm going to fuck off to bed, unless there's more to sort?" He gave everyone a quick look, caught my eye, and nodded at the door out to our mattress.

"Sleep tight, you drek!" I gave hugs and kisses all around, then followed Jonny out. Good riddance to yet another day. May we finish shaking off the Peaceforgers as easily.

The heating was weak back in the area where we kept our mattress. The contrast of the chilly air and our steaming bodies heightened my senses. Made every bit of skin-on-skin even more desirable.

I sent off the frustrating day shagging my...boyfriend, I guess. We hadn't named it, but that seemed a fair label for our relationship. Especially since we'd talked about living together. On purpose. No kidnapping or captivity involved. I'd call him any non-demeaning label he wanted if we both just made it through this alien shit-storm alive and able to do this every night.

CHAPTER 20

I slept away most of the day Wednesday. It wasn't good sleep by the end, more just refusing to deal with the world. Refusing to go out and do another real-world action. Once this whole thing was over, I wasn't going to do anything that wasn't online or in my bed. At least nothing that required me to leave whatever flat (or house, since Gran's was now mine) I ended up living in. Not for at least a few months. That was a big enough, real enough world for me.

I rolled over to look at Jonny, who was already looking at me in the faint light of my mobile screen and its news feed. "Listen," I informed him, "this is it. No more real-world shit after this, okay? We stick to what we're actually good at, online shit, and let the people whose fucking jobs it is take care of the meat stuff. Okay?" I grabbed his hand. "Our minds aren't made for this, for planning it or for handling the psychological impacts of doing it. And I'm not made for losing you, got it? These lives are *ours* to make the most of. Okay?"

I don't know if it was because he already felt that way or because I'd gotten kind of intense there, but he just gently nodded, touched my cheek. "Yes. I am entirely on board with that."

Had I been holding my breath? I must have been, because I exhaled in relief. And kissed him. This (and food, let's be honest) were really all I needed the meat space for.

We were interrupted by Riles, who bounced onto our mattress, begging, "Can I hide here with you? I don't want to do tonight."

So we made room for zir and huddled under the covers with Rye's flashlight, like kids in a blanket fort, talking about what we'd rather be doing. You know, instead of breaking into an aliens' manufacturing plant for mind control devices that would help them take over the world. Oh, where there was also biological weapon stuff ('cause purposefully infecting someone is *totally* biological warfare, whether we're talking smallpox blankets, AIDs unleashed in minority populations, or a world epidemic of beat down flu).

But we weren't actually kids, and hiding under our covers never held back trouble. Not really. So we gave ourselves a sort of communal group pep talk and inspired ourselves out into the world on the other side of the blankets. Ugh.

Out there, we found Bryan and Quinn making sure guns were ready and laughing about some past escapade. When they saw the three of us standing in the door, probably looking sullen (I felt that way...a little...), they greeted us heartily.

Bryan jumped up and headed for the tiny stove that was in the kitchen-ish corner of the break room. "I've made pasta and dumped on meat sauce. Come get carb loaded before we do this thing. Let's stuff our faces!"

"But not enough to weigh you down," cautioned Quinn. "If your pasta gut compromises your abilities, I will kick your asses." He laughed.

I laughed along, but I kept thinking, *Fuck you guys and your jovial attitudes. And fuck your pasta.* I mean, sure, I ate it and I enjoyed it...but fuck it, nonetheless. Stupid, jovial pasta.

I crouched in the shadows of the alley behind the plant, trying to breathe quietly. I knew I had to keep half an eye on the world around me and half an eye on Quinn, our leader for this excursion. I kept a hand on my gun and tried not to tug at the balaclava I was wearing. I hoped that the little bit of healing I'd done since demo day and the films I'd watched with people doing sneaky shit had adequately prepared me. I knew full well they hadn't.

The lock on the door needed a passcard. Fortunately, this was the sort of hack that you could buy a (quite illegal) gadget to handle. And Quinn had one. So, mentally, I ticked this off as a win. I was trying to keep a pep talk going in my head without becoming too distracted to get it right *outside* my head. Yay! Obstacle down! We can do this! Woo! Some shit like that.

Entering from the alley, we were coming in through the stock area. Fortunately, it was dimly lit and stacked with crates, so we had plenty of cover for getting our bearings. Realizing Jonny's bug had a little juice left, we'd set it as a bit of a very shitty sentry. Perched on the door frame of the office and pointed out, we could get a blurry sense of where people might be. Crowded around Jonny's mobile screen, we thought we could make out three people. Only three. Though we thought we could hear a fourth person in the stock area, shifting crates as they were filled.

We hugged a wall, moved in the opposite direction of where the completed (tainted) doses of the cure rolled into the space. I had to remind myself that not breathing, however *silent* an option, was not a *viable* option. Quinn led the way, with Jonny close behind (since he had our other set of eyes on his mobile screen). Then it was me, Riles, and Bryan bringing up the rear, watching our arses.

Make it through the stock area. Check. Realize the supposed fourth person in the stock area is an automaton. Bonus! Carefully crack the door, confirm no one is watching, and ease out into the main area. The horrifyingly brighter main area. Check. Creep quickly around, towards the office, avoiding being seen by the three people we know are in there. Check! My heart was leaping in my chest, and my mental pep talk was going wild. We were stealthing the shit out of this mission. Holy hell, there was hope!

The creep to the office was the worst of it, too. It wasn't *glaringly* bright, but our black-clad selves didn't have any truly dark shadows to hide in. It was a ridiculous eternity (that probably only took 5 or 10 minutes) of creeping, finding something to pause behind when one of the three employees seemed to be turning our way, and then doing it all over again. When we finally found ourselves at the wall that separated the office from the factory floor, my instinct (built on vidgames) was to shout something like, "Fuck yeah, bitches!" Fortunately, I knew the difference between a game and reality.

As Quinn dashed to use his passcard tool on the lock on the office door, the rest of us smashed back into the near-shadow of a corner. Jonny watched his mobile monitor for what the bug saw, I watched Quinn for a signal, and Bryan and Riles watched the people. Quinn waved, ducked inside, left the door barely ajar. One by one, we'd take a deep breath, scurry for the door, and duck inside. Each time, we had fewer eyes to watch with us. Bryan, last to go and with no one to watch, must have seen someone turning and hit the floor; through the windows that made up the top half the wall, I saw him drop down quickly. I didn't breathe again until he was through the door and it was closed behind him. He had dust all across his front and flashed us all a grin and double thumbs up.

"Quinn," Jonny whispered, "crack the door so I can grab the bug. We don't dare leave it behind."

"Are we okay to make the run for the door out without it, though?" asked Riles.

Quinn cracked the door, just enough for the bug to scurry in. "We have to be. He's right. We can't leave that kind of evidence."

Jonny pocketed his bug, and we all crept to our digital responsibilities. Jonny grabbed data from the external drives and stayed out of sight by putting his back to the wall where the windows were. The three of us grabbing data from computers hid under the desks. This part was the easy part.

I didn't need much of my brain to do this, so I spent the time patting us on the backs for being such capable badasses. Who knew that someone like me could, in the real world and not just in a film or vidgame, manage to not fuck up a bit of physical action? I was going to buy us all champagne and crowns. We were just too awesome. Etc.

I finished grabbing all my computer had to offer and went over to help Jonny finish external drives. I saw Rye looking through desk drawers, zir desk and mine (because I was too busy thinking we were smart to actually be thorough). When Bryan poked out from his desk, we exchanged looks and nods, and he whispered Quinn's name. When Quinn looked, we all gave thumbs up. Mission accomplished. Well, we hoped. At the very least, we'd grabbed their files. Whether any were going to be useful was something we'd have to wait to find out back at our lair.

We crept around until we sat in a row, backs against the half wall that separated the office from the factory floor.

Quinn whispered, "Anyone find their camera system to delete our sneaking in and turn it off for our sneaking out?" When we all shook our heads, he said, "Okay, don't freak out. I've gotta do some things to cover this. Because I don't see cameras in here, but someone will notice us on the cameras out there for sure."

The rest of us exchanged "what the hell?" looks. It would have been nice of him to clue us in before.

Quinn took out a small can of red spray paint and painted an upside-down pentagram on a wall, then used a red paint pen to write "Hail Satan!" under it. What the fuck? I checked, and mine was not the only mouth hanging open. He also threw some papers, that appeared to have the same kind of shit on them, all around the office. Apparently, he'd come prepared for this.

When he rejoined us at the wall, he said, "There's no way someone doesn't notice us at some point. If nothing else, when the computer tells them that some unknown code opened the door. So, now they'll think it's about vandalism by a hate group."

I could have hit him, because what about being ninjas? On the other hand, this was his thing. He didn't tell me how to hack; it did me no good to argue with him now. Right or not, this was more his area of experience than mine, and we'd agreed he was taking lead on this. Dammit.

Though, seriously, if I'd known vandalism was a thing we were going to do, I could have brought in Lex's people. At least we hadn't gotten into a fight with security or other church personnel...Probably hadn't really needed Lex's guys...I tried to let it go, keep my head in the moment, focus on getting out.

"One at a time back to the corner," Quinn instructed, then cracked the door, took a look, and went, drawing more upside down pentagrams as he went. Seriously.

Then Bryan. Then Riles. No shouts from anyone catching them. Cool. I gave Jonny's hand a squeeze, checked that no one was looking my way, and made my own run. Jonny followed right behind.

Oh shit, son! We were going to do this thing!

Again with the excruciating scurry, pause behind things (discover Quinn left graffiti on each thing when he was the one paused behind it), scurry again to the wall, follow it back to the stock area. Into the stock area. We paused a moment to breathe in the shadows. We just had to get to the door and then to our vehicle. I was buzzing. We were going to do this. We were we were we were!

Still in a row—Quinn, Bryan, Riles, me, Jonny—we crept through the shadowy stock area. There was the door. Big thumbs up and a grin from Quinn. We knew we had to rush out the door, into shadows, sticking to them until we got to our vehicle, parked in another shadowy alley a block away. I watched Quinn lift his head, like a "ready, set..." signal, and then crack the door open to go.

Which was when we learned that someone had already seen us on camera.

A bright light shone in through the door, clearly outlining Quinn.

Quick-thinking Quinn, who directed a whisper at us so fast we could barely hear. "I'll draw them. Run, you fuckers!" And then he threw the door open, shouting, "Hail Satan!"

Instead of running into the shadows, he ran for the people with guns. The light made it so I couldn't see the people, but I could hear guns being readied. Not just handguns.

Quinn went mental, shouting all sorts of anti-religious things and running around, batshit, getting in faces. They must have had instructions to try to capture us alive, because the men just shouted at him, maybe moved slightly in to engage him, didn't shoot. But his crazy act threw them off for just a moment, and we dashed for where the shadows should be. Away from where Quinn had thrown himself to engage and distract the armed and armored bodies that would otherwise have cut us off. It was a small opening, but we dashed like fucking mice for a hole in the wall.

It was all so quick and stupid and Quinn was pulling them in...In less than a breath, Bryan was through, Riles was through, I was through, Jonny...There was a shot and Quinn's shouting stopped. Jonny must have paused for a split second. Not long enough to be stopped. Soon after, he was running with me. The over-confident pricks hadn't kept anyone on the street. And Bryan used the remote to have the vehicle started, unlocked, rear doors opening (so only the driver had to pause to open a door; the rest of us could just throw ourselves in).

There were shouts and boots on pavement behind us. Did we duck into the alley before they saw us?

We were speeding away, Bryan trying to be circuitous and lose them, assuming they'd gotten to vehicles and were following us. Rye scrambled up to ride shotgun.

I was crying for Quinn and trying not to distract Bry as he drove. The pain from my not-yet-healed body adding fuel to my tears.

Riles frantically asked, "Was that cops? Feds? Anybody see markings?" Zie had zir mobile out. "I'm going to try to find any cams they had on them, but I have to know who they are." When no one answered, zie replied to the silence, "I'll take that as 'no.' So, will one of you piggyback with my work? I'll grab camera footage that shows them moving in, and you—" zie stopped short as zie turned to speak to us, and just stared at Jonny. Zie mouthed, "Oh fuck," but didn't say anything aloud.

And that's when I saw that he had his hood up. Hood up and no balaclava.

My eyes must have gone wide, because he whispered, "They grabbed it." He looked mortified and terrified and probably petrified and other words that rhyme with those three and aren't good.

I barely noticed the insane movement of the vehicle as Bryan tried to accelerate us to safety.

"Your family," I whispered to Jonny.

Jonny pulled out his mobile. He tapped it as he talked, voice intent and brow drawn. "I'll tell them to leave everything, including mobiles, and run immediately. I'll tell them where to go and I'll send someone for them. Or something. Shitshitshit."

"Rye, I'll piggyback and make sure that anything cameras might show of us is scrubbed. Right?" I tried to sound like I wasn't freaking out. I didn't want to worry Bryan or distract him from the task at hand.

Riles nodded, and we went to work.

We all worked in tense silence until Bryan's driving got less running away-like. For Riley's part, trying to figure out who'd come for us, the cameras on other buildings or streetlights showed only a nondescript black vehicle, filled with humans who wore no insignias or identifiers—much like the handful of people who'd broken into my flat twice in October—all suited up with guns and black clothes. Zie tried to follow them back, to find out where they'd come from, but they eventually disappeared in (exited from, if you weren't watching in reverse) an area with no working cameras in a neglected part of the International District. We'd have to remember that area for our own possible use.

My work was somewhat easier. I had fewer cameras to hit, and only a couple had gotten any footage in which you might see Jonny's face. One did capture the moment when one of the armed men swung around, reaching for Jonny. Jonny ducked...and the guy came away with just a handful of balaclava. I knew Riles was already grabbing footage that might help, so once zie confirmed zie'd gotten it from the streetlight camera in question, I gave it the same blip of dead space as every other. A few seconds of black to hide Jonny's identity. Thanks to his quick move, pulling up his hoodie (and to the fact that hoodies made for guys have roomier hoods), there wasn't much for any other camera to catch. Except, perhaps, for whatever the armed men had caught on their own cams. Dammit.

In a parking lot with broken lights, Bryan stopped at last. He turned to talk, saw Jonny's face instead of Jonny's balaclava, and said, "Shit." He took a breath. "Okay, here's the deal, we're going to go back to the warehouse. I think I lost them. But, just in case, as soon as I get there, you're going to pack bags like we ran with the first time, and dismantle everything possible into the vehicle. And you're not going to leave anything behind that isn't on fire. Okay? I want us to hit it running."

"Then why the fuck are we just sitting here?" Riles demanded, adrenaline turning to anger in zir throat.

"Because, Riles, if they're on us still, I wanted them to hopefully grab us out here, not back at HQ where they might figure out we aren't just out for religious persecution." Bryan was gritting his teeth.

It all sounded stupid to me, but I didn't have better ideas. Once again, we were all just guessing. Out of our depths. The one person who might have had half a clue had been shot. (And was it better to think of him dead or alive and able to be tortured into giving us up? I hated myself for even wondering that.)

Bryan turned back around, didn't turn the vehicle's headlights back on, and drove us back to the warehouse.

As we drove, I asked Jonny, "Did they run?"

All this time, his family had been safe because nobody had seen Jonny's face. As far as we knew, no one knew he was involved in the SWS thing. And, until tonight, no one had known he (or any of us) was involved in this Divine Community thing either. At best, we might have made it impossible to hunt down any kind of camera footage that caught him unmasked. At worst, and if they were smart, they had cameras on their bodies or in their vehicles and already knew who he was.

Jonny nodded. "I think so. They said they would and abruptly stopped answering messages. I won't know until my person gets to them. I guess maybe the shock of me suddenly showing back up and just telling them to go because someone was coming to kill them had the impact I hoped." He put his face in his hands. "Shit. This wasn't supposed to touch them."

I put a hand on his back, but addressed my words to Bryan. "Bry, I know it's late to ask, but you guys switched off the license plates for the vehicle before we headed out, right?"

"Lucky for you," he replied, "we thought of that *before* we left, not after all was said and done." He sounded irritated and I had to bite back an urge to tell him to fuck off with his attitude.

We still had shit to sort out. I'd yell at him after, if I still felt like it. Adrenaline and fear weren't exactly social lubricants.

Back at the warehouse, it was all just a blur. We stuffed our bags full and fit all else we could into the back of our vehicle, stuffing every spare space. It was good that we hadn't bought loads of extra stuff since we moved in.

When that was done, Bryan had us lean our mattresses and the tables at which we'd spent so much time up against walls.

"There's going to be loads of DNA all over this place, too much to make it clear ours is important. Except for the fact there are these mattresses and these tables. So, we're going to carefully wipe the tables with bleach and light the mattresses on fire."

"What the fuck?" Rye stopped in the middle of making sure a mattress was balanced as it leaned. Zie didn't quite shout, "Are you fucking serious? Because there's nothing like a random warehouse fire the same night their plant gets broken into to make sure the Peaceforgers don't look carefully here."

"Calm down. Look." Bryan pointed up, where there was a standard, industrial, automatic fire suppression system clearly installed on the ceiling.

"Hate to poke holes, mate," Jonny actually didn't sound too sorry, "but those usually also send out an alert to the closest fire department."

"Right. And if we can't hack into this system or the fire department system and stop that messaging from being delivered, we're not the badasses we think we are," retorted Bryan.

"We *aren't*," I mumbled. I looked up to face Bryan's scowl. "At this point, I think there's sufficient proof that we *aren't* badasses. We're just a bunch of...fake adults with code smarts who are, otherwise, fucking useless. Unless you count getting our loved ones killed as 'useful' in some fucked up way."

Bryan held his scowl just a moment, but then it dissolved. His face went soft, and I thought I could see the memories of all the people we'd lost since everything started in October in his eyes. "Point taken. But," and he turned to face the room of us at large, "we *are* badasses with code. We *can* stop that message. And this," he gestured to the fire suppression system, "should kick in quickly enough to stop the whole place actually burning down. Hopefully after the mattresses have burned enough and caused enough smoke damage that they'll at least have a harder time getting us."

Jonny argued, "But those sensors are usually really fucking sensitive. The mattresses won't burn enough. Plus," and he smacked our mattress, which was leaned up by him, "these are made to *not* burn easily." He scanned our now-stripped room. "And I think our only accelerant is the fuel in our car."

"Or what little alcohol was left after the other night," I reminded him.

"Or we could just do a quick 'Net search to see what destroys DNA and what might let our mattresses burn well. Narrow down to something easy to get." Riles looked up from the portable on which zie had surely just done what zie was suggesting. "For one thing, we're going to use that bleach Kot and I made us buy the other night, use it liberally on most everything. Not forgetting the bathroom. It will corrupt DNA, as well as mess with most equipment that they would use to look for DNA in the first place. Show up as 'body fluids everywhere!' sort of thing. Though," zie cautioned, "remember that a big fire and bleach could create chlorine gas, so that's a 'throw fire and run' situation." Zie scanned a page quickly, then said, "Hear me out on what I'm about to suggest." When we nodded, zie continued, "In trying to sort out spontaneous human combustion by using pigs, it was found that the...basically the lard from the pig gave a long, slow burn that would destroy stuff like trace DNA or whatever was soaked with it, but wouldn't actually light carpets or rooms on fire. So, some of us wipe stuff whilst some of you hit a market in the International District to pick up plenty of lard stat."

Bryan laughed, a surprised bark. "How the hell did you even get to spontaneous human combustion as a starting point?"

With a cocky little grin, Riles replied, "I guess I'm just cleverer than even you ever imagined."

All of which led us, more minutes later than we'd have liked, to be sitting in our vehicle, taking control of the fire suppression system, just in case. Making sure no message was sent to the fire department as our mattresses, soaked with bleach like the rest the room *and* smeared with lard, sizzled. Who would have thought spontaneous human combustion would be more than an interesting story?

"At least if we've misjudged," I noted, "there's plenty of parking lot to act as a fire break."

On 6 June, 1889, Seattle was razed by the Great Seattle Fire. At that point, the city was about 25 blocks of mostly-wood buildings. None of which, due to a lack of time travelers peddling technological marvels, had had what we might consider even a bare bones (and, depending on the decade, often legally mandated) fire suppression system. They hadn't even really been set up well with buckets of water sufficient to handle the situation. Basically, their destruction by fire wasn't exactly inconceivable.

After the fire took down the first attempt at a city, the second attempt to build Seattle had a bit of an uneven start due to the city's natural, swampy terrain. Fire and water were Seattle's heritage. Those who were quick to start rebuilding their shops and hotels and such (this time, with bricks), who had their buildings going back up before the people in charge sorted the swamp issue, found that the final plan, which involved elevating the streets and sidewalks above the mess, meant their newly built ground floors—and sometimes their second floors—were facing walls used for said elevation and weren't actually accessible via the street. (And that's why procrastination is a virtue, bitches. Or patience. Call it what you like.)

Soon enough, they just built yet another floor up, and then found themselves at street level. But none of them really bothered to demolish or fill in that first go at rebuilding (or even just wall off the doors that led outside and create basements), which left Seattle with an underground ghost town. Main streets, former first floors of department stores, and so forth. All under the busy neighborhood of Pioneer Square, just south of the city's downtown core.

For a number of years, you could take an official tour of the underground. If you chose to go later in the day, you even got the adult version, where you'd learn how Seattle was built on the hard work of its prostitutes. Ah, the true "city mothers." However, in the 2030s, the underground tour went away. The desperately poor had started trying to take over the area as compassionless neighborhood committees full of NIMBYs (claiming they were full of the milk of human kindness, but "not in my back yard") made sure more and more tent cities and such got closed down. And the under-housed people had soon been followed into the underground by a certain pack of rich kids who thought that hurting or killing homeless people was both fun and a way to clean up the city. (Plus, a disproportionate number of the homeless people were people of color or immigrants, so the racism that had started to be fed and stirred up more than usual in the country starting in the 2010s had these rich kids feeling pretty sure that it was their right to kill or abuse these folks. And had plenty of law enforcement not really giving their all to true law enforcement efforts in these instances. It was a perfect storm of the worst in humanity.) By the time anyone bothered to catch those psychopathic assholes, the underground had become too much a horror story for anyone to go there who felt they had a choice.

Which is all to say that, on the other side of our own fire, we found ourselves in need of fleeing somewhere without cameras (now that Jonny's face was known) but near food. Plus, it was late autumn. And whilst November in Seattle is a milder experience than some other places, it's still not a healthy choice to sleep rough. And, so, we ran from the site of one fire to the site of another once we'd ditched our vehicle in Zane's parking spot.

Zane's parking spot. A bit of good luck there. To find a spot in Seattle where we could just *leave* the car, a spot big enough for our mini-SUV, that we didn't have to pay for. A spot included in the rent of a flat but neither in use by the renter of said flat nor sublet out to anyone else. And a renter who happened to have mentioned, as part of trying to make Bryan feel welcome at their place, that they even had a spot he was welcome to park in, you know, should he ever want to come up and see them instead of just meeting at a random place. (Yay for love and/or lust...Whatever it takes!)

So, we dropped our vehicle there, waited for Bryan to finish snogging Zane in thanks, and made sure our g/ap masks were doing their job of making it harder for cameras to spot any of our faces (can I get another hallelujah for flu season making this unremarkable?). They offered to let us stay with them, but that didn't seem like the wisest option at the moment. We shouldered our bags and headed out to make our new "home."

That gave me the whole walk to go around and around in my head. I just sort of trudged along, counting on Jonny's hand in mine to pull me the right way. Counting on my friends to make the choices. Counting on myself for nothing more than putting one foot in front of the other whilst, internally, I spooled up. Freaking out over our losses and the enormity of the task we still seemed no closer to completing.

We were hunkered down in a dirt and brick corner of the underground, the place that Bryan and Jonny had thought best. Bryan was explaining how he thought things should go in the even and confident tones of a man who knows that the rest of us would readily admit to having little to no fucking clue.

"We'll do sleep shifts, for safety. And we'll just start sifting through all the files we got from the plant. Probably make sure we do a serious virus scan on all of it first. It shouldn't take *too* long. Take breaks to see what we can manage with getting us trained on drones. If the Wi-Fi we can get here is sufficient for it. Uh, ditto efforts to hack into satellites or figure out transmissions to and from the ship and Rye's mobile."

He might have had more to say, but I couldn't bear to hear it.

"I'm done." I looked up from my fingers, twisting each other in my lap. My voice was flat; there was nothing left in me to put into tone. "I just...can't anymore."

Bryan and Jonny looked surprised, but Riles scooted over to put zir arm around me.

"This bullshit where...where we run, where we don't have homes, where we sleep in fear and watch our loved ones die? This will *not* be my new normal. I mean, this shit again? Fucking compromised by armed men in black, so we flee and hide out? This time, not even to a crowded but tidy flat. No, it just keeps getting worse. Live in filth! Live in fear! Live with knowing that the fucking people you love are motherfucking dead, and it's because they knew you." Somewhere in there, I'd started crying, but my voice had held on until that last thought. So I half-sobbed, half-raged, "So, fuck this. I was *not* made for this. And I can*not* handle this. I'm done. I'm out." And then I just shut up and tried to keep my sobbing sounds quiet, face buried in my hands. As I did, I felt ashamed of my outburst, which only made my sobbing worse.

I'd tried to make myself believe I could do this. That I was somehow up for this. I had let Gran's death and my sense of responsibility make me think that I had to, and that I *could*, do something. And maybe all I *had* to do was stop putting other people in the line of fire. Stop trying to do things I was bloody well *not* trained or suited for. I hated myself for believing I could, for admitting I couldn't, for failing to make any progress or stop any deaths. For falling apart at a moment that was clearly not ideal.

I'd expected immediate lectures, but nobody said anything for a few minutes. I could hear that at least one person was on their portable, and Riles stayed by me. After a few moments, Jonny sat on my other side with a hand on my leg. When I finally stopped crying and took my hands from my face, Bryan was sitting on the dirt at my feet. He had his portable in his lap, but was now watching me. I couldn't read his face, but it didn't look angry. So, there was that...

My little freak out hadn't changed what needed to be done. Hadn't changed that this was my team, that these were my friends. So, I made sure my post-cry face was resolute. Specifically, I was going for "quietly resolute but not angry." I *was* angry, but not at anyone here. They weren't actually the bad guys, and nobody had forced me to stay.

It was no surprise that it was Rye who spoke first. Delicately. "You know that I'm with you. You know that you and I are Team Run the Fuck Away. And I'm also totally with you on being done. Because you are *so* right. We are in so far over our heads that I don't know if we'll ever surface. We *are* the wrong people for this. We lack a whole section of skills that are actually pretty necessary for what we're doing. And..." zir voice faltered, "we've lost people. So, again, I am entirely with you on Team Run the Fuck Away. I will buy us, just you and me, shirts when this is over."

That drew little smiles from everyone, even me.

"But," I whispered. Acknowledging that I knew it was coming and that I was listening anyway. Maybe even acknowledging that part of me wanted to be talked into not quite being done. Rabbi Tarfon's words in my head: *You are not free to desist from it either.*

"But, until we finish this phase of things, we are literally the only ones standing between humanity and a possible alien overlord situation. Which sucks so much ass that there aren't words to encompass it. And just makes me want to run even faster. But we'd run, and then we'd live with guilt until we died or until a Peacemaker got put in us and forced us to feel nothing but 'peace.' Or until they decided humans are too difficult and they blew us up. But! And this is a better 'but,' my dear. But we are now almost certainly down to just the digital phase, to no more meat stuff we can reasonably be expected to do. Even the boys would agree that any remaining meat stuff is for others." Zie paused so the boys could nod, then went on. "We're at the part where boredom is our worst threat. Or sucking at drone training. We just go through the shitloads of data we stole, find the handy bits to prove what's going on, manufacture shit to fill the holes that the documents don't, package them up, and send them off. And *that* is shit we can do in our sleep. Without leaving the house or, uh, the hideout, as our case may be." Zie took zir arm from around me, and half turned, holding my hands. "Kot, you *can* do this last part. And it's the last fucking part we need to do. And we wrap it up in, what? A day? Two days, max?" Zie looked at Bryan and Jonny, who considered and nodded. "Okay, so, we just do *our* thing, the thing we *are* good at, for a day or two. We send the email, and then we disappear. We let the authorities finish the job. Let the experts sort it out. Okay?"

This time, zie was looking intently at me, only me.

The petulant brat in me sulked and kicked. I tried to breathe past her. She beat at my heart and made me want to scream for a moment. Breathe. Breathe. Think of who was actually to blame for Gran. For Quinn. For Kitty. For 'Randa. For Huw. For those kids that girl shot back when it was just Jonny noticing stuff, and for the girl herself. For deaths we probably didn't even know about. And for a host of smaller wrongs. You know, smaller than death. And all I had to do, I told the brat, was sift through data and send an email, maybe fake a memo or two. And, this time, there'd be no surprise alien to show up and tell us it was bigger and we'd made it worse. This time, we'd know there was more to come, but that it wasn't ours to do.

Just sift data. Just send email.

If there was any kind of afterlife where I would have to face Gran...Even if I just believed in honoring the dead...How could I face Gran or the memory of who Gran wanted me to be if I didn't just do this last, simple thing?

"If we do this, can we send the email from the vehicle? On our way out of town? Watch the rest unfold on the news or, more likely, via some hacked official email? Promise?" I didn't actually let them answer. "Sift data, send email, sit on our arses to watch the rest go down. That's it? 'Cause I can agree to that."

Bryan nodded solemnly. "It's all I'm asking. It's all we need. And...even if we needed more, at least for me, I'd take whatever you're willing to give. Even if that's nothing." He put his hand on my ankle like he might put it on my shoulder if he were standing.

Jonny took one of my hands from Riles. "That sounds like the right plan to me. So, yes, I promise. That's it." He shrugged. "That's about all I'm up for too."

Riles just squeezed the hand zie still held.

"Right. Sorry for yet another freak out. Let's divide the files. And, if we have a signal down here, we should check the news or the fire department database to see if we let the fire suppression system turn on in time to keep the warehouse from burning down, but also if we managed to totally suppress the outgoing signal from that." I could hear the deep weariness in my voice.

But I could also hear the quiet voices of the heroes in the stories I loved, the ones who'd pushed through the shitty times, who'd kept fighting the fights they seemed unlikely to win. And I could hear Gran's encouragement and belief and all her attempts to help me grow up to be something other than a useless drain on society. And I promised myself to try to just listen to those voices until we were done.

CHAPTER 21

Even in the underground, we could get a Wi-Fi signal. It was weak (too weak for drones or satellite hacking), but it was there. After so many other infrastructure failures, Seattle had at least managed to do well with making sure that anyone could be online. Even if that anyone was, technically, in Seattle version 1. Fortunately, we shouldn't need more than access to email and the ability to keep an eye on the news. We might *want* more, but we were learning—even if I wasn't doing it gracefully—to live without our wants.

Thursday morning, Riles reported, "Kitty can get through too. Not that she knows where we are. But she hasn't complained about it being harder." Zie sounded relieved.

On the news and elsewhere...The good news was that nobody seemed to be showing Jonny's face at all, much less in a "connected to a crime; please contact authorities if you know where he is" way.

The good news was that there was no news on our warehouse. (And a quick peek at action on the servers of the fire station nearest the warehouse didn't show anything to do with us.)

The good news was that, due to hackers working hard to nuke any new SWS data...It looked like there *had* been body and vehicle cams on the team that came for us, but it got corrupted even as it uploaded. From little things we could recognize in code, having done a few online raids and shit with other hackers, we were pretty sure the nasty bit of code that might have saved Jonny's ass was written by someone we knew SWS had tried to force into working for them. Three cheers for vengeance!

The good news was that Jonny's person had checked in. She had his family tucked into a safe house until he let her know what to do. And she'd set up a crew to keep watch so they could see if anyone tried to get into the family home or whatever. Now that Jonny had access to more funds, thanks to us draining SWS accounts, he could do everything necessary to keep them safe and get them into a good life (hopefully back to a slightly comfier version of their old one) ASAP.

The *bad* news on the news was a "local guy makes it big" story. Or, rather, as the perky anchor explained, "In a case of local church makes it big, or mega, the Divine Community Church has some mega big friends. You might recognize the name of the megachurch, which has funded the development of a cure for the so-called beat down flu and is *giving away* doses of the cure to any and all who want it. Well, after they reached out to make sure the CDC and the World Health Organization would be able to use the cure now that beat down flu is spreading widely, they caught a very important eye." A picture replaced the anchor's face, and she explained what it was to those who might not see so well. "Yes, that's right, that's Seattle resident and church leader Shepherd Michaelson, leader of the Divine Community Church, meeting the President of the United States! Sources say the President wanted to thank Shepherd Michaelson for the generosity of the church, and that he also spent some private time counseling with the shepherd. As you know, the President's lifelong pastor and spiritual advisor passed away last month. Could it be our own Shepherd Michaelson will fill the role?"

I'd never really worried about the religious life of a U.S. president, but I suddenly felt an urge to only support atheist presidents from now on. Shit.

"I hope he wasn't on your list of people to email," I mumbled to Rye. Glum. Oh, man, glum like I was 15 and grounded.

Fortunately, to balance out that news, we had all the data we'd stolen from our raid of the Divine Community plant. And it was just as tasty a score as we could have hoped. Our initial search of the files for "Peacemaker," turned up an array of specs. They weren't proof of ill-doing, but some of them were labeled differently than what we'd seen from SWS. In an alphabet we *did know*, it confirmed there were beta and release versions of both the vI and the vII. We shifted those off to Doc and Engie posthaste, just in case there was useful stuff in there that wasn't in the SWS files. They'd had no luck figuring out the kill switch issue yet; they couldn't find enough in the specs to figure out exactly how it worked, much less how to disable it. They *were*, however, able to let me know with a reasonable degree of confidence just what size of...sieve or filter or something the cure could be passed through to make sure people got just cure and not a vII as well. Maybe we could still keep the cures rolling out in time to save people, rather than having to shut that down until we could get clean doses.

In addition to that useful information, we had all the proof we needed to show that, indeed, Divine Community were putting a vII in each cure. That stuff took us longer to find, because only some of it was easily found searching for "Peacemaker" or "SWS" or "vII." But what we found was carefully tucked away communications with SWS, some laying out how many units of the vII the Divine Community could expect until they had their own equipment set up to manufacture them, one memo dated after we blew HQ that was SWS letting the church know they'd need to increase their own vII manufacturing now, and memos confirming both that a vII would be fine if it sat in the cure a long while and that it could be delivered via an injection in the arm. We found iterations of maps and plans for how to best stage rollout of their disease, as well as the documents we'd previously had that showed the different attempts at manufacturing an appropriate disease and cure. We found lists of people, Peacemaker unit numbers, locations, and injection dates. The early dates were all clumped in Seattle, then spread outward through (a little research showed) poor communities and neighborhoods, until it was finally given the wider release. Hell, they'd kept orderly records of the shipment of both the infecting agent and the cure to their faithful employees in other countries. We found the note we'd had before, where Shepherd Michaelson specifically called out unleashing the disease and offering a cure as a way to get people to let them in. Basically, we found the proof that they'd made beat down flu, released it on the world in order to get converts, and then contaminated the cure with the vII in alliance with SWS. And we did it all in about a day. Fuck yeah!

Which left the question of proof that might convince the authorities they had an alien problem, not just a religious one.

As we sat to discuss what to do about proving the aliens were real, we heard back from Doc and Engie. What we'd sent was exactly what they needed to revise their instructions for removing Peacemakers of every type represented by the specs. They'd even sorted out ways for doctors to tell which version of the vI or vII they were removing (looked like there was a vI.0 and vI.1, as well as a vII.0 and vII.1; hopefully no others, because we didn't have specs for anything more), which clearly mattered for more than things like the vI.0 not detecting drug use. They were relieved to discover that only the vII.1 included a kill switch. It looked, from related memos, like the Peaceforgers added that when they started seeing indications that people were having Peacemakers removed. Because of course they did.

We quickly (and anonymously, of course) emailed all their updates to the same doctors and other people who'd gotten all the other instructions in previous mailings. I made sure to drop a note for Lex that it was now time to get Marleina (and herself; couldn't forget that she still had a bug secreted in her brain) to the doctor. Big checkmark next to that whole issue. I was feeling optimistic about our chances to wrap this whole mess up soon.

Riles gave my arm a squeeze. "Just need to get the proof and get the rest of the info out. Almost there."

"So, your list of who to send to is done?" I asked.

Zie sighed. "Yeah. Just...a heads up for you all. You know how, after World War II, certain countries we won't name took in the Nazis' scientists? Probably didn't look closely enough at the politics of those scientists, just at how the countries might profit or do better in war with those scientists' brains working for them?"

Nobody nodded, but the narrow-eyed looks we all exchanged told zir that, yeah, we knew what zie was talking about.

"Well, let's just say that plenty of countries threw themselves at SWS scientists—who may or may not be Peaceforgers—once they learned that mind control was possible." Zie made a disgusted moue. "It's not like there's nobody on my list; it's just shorter than you'd hope. Enough people, but...What the fuck, humans?"

With the end in sight, it was suddenly easy for me to be encouraging. "Okay, but we have enough people. There's hope. Especially, I mean, we have people in the U.S., right? Where we can most easily attack their ship from?"

Riles nodded.

"The problem," Jonny said, "is that any video or photos we send to try to convince the authorities they've got an alien problem...We can show them the writing, but they can write that off as...Didn't one of you mention at the start that it could just be people making up a code language?"

I nodded. I thought that might have been me. It was a reasonable point.

"And," he went on, "we can point them at the satellite thing to see the fishes swim to avoid an object, but can they get any sort of thing down there to confirm? If I were the aliens, I'd have sensors to detect things like Riley's fish broadcasting back to us. Or to notice if a sub got too close."

Bryan nodded, conceding that, yeah, using the unmanned subs for that might not actually fix things. He added, "Or they could decide the ship is just something new from another country."

Jonny shifted, clearly uncomfortable with what was coming next. "But...I feel pretty sure that to even get them to check for the ship or at all consider the possibility that this isn't a joke, we're going to need to give them something...substantial. We're going to need...Zane to take a big risk."

"Yeah, but even if Zane goes on video, they'll assume it's good special effects or that pics are done with photo manip, won't they?" asked Rye.

"I think they will. I think...We need to ask Zane, to persuade Zane, to let us use them, video of them, anyway, but we also need...more." Jonny hated where he was going; it was written all over his face.

Based on the way he replied, with a hint of defensiveness and another of aggression (ah, and here was the downside of his interest in our alien friend and of shitty sleep making us all a little more on edge), Bryan also hated it. "Even just asking them to let us use video...That's just huge. That fucks them. What do you think we should ask Zane for? What more than they've already given? I thought there was no more killing. I thought—"

"Oh, for fuck's sake," I cut him off. I took a breath and tried to be calmer. "Listen, Bry, I know that Zane is great. And I doubt anyone's asking them to give up a finger or turn themselves over. Try to remember that we're actually not the sort of assholes who enjoy people dying or getting hurt. And I think we all like them. Nor do I think that one person is responsible for taking on themselves the crimes of their so-called race or species. But, we're out of options. Unless you have some. Asking for video, asking for...blood or a cheek swabbing or some totally basic shit like that is reasonable given the situation. This is one life made harder in order to literally save all of humanity."

Jonny nodded and said, as I took a breath, "Exactly. Just some DNA. That's all I was going to suggest." He was managing to keep a much more neutral tone than I was.

I continued, still feeling surly. "Especially when...when certain humans we know have taken much more difficult actions because they were the only ones who could...Similarly, Zane is the only Peaceforger we seem to have to help in this. Though, if someone else in their rebel group wants to give up the DNA or the video, I'm good with that. But somebody has to do that stuff." I gestured at our dirty grotto and said, "I didn't get stuck living here and risk everything just to be set back over proving that they're real." I folded my arms tried not to glare as I admitted, "And none of my actual ideas for manufacturing evidence have turned out at all persuasive."

Through clenched teeth, Bryan replied, "You do fucking realize that, if the Peaceforgers get hands on whatever DNA evidence or vids we send, Zane is dead? Or at least totally fucking cut off from their people, their family? But probably dead."

With painful and frightening calm, calm with a hint of kindness somehow, Jonny replied, "Just like, if we get caught, we're dead. And just like we're cut off from our families. Some of us even walked away from our families specifically to help...well, at that point, I didn't even realize it was the whole damned world; I thought it was a smaller set of people. So, you know...I'm sure we all feel for Zane, but I'm also pretty sure that we kind of feel like what we're asking is...pretty reasonable and something we'd all be willing to do. Given the stakes."

Stared down by all of us, Bryan narrowed his eyes, seemed ready to dig into anger, then quietly acquiesced. "I'll ask them. But I'll defend them against you if they don't want to. Clear?"

"Fair enough." I said it, I tried to sound like I meant it...but I didn't mean it. If Zane wasn't being more logical about this than Bryan, I'd sort out some damned DNA on my own, thanks. I really hated how quickly living down here and generally living with constant pressure for almost a month had turned us mean.

"Get me something sterile to collect DNA and I'll go talk to them. And I'll get permission to release the video of them talking, explaining everything." Bryan turned back to his portable. "Hope you're all ready to fit one more person in here. Because they're obviously going to have to run now too."

With forced enthusiasm, Riles said, "Now our fake band has enough people to have a horn section!"

Bless Riley. We all snickered the tiniest bit. Bryan and I even exchanged kind shoulder slaps, as if reminding ourselves and each other that we were actually friends.

Because I was worried they'd object, I hadn't told anyone exactly how I was going to get DNA collection supplies. Because I was tired and eager to be done, I had ignored my paranoia, taken a chance. And it wasn't until I was sliding into the shadowed booth in the back of a Mexican joint, face-to-face with Detective Engalls of the Seattle PD for the first time since we'd reported 'Randa's murder, that I came to my senses. Well, fuck...

Engalls scrutinized my face. "You kind of look like shit. Like you've been making hard choices and on the run." He pushed the plastic basket of chips and salsa at me, like he thought that might actually help.

I helped myself to a chip as I replied. "I kind of feel at least as shitty as I look. Whether or not it's for those reasons, I couldn't say." I looked around. I didn't know what I was looking for, but I wanted to believe I'd notice something was amiss if he was there with intent to get a confession or capture me. Obviously, I noticed fuck all.

"Why did you decide to trust me?"

I sighed. "Part desperation, part stupidity. Part keeping an eye on things and you seeming to be a guy who maybe isn't out to stop people who are actually doing good, keeping this so-called free nation free."

"Sounds more like a whole lot of stupidity." He held up his hands. "Not that I'm unhappy you messaged me, but it definitely wasn't an objectively smart move."

"Yeah, well, as established, I am in a shitty way. And, as you might also have established through investigation, I'm not exactly used to all the things that have made life shitty lately." I sighed, thinking of our losses and hard choices. "Not at all."

Engalls passed me a bag. A quick peek showed that, as requested, he'd set me up with the stuff I needed to do cheek swabs and get quick blood draws for collecting DNA samples in the field. "Thanks. This should be the last piece in theoretically making a convincing show of evidence about a...a pretty fucked up threat from an unexpected source."

"I guess asking you about it would be a waste of breath?"

I nodded. "But, listen, if you felt like doing me one more solid...if you heard some crazy rumors about...things that either sound like science fiction or like maybe there was more to the Peacemaker shit show...If you heard stuff like that and could at all casually help people believe that maybe it's true...Well, that would be fantastic. And, if I make it through this and can show my face in this town again, coffee and a long tale are on me. Off the record, of course. Purely a fictional tale of what maybe was done by those unknown people who've shaken things up lately."

It was Engalls's turn to nod. "Sounds good. And, since it's relevant to one of your past interests and this DNA thing reminded me of it...There were rumors flying around the station, the day after the SWS HQ thing, that the medical examiner had found weird stuff she couldn't explain while trying to identify some of the bodies. I didn't pay attention to details, because I try to ignore office gossip, but..." He shrugged as if to say, "Can't help the shit I hear."

"Oh, that's *very* interesting. And definitely probably relevant. Thanks!" I was going to have to poke at the ME's files, it appeared.

"And, Katja...Thanks. Not sure if you knew, but I have a kid whose stepdad freaked out and got a Peacemaker put in her head. That could have been my girl killing kids, out of her mind and brainwashed." He sounded almost like there were some real emotions in his fascist pig heart.

"Some things just have to be taken care of, even if one isn't the person with the right skills or experience. I'm glad your kid is okay. That the skills that someone *does* have were enough to take care of things." I paused a beat, then did the responsible thing. "Did...did you hear the updated news? About the vII? Because, if not...It's not quite over yet. But the information for finally sorting it out has just been found and delivered." I shrugged and too-casually said. "You know, according to my theoretical friend who knows about this stuff. Just make sure your doctor has the info about the kill switch."

"Oh. Shit. No, I hadn't heard." He pulled out his mobile, then paused. "Hey...I hate to ask or mention it, but...When I called down to make sure I understood what to tell you had happened to your gran, the examiner I spoke to said...Listen, your gran's doctor confirmed that she'd had beat down flu and there can be complications. But it also almost looked like someone had done brain surgery recently on her..." He trailed off.

I swallowed the grief that was reaching out, cleared my throat. "My gran was an amazing woman, and you've almost got all the pieces. Just...someone had to be how we found out about the kill switch..." I tried to cough away the emotion. "I'm sure Gran would be glad to have saved your kid's life." I rubbed at my face, needing to be gone and to not cry in public. I slipped out of the booth.

"Shit." It was a hoarse whisper. He spoke up, and his voice had an edge of emotion as he said, "Seriously, Katja, thank you. Be safe, okay? I'm looking forward to a drink and a tale."

"Will do, Johnny Law. Will do." I made sure my mask was on and got my arse back to my friends.

As soon as Bryan left to meet with Zane, the DNA-collecting gear in his hand, I asked, "Does anyone's bug-detecting watch still work? I want to go make sure Gran's house is okay. Just in case I get to come back and actually live there."

"As much as I'm into the idea of reclaiming our lives and settling down—" Jonny started.

"Mine works." Riles interrupted. "I'm totally up for some house time." Zie stood and smacked at the dirt on zir ass.

I stood too. "You coming?" I quirked an eyebrow at Jonny.

He sighed and shook his head, but he stood to go. "Maybe we can at least grab showers while we make this inadvisable stop."

Riles slipped zir arm through his. "Mate, it's not like we're going to one of *our* places. This is minor league inadvisable."

So, we shouldered our bags, put on our masks, sent Bryan a quick note (so he wouldn't be worried when he came back and we were gone), and grabbed a cab.

Once I was in Gran's house (my house now), with no alarms from the watch, I didn't know what to do. I was overwhelmed with emotion. This was where I'd grown up. This had been Gran's. And, depending on how things went, this might be my last time standing here. I was so tangled in the emotion that I'd forgotten Riles and Jonny were standing behind me.

I jumped a little when Jonny reminded me, "You could stay here. You guys are all clear of actual charges and probably of real suspicion now. Just Zane and I have to run at this point."

I sighed. "Part of me wants you just to hide out here. But I know that's ridiculous." I turned to face him. "And I'm pretty sure that I'd never forgive myself if I just let you ride off into the sunset without me. With a good looking alien to hold you at night. Especially when I *am* on the Peaceforger radar." I snorted. "The civilians might believe CFO Williams blew things up, or that Kitty was MK, but I kind of doubt the Peaceforgers have actually decided I'm entirely okay."

"Well, listen." Rye's tone was thoughtful. "We set Gran up with all that smart home kind of shit, so we can program the house to turn on lights. We can leave cameras to keep an eye. Set up an alarm. Try to tuck some shit out of the way so it's not an easy steal." Zie nodded. "It's possible we could come back if the soldier boys hop to and take out the aliens quickly." Zie headed into the office where Gran's computer was. "I'll get working on that."

"You should grab some things, make sure there's nothing it would break your heart to leave behind or...maybe there's something that would give you good feelings just to have around." Jonny, as usual, had a good sense of belongings.

He kindly followed me from room to room, asking me about the meaning of each thing that made me pause. It kept me on track. In the end, I grabbed some of Gran's old t-shirts (she had a collection of shirts she'd held onto from as early her teens and 20s, a mix of band logos, culture jokes, and some film merchandise). Every time I wore her Banzai Institute shirt, I'd feel a little bit of Gran with me. I also took a few pieces of jewelry that either had deep sentimental meaning or that I'd been coveting my whole life. Nothing expensive; Gran didn't believe in wasting money on spendy jewelry. Basically, I seemed to have gathered up some stuff that would let me look a bit like the coolest version of Gran. She'd had a thing for aesthetics, so I figured she'd approve. (On an impulse, I threw in a wine-colored cardigan and a cheap black velvet jacket to complete the look.)

We knew we shouldn't stay long, but we grabbed quick showers anyway. If only cleaning clothes were something we could do quickly...It seemed a shame to put the dirty shit back on, but my life was all about shame for the moment.

I used up all my willpower to hold back tears as we locked up, sending something like prayers to that higher power I didn't believe in that, someday soon, I'd be back here for good.

We beat Bryan back. Weird. I sent him a quick message to make sure he was okay. All he had to say in reply was:

Yep ;-)

Right. Okay. I'd be sure to sort out why the winking emote later. Riley, of course, immediately asserted it was for sex. Either way, he was fine. Or someone who could crack his mobile was, and I was going to leave it at that.

Whilst Jonny and Rye finished researching who to send DNA samples to, I dug into the files from the medical examiner's work after we blew the SWS HQ. Hat tip to Engalls for pointing me that way. Anyway, the shitty news was that most of the people who'd died that day seemed to be human. Fuck. I found myself very purposefully setting aside those who would have been in Conference Room Beta. Those were *not* on us. And, much as my guilt wanted me to linger on the others, like the CorpSec people who were human, I knew I needed to stay on target.

By the time the building blew, the SWS executives who'd been in Conference Room Alpha had all been rushing from the lift to their cars. It looked like the first bodies the ME saw were CorpSec, easy to identify, quick to issue a death certificate for. It looked like the execs were the last to be dug out and tagged, aside from the humans in Conference Room Beta. So, it was late when the ME got to them.

Initially, if they were easy to identify, like CFO Williams, she just wrote up the death certs; she didn't pause to poke at kind of weird stuff like blood that didn't seem to be quite the right color. Even if some biological attack had done that, it was pretty damned clear that the explosion was the cause of death, and there were a lot of bodies to process.

When she hit her first exec who wasn't as easy to ID, she slowed down. She discovered the lack of fingerprints and admitted that there were definitely no pores in the skin. She opened mouths and eyes to try to compare dental records and retinal scans. Basically, she actually finally took a close look.

And you'd think that would have been enough that *she* would have blown the whistle on the whole alien thing. Nope! I listened to her audio log, the one she'd made as she did the exams, and it was pretty clear that she had opted for the answers that didn't make her look crazy. Which is to say that she used the info that was already out to narrow down which execs *should* be on those slabs, looked up the execs online to make closest matches, and wrote the death certs that could all accurately pin their deaths on the explosion.

But she *knew* something was up. I could hear it in her pauses, her verbal stumbles, the quiet mumbling to herself that she stopped when she realized she was doing it. And, when her assistant tried to point out what she was avoiding, she cautioned him to think long and hard about what he was about to go on record saying...and then she sent him home. She went from "what appears to be, but must actually be" when she found weird (alien) shit to just not mentioning it. There were pauses. "I'm opening the chest cavity and..." But she kept going, kept doing the exams.

And those bodies had long been released to their next of kin for...well, a quick search told me that every single one of them was cremated. Imagine that...

Shit. Sure would have been nice to get our hands on *those*.

It looked like any pics or samples the ME had taken were gone. Had she deleted them or had someone else?

I grumbled, cranky and incoherent, then let myself into the ME's personal computer and mobile. I felt like, if she wasn't corrupt or some bullshit like that, she could be helpful, someone to pull into the loop. And, if she *was* corrupt, then fuck her for not pointing out that some of the people weren't humans when she'd had a chance. If that were the case, I'd be sure to take some kind of revenge. It felt like revenge was about all I had these days.

It took some digging, but I found a folder...For whatever reason, she hadn't deleted the pics she'd taken. Maybe she'd also kept the samples somewhere? She definitely knew that there were ridges under the hair, that the skin was poreless, and that the eyes weren't, well, human. She fucking *knew*. I sighed, frustrated. And I saved all that shit to my own drive. I was happily going to let her submit evidence to our cause.

The question was whether she knew and would help or knew and had the kind of loyalties or selfishness that would allow her to just let the human race get fucked. And how was I going to figure it out?

I chewed the inside of my cheek and considered.

Right. I could go through her mails and messages from the night until now. I could randomly eavesdrop via her mobile or cameras in her vicinity. I could...Oh, hell yes! I could luck into a woman who kept a journal on her portable, words and doodles and random voice memos. It was encrypted. She'd sprung for some nice encryption, actually. One that, if I'd been a clumsier hacker, would have deleted the whole thing when the safety on it got tripped.

Clever me, I got in. I got what I needed. It was a drunken bit of babbling at her computer the day after she'd worked on all the bodies.

"I found some weird stuff, fucked up stuff...shit...I should just pretend it didn't happen. Best case, they call me crazy. Worst case, whoever now runs SWS goes after me. Right? Dammit. Just...let those bodies go. Great scientific discovery, right? But, oooooooh no, can't do shit with it. Nooooooo. Because it fucks up my life if I do. You think...You think, hey, I have the bodies. That's enough, right? But noooooo. No. Sorry, bitch. They had to be bodies of powerful people. Shit. Maybe I show someone in charge the bodies? Yeah. Okay. Yeah. I do that tomorrow."

The next day wasn't a voice memo, just a quick little bit of text.

Came in to find bodies immediately claimed and shipped. Fast. Way too fast. Bodies of powerful people, right?

So, maybe she wouldn't be a great asset, but she might. Maybe. And it probably wouldn't *hurt* to get her the info that she probably already had.

I added her to the list Jonny and Riles were building and brought them up to date on why.

By the time Bryan returned, we'd researched which doctors and biologists we should send DNA samples to. We had addresses ready and, the instant he stepped in the door, we headed right back out to package the results and send them via overnight post. Bryan was quiet through it all, so I didn't ask questions. I figured that, at this point, it just mattered we had the samples and they were on their way.

Bryan stayed quiet as we finished the next step too, sending emails to the experts who'd be getting the packages, making it look like they were sent by the authorities we needed to convince of the threat.

Please analyze the samples I've sent you (via overnight post) *immediately* upon receipt. It's very important that you let

me know the composition of the DNA first thing in the morning. Apologies for such an ask Friday night/Saturday morning.

We made sure to do plenty of Cc-ing and Bcc-ing and to keep an eye on computers...Computers receiving email, computers on the networks of our DNA experts (hoping to see their work). We kept our other eye on those who would get the package we had pulled together, documents and video to send to our chosen legal authorities and military personnel (and the few politicians who we thought could be counted on to discretely push the rest to take action). At this point, it was just hours until we sent our email to these carefully-selected law enforcement, etc. Hours until they got an eyeful of "here's how Divine Community is bad and proof of their scheme; here's the spec for a functioning Peacemaker detector, in case you missed it, and how to clean that shit out of the cure; and here's an alien to tell you that *they're fucking aliens*, and also this alien wants you to know you gotta be sneaky ninjas in what you do because this is literally the fate of the fucking world (please see attached SWS self destruct docs and building plans with underwater door to see that we're totally serious about them being dramatically villainous)."

As soon as the DNA experts started sending their emails, we'd send ours and, finally, be done with things. Not nearly as dramatic a resolution to our actions as blowing up a building, but I wasn't going to complain about lack of drama ever again.

Riles was the first to drag me out for a "walk."

"Kot, I'm worried. I'm worried about Kitty."

We were walking arm-in-arm, so I gave zir arm a squeeze. "Why're you worried, poppet? I mean, besides the fact that she's in the dark and that's all we know."

"Logically, Peaceforgers have her, right?"

I nodded. "Sounds like a valid assumption."

"That probably means she's local, even if 'local' means 'in the Pacific Ocean,' right?"

"Yeah. Yeah, I hear you."

"I know we don't know *where* she is, but how do we break her out if we're far away?" The g/ap mask muffled plenty, but it couldn't muffle zir despair. "Are we abandoning her again?"

Oh. Man. That was a tough and valid question. Shit. I chewed the inside of my cheek (this whole aliens bullshit was going to leave me with a hole in my cheek) and tried to think of the right answer. A true answer that didn't somehow fuck things up for Rye.

"What if I promise that, as soon as we can figure out exactly where she is, I'll come back with you? Whether we're one day out or already settled in our new place."

"Maybe."

"I'm just...I'm worried that, if we don't go, we'll somehow end up caught before we can save her. Or...How much longer," and I tried to make my voice kind, make my voice acknowledge that this applied to me too, "How much longer can you sleep in the fucking underground before you can't function? Or before some sadistic frat boy decides to take a hunting trip and finds us?"

Zir sigh barely made it past zir mask. "Okay. Fair. I just...she seems to really be getting more aware and capable every day. Literally any day now, she could figure it out."

I squeezed zir arm again. "And when that day happens, I'm with you. I promise." I promised even as I knew that meant more damned meat stuff. I'd live to regret it, I was sure. But not as much as I'd regret abandoning Riles to do it alone or abandoning Kitty to whatever the dark was.

I hadn't been sitting down for 5 minutes when Jonny wanted to take a walk. It was a good thing the real work we could do with our current Wi-Fi access was done.

"What was up with Riley?" he asked.

"Just Riley stuff. Not my business to spread zir business," I shrugged.

"I'm just worried about zir."

"Worried?" I was too, obviously, but I didn't want to accidentally give anything away by admitting it.

"It's just that we still haven't figured out the Kitty thing. I'm worried zie'll break or refuse to go or...something. I don't know." He put an arm around me, pulled me closer. "Not like I wouldn't do the same, of course."

"Good save," I teased. Then, more seriously, I said, "Your concerns make sense. And...I feel pretty sure Riles will do what zie needs to do. But...If zie figures out where Kitty actually is, wherever it is, I need you to know that I won't hesitate to help Riles plan and act to save her."

With faux shock, he said, "Even if it takes meat stuff?"

I softly punched his shoulder. "Fuck you. Yes. Just don't tell Bryan. I don't want anyone getting the idea that I'm actually made for anything that isn't digital."

He let his hand slip down to give my ass a quick squeeze. "Oh, I think the word is already out that you're made for at least one or two anythings that aren't digital."

"Bastard."

"I am. But, also, count me in. If we can figure out where she is, I'm on Team Kitty Rescue."

I grinned, not that he could see it, behind my mask, and said, "I know." I also felt pretty sure Bryan would be as well. If she was more than a glitch or a lure, someday, we would save Kitty.

After an evening of silence, Bryan finally spoke up. "Zane was completely willing to give DNA and to let us use their video. They're a better person than plenty of humans. Totally graceful about it, even knowing what it meant for their life."

With undeniable sincerity, Jonny responded, "Then I'm glad they were the one who found us. It's good people who will make this thing end alright."

To me, that left the question hanging in the air: How many of those getting a DNA sample or emails were good people? For my part, I hoped enough of them were, but I feared that wouldn't be the case. Again I realized that the species I was working to save might, indeed, be just as fucked up as the Peaceforgers thought.

Of course, our Rye had questions too. Different questions.

"You sure took plenty of time to get a little DNA, Bry," zie said cheekily, pretending to concentrate on zir cup of noodles.

"Uh-huh." Bryan blushed.

I knew zie was onto the scent of sex, because zie used zir most innocent tone to ask, "Anything you want to share? Hmmm? Anything about all the ways you might have interacted with potential sources of DNA samples?"

When Bryan didn't reply but just became much more invested in examining his meal, Riley scooted over, put an arm around him, and said, "I think we all realize that I am going to be adorably annoying until you tell me about sex with an alien." If voices could flutter their eyelashes, zirs did just that.

"Normally, I'd consider your business, well, *your* business," Jonny said. "But, one, this involves an alien and, two, you were gone an impressively long time. If I could make my voice do what Rye's just did, I'd help zir flank you."

Bryan looked at me as if asking for help. Oh, a wee chance to be a bitch in return for his morals and shit keeping me involved in the Peaceforger shit. I almost grinned.

Instead, I shrugged casually. "Mate, I've got to side with my Team Run the Fuck Away teammate." I threw a conspiratorial smile at Riles. "Annoy away, poppet!"

With a resigned sigh, Bryan grumbled, "It's not like I didn't know this conversation was coming. I just figured maybe we could do it on the way to South Dakota."

He paused, as if he expected somebody would take him up on that alternate timeframe. I mentally snorted. Did he even know us?

Ever the helper, Riles noted obligingly, "Sure. We could wait to ask you until Zane's also trapped in the car with us for hours."

That was enough. Bry got a slightly panicked look. He'd known this conversation would happen, and I could see the gears turning as he stumbled through bits of the unfinished reply he'd been trying to put together.

"It wasn't like I could just fall into bed with them. First, I wanted to make sure we both had...compatible goals for sex. Without a shared cultural context or understanding of each other's contexts, can you really have consent? So, made sure first it was about wanting to express physical and emotional attraction via sexual pleasure..." He cleared his throat. "And then we had to educate each other about erogenous zones and what stimulates those places in ways we like. And, finally, we had to sort out how to use the, um, gear at hand to make it happen and leave everyone happy."

"But they knew about your erogenous zones, right?" asked Riley, ignoring the sensible and mindful parts about Bryan's answer.

"Mate, do you think that TV and movies actually give a complete picture of human erogenous zones?" Bryan snorted.

"Good point." Riles nodded sagely. "I wouldn't trust TV to teach me how to kiss someone, much less fuck them."

After a moment of expectant silence, Riles said, "And then?"

Bry shook his head. "Nope. That's all you get."

"But you enjoyed yourself?" Riley asked.

The only answer zie got was a wink and a grin.

I imagined that, somewhere, Zane was feeling relief, a sense that they'd dodged a bullet. Of course, that would just mean they didn't know how persistent Riles was when curious about sexual things. For Bryan's sake, I'd cross my fingers Rye kept a leash on it until we were on the other side of the long drive. Nobody does awkward quite like *we* do awkward.

CHAPTER 22

The plan for our day was very simple. The DNA result emails would come in, we'd send our informative email, we'd go to Zane's (for them and our vehicle), and then we'd drive east. Obviously, we'd keep an eye on things as we went, hoping we'd watch the people sworn to protect assorted chunks of humanity in the United States spring (covertly) into action. If they weren't covert, we'd be able to move from watching by spying on them to watching it on the news. That's how we understood it.

If they didn't spring into action...well, then we had no idea and would regroup. It would probably involve using the drones and unmanned craft *they* should have used. But, we all agreed, we'd done all we could do in Seattle. At least until we knew what the deal was with Kitty. Time to move back from the geographical front of this secret invasion and work from a safer place. Preferably, somewhere we wouldn't have to wear masks even into the summer to keep our identities safe.

The DNA result emails came in. The experts were baffled. Some hedged around it, but others flat-out said that the DNA was alien to anything they were aware of on Earth. A couple even mentioned some extraterrestrial DNA collected off-planet, noting that the sample they'd received, whilst not like that DNA, was just as different from any life on Earth.

We sent our informative email. We spied a bit, just for a moment, on a few key people's computers. The pattern seemed to be that they'd read the DNA email, check their Sent email folder, re-read the DNA email, start working on our email. And, depending on the order they opened attachments, they might go back to the DNA email or they might look up things like where beat down flu had first appeared, how many had gotten the cure, or the history of Divine Community. Some ran checks on Shepherd Michaelson and other key leaders. From our side, we couldn't tell much yet, but at least they weren't just blowing us off.

We went to Zane's. On the way there, I got a message from Lex. Marleina was now bug-free and, once she was awake, Lex would get her own bug out. Excellent. That meant our vII plans, both sets, lest we forget that Marleina had a beta version and the release version in her head (thanks to the cure), were good. I shot a note to let Doc and Engie know that their plans had already been verified. When I showed everyone the message on my screen, we had a mini-celebration (quietly, lest we fuck ourselves over by talking about things in public) of high fives and grins. (I'm assuming they grinned too. Damn the masks.) Fortunately, we'd be celebrating our way the hell out of town very soon.

Anyway, we went to Zane's. They met us down at our vehicle with a bag of, I assumed, their own necessary belongings.

After greetings, I made sure to say, "Thank you so much for...your DNA and for letting us release the video. We know that, like us, that means you're going to have to leave everyone and everything behind."

Zane blushed blue, but graciously said, "It was the right thing to do. At least this saves me having to decide whether to just never commit and always be questioned or to pretend to commit. Time for me to choose to take a bolder stand."

I saw Bryan give their hand a quick squeeze and hoped that it was a sign of peace to come. Obviously, there was no biological mandate that kept our two species from being able to sort shit out.

"Okay, ready to go?" Jonny asked, much less impatiently than I wanted to ask.

But no harm in me quickly, cheerfully, replying, "Aye! Let's go!"

And Riles enthused, "Definitely! Team Run the Fuck Away approves of this action." Zie and I exchanged grins (we did; I saw it in zir eyes). *Finally.*

"Actually..." Zane seemed to cringe as they said it. "I have, uh, one last thing to do. It...it will be quick. I just...I have to make sure that the leader of my 'heretical' group knows what happened to me. In a very general way, of course. Otherwise, they might assume the worst and rush to put a lot of unnecessary emergency procedures into effect." They looked pleased with themselves as they said, "I wanted to wait until the last minute, just to be careful."

"Good thought," confirmed Bryan. "How long should we wait before we worry?"

"It won't be long. If you're refueling, we could meet there. It should take me less than an hour from here to...wherever you're stopping."

Okay, so it wasn't exactly "go to Zane's, and then drive east," but it basically was. So Bryan and Zane kissed, we humans all hopped into our vehicle, and away we went.

Obviously, refueling didn't take an hour, but we took the time, once we were done, to poke in on people's computers, grab snacks, and use the loo. Thoroughly prepped for a cross-country road trip. Onwards to Rapid City, as we'd originally planned to do after the SWS explosion.

"You know what I want to figure out?" Riles mused. "I want to figure out how to hack the Peaceforger's ship computers, then fly them off Earth and into the sun. Once we make sure Kitty's not there, of course."

Jonny joined in, "Or at least wipe everything about Earth from their databanks and fly them way the fuck away from us."

"Remember that you're talking about Zane's people," reminded Bryan. "So, I'd vote for Jonny's ending. Or at least not mentioning it in front of Zane if we're opting for Rye's."

"Mate, at this point, I'm happy to consider any plan that gets them gone. As long as I do it from a safe distance. Sitting in a comfortable living room. After a nice shower and change of clothes. And some good sleep." I liked the idea of the challenge hacking an alien computer would be once we figure out how to even interface with it, but not nearly as much as I liked that we could do it from somewhere safe and comfortable. At last.

Holy hell...We were finally out.

As promised, about an hour after they'd left us at theirs, Zane made it to the refueling station. They looked grim.

Looking around to be sure only we were listening, they quietly told us, "I think somebody talked. Somebody you sent your email to."

We froze, and Bryan delicately asked, "Why do you think that?"

"Because...the person I went to tell I was leaving got a message while I was there. And the other Peaceforgers, or at least those at the top, know about your email and the DNA samples."

"Holy shit." I was stunned. We'd been careful, and we hadn't seen anything that seemed like some dumbass human had sold out the species. It now looked like the stealth we'd hoped they would use *was* being used, but not for the right cause. Dammit, humans!

"Well, we all agreed we were out. So, not to be an asshole, but I'm taking one last piss and then heading east. I can't see what else we can do here. Or what requires us to be here to do it." And, without waiting for an answer, Riles turned and headed back to the toilets.

Before I could say pretty much the same thing (Team Run the Fuck Away!), Zane hesitantly said, "I may be dead if we stay. I'm also going to, uh, to piss." With an apologetic look to Bryan, they too walked to the toilets.

I didn't even bother saying anything, just gave Jonny and Bryan an apologetic shrug and headed that way myself.

I was standing at the sinks in the bathroom, exchanging "I can't believe this is finally fucking done" small talk with Riles and Zane (who both chose the ladies' toilets because, in general, they got less shit for their contempt of the gender binary in there than in the men's, regardless of what sex people might guess they were), when two things happened.

First, Kitty barraged Riley's mobile with messages. Zie held it up, looking concerned and confused. Row upon row, all it said was:

DANGER! RUN!

And, second, we heard gun fire. Shit.

We dashed out, but then crouched low as we moved from the back of the building to the side. We inched towards the front of the building. Whilst Riley and I tried to carefully take stock of the situation from around the corner of the service building, Zane dashed straight out.

I whispered, "Shit," and drew my gun, but I didn't follow.

From our careful vantage, we saw that three large, black vehicles (like the ones from the ambush at the plant) had pulled into the refueling station, blocking in our own smaller vehicle. It looked like there were over a dozen people (all masked, so I had no idea whether they were human or Peaceforger), all big and heavily armed, standing in front of those vehicles and shooting at ours. It was a wall of black and guns momentarily blazing, impossible odds and chaos. And it took me a moment to parse it, to realize that Jonny was on the ground.

Oh fuck oh fuck oh fuck! Jonny!

Riley must have known what I was going to do before I did, because zie grabbed me and stopped me just as I was diving out of our undetected space.

"What the fuck do you accomplish by going out?" zie hissed.

"What the fuck do we accomplish hiding back here?" I growled in reply.

Before zie could answer me, Bryan fell. Oh. Oh shit...Rye's grip on me increased, and I could hear zir breathing heavily, roughly.

An authoritative voice behind the armed meatsacks called out, "That's enough."

Zane was between us and our vehicle, just feet from the bodies of our friends, standing stock still, gun (Bryan must have given them one) pointed forward. Staring in the direction of the voice.

As a few of the men stepped forward, moving towards Jonny and Bryan's bodies (there was blood blossoming on Bryan's chest and running down Jonny's face...did I even have room to hope it was more than just bodies?), the source of the voice also stepped forward. Zane's gun was still up, but they didn't pull the trigger.

The Voice and the meatsacks must have felt sure they wouldn't, because nobody moved to take the gun. Zane was shaking, and then I saw why. The Voice was their broodmate, Shay.

Shay strode forward, right up to the gun pointed in her direction. She coolly stared Zane down. When they lowered their gun, Shay sneered, "You can't even fully commit to the wrong side, can you,? Traitor."

I was distracted by movement. I saw Bryan start to lift his hand and felt a surge of hope. But Shay had also seen it, and she turned, raising a gun of her own.

Except that she didn't have to pull the trigger, because Zane's tongue flashed out, hit Bryan's neck, and Bryan's hand and eyelids dropped in unison. I could feel a mutual fury of betrayal rise off both Riles and me.

Shay lowered her gun, and I could see the smirk as she watched Zane go over to the bodies. It looked like they were taking the guns off the bodies, off our friends, before they started trying to lift Bryan.

Shay barked, "Help them. Get the bodies in the car." She said more, it seemed to be aimed at Zane, but it was in their language.

Once Jonny and Bryan were loaded into a car, Shay stopped, her hand on Zane's cheek. "You had me worried, broodmate."

They gave her a small smile. "Timing is important. You know you and the others mean everything to me."

"The Divine shines through our kinship," she said, smiling broadly.

Zane returned the smile and, without looking back, climbed into Shay's vehicle.

What the hell?

Riley and I didn't move until we were sure they wouldn't even see us in their rearview. But then the spell of paranoia and fear broke, and Riley and I rushed out together, just to end up staring down at puddles of blood. I was on my knees, sobbing on the dirty concrete.

It didn't take us long to stop sobbing, to move to rage.

"That bitch betrayed us," snarled Riley.

Numbly, I asked, "Why didn't they tell Shay about us? I'm beyond confused."

"Don't care. I'm going to kill them." Riles was shiny fury, pacing tiny, agitated circles.

I'd tried to stop panicking, to start thinking. I put the boys' guns, left on the ground, in my pockets. Okay. They had our boys. I didn't have the luxury of grieving yet. Dammit. (What the fuck sort of life was this?)

I started taking stock. Trying to figure out if the amount of blood on the ground was too much. Whatever the hell "too much" meant. Should I take a pic, send it to Dr. Scott and ask *her* if it was too much?

My eyes caught on something under our vehicle. I moved carefully, avoiding the blood, and found two mobiles. Jonny's mobile. Bryan's mobile. My first instinct was to hug them to me like they could somehow comfort me. Hell, given how connected we were to our mobiles, it *was* pieces of them. I let a convulsive sob fall out of me.

But I pushed through, because I suddenly realized, "Riles, Zane didn't just leave their guns. I think they made sure the boys' mobiles got left." I held them up to show zir.

Zie stopped, face confused. "What the hell?"

And then zir mobile was pinging, over and over. Zie stopped to look. "Huh. Kitty's asking if I'm okay."

"Kitty who tried to warn us right before?"

We both froze, looked around and up, like somehow Kitty was, I don't know, a benevolent satellite? Or maybe lurking on the fueling station cameras?

Slowly, I stood. I got up to walk around our vehicle, see if it was driveable. The tires had made it through. Nothing obviously wrong. Bry seemed to have sprung for some bulletproofing, 'cause it didn't look as bad as expected. It still even had all its windows. Okay. I got in the driver's seat, relieved that the keys were in the ignition. And I just sat and stared at the windshield. Not through the glass. I didn't have the mental power for that yet. Eyesight stopped at the dirt and at the crack where a bullet had probably dinged it.

Quietly, Riles climbed into the passenger seat. The silence was thick.

Riles broke it, asking, "Did we check yet which human betrayed the planet?"

I shook my head. Then acknowledged, "We need to take stock. We need to figure this out. We need to take care of the practical things."

As if it would make much difference, I started the vehicle and pulled into the shadow between the back of the fueling station and the trees behind it. Riles tapped away on zir mobile whilst I did so.

"Okay. It was a senator. Messaged Michaelson." Zir tone shifted, clearly reading, imagining and mimicking how the senator might sound. "'Michaelson, get your house in order. You've got 5 minutes until the troops show up. Too many people got tipped off this morning. Unfortunately, not enough people put off by some bullshit about aliens. I expect this courtesy to be paid back.'" Riles looked up, zir face stony. "I fucking hate humans."

I growled. "I'm so over trying to save them all."

We simmered in silence. Well, silence outside. Inside, I was roiling. A storm. Rage and grief and fear and loss and howling fuckfuckfuck. We were almost out. We were almost done. We had done all we fucking could. We had given every-fucking-thing. (And, now, more of every-fucking-thing, dammit.)

Did we run? Did we stay?

Were our friends alive? Could we even find out? Could we get them back?

Could we fucking blow up the whole fucking Peaceforger ship? Because to hell with just erasing their computers if they'd killed more of our people, if the one Peaceforger we'd trusted had betrayed us.

And, even pulling it back, before the grander plans, where the hell did we stay? It was getting colder out and the underground was a shitty long-term solution, especially now that our better fighters weren't there to make sure no psycho frat brat jumped us, and there was no way to know whether our faces could be shown in public. (There was. Okay. I knew there was. But it would take time and research to be sure.)

Riley's mobile pinged insistently. "Kitty," zie reported.

"We have to try to save Jonny and Bryan," I noted.

"And beat the shit out of Zane. And hopefully their sister. And those fucking SWS execs. And Michaelson," Rye agreed, adding to our to-do list.

"But first, we have to figure out where we stay. Because, we stay, don't we?" Did I sound as defeated as I felt? I turned to look at zir.

Resigned, zie nodded. "We stay. I don't know how we do it all, but we stay."

My mobile was now pinging insistently too. I looked, and it was actually fucking Zane. "The fucking gall..." But I quickly shifted from annoyance and gave Riles a confused look. "Zane. What the hell?"

Riley grabbed it to read the message that kept repeating.

Please let me explain.
Also, my people are now debating scorched Earth. Be careful.
Please let me explain.
My People are talking scorched Earth.
Be careful.
Please let me explain

Over and over. Variations on the same message.

Riles was in rant mode. "Well, first, you're not replying to this bullshit. Because who the fuck are they to even try? And, second, 'be careful'?! From them?! I just...I can't even!" Zie threw my mobile in my lap and then threw zir hands in the air.

Zir mobile kept pinging.

We both just stared at the windshield.

Finally, Riley said, "But it's just us. And we're out of options. And only have what we have. We don't have Bryan's weapons contacts or..." Hysteria was lurking around the edges.

I put my hand on zir shoulder. "Okay. Yes. But breathe. One step at a time." I took a slow, careful breath of my own. "We have to be our own Bryan."

Zir mobile was still pinging.

"Still Kitty?"

Zie checked. "Yeah. But now...With the warning she sent...It feels even more off. Definitely not right. How did she know to warn us? It's like Zane. It doesn't match."

"Might as well see what's up. Before we go find a home. See if we need to ditch or wipe your mobile before we do that. Yeah?" I was feeling the dread calm that my mind reserved for big troubles. Like my building exploding or, apparently, my friends being shot and taken by a malevolent alien force.

Riley's brows were in a confused V.

"What does she say?"

"It's the same message over and over. 'Turn on your 3D.'" Zie looked at me. "What the hell?"

"I mean, first, silver lining here is that, whoever it is, they can't control your phone. So...what's our danger if you turn on 3D? Do you have yours hacked to do something odd?"

Zie shook zir head. "Shouldn't be any danger. It's just passive projection."

I shrugged. "What the hell? I'd turn it on." I could see the same message, pinging onto zir screen over and over.

Zie mumbled the reply as zie tapped it out. "Ok. Chill the fuck slowly out. One sec."

One more look at me, like zie wanted to make sure I was sure. I shrugged. Zie held zir mobile with the screen facing up, no cameras pointed towards us, and pushed the button.

CHAPTER 23

A wee projection of Kitty sprang up from Riley's mobile. In a tiny version of her voice, Holo-Kitty said, "Holy shit, baby. That took forever."

We both stared at the little Kitty, mute. She didn't look like Kitty had when last we saw her. She wasn't in a business suit, but was, if previous Saturday nights were a hint, in one of her favorite going out outfits, complete with hair and makeup. And a possibility that had been tickling the edge of my brain started to solidify. If that tickle was right, if this was an AI built on the person we knew (which would be a pretty damned awesome thing), she was, I reckoned, Kitty's ideal image of herself.

She swiveled, as if unsure where Riles was. "Can you hear me?"

Riley looked torn, like zie didn't know whether to feel relieved to see zir bae again or worried about this entirely new and unexpected manifestation. Quietly, zie replied, "Yeah. Yeah, I hear you."

Holo-Kitty asked, "Hey, will you turn your mobile? If you hold it like we're vid-chatting, I can see you too."

I nodded and shrugged. Do it. Sure.

Riles carefully held the mobile up, making sure the back camera cover was on. Making sure the front camera would only show zir.

Holo-Kitty shrieked. "Baby, you look shitty! Did they get you? Are you okay?"

When zie just watched Holo-Kitty with narrow eyes, she said, "I figured it out. I know where I am. I...Listen, baby, when you told me they were aliens—"

Zie was facing zir phone cam/Holo-Kitty, but it was clearly for my benefit that zie clarified, "Not very long before they attacked us. Definitely after everyone got emails. Definitely after we got fucked by a senator."

Holo-Kitty's face scrunched in confusion. Then she got it. "You're not alone! Someone else made it, and you don't want to get in trouble for telling me after you've been so careful not to tell me anything that could mess you up. Uh..." She turned, mumbling to herself, orienting herself as if she was in physical space. "Okay, you're in the passenger seat, so...over this way. Probably one of the others in the driver seat." Little Holo-Kitty turned as if looking at me. "Zie has been tight-lipped. And definitely didn't tell me until somebody else betrayed you."

She turned back to face Riles. "Once you said it was aliens, I remembered I'd found, like, a dictionary. Really, a lot of them. One each for all the languages there are on Earth or something, to convert to the alien language. To the language that I couldn't read. But I thought I was a body when I found it at first, so I thought it would be a waste to try to use it. But then, when I found it again, when I knew it was aliens and accepted something might be weird with me, it was like I suddenly knew it all in one look. And it all made sense."

Very seriously, she told zir, "Baby, I think I'm...I'm in their computer. For real. Like a soul trapped here or AI maybe?"

Riles shot me a look, eyebrow up. Kitty was AI? In other circumstances, this would be fucking fascinating. (It *was* fascinating, but this wasn't the time to feel or deal with fascination, sadly. Or even to give my brain a gold star for suspecting correctly.)

"I can tell you all about it. I can tell you now, because I get my paradigm. And I'll tell you everything. But first, I need to tell you something more important than my story."

She leaned forward, as if she were about to tell Riles an important secret, and we both leaned towards her instinctively.

"Baby, now that I know what's going on, I can help you. We can finish the job, the real job, the one behind what we were doing in October." She beamed and, in her tiny approximation of Kitty's voice, she assured us, "They're badasses, but we're badder. And we can win."

I had never in my life so badly wanted to believe the reality a hologram promised.

END

ACKNOWLEDGEMENTS

This book struggled to come to be as changes in the world (2016-2020 have been wild) and challenging life things bombarded all involved…and probably made me extra "delightful" to work with or be a friend and support to. Which is why special, massive gratitude and love must go to Clarissa C.S. Ryan and Sarah Keliher. Thank you for your persistence, valuable feedback, encouragement, and deep wells of patience. I'd swear I'll get better, but I think you've known me long enough to know the truth…

With all that hard stuff to overcome, I'm quite grateful as well for all who showed their love for *Peace Fire* and their eagerness for the sequel. Who left positive reviews, gave it as a gift, dropped me notes, recommended it to others, and so forth. If that's you, you've helped it seem worth continuing the work on hard days. (The final book is just coming back from beta readers as I write this, so I hope you won't have to stretch out your eagerness for so long this next time.)

One particularly amazing champion of my work (in word and deed), who's also been liberal in sharing her relevant expertise with me, has been Sarah Caseberry, and so I'm going to note that here for all the world to see. Thank you for your generosity. So much love for you always.

Thanks to George Cotronis of Ravenkult Studios for, once again, making excellent cover art. I realized too late that I thanked you on social media for the *Peace Fire* art, but not in the book. That was a gross oversight for which I hope you'll forgive me. (Fingers crossed you'll at least forgive me enough to make sure the final book in the trilogy has your art for the cover.)

Thanks to Jana Wright for being clever about forensics (lard and bleach FTW!)...just like I knew you'd be.

Thanks to people who were upset about Kitty at the end of *Peace Fire* but trusted me enough to buy this book anyway. (Shout out to the Justice for Kitty! club.)

Thanks to Shawn King for the 'nym D3AD_L1NX.

Love and gratitude to Simon, the most patient cat a writer could ask for. A decade with you was not enough, and my writing time was only improved by having you as my constant companion.

Loads of respect and love to the amazing people at TinyKittens, non-fictional heroes rescuing, doing TNR for, and otherwise helping feral and abandoned cats and restoring my faith in humanity. For Katja, it was one related mention in one sentence; for me, it's a real, daily inspiration. Shelly and her saintly crew have kept me from drowning in the darkness of this world and the inhumane acts of humans some days...especially after my own beloved cat passed and I had extra need of some kitten therapy. (If you need some of that, they have a 24/7 live video stream.)

And, of course, thank *you* for joining me for this next book in the trilogy. One to go! Hope you'll join me for that as well.

Photo by Jesse Means

Amber Bird is...A writer, a rockstar, and a sci-fi simulacrum...The author of the Peaceforger books, a published poet, the front of post-punk/post-glam band Varnish, half of transatlantic Autistic musical duo The Companions, and an unabashed geek...An Autistic introvert who was saved in many ways over the years by music, books, and gaming...An idealist and dreamer who now writes (books, poems, lyrics, blogs) and makes music in hopes of adding to someone else's escape or rescue...And, yes, the model for that Magic card.

Learn more about Amber-related things at amberbird.com.

9 781945 636158